A KILLER DOES HIS JOB

"I'm afraid I can't let you leave," the man said.

Sheri whirled, struggling to maintain her balance. *The gun*, something in her head whispered. *Use the gun.* Her hand obeyed and pulled the gun from her purse.

"Get back," she said, "or I'll blow your head off."

"Nothing personal," he said, "but you have to die today."

"Keep away from me, you—"

His foot rose sharply and knocked the gun from her hand. It fell on the floor between them. The man picked it up. "I'm an expert," he said.

Then, before she could scream, he clamped a hand over her mouth and moved her into the bathroom.

He pushed her into the shower.

It was then that she saw the knife.

It was the last thing she ever saw.

When he was done, he used a red felt-tipped marker to write the letter *W* on the smooth white flesh of her thigh. *W* for Whore.

Are you getting my messages, Cotter?

*MAYBE YOU SHOULD CHECK
UNDER YOUR BED... JUST ONE MORE TIME!
THE HORROR NOVELS OF*

STEPHEN R. GEORGE

WILL SCARE YOU SENSELESS!

BEASTS   (2682-X, $3.95/$4.95)

BRAIN CHILD   (2578-5, $3.95/$4.95)

DARK MIRACLE   (2788-5, $3.95/$4.95)

THE FORGOTTEN   (3415-6, $4.50/$5.50)

GRANDMA'S LITTLE DARLING   (3210-2, $3.95/$4.95)

Available wherever paperbacks are sold, or order direct from the Publisher. Send cover price plus 50¢ per copy for mailing and handling to Zebra Books, Dept. 3939, 475 Park Avenue South, New York, N.Y. 10016. Residents of New York and Tennessee must include sales tax. DO NOT SEND CASH. For a free Zebra/Pinnacle catalog please write to the above address.

SERIAL BLOOD

ALEXANDER BRINTON

ZEBRA BOOKS
KENSINGTON PUBLISHING CORP.

*To Dan Monte,
for being my number one fan*

ZEBRA BOOKS

are published by

Kensington Publishing Corp.
475 Park Avenue South
New York, NY 10016

Copyright © 1992 by Alexander Brinton

All rights reserved. No part of this book may be reproduced in any form or by any means without the prior written consent of the Publisher, excepting brief quotes used in reviews.

If you purchased this book without a cover you should be aware that this book is stolen property. It was reported as "unsold and destroyed" to the Publisher and neither the Author nor the Publisher has received any payment for this "stripped book."

First printing: October, 1992

Printed in the United States of America

One

"Morning, big guy," Cindy Brekke said, rolling over and slipping her arms around the man who'd spent the night with her.

"Mumpf," he said.

"Mumpf? Is that all you can say—mumpf?"

"Double mumpf."

"Lucky me. I've got twice the mumpf I had only a moment ago."

"Our best customers get a second helping free on Wednesdays. It's sort of like double-stamp day."

"But this is Friday, and—"

"Our very best customers get their mumpf a few days early."

"And no one's given away Green Stamps in years. I don't think they're in business anymore."

"Mumpf."

She sighed. "Let's start this conversation over again. I'll say, 'Good morning, big guy,' and you say, 'Good morning, darling, you were wonderful last night.'"

"Good morning, darling. You were wonderful last night."

"Could we try for just a little more sincerity?"

"I was sincere. I just don't like to gush, that's all."

"No one would ever accuse you of gushing."

"Mumpf."

She slugged him in the back. He didn't seem to notice. Or he refused to let on. She was tempted to hit him again, but she didn't.

Dawn light was seeping in around the blue curtains, bathing Cindy's bedroom in a dim grayness, as if she and Cotter were floating along inside a dark cloud.

A few months ago, had anyone suggested that she'd be sleeping with someone like Cotter, Cindy would have thought the person was crazy. She was a successful, independent woman, a feminist, a political liberal. She had a master's degree in marketing. How had she come to have a relationship with a cop? Never in her wildest imaginings had she contemplated such a thing.

"How come I'm involved with a guy like you?"

"Can't resist good looks and charm, I guess."

"Oooo!" She hit him again.

"Ouch."

"Felt that one, huh? Good, you deserve it."

"For what?" he asked in mock innocence.

"Don't push your luck, or you may get another one."

"All the gentle women were taken."

That was one of the things that attracted her to Cotter, Cindy supposed. She could be foolish around him; he brought out the little girl in her.

It was an odd reaction for someone who'd resolved she would most likely never marry and absolutely, positively never have kids if she did. Career, success, independence. These were the things she wanted.

And a guy who needed her, gave her the chance to feel like a little girl from time to time. Inwardly she sighed.

"Where did you come from?" she said softly.

"Texas."

"No, you big lug. I mean how did you find your way into my life?"

"I was lucky that day."

"You mean that?"

"Definitely. Luckiest day I've had in a long time."

Cindy met him six months before, when he'd knocked on her door one evening, showed his badge, and said he was looking for a guy named Manwaring, who had lived in the apartment across the hall. She told him Manwaring hadn't informed her he was leaving, much less said where he was going. Instead of departing at that point, Cotter had hesitated, seeming to be momentarily at a loss for words, and then he'd asked her where she'd bought her couch. She told him, and he asked how she liked living here. It wasn't until after he'd left that she realized he'd been trying, in his bashful way, to make a pass at her.

Two days later, he'd showed up again. Standing in her doorway with a big silly grin on his face and a bouquet of flowers in his hand, he'd taken a slow breath, confessed to being smitten with her, and asked her out to dinner. Cindy surprised herself by saying yes. She didn't really know what she'd expected—Dirty Harry, she supposed—but to her astonishment Cotter turned out to be one of the sweetest, most sensitive people she'd ever known. Two months later, they were living together.

"I like you," Cindy said.

He rolled over, taking her in his arms. "I like you too," he said softly.

He squeezed her tighter, and she kissed his nose, then his eyes, then his lips, not really sure whether she was feeling amorous, but willing to see where it led. It led nowhere because they both began drifting off to sleep.

The phone yanked them out of it. It was on the table on her side of the bed, ringing impatiently because Cindy was unable to get her arm untangled from the covers so she could answer it. She finally succeeded, mumbled a sleepy hello into the mouthpiece.

"This is the police department," an efficient-sounding woman said. "Detective Cotter left this number."

"Well, he shouldn't have."

The woman hesitated, then said, "You mean he's not there?"

"No, I mean that if he hadn't left this number you wouldn't be calling us at such an uncivilized hour."

"I'm sorry, but he's the on-call detec—"

Cotter took the phone from her hand. "Cotter," he said. He listened a moment, then said, "Okay, Bev, I'm on my way."

Cotter climbed out of the bed. "Mrs. Peel, I'm needed."

"I used to watch *The Avengers*," Cindy said. "And as I recall, Steed would tell Emma *we're* needed, in the plural, but I never get to go."

"You wouldn't want to go," he said.

"Bad one?"

"Clerk at a convenience store was killed. Shield your eyes. I'm going to switch on the light."

Cindy watched as he hurriedly dressed. He was tall and broad shouldered, with the muscular body of an athlete, his tummy and butt firm, his thighs smooth and hard. His chest was covered with thick hair, brown with a lot of gray mixed in. The hair on his head was salt-and-pepper as well, still full and healthy looking, but starting to recede at the temples.

She said, "With a bod like that, you should be in the movies, stomping on evil aliens or something, flexing your biceps for the benefit of all the little girls in the audience."

"Me? I'm just a middle-aged working stiff."

"I know, but you look so good I tend to forget."

"You trying to sweet-talk me?"

"You bet. So I can get into your pants."

"My pants are much too big for you."

"You're hopeless," she said. "Absolutely hopeless."

Cindy watched as he strapped on his shoulder holster. She hated guns, hated having the evil thing in the house. On the other hand, she was glad he had it, for she knew someday the weapon might be all that stood between Cotter and a robber's bullet or a drug pusher's blade.

"Have you ever had to use that?" she asked, looking at the gun.

"No, thank goodness."

"Never?"

"Never."

"I . . . I'm glad."

He slipped on the black-and-white hound's-tooth sportcoat. Pushing the bedroom door closed to reveal its full-length mirror, Cotter patted the material below his left arm, making sure the gun didn't show. His paisley tie still hung from the doorknob. He hadn't bothered to put it on.

"Gotta go," he said, stepping over to the bed and giving her a kiss.

As he switched off the light and left, Cindy silently implored him to be careful.

Cotter took the elevator from Cindy's twelfth-floor apartment to the underground parking area. The sign out front said BAY VISTA LUXURY APARTMENTS. Cotter could never afford the rent here on a cop's salary. Cindy owned a highly successful advertising agency. She didn't worry about the rent.

His car, an unmarked brown Dodge, looked dowdy compared to the BMWs and Porsches and top-of-the-line Japanese models that gleamed expensively in their assigned parking spaces. As he pulled onto the street, Cotter picked up the microphone.

"Unit 338 to Central. I'm ten-eight, en route the one-eighty-seven." A one-eighty-seven was a homicide.

Cindy's apartment was in a neighborhood of luxury complexes, all of them fairly new, with swimming pools and assigned parking; some even had guards to keep out the less desirable element, make sure no one's Ferrari had its tape deck taken or its windshield smashed.

Cotter drove along a wide tree-lined street that led through a neighborhood of houses that cost from five hundred up. When referring to California real estate, Cotter had discovered, no one ever bothered to say five hundred what. He supposed the price of a multi-million-dollar house would be "two" or "three." Never having looked at a place in that price range, he could only assume. It would be something to do as a lark someday, wouldn't it? Go out and look over the really expensive places, tell the real estate agent you could go one-and-a-half, maybe two.

Tres Cerros was one of the numerous bedroom communities located between San Francisco and San Jose. In the past fifty years it had grown from an uninspiring community of forty thousand to a gleaming city of nearly two hundred thousand. Everything here was new. The trees lining the streets were young, still reaching out across the pavement toward each other in hopes of creating a leafy tunnel of shade someday. The asphalt on the city's streets was pristine, uncracked, free of potholes. There was no business section, since the people living here nearly all worked somewhere else. And those who did work here—mostly people in what were called service occupations—lived somewhere else.

Cotter had come here fifteen years ago, after—

After he'd decided to leave Texas.

He pushed the thought away. He didn't want to remember what had happened in Texas.

Parked across the street from Cindy Brekke's apartment was a shiny new Lincoln that fit right into the neighborhood. The man behind the wheel watched as the brown Dodge's taillights faded into the distance. *Have fun at the convenience store, Detective Cotter,* he thought. *Enjoy what I've left there for you. See if you get the subtleties.*

Then he shifted his gaze to a window on the twelfth floor. A few moments ago the window had been a bright yellow rectangle. Now it was dark.

Sleep tight, Cindy, he thought. *Sweet dreams.*

The convenience store was on San Carlos Avenue, one of those places that sold pump-your-own gas, newspapers, and almost any snack you might get a craving for when the regular grocery stores were closed. It was located between an auto parts store and a branch bank. The scene out front was a display of flashing lights dazzling enough to delight a hippie's psychedelic heart—if there were any hippies left.

The uniformed sergeant in charge of securing the scene joined Cotter as he got out of his car. "Cash register's empty," he told him. "The perp either panicked or decided not to leave any witnesses. Or maybe it was one of the crazies. You know, the kind that enjoys killing."

"ME been called?" Cotter asked.

"On the way. So's the lab." The cop's name tag said HART. Cotter had seen him around, but he really didn't know him. Hart was young to be a sergeant, a wiry fellow with blond hair cut in a flattop and the ramrod-straight posture of a military cadet. Cotter could see him snapping to attention, answering "Yes, sir," "No, sir," or "No excuse, sir."

The two men entered the store. The clerk was a thin black woman. She was lying face down behind the counter, her head in the center of a darkening puddle of blood. She was wearing a dress, gray with orange flowers. Her hair was done in a series of small, tight cornrows that must have taken forever to get right. Cotter wondered whether someone helped her do them, a daughter or a sister or a neighbor. He put the thought away, forced himself to be the detached professional he had to be.

Cotter didn't know how the woman had been killed, because she was lying on the wound. He'd wait to move her until the lab guys took photos and the medical examiner checked her over. There was no rush. The woman was dead, the killer long gone.

"Any witnesses?" Cotter asked the sergeant.

"No. Came in as an anonymous call. Apparently whoever found her didn't want to get involved."

Cotter nodded. Stepping back, he surveyed the scene, taking it in in its entirety, absorbing impressions. Directly above the victim was the cash register, its drawer open, empty. Nothing else in the store seemed to have been disturbed. Bags of Fritos and cans of Austex chili-with-beans were lined up neatly on the shelves. Half-and-half, milk, cheese, and tortillas were in a refrigerated case. Cold cuts and soft drinks filled another.

Cotter studied the body, the cash register, the neatly arranged shelves. It didn't feel right. He looked the scene over again, trying to get a handle on what was bothering him, but it eluded him.

The lab guys tonight were Gonzales and Wu, known in the department as Cheech and Chong. They took pictures, then checked for prints, their equipment giving off flashes of green laser light. Then the ME showed up. He was a corpulent gray-haired guy named Thompson who had a large, rudder-shaped nose crisscrossed with red veins.

"I'll need to roll her over," Thompson said, looking at Cotter with tired, bloodshot eyes.

"We're done," Wu said, and Cotter told the medical examiner to go ahead.

Thompson rolled her over. "Jesus," he said.

A chill slid through Cotter's insides, sending out icy tendrils as it went. The woman's throat had been slit. Not hurriedly, but carefully. Deeply. Cleaving the throat all the way to the neck bones. Like a butcher cutting through a roast.

Then the wound had been pulled open, like a big, bloody mouth where no mouth should be.

The icy feeling in Cotter's gut intensified.

"It doesn't make sense," Gonzales said. "Most of the money in one of these places goes into the night safe. The perp gets fifty bucks if he's lucky. Usually only addicts are desperate enough to take the risk. They grab the money and run. So why does some junkie stop and go to all the trouble to do something like this?"

"Who the hell uses a knife to rob a store in the first place?" Wu said. "Where I come from, they use guns."

"This *is* where you come from," Gonzales said.

"The point is, who uses a knife to knock over a convenience store?"

Exactly, thought Cotter. *No ordinary robber did this.*

He knew of a man who slit people's throats.

The thought hung there.

"Cause of death was loss of blood due to severing of the major vessels in the throat," Thompson said.

"And here I thought it was a heart attack," Gonzales said.

Ignoring him, Thompson said, "Been dead about an hour and a half. Anything else I can tell you?"

"Yeah," Wu said, "who did it?"

Thompson sighed. "Crazy, bloodthirsty son-of-a-bitch with a sharp knife."

Cotter knew a man who fit that description perfectly.

The ambulance came and took away the woman with the braids and flowered dress, who no longer had to work nights in a high-risk job for the minimum wage. For she had met someone tonight. Someone demented and deadly.

The medical examiner and the lab guys left. Then so did Cotter and Sergeant Hall. Only a single patrolman remained, keeping an eye on things until someone from the store could be located. As often happened, no one answered at the emergency number listed on the door.

They'd found her purse behind the counter. The robber apparently hadn't thought to look for it, or hadn't bothered. Her name was Wanda Grant, twenty-three, address in Colmer, Tres Cerros's less prosperous neighbor to the north.

The killer had taken the time to cut her throat. But why would a robber do that? Your chances of getting caught increased dramatically with every second you lingered at the scene of the crime. And it would be messy; the perpetrator would have to get bloody.

Sure, Cotter could come up with a scenario that fit, the robber not having a gun but still wanting to eliminate the one person who could identify him, for instance. A lot of robberies were spur-of-the-moment decisions. Some junkie needs a fix, sees a convenient 7-Eleven, goes in with a knife because it's the only thing he has handy.

But Cotter didn't like it.

Just because this appeared to be a murder committed as part of a robbery didn't make it so. The reality could be the other way around, a murder made to look like a robbery, with killing Wanda Grant the true purpose. She could have a fat life insurance policy. She could have had an extremely jealous and insecure lover, someone who refused to let go when she decided she wanted out of the relationship. Cotter would check out those possibilities and others.

He hoped he'd find a greedy beneficiary or a jealous lover. Or even a crazed knife-wielding robber who'd gone into a sanguinary frenzy. Something he could understand. Something he could deal with. Not like . . . like what had happened in Texas.

Cindy would be on her way into San Francisco now, so there was no reason for Cotter to go back to her place. There was a pancake house a few blocks away, and Cotter headed for it. He could use some coffee, and a few moments to simply sit and think.

The sun, hanging over San Francisco Bay, was shining in his eyes. He pulled down the visor.

Suddenly Cotter felt cold all over, as if an Arctic wind were blowing through his soul. He shuddered. And then he couldn't stop shaking. His teeth were chattering, his hands gripping the wheel as if they were frozen to it. He was passing the Three Hills Mall—"More than two hundred merchants to serve you"—and he pulled into the parking lot. It was too early for any of the stores to be open, and the parking area was like a great asphalt plain stretching off in all directions. Cotter pulled to a stop, and rested his head against the steering wheel, shivering uncontrollably.

The similarity was coincidence. Just coincidence.

Fifteen years had passed. The madman was locked away in Texas, would always be locked away, forever. And Cotter had changed his name. Only a handful of people knew he'd been that unfortunate rookie cop whose horrifying story had stunned the citizens of Houston and made national news a decade and a half ago.

Finally the shivering subsided. He was making entirely too much of a woman's throat having been cut. After all, it was an act that had been committed thousands upon thousands of times since some enterprising primitive ancestor had discovered that the sharp edge of a rock could cut.

It was psychological, his reaction, a predictable response to an event that triggered the memories of . . . of what had happened in Texas fifteen years ago.

He forced himself not to recall the things he had seen then.

They were images he could not endure.

Two

The hacker's address was 7701 Hillside. It turned out to be an attractive split-level house in Vista de las Colinas, a sprawling subdivision on the south side of Tres Cerros. The neighborhood had probably been built in the fifties or sixties. Driving along its tree-lined streets, passing all those manicured lawns and concrete driveways, had made him think of the Anderson family, Beaver Cleaver, Ozzie and Harriet Nelson.

He parked the Lincoln at the curb and followed the flagstones to the front door. A bed of rosebushes paralleled the walk on one side. Not yet in bloom, the rose garden was nothing but a collection of leafless brambles. He wondered what colors would be displayed when they were in bloom.

He pushed the button on the wall beside the door and chimes sounded from within the house. A second or two later the door was opened by a pudgy man with reddish-blond hair. He wore a white shirt and gray trousers held up by red suspenders. His red-and-white rep tie had been draped around his neck and was still unknotted. He glanced impatiently at his watch: he was clearly on the verge of being late for work.

"FBI," the man on the stoop said, flashing an official-looking ID case. "You Thornton Hollingsworth?"

"Not again."

"You Hollingsworth?"

The chubby man nodded.

"May I come in?"

"I didn't do it."

"Do what?"

"Whatever it is that brought you here. Someone else did it. I learned my lesson. Believe me."

"I have to ask you a few questions."

"I'll be late for work. Can't we do this some other time?"

"It'll only take a few moments."

Looking resigned, the pudgy man stepped back from the door, waving the visitor inside. The living room was early American, Ethan Allen-type stuff. An RCA big-screen TV occupied one corner. Thornton Hollingsworth wasn't wealthy, but he lived comfortably.

He didn't seem at all like an ex-con.

"Do you have a computer?" the visitor asked.

"Yes, but—"

"With a modem?"

"Of course. But—"

"Let's take a look, shall we?"

"What for?" Hollingsworth asked, his eyes filling with worry.

"It's a good place to talk."

Hollingsworth stood there in his living room, staring at the floor, fidgeting like a guilty child. "I learned my lesson," he said. "I spent six months in jail. Not that I deserved it—the judge wanted to make an example of me. He wanted to scare all the hackers."

"Let's go where your computer is. That's the right place to talk."

Hollingsworth nodded miserably. "This way," he said, looking confused and hurt, like a dog who'd just been scolded but had no idea why.

As they moved along a carpeted hallway, a woman's voice came from another part of the house. "Thorny, is someone here?"

Thorny. It figured, somehow.

"Yeah," Hollingsworth answered. "It's for me."

"You'll be late."

"It's okay. Don't worry about it."

He led the visitor into a bedroom that had been converted into an office. It contained a desk, bookshelves, filing cabinets. The shelves were laden with plastic storage cases full of floppy disks. There were two computers, a Macintosh and an IBM clone.

The visitor said, "Which one would you use to enter the computer at the First National Bank?"

Hollingsworth went rigid. A slight tremor worked its way

through his midsection. "I . . . I wouldn't. Not after—"

"Not after you illegally broke into the computers of some of the biggest corporations in California, not to mention the Alameda Naval Air Station? Yes, I know."

"I . . . I . . . I . . ." Hollingsworth could only stammer. His eyes bulged.

"It's all right, Mr. Hollingsworth. That's ancient history. You were caught and served your time, and now your life's back in order."

Hollingsworth nodded vigorously.

"I'm not here to accuse you of anything."

Hollingsworth continued nodding.

"You have a gun?"

"Just . . . just a twenty-two automatic."

"Would you get it, please."

"W-why?"

"I just need to see it. Look, there's no problem here, okay? I just need to see the gun. As soon as I do, I'll explain everything, all right?"

Hollingsworth was nodding again, his eyes brimming with terror. He would do whatever an FBI man asked him to do. He didn't want any trouble.

"That time in jail," he said. "It was the worst six months of my life."

"Don't worry. I'll look at the gun and be on my way."

"It's in the bedroom." He stepped toward the door.

"Oh, I also need to talk to your wife. Could you call her in here."

"Laura?" the man asked him.

"Yes, Laura. I need to see Laura and your gun—also any ammunition you have in the house."

Hollingsworth hesitated, uncertainty flickering in his eyes.

"Unless you'd rather do this down at the Federal Building."

"No," Hollingsworth said quickly, fear instantly replacing whatever misgivings he had. "I'll get the gun." As he stepped into the hall, he called his wife's name.

The visitor heard a hurried conversation conducted in whispers, and then Hollingsworth entered into the room accompanied by a petite brunette with inquisitive blue eyes. She was dressed for work in a white flowered dress. Her hair was cut in a short, no-nonsense style.

"This is my wife, Laura," Hollingsworth said. He was holding the .22 automatic at his side.

"May I see that, please?"

"Oh, sure," Hollingsworth said, handing over the weapon and a box of cartridges. "It's loaded. We keep it that way in case . . . well, just in case."

"What was your name again?" Laura said, studying him with her intelligent blue eyes. There was wariness in them.

"I didn't say," the visitor replied. Abruptly he stepped forward, pinning the woman to the wall with his weight and pressing the gun into her neck with his good hand. The other hand dangled uselessly at his side on his worthless left arm.

"Hey!" Hollingsworth shouted, but he made no move to intervene. He seemed bewildered by this sudden turn of events.

"Thorny, I want you to sit down at your computer and find me a large sum of money. Make it a hundred thousand. You're going to make it disappear without a trace. Then you're going to put it into an account at First National."

"I . . . I can't do that."

"Sure you can. Computer expert like you."

"It's . . . it's against the law."

The woman was still pinned against the wall. He could feel her trembling. She was tiny, all bone, probably weighed less than a hundred pounds. "Please," she whispered. "We haven't done anything to you. Don't hurt us."

"You do as I ask, and I won't. It's up to you."

"You promise?" she asked.

"I promise."

She nodded, latching on to the hope. A little careful analysis would have made her realize that her husband would know where the money came from and where it went, information he could not be allowed to pass on to the authorities. But Laura Hollingsworth clearly didn't want to think about that. She wanted to hope.

"Better get busy," the phony FBI man said.

"Okay, I . . . I can do it. But you've promised you won't hurt us if I do."

"Hey, would the FBI lie?"

The irony was lost on Hollingsworth, who sat down at the IBM clone and went to work.

The man was indeed a whiz with computers. It took him only an hour to locate $35,000 in an oil company's account, $31,500 belonging to an insurance company, and $40,000 in the State of California's payroll account, and send it all into untraceable electronic oblivion, then bring it back to life and transfer it to an account in the First National Bank of Tres Cerros.

"How did you do it so quickly?" the bogus federal agent asked. He was impressed.

"I . . . I already knew the numbers to dial and the entry codes for the computers."

"Couldn't quite give up hacking, huh?"

"I didn't do anything. I . . . I just entered, then left, without changing a single thing."

"Let me go," Laura said, struggling against his weight. "You have what you want."

"There's just one more thing." He was still holding the woman against the wall. He felt her stiffen. She knew what was coming. Anticipation, hot and tingly, coursed through the fake FBI man's system.

"What?" Hollingsworth asked. "What now?"

"We have to have a murder-suicide."

Before either of them could react, he shot the woman in the head, turned, and stepped toward her gaping-mouthed husband.

Three

Through the window by his desk Cotter could see the two-story brick-and-glass City Hall. It was separated from the police department by a grassy area where secretaries ate their lunches when the weather was nice. A brick walk lined with flowerbeds connected the two buildings, which were twins. The police station also contained metro court, the city jail, and a city-county juvenile detention facility. The detective division was on the second floor.

Cotter watched a squirrel scamper over to one of the now unoccupied wooden benches, poke around for crumbs, then scoot away for the safety of a tree as a man in a blue suit walked by, gently swinging his briefcase. A light fog hung in the air, making things in the distance look spectral, as if they existed in some other reality and had no true substance in ours.

Cotter was on long-distance hold, listening to the subtle electronic "presence" that lets you know the phone is actually connected to something and not just a hunk of plastic in your hand.

Although it occurred fifteen years ago, he recalled the conversation with Dr. Waters with the precise, vivid detail of a videotape recording.

"The prognosis hasn't changed," the psychiatrist had said. He was tall and thin and gray-haired, and he wore metal-framed glasses that made his gray eyes seem smaller than they were. He was calm and professional, saying the things he had to say in a tactful but businesslike manner.

Tactful or not, he was tearing Cotter's heart out.

"Coming here's not doing any good whatsoever. She doesn't even recognize you."

"But she might . . . someday."

The doctor sighed. "That seems unlikely at this point. You have to understand that."

"But—"

"You're killing yourself. You're not doing a bit of good here, but you are doing a lot of harm—to yourself."

"But maybe someday . . . maybe my presence will trigger something."

"If there are any signs of recovery, I'll contact you immediately, but in this case . . ." He let his words trail off.

"But . . . how can I just desert—"

"I don't want you for a patient too." Dr. Waters took off his glasses, folded them, and placed them in front of him on his desk. "How do you feel after coming here for a visit?"

"How do you think?"

"It's destroying you. And it's accomplishing absolutely nothing."

"But . . . but I have to come. I just have to."

"You continue, and we'll have two members of your family here instead of just one. I've seen what it does to you. And I know you can see it too. There's no way you couldn't."

Cotter nodded.

"Go away," the psychiatrist said. "Put all this behind you. Start fresh. Please, for your own sake, do it."

"I'd be . . . abandoning—"

"No, you wouldn't. You can't abandon someone who's beyond reach. It's time to save yourself—while you still can."

Cotter had simply sat there shaking, uncertain what to do.

But that had been a long time ago. One healed, even after something like that. The past few months with Cindy had shown him that he could live a normal life again, be open again, share again. He had no secrets from Cindy—except the events of fifteen years ago. That was his own personal horror, and no one else could help him live with it.

After what seemed an interminable wait, a click came over the line and a woman said, "Hello, Mr. Cotter, this is Dr. Lockwood. How are you today?"

Philippa Lockwood had replaced Dr. Waters as the director

of the Hennepin Psychiatric Hospital outside San Antonio. It was a facility for mental patients who were unable to care for themselves. Admission was usually for life, since none of the patients was expected to recover.

"Fine," Cotter said. He took a slow breath. "I don't suppose there's been any change."

"No. But then, none is expected; you know that."

"But it's not impossible."

"Nothing's impossible, Mr. Cotter, but some things are highly improbable."

"I know. But . . ." But what? He had to ask because to stop asking would mean he had given up. But then he'd given up already, hadn't he? Otherwise he'd have stayed—no matter what it was doing to him.

"Is that all you wanted, Mr. Cotter?"

"Yes. Thank you."

Leaning back in his chair, Cotter looked out the window. Three squirrels were out there now, darting from one spot to the next, picking things up and examining them, moving on. Little gray bundles of energy, concerned only with simple squirrel affairs, unaware of all the unspeakable things humans did to each other.

Unlike the squad rooms on television cop shows, which were usually open rooms full of desks, this one was partitioned into cubicles. They had no doors but still provided enough privacy for some of the guys to bring in pictures and other personal things. Don Tuffle had a collection of bowling trophies in his. It was a detective division rule that prisoners were processed and interrogated downstairs, never here. In the us-against-them mind set of police work, this place belonged to us.

Cotter made himself think about business. It was how he'd gotten through the ordeal in Texas. Focus your thoughts, concentrate on a task. Commit yourself to it with so much determination that you drive everything else from your mind.

So how was he going to handle the Wanda Grant murder? There were no doors he could knock on to ask residents whether they'd seen anything. The store was in a commercial district, surrounded by other businesses, none of which had been open when Wanda Grant was murdered.

His next move, he decided, was to find out about Wanda Grant, try to determine whether anyone might have had reason to murder her, then disguise it as a robbery. She had lived in Colmer, a twenty-minute drive if the traffic was light.

Cotter stared out the window for a moment, thinking how all the seasons here were so much alike, never terribly hot, never cold enough to snow. There were two dominant weather conditions: cool-and-foggy, and cool-and-rainy. The only truly extreme natural events were earthquakes.

Cotter headed for the parking area, thinking that in Houston there had been seasons. No, not like in the North, but summer anywhere on the Texas coast was basically unbearable, fall was hurricane season, and winter provided a few months relief from the mosquitoes and the oppressive heat.

At the Hennepin Psychiatric Hospital near San Antonio, Dr. Philippa Lockwood was making what she referred to as her morning rounds, although the activity had little in common with rounds as they were performed at a medical hospital. Here no cardiac surgeons performed bypasses, no tumors were removed, no fractured bones were reset. Dr. Lockwood's rounds were performed simply to make sure things were as they should be, not to check on the progress of the patients. Here the patients made no progress; they either remained as they were or they deteriorated.

Absently she ran her hand through her thick blond hair. Realizing what she was doing, she frowned, annoyed with herself. Fooling with her hair had become a habit, and she was trying to break herself of it. She was in a position of authority and responsibility, and she should be acting in businesslike, professional manner. Fiddling with your hair was something cute little air-headed high school girls did.

Though forty-two, Philippa Lockwood still had the lithe form of the cheerleader she had been as a teenager. She still had the hair, too, fashion model hair, which made it all the more imperative that she not constantly fondle it as if she were some sweet little thing out to catch a husband. If she wanted the respect of the staff and her colleagues, she had to be serious, exacting, professional.

It annoyed her no end that men didn't have these kinds of problems.

Smiling at her secretary, a frizzy-haired woman named Grace, Dr. Lockwood left the administrative wing of the building and entered the portion occupied by the patients. A variety of odors washed over her—disinfectant, medicine, human waste, desolation.

She was in a long corridor with beige walls and brown-and-white floor tiles. Most of the rooms she passed were empty, their occupants in the TV room or milling around the areas to which they had access. They did a lot of that, milling around. They were aimless in everything they did, staring for hours at the television set and never really seeing it, gazing for hours at a wall and never seeing it, either. A lot of it was because of the medication; Dr. Lockwood knew that. But without the tranquilizers, the patients could become agitated, even violent.

She stopped at the open door to room 110, in which a middle-aged man sat in a chair, his eyes fixed on the floor in front of him. Although it was barely perceptible at first, after you'd watched him for a moment you noticed the head movement, slowly tilting to the right, then the left, as though he were listening to his own private orchestra playing something soft and ever so slow. He had the sort of extremely pale skin that burned at the first touch of a summer ray. His thick dark hair was uncombed, and it hung in his eyes. He wore the same white pajamas all the patients wore, clothes that could easily be removed and washed in the event the wearer soiled himself.

The man's name was Carl. Should his medication wear off, he would begin masturbating, not stopping until he was restrained. Before coming here he had frequently done it until his penis was bloody. As she watched, liquid appeared beneath him on the plastic seat of the chair, then spilled off onto the floor.

Doctor Lockwood made a mental note to tell the nurse that Carl needed changing.

She moved on to room 112, looking in to see a young woman sitting on the floor just inside the doorway, gazing up at her. The woman wasn't actually looking at her, of course; she never looked at anything. Not with comprehension. The psychiatrist moved to the left, and the woman's eyes did not follow her. The patient was known as Dawn, although that wasn't her real name, which was known only to Dr. Lockwood. Dawn would have been a pretty girl under other circumstances. She had dark brown eyes, light brown hair with a natural wave, a small nose, flawlessly smooth cheeks. Words like "perky" and "cute" came to the psychiatrist's mind. But those were would-have-beens. The young woman on the floor was none of those things. She was scrawny, her skin as thin and fragile-looking as a ninety-year-old's. Dawn reminded Dr. Lockwood of those scenes of African famine you saw on the news, often preceded with a warning: *The upcoming scenes are not pretty, and if there are any young people watching* . . .

Well, they didn't have to go all the way to Africa to find things that weren't pretty, did they?

Dawn was still sitting there, unaware of the doctor's presence, unaware of the room, unaware of her existence on the planet—so thin she seemed an illusion, so lacking in substance the psychiatrist could imagine a light shining right through her, silhouetting her skeleton like a shape seen through a shade drawn over a lighted window. She wouldn't eat. If you put the food in her mouth, it would simply dribble out again, spilling down her chin, dripping onto her clothes. She was kept alive through the tube permanently attached to her stomach. And even that nourishment was accepted reluctantly by her body, as if the brain refused to tell her to digest it, as if the only portions of her mind that still functioned were operating solely for the purpose of shutting her down so she could die.

Although she had not been in charge here at the time, Dr. Lockwood knew that the woman's father had been unable to deal with this on top of the other unbelievable horrors he'd endured. He'd been heading for a breakdown, to use the common term, or maybe something worse. The psychiatrist could understand why.

The woman on the floor had been a child when she'd come here. Physically she had grown into an adult, even if not a terribly normal-looking one.

She smelled of fear.

It was a notion Dr. Lockwood would share with no one, because it was so unscientific. Yet every time she came to this room, she was sure she smelled the essence of pure terror.

There was nothing physically wrong with Dawn. She had neither hit her head nor suffered a stroke. Dawn had simply escaped into herself so completely that she could never return to the real world. For Dawn, reality had proved so horrifying that her mind had escaped it the only way it knew how. It had simply exited stage right. There was a saying about wanting to jump in a hole, then pull the hole in after you. In a manner of speaking, that's what Dawn had done.

She had been like this for fifteen years.

She would always be like this.

Three different psychiatrists and a psychologist who used behavior modification techniques had worked with her extensively, to no avail. But then, most of the patients here had been worked with extensively to no avail.

As the psychiatrist was turning to go, Dawn's expression abruptly changed. The lips pulled back in a grotesque grin that was part grimace and part snarl. Then her eyes opened wide, filling with terror so icy pure it turned the psychiatrist colder than a January wind.

Dr. Lockwood told herself to look away, but she couldn't.

The young woman's mouth opened and a silent scream came out, a soundless primal screech Dr. Lockwood could hear and *feel* even though the room was still. The psychiatrist resisted the impulse to clasp her hands over her ears.

Although it was spring, and already stifling in Texas, Philippa Lockwood shivered. She still felt cold when she returned to her office thirty minutes later.

* * *

The prosperity that extended down the peninsula from San Francisco and up it from Silicon Valley seemed to peter out in both directions before reaching Colmer, which consisted of a lot of old wood houses that would have looked right at home in the less affluent neighborhoods of Des Moines or Birmingham or Buffalo. This was not what people usually pictured when they thought of California.

Wanda Grant had lived on Rinley Court, a narrow street with grass growing from the cracks in the asphalt and no curbs or sidewalks. The neighborhood was primarily black, and preschool-aged children stared at him suspiciously from their tricycles, already old enough to wonder what a white guy in a plain brown car with two antennas on it was doing here.

Wanda Grant's house was better maintained than some of the others, which led Cotter to wonder whether they owned the place while the homes in the greatest disrepair were rented. It was a small house, white with a blue roof, blue trim. Unlike the neighbors to the west, whose yard was a tangle of weeds, the Grant property had a recently mowed lawn and was largely weed free.

The place was surrounded by cars, which meant the Colmer police had delivered the death message as requested. Someone in the family would have to identify the body, but there was no hurry about that. Wanda Grant's corpse had matched the photo on her driver's license. There was no doubt that it was she.

The detective parked his car and followed the concrete walk to the front door. It was opened by a young black man whose eyes displayed open hostility when Cotter identified himself.

"What you want?" he asked, acting as though he hadn't decided yet whether to let Cotter in.

"I'm investigating the murder of Wanda Grant. I need to talk to her family. You a relative?"

"She was my sister," the young man said.

Cotter realized that he looked like Wanda, the same slight build, the same high cheekbones. His eyes were large, a very warm shade of brown. They would have been friendly, winning eyes if they hadn't been filled with so much animosity.

"Steven, who's there?" a woman's voice called.

"The police."

"You gonna let 'im in, or you gonna keep 'im standing out there forever?"

Steven stood aside, resentment radiating from him like heat from a hot oven. Cotter stepped into a small living room in which nearly all the furnishings had a floral pattern, including the carpet and drapes. The room was full of people, most of them dressed nicely but inexpensively. As a group they probably shopped at Wal-Mart but did so with care.

A slender gray-haired woman sat on the couch. Surrounded by other women, she was holding a crumpled handkerchief, and she looked at Cotter with eyes that were red from crying. "I'm Belinda Grant," she said. "You here about what happened to my little girl?"

"Yes," he said, identifying himself again and displaying his shield. "You're Wanda's mother?"

The woman nodded, holding back more tears. Around the room eyes not as hostile as Steven's, but wary stared at Cotter. This was a neighborhood in which police officers were regarded with suspicion. Maybe these people had good reason for feeling that way. Cotter had heard some bad things about the Colmer force.

"You catch the killer yet?" Steven demanded. He was standing by the door, his eyes full of malevolence.

"No," Cotter said.

"You won't, neither."

"Steven . . ." his mother said, her tone making it clear she wanted him to back off.

But Steven had no intention of obliging. "We don't get a whole lot of help from the police around here," he said. "Like with the crack house down the street. Called the cops about it I don't know how many times. Nobody came. Nobody gave a shit. Cops figured this was a good place for a crack house. If it blew up, nobody important would get hurt."

"Steven . . ." his mother said again.

"You know what happened to that crack house? The people in the neighborhood got together. Including the ones who rent, because even if they don't own their homes, they've still got to raise their kids here. Got our shotguns and hunting rifles and went over there in a group and ran the people in that house out of the neighborhood."

A heavyset man sitting in an upholstered chair spoke up. "Steve, I don't think this gentleman needs to know about that."

The message was that Steve was talking too much. Apparently he got it, because he fell silent and began staring sullenly at the floor.

"Why don't we go in the kitchen," Steve's mother said, "so we can talk privately."

The kitchen was tiny, with almost no counter or storage space. The counters, floor, walls, and curtain on the window over the sink were all in various shades of yellow. A big cast-iron pot sat on the small gas stove. They sat down at a table covered with food that had been brought by friends and family. The moist chocolate aroma of the foil-covered cake in front of Cotter rose to meet him.

"I'm sorry about Steven," Belinda Grant said. "His father ran off when the children were just babies, and sometimes it's hard for a mother to have all the control she should. He tries hard. He's a draftsman now, but he's taking college courses at night, and some day he's going to be a civil engineer." There were traces of the South in her speech. Alabama, maybe.

"Tell me about Wanda," Cotter said.

"Not much to tell. She wasn't as ambitious or hard working as Steven, but she was a good girl. She just hadn't figured out what to do with her life. When I asked her why she didn't get a better job than working nights at that store, she said if she got a good job she might get stuck in it, and she wasn't ready for that yet. This was a job she wouldn't mind quitting when the time came." She frowned. "That make sense?"

Cotter said it did. "Is there anyone who would gain from her death?"

She looked puzzled. "Gain from it?"

"Life insurance policy, maybe."

Belinda Grant laughed. "Life insurance. You gotta be kidding. You know what that costs? Besides, it only pays off if you die, and what good's it going to do you then?" She shook her head.

"Did she have any enemies?"

"Wanda? Heavens, no. Everybody liked Wan—" She fought back tears. She wasn't enjoying this interview, but it was something she had to do, and Cotter suspected that Belinda Grant always did what she had to do, whether it was supporting her children or talking to the police.

"Wanda was real lively. She had a good sense of humor. Nobody would want to hurt her."

"How about boyfriends?"

"Last one was Denver—Denver Jones. But she broke up with him at least six months ago."

"Were there hard feelings?"

"Not that I know of. I'm sure there weren't. The relationship didn't end all at once. It just sort of died from lack of interest."

"Sometimes people get hurt but don't let it show."

"Not in this case. Wanda would have told me."

Wanda Grant had never been arrested; he'd checked. "How did she spend her time? What did she like to do?"

"Go shopping with Leona. She did that a lot. And lately her and Leona had gone to the ballgames a lot. Baseball. The Oakland Athletics. I don't know why they liked it as much as they did, but they did."

"Who's Leona?"

"Leona Roberts. Lives two blocks over. They've been friends since high school."

"Was Wanda ever married?"

"No, and I worried about that some. After all, she was twenty-three, and she didn't seem to have any idea what she wanted to do with her life. I know at twenty-three there's still plenty of time, but she was just so . . . so . . ." Belinda Grant paused, working hard to hold back the tears that had pooled in her eyes. Her lower lip quivered, a tear trickled down her cheek, and then she was in control again. "She didn't want to think about her future. I'd ask her about it, and she'd say, 'Don't worry about it, Mamma. Whatever comes your way, that's what you do. No point thinking about it before it gets here.' That was her attitude."

"Did Wanda have any arguments with anyone lately?"

"No. Nobody was mad at her; she wasn't mad at nobody."

"How about at work? She have any trouble with her boss or other employees?"

"Not that she ever mentioned to me."

They talked for another few moments, Belinda Grant straining to maintain her composure. Cotter decided he'd gotten enough. He asked for Leona Roberts' address, then thanked her for her help. Before leaving, he asked the people in the living room whether any of them knew why anyone might want to kill Wanda. None did. Though he remained silent, Steve glared at Cotter until the detective left.

Cotter was on his way down the walk when he heard the door open, then rapid footsteps behind him. Turning around, he found Belinda Grant.

She said, "Do you think it wasn't a robbery, that someone killed Wanda on purpose?"

"It looks like a robbery," he answered.

"Then why you asking about her enemies, things like that?"

"I have to check out every possibility."

"There's one thing I didn't tell you. Maybe it doesn't mean much, and maybe I shouldn't say anything about it, but . . . well, I want you to know everything."

"You never know what might help."

She nodded. "Steven wouldn't like it if he knew I was telling you this. He'd say I was spoiling Wanda's reputation." Again she had to pause, struggling to maintain her composure. Finally she said, "Wanda used to shortchange people. Not people who needed the money, but people wearing expensive clothes, driving fancy cars. She'd hold back a dollar or two. Usually they didn't notice. If they caught her, she'd just look embarrassed and say she made a mistake."

"She do this a lot?"

"All the time." She looked ashamed. "I told her not to do it anymore, but I know she didn't stop." Her eyes, the same warm brown as those of her children, locked onto Cotter's. "A person wouldn't murder someone over something like that, would they?"

"People have been killed for a lot less," he said, and let it go at that.

Four

He jogged along Dalton Avenue in Colmer, his good arm pumping, his other arm swinging limply at his side. Although the arm was nearly as useless as an old piece of hose, he had learned how to hide his handicap when the need arose. It was a lot like prestidigitation, the hand being quicker than the eye—except in this case it was the arm. He had become quite adept at it, having worked even as a bellman, handling heavy luggage as smoothly as his able-bodied co-workers. But then, people were remarkably easy to fool. All it took was a little observation, a modicum of intelligence, a pinch of *chutzpa*.

He smiled, pleased with his success.

Dressed in a worn gray athletic outfit, he was sure he didn't look like a man who had more than a hundred thousand dollars in his bank account—an account that early that morning had held a mere three hundred bucks. Ah, but then, such was the magic of electronic banking. Money, as such, didn't really exist anymore. It had been replaced by electronic impulses stored on microchips. Someday some enterprising soul with a computer was going to take all the electronic impulses and claim them for his own. And what would the world do then?

He jogged on, breathing in . . . out . . . in . . . out . . . his good arm pumping. He'd bought the athletic outfit at the Salvation Army thrift store. Some yuppie's old workout clothes, donated to the less fortunate. Though not expensive, his shoes were new. They'd had running shoes at the Salvation Army, but donning footwear that still reeked of someone else's sweaty feet was farther than he was willing to go. Clothes could be laundered; shoes had to be new.

Dalton Avenue ran through a neighborhood of small apartment buildings, mainly one- and two-story structures with gravel parking lots which doubled as playgrounds for the surfeit of children in the neighborhood. Who was it said the rich get richer and the poor have children? He couldn't remember, but it was apt.

The neighborhood was a study in integration, its residents white, black, Hispanic, and Asian in roughly equal proportions. It proved that people of any ethnic background could end up living at the bottom of the socioeconomic ladder, even here in the Golden State, the embodiment of the American Dream.

He didn't like this neighborhood, didn't like the people, didn't like the cheap motel where he lived. But then, it suited his purposes. It was an ideal place to keep a low profile. People were transient in a neighborhood like this, nameless and faceless to those higher up on the economic scale. And, should he decide the time was right to begin that part of the plan, the motel would be the ideal place to leave a few tantalizing clues for Cotter.

Across the street, a blond woman was taking groceries from the trunk of a dented gray car. She weighed at least three hundred pounds and wore a green dress that hung on her like a gunnysack. Dull cow eyes glanced at him from her fleshy face, then quickly darted away.

By jogging he called attention to himself, he knew. But his appearance and physical condition were important to him. He liked to look good. And he liked to stay in fighting trim. The blond woman with the dull eyes was an example of what could happen when you didn't take care of yourself. Looking over his shoulder, he spotted her trying to juggle her groceries while she unlocked the ground-floor door of an apartment. A boy of about three, as chubby as the woman, waited behind her, kicking the gravel impatiently. She probably lived on welfare, watched soap operas all day while nibbling cookies and chips and the like. How could people let themselves go like that?

He jogged on, one arm pumping. His mood continued to darken, and he felt the stirrings of other, more volatile emotions. He kept his speed up, feeling the tiredness in his legs, but not giving in to it.

He thought about the money in his bank account, right up to the limit of the FDIC insurance and even a little beyond. He had the time and the wherewithal to do exactly what he wanted to do.

At a cross street he turned right, then right again at the next intersection, jogging back toward the motel. The streets in this neighborhood seemed interchangeable. Everywhere he looked were bland apartment buildings occupied by people who devoted their insignificant lives to populating the world with their progeny. The odor of hot grease wafted to him from the building on his right. In places like this, food was always fried. Give these people some lovely jumbo shrimp or a nice filet of fresh fish, and they'd bread it and deep-fry it, turning it into a grease-laden, artery-hardening mess. Here people probably saved the bacon grease, added a dollop or two to their overcooked green beans.

A stone bounced into the gutter not far from his feet. Looking in the direction from which it had come, he saw a pair of boys, four or five years old, standing on the sidewalk on the other side of the street. Wearing filthy T-shirts, they eyed him defiantly, their eyes saying, *What you going to do about it, asshole?* He thought it was too bad that you couldn't call the Orkin man, have him rid the world of such obnoxious pests.

Pointedly ignoring the brats, he continued jogging in the direction of his motel room. He checked his watch. Plenty of time to shower, then drive to Tres Cerros and position himself outside Cindy Brekke's apartment before she returned from work.

He thought, *I'm your secret admirer, Cindy. Always watching, but just too shy to come up and say anything to you.*

He chuckled, amused by the image of himself as a bashful suitor.

As he neared the motel, his surroundings changed from seedy residential to seedy commercial. As he passed a place that sold industrial cleaning supplies, a man stepped out of the grimy doorway and said, "Hey, I got what you're looking for."

Wearing a faded Oakland Raiders jacket, he had curly light

brown hair, two days' worth of stubble, and breath that smelled like canned cat food.

"What is it you think I'm looking for?"

"How about some numbers—Visa, Master Card, American Express."

"Just the numbers?"

"Better that way, man. People notice the card's gone, but they don't know anyone's got the number till the bill comes in. Just use the phone. You can order all kinds of shit."

"How do I know you didn't just make up a bunch of numbers?"

"Hey, man, I've got to stay in business here. If I did something like that, what would you do? You'd come looking for my ass, right? Well, I don't need that shit. I sell them by the list. Each list has ten numbers. That way, if a couple of them are bad for any reason, you still have others to use."

"Where do they come from?"

He knew the answer to that. Sometimes people raided the dumpsters behind businesses and collected the carbons from credit card transactions. Another way was to run an ad for something, a real bargain, credit card orders taken over the phone. The merchandise was never sent, for it had never existed. The whole thing was just a scam to get the card numbers.

The man in the Raiders jacket grinned and said, "Hey, you know, that's like a trade secret."

"How much?"

"Fifty."

"Too much."

"Hey, we can negotiate."

They settled on twenty dollars.

He continued jogging.

35

Five

After talking to Leona Roberts at the clinic where she worked as a receptionist, Cotter headed back to Tres Cerros. He'd learned nothing new from Leona except that she and Wanda shared a crush on Dave Stewart, star pitcher for Oakland. Silly, she admitted, but fun. Both had gotten his autograph.

She had known that Wanda shortchanged certain customers, but figured that if they were well off, then no big deal. That was the trouble with being affluent, Cotter supposed—all the little people wanted a piece of your hide.

Back in Tres Cerros, Cotter talked to Wanda's boss, a young man named Levitt, who said he knew of no one who had a grudge against her. The only complaint had come from a woman Wanda had accidentally shortchanged.

"She make a habit of that?" Cotter asked.

"No, of course not. It was just a mistake. Wanda apologized, but the woman wasn't satisfied. It's like that in the retail business. Some people are just never satisfied."

Cotter didn't tell him about Wanda.

The woman who'd complained was named Darleen Noble, and her apartment was vacant. The manager said she had moved. Forwarding address was in Baltimore. Cotter headed for the station.

Ted Kozlovski grabbed him as soon as he stepped into the squad room. Kozlovski was a potbellied detective who was partial to polyester sportcoats in pastel colors. Today's was a chartreuse plaid. He was the only guy Cotter could think of who probably missed leisure suits.

"Hey, Cotter, you're from the South, aren't you?"

"Texas. You usually get an argument as to whether it's part of the South."

"You know what okra is?"

"Sure."

"Well, what is it?"

"A vegetable, a green pod that tapers to a point. It can get slimy when you cook it, and not everybody likes it."

Kozlovski nodded. "Thanks." He headed in the direction of his cubicle, then stopped, turning to face Cotter again. "Captain's looking for you. You might not want to mention okra." He chuckled.

Captain Zinn's office was to the right as you stepped into the squad room. Black lettering on the door said COMMANDER, DETECTIVE DIVISION. It was open, and Cotter walked in.

"You wanted to see me?" he said.

Although Cotter had never known him to be in poor health, Captain Tony Zinn had the gray pallor of someone recovering from a serious illness. His expression was usually one of weariness, the look of a guy who had taken on more problems than any man could endure. He was completely bald, with not so much as a single strand of hair protruding from his scalp. If he hadn't been so thin, he'd have reminded Cotter of Kojak.

"You know what okra is?" he asked Cotter.

"A vegetable, a green pod that tapers—"

"Never mind," the captain said, cutting him off. "Does it look like marijuana?"

Cotter considered that. "Well, there's a similarity in the leaves, I guess—at least, if you don't look too close. Why?"

"Because Tuffle and Morikawa just pulled up a whole greenhouse full of it."

"They thought it was marijuana?"

"Yeah. A patrol officer spotted it growing in a greenhouse over on Santa Fe Street. Tuffle and Morikawa went over there, decided it was definitely marijuana, and got Judge Ortega to issue a warrant, then went in and pulled up all the plants and arrested the guy who lived there when he showed up."

"But it was really okra."

37

"Yeah. And the guy is really pissed. Turns out he's from Louisiana, and he absolutely loves the stuff. That was his supply for the year. He freezes it. We've already heard from his lawyer."

"At least they got a warrant," Cotter said.

"Yeah. With the wrong address on it." He sighed, rolling his eyes heavenward as if pleading for the Almighty to save him from all the world's incompetents.

"Is that what you wanted to see me about?" Cotter asked.

"No." He handed Cotter a manila envelope. "Preliminary autopsy report on Wanda Grant. You weren't here so they delivered it to me."

"That was fast. It's always taken at least twenty-four hours to get them to so much as admit the victim is dead."

"Wanda was the only customer. Besides, it's Friday, and everyone over there likes to get away early on Friday." He ran his hand over the shiny smoothness of his head. "Only thing out of the ordinary in there is that she had a letter on her stomach. A large red *C* written with an indelible felt-tip."

"Could they tell when it had been put there?"

"No, not reliably enough to say whether the killer could have done it."

Cotter mentally ran down the list of Wanda Grant's friends and relatives. No *C*s. What else did he know about her? She was a fan of the Oakland Athletics, especially of Dave Stewart. She liked shopping, her favorite spot the Three Hills Mall.

"What was her middle name?" the captain asked.

"Jane."

"Hmmm. You think there's a connection? I mean, not many people go around marking their tummies with a felt-tip."

"I'll check it out, see if any of her friends or family ever heard of her drawing letters on herself."

"You got any suspects?" Zinn asked.

"So far, I've narrowed it down to the entire population of northern California."

"And in only a single day."

"But then, I'm one hell of a hard worker."

He was on his way back to his cubicle when a uniformed lieutenant named Rosenbloom grabbed him. Grinning, he said, "Hey, Cotter, you know what okra is?"

"That's that woman on TV, right? Okra Winfrey." He left Rosenbloom staring at his back as he continued on to his cubicle.

He phoned Wanda Grant's mother—Steven's voice in the background proclaiming loudly that she didn't have to talk to the cops if she didn't want to, and why the hell didn't they leave her alone in the first place. He wasn't making any of this easier for her to deal with. The world would be a much better place, Cotter thought, if all the hot-headed young men were sent off to mellowness camp until they learned to behave.

Wanda's mother had never known her daughter to draw letters on herself. Nor had her best friend, Leona Roberts. Neither of them could think of any special significance for the letter *C*.

Cotter hung up, feeling certain the letter had been left by the killer. An uneasiness skittered through him, as if something with hundreds of prickly little legs were crawling around inside his rib cage. Anyone who'd slit Wanda Grant's throat and then draw a letter on her flesh was no ordinary killer. This was a calculated act, the product of madness, and the reasoning behind it would be incomprehensible to the rest of us.

Cotter had encountered a killer like that.

A person who should have been no challenge for a man in Cotter's physical condition but who had turned out to be a very worthy opponent. Cotter had broken the man's arm.

And he wished he hadn't. Wished it desperately.

For he had paid a terrible price for what he'd done that day. An unimaginably terrible price.

He slipped the preliminary autopsy results from the envelope. Time of death was about what they'd originally believed. Wanda Grant had eaten some junk food before her death, sour-cream-and-onion flavored potato chips. No alcohol or other drugs in her system. No indications of serious health problems. She hadn't been sexually assaulted. No signs of a struggle. Apparently her killer had simply moved in and done it, before Wanda had been able to put up a fight.

Or was it someone she'd known, trusted?

No, he thought—this was the work of a stranger.

The *C* had been applied with a red felt-tip. The lab would eventually give him the brand, although the information might never prove useful. Why red? So it would show up on Wanda's dark skin, or was there some other reason?

A scarlet letter.

But then *the* scarlet letter had been an *A* for adultery. What was the meaning of a scarlet *C*? Crackpot? Criminal? Cretin? He turned it around and around in his head, coming up with nothing. Still, he was convinced that there was a message in that red letter, that it had been put there by the killer to say something.

Was this going to be one of those cat-and-mouse things, with some lunatic trying to make a game of it, leaving tantalizing clues just to see whether anyone got them? It was too soon to assume that. And yet the many-legged thing inside Cotter continued to skitter about in his most sacred and private places, for a part of him believed that whatever was happening here was just beginning.

When he was sure Cindy had had enough time to commute home from her San Francisco office, Cotter phoned her. "Hi," he said, "it's me."

"Hi yourself. You coming home, or is this going to be one of those long days of gumshoeing?"

"No more gumshoeing until Monday. The weekend's ours. You hungry?"

"Famished."

"How does seafood sound?"

"Wonderful."

"The Harbor?"

"The Harbor."

"Meet you there."

* * *

Hanging far enough back so he wouldn't be noticed, the man followed Cindy Brekke's silver Mercedes. He'd swapped the Lincoln for a tan Oldsmobile that had been left in a supermarket parking lot with the keys in the ignition. He'd switched the Oldsmobile's plate with one from a Honda Civic, knowing the Civic's owner might not notice the change for days or even weeks. Not foolproof, of course, but at least he wouldn't be driving a stolen car easily identifiable as such because of its license number. And within a day or two he'd swap the Oldsmobile for something else.

The silver Mercedes turned right on Mantara Street, passing a white windowless building with the flag flying out front—the First National Bank of Tres Cerros. An electronic sign flashed the time and temperature and urged passersby to have a nice day. Cindy continued heading west on Mantara. She passed a used-car lot. Flags suspended on wires waved colorfully. A Ford Escort had $3995 written on its windshield in huge cream-colored letters.

Hey, Cindy, where you going? You meeting our mutual friend?

He had his answer almost immediately, because the silver Mercedes pulled into a restaurant called The Harbor and parked beside a familiar brown Dodge with two extra antennas on it—Cotter's allegedly unmarked car. It might as well have huge neon letters that flashed the word COP. But then, it wasn't his concern. Cotter was not after him. In fact, no one was after him. No one knew he was here—not yet.

The man pulled to the curb in a no parking zone. He watched as Cindy Brekke got out of her car. She was thirty-something, but he was willing to bet she could still don a bikini any time she wanted. She was trim, with long legs. She didn't flaunt it. Not her style. Her blue and white dress was expensive but tasteful, her shoes sensibly low-heeled but of good quality, her pearl necklace most likely the genuine article. All her clothes, he was sure, were made of natural fibers, no polyester for Cindy Brekke, successful businesswoman. In a word, she was elegant, with the natural grace of one who knows how to display quality by understating it. He wondered whether Cindy Brekke knew that about herself.

That Cotter should have such a woman was startling. The policeman had always seemed the family type, lots of kids, big, furry dogs, vacations to Disneyland. That's what he had been before. But then, people changed, didn't they? Sometimes they grew.

Good for you, Cotter, he thought. You've surpassed my expectations for you.

Cindy Brekke disappeared into the big carved-wood door of The Harbor. *'Bye,* the man thought. Then he drove away from the restaurant. He had other business to attend to.

In bed that night, Cotter was drifting off to sleep when Cindy's hand slid over to his chest, her fingers gently gliding through the thick hair.

"Must have driven all those Texas women crazy," she said, "all this sexy chest hair."

"Ummm," he said.

Her hand began moving downward, following the hair. "It's like a furry road. I wonder where it leads."

"You copping a feel?" he asked.

"No. Feeling a cop."

Cotter laughed. "I can't believe you said that."

Her hand found the spot where the furry road ended, and Cotter heard himself groan. A moment later he was conducting some exploration of his own, and it was Cindy's turn to moan.

They did it with Cindy on top. He looked up at her, dimly seeing her slender shape in the dark room, her small firm, breasts, her shoulder-length brown hair. And he wondered how such a woman had ever fallen for someone like him.

"Where'd you ever learn to do a thing like that?" he asked.

"Marketing school."

"Must have been quite some school."

"Taught us how to bed clients."

"You ever done that?"

"No. Well, not because he was a client, but because he was a damned sexy guy. So that doesn't count."

"Ummm."

"What's that supposed to mean?"

"Nothing. It's just my way of letting you know I'm listening."

"Uh-huh."

"Well, it is."

"Are you suggesting that I went to bed with this particular client for reasons other than the ones I stated?"

"You can get all that from a perfectly innocent 'ummm'?"

"Well, are you?"

"No."

"Oh." She was silent a moment; then she said, "Does it bother you that I've . . ."

"Been to bed with other guys? No. Why should it bother me? At our age we're not supposed to be virgins. Jesus, why would a guy my age even *want* a virgin?"

"Good question," she said, snuggling up against him. A few silent moments passed; then she said, "Why do I act so . . . so little-girlish around you?"

"Maybe it's not little-girlish," he said. "Maybe it's just relaxing, having a good time."

"Yeah," she said. "That must be it."

They talked about this and that, and then Cotter found himself telling her about the Wanda Grant case. Earlier in their relationship Cotter had been uncertain about just how much he should say about the grim world of police work, but Cindy had seemed genuinely interested in what he did, so he'd started describing his active cases. She usually asked intelligent questions, occasionally challenging his assumptions, but even when she just listened, Cotter frequently found himself rethinking a situation, looking at it from a fresh perspective. Just one of the many ways his life had been better since Cindy had entered it.

After telling her about the red *C*, Cotter said, "I'd be willing to bet that the killer put it there, but I have no idea what it means."

"A scarlet letter," Cindy said.

"Yeah, that's what I thought." He told her the things he'd learned about Wanda Grant.

"Canseco," she said.

"Huh?"

"With the A's."

"That Canseco."

"The letter C. Maybe she had a secret crush on Jose."

"She was a Dave Stewart fan."

"Oh." Cindy mulled that over a moment, then said, "Why'd she go all the way to Oakland? Candlestick's a lot closer."

"I guess she didn't like the Giants."

"Me neither."

"You don't like the Giants?"

"No. I like the Dodgers."

"LA? Why LA?"

"I like Tommy Lasorda. I think he's cute."

"Ah. That explains everything."

Cotter was dozing off when she said, "Mike . . ."

"Hmmm?"

"What is it you're not telling me?"

"Not telling you about what?"

"I sense that something big happened to you in the past, something that had a tremendous effect on your life. Whatever it is, it just sort of hangs there between us sometimes."

"There's nothing hanging between us," he said.

"Mike . . ." She paused, apparently collecting her thoughts. "Look, we seem to have a relationship here that's . . . well, if not forever permanent, at least permanent for now. And when I think about that, about us, I realize that I really don't know anything about you. Every time I ask you anything about your background, you put me off. You change the subject, or you suddenly have to run out and pick up something at the store, or . . . or something. You have more ways of wriggling out of talking about yourself than Imelda Marcos has shoes."

"What do you want to know?"

"Everything."

"Everything?"

"I'm sharing my life with you," Cindy said. Her eyes grew moist, and she looked away. "I care about you, damn it. I love all the silly conversations we have, but in a way they seem designed to avoid any serious talk. I want more than that from someone I care about as much as I care about you." A tear slid down her cheek.

"Cindy . . ."

She wiped the tear away. "Mike, I want to know you. I want to know all there is to know about you. I want you to share yourself with me, the good and the bad."

Cotter gathered her in his arms. "You ask, and I'll do my best to answer," he said.

"Now I feel guilty."

"Guilty?"

"For forcing you to do this when I know you don't want to."

"You couldn't force me. I'm a lot bigger than you are."

"True."

"So ask your questions."

"You sure?"

"I'm sure. Hurry up before I think of an errand to run."

She laughed. "Okay. Let's start with what you did before becoming a cop."

"I drove a truck."

She shook her head. "A truck driver. Probably slapped waitresses on the behind and called them honey. Played Hank Williams records while you drove along picking your teeth."

"Can I get a word in here?" Cotter said. "First of all, it's not good manners to pat women on the behind, even at truck stops. Second, I didn't play Hank Williams, and I don't pick my teeth."

"What did you play?"

"Mostly classical."

"Really? What do you like?"

"I guess my favorite's Vivaldi's *Four Seasons*. I like the baroque and early classical periods a lot. Boccherini's third sonata for cello and harpsichord is fantastic."

"Jesus."

45

"I also like ballet, although my exposure to it has been minimal. Of those I've seen, *Swan Lake* is my favorite."

"This just proves my point," Cindy said. "Here I am in a relationship with you, and I don't even know you."

"Is it that important?"

"Of course it is. Let's trade information, what do you say? I'll tell you about me, and you'll tell me about you."

"Knowing about me won't change anything. I'll still be the same guy."

"But I want to know that guy."

Cotter sighed. He did not want to have this conversation.

Cindy said, "I was born in Madison, Wisconsin."

"Liberal, Kansas."

"I grew up in Wisconsin and Minnesota."

"Houston. Watched it grow into one of the biggest cities in the country."

"I attended the University of Minnesota where I earned a master's degree in marketing."

"University of Texas. Bachelor's degree. That's when I was driving a truck, by the way, in college. I worked my way through."

"I did it the easy way," Cindy said. "My family paid for it."

"My dad offered to help, but I wouldn't let him. He didn't have that much money, and I was the one getting the education, so I thought it should be my responsibility to pay for it."

"After college, my first job was with an advertising agency in Minneapolis."

"I became a Texas state police officer."

"I've never been married," Cindy said. She let it hang there.

Cotter hesitated, then said, "I'm not married either."

"Were you ever?"

"Yes," he said.

The silence stretched out; Cindy waiting for him to say more. Finally she broke it. "Are you divorced?"

"No. My wife's dead."

"I'm sorry. How did it happen?"

Cotter didn't answer.

"It bothers you a lot, doesn't it, what happened to your wife?"

Again Cotter didn't say anything.

"Talking about it might help," Cindy said gently.

"I'm not ready to talk about it."

"Well, when you are . . ."

"I'll know where to come," he said.

Cindy asked nothing further on the subject for the rest of the weekend. On Sunday, she surprised him with tickets to a chamber music concert in Palo Alto, featuring works by Telemann, Handel, Boccherini, and Bach.

"When did you do this?" he asked.

"While you were washing the breakfast dishes," she replied, grinning impishly. "I phoned for them, used my credit card."

The chamber orchestra performed beautifully.

Had there been anything developing on the Wanda Grant murder case, he would have spent Saturday and Sunday on the job, but nothing was shaking. He'd sent inquiries to both Washington and Sacramento concerning killers who drew letters on their victims, but there'd be no replies until next week sometime, and he had no local leads to follow up.

He was at his desk Monday morning when Captain Zinn stepped into his cubicle.

"You better see this," the captain said, dropping a clear plastic bag on Cotter's desk. It contained a single sheet of paper and a slit-open envelope with a local postmark. It was addressed to the Tres Cerros Police Department. Typed on the sheet of paper was a one-line message:

C is for cheat.

Six

"She shortchanged customers," Cotter said.

"You think she was killed for that?" Zinn asked.

His words reminded Cotter of what Wanda's mother had said: *A person wouldn't murder someone over something like that, would they?*

Cotter sighed. "Somebody getting so mad over being shortchanged they slit a person's throat? It could happen—crazier things *have* happened. But in this case it just doesn't feel right. Something else is going on here."

The captain frowned. "Why does it have to be anything more than it seems? She shortchanges some weirdo, and he slices her for it, draws the letter on her, then sends us a note to make sure we know why he did it."

Cotter nodded. "It could be like that. I'm just not comfortable with it."

"Anyone other than us and the medical examiner's office know about the red *C?*"

"No. It wasn't released to the media."

"So you think this is the genuine article, then?"

"Yeah," Cotter said. "I think it's from him."

He could *feel* the killer's presence in the room, as if lunacy and death were rolling off the letter like a vile fog. Cotter imagined it sticking wetly to his flesh and broke out in goose bumps.

"I'll get this down to the lab," Cotter said.

"Tell them to expedite it," Captain Zinn said.

As he carried the plastic bag down to the basement, where criminalistics was located, Cotter continued to feel as though some sort of link had been established between him and Wanda Grant's killer. It was as if he could mentally reach into a dark hole and find something waiting for him there. It was not a comfortable sensation, for when you reached into dark places you often found spider webs.

And spiders.

That morning he spoke with Denver Jones, Wanda's former boyfriend who turned out to be a loan officer at the Bank of America. He said he'd wanted to marry Wanda at one point, but in hindsight he was glad it hadn't worked out, because Wanda hadn't known what she wanted out of life, and the quiet, conservative existence he'd have offered probably wouldn't have satisfied her for long.

He had no idea who would want to kill her.

Nor did he know she was in the habit of shortchanging customers, although she wouldn't have told him about that because he would have disapproved. A banker, he said, had to be scrupulously honest.

Just like those guys running the savings and loans when the Reagan administration deregulated them, Cotter thought.

That afternoon, Sacramento faxed the information he had requested concerning people who had marked their victims with letters. There was a man in Los Angeles who'd painted the word "bitch" on his girlfriend, another in Fresno who'd held his wife down and cut the word "whore" into her hair with barber tools. Someone in San Diego had stabbed a vagrant to death and put his body into a dumpster, spray painting "garbage" on the back of the victim's shirt just in case anybody had any doubts about the significance of the body's being in a dumpster. No one had been charged in the San Diego case.

There were fifty-one incidents on the list, including a man who stepped around a corner in Oakland and accidentally got sprayed by a kid applying graffiti to the wall.

Most of them either had no relevance to Cotter's investigation or had been committed by people currently in jail. Cotter decided to request more information from the San Diego PD on the bum who'd been labeled garbage, since that homicide and the Wanda Grant murder both were committed by someone who wrote his or her reasons for the act on the victim.

Garbage.

Cheat.

The same kind of thinking prevailed in both cases. And both had involved the use of a knife. Again Cotter had the feeling that he had somehow moved closer to Wanda Grant's killer, that if he really tried, he could establish a mental link, peer into the perpetrator's mind. He shivered, for he sensed the madness there, hot and volatile, and he knew that looking upon its source, seeing first hand the evil, the bizarre system of fantasy and tortured logic, would be like stepping into the mental equivalent of the funhouse, a place in which mirrors reflected distorted, hideous images, and monsters lurked in every corner.

Cotter could not survive in that place.

Not if he wanted to remain sane.

He wondered why he felt this way. There was no firm link between the Wanda Grant murder and the incident in San Diego. And it was ridiculous to believe that he had some sort of psychic connection to either killer. So why was he feeling like this?

But then the answer was obvious, wasn't it?

He had looked upon the face of madness. When he was a rookie cop in Texas.

And later he had experienced its fury.

After half an hour of being transferred from one San Diego detective to another, he was connected with one named Houghton. He told Cotter that no arrests had been made in the murder of the vagrant, no suspects had ever been identified, and the case was considered inactive.

"Let's face it," Houghton said, "manpower and money are tight these days, and nobody gets that upset about what happens to a vagrant."

Cotter did. He cared about Wanda Grant, who never got a chance to find what she wanted in life. He cared about every victim he'd ever seen. He didn't let it get him so emotionally involved that he couldn't do the job, but at least on some level he cared. Maybe it was because he knew death and suffering so much more intimately than those officers who viewed victims strictly from the safety of professional detachment.

About four o'clock, the initial lab report on the letter was hand-delivered by Wu, who said, "No prints on the letter itself. The envelope was covered with them."

"All from postal employees, no doubt."

"Probably," the lab man said. Though in his early thirties, Wu had the smooth, youthful face of an eighteen-year-old. He attributed it to clean living and *mapo dofu*, a spicy Szechuan bean curd dish he was fond of.

"Paper's the cheap sixteen-pound bond stuff they sell in hundred-sheet packages just about everywhere," Wu said. "We can narrow it down, but it's going to be a brand sold by K-mart or someplace like that. Same for the envelope. Wal-Mart or K-mart. Typewriter was a manual, an old Adler. Even with just the few letters that were used, we found four keys with unique patterns of wear. You find the typewriter, and we can show it's the one the letter was typed on."

"Fibers?" Cotter asked.

"A few. Cotton-polyester blend. Presumably from the author's shirt. White and blue."

"Anything else?"

"Would you believe a signed confession in invisible ink?"

"No."

"I didn't think so."

"I can feel him," Cotter said as he lay in bed with Cindy that night.

"The person who killed Wanda Grant?"

"Not person. Man. It's a man."

"How can you be sure?"

"That's what I feel, a man."

"Cop's hunch? No," she said, answering her own question, "it's more than that, isn't it?"

"I don't know. I just know I feel this guy, and I've never done that before."

"What do you feel? What exactly?"

"Like I'm standing at the edge of some drop. Below is blackness. And something is pulling at me, saying, 'Hey, come on, join me. Just take a step, one little step, and I'll share all my secrets.' " He shuddered.

Cindy hugged him. "This . . . this feeling must be very strong."

"Very."

"These feelings relate somehow to this thing that happened to you, don't they?"

"I looked into the eyes of madness," he said. "Looking back on it, you could say I met the devil, and he was an ordinary-looking guy with dark hair and dimple on his chin."

"Are you religious?"

"No. But I met the devil that day. Maybe not the same one the preachers talk about, but it was the devil just the same." Cotter listened to the whine of the elevator as it rose to a floor somewhere in the upper reaches of the eighteen-story building. Somebody coming home late, he thought.

Or the devil, coming to pay a visit.

He said, "Texas is the Bible Belt, lots of fundamentalists. For some people, church is a whole way of life. Everything they do socially is connected with it—Bible readings, church picnics, rummage sales, you name it. Creationism, book banning, right-wing politics. Loved the hell out of Reagan. Probably still miss him. Anyway, that's why I'm not religious. I rebelled against all that."

"Was your family fundamentalist?"

"No. My dad referred to himself as a wishy-washy Methodist. Went to church on Easter and paid lip service to it the rest of the time."

Softly, Cindy said, "Do you realize that I don't even know what your father did? You're so reluctant to talk about the past that you won't even ask me about mine. You're supposed to wonder about my childhood, whether I rode a bicycle, whether I was ever a cheerleader. It shows you care."

"I care," Cotter said.

"I know. And I care about you—very much. But we've got to share ourselves. Otherwise we're just two strangers who happen to be living together."

"My father managed a grocery store," Cotter said.

"And your mother?"

"Died when I was a baby. My dad raised me."

"Does he still live in Texas?"

"He's dead. Drowned about five years ago when the fishing boat he and some of his friends rented sank in the Gulf."

"I'm sorry."

"It's one of those things that happens." He hesitated, then said, "How about you? What were you like as a little girl?"

"I wore glasses and was entirely too serious. None of the boys liked me."

"I'm a boy, and I like you."

"You do?"

"Yes, let me show you."

"That's not like, that's lust."

"Does that mean you want me to stop?"

"Don't you dare stop."

The fog had wrapped itself around the city like a shroud.

Sheri Vanvleet liked that image, something from a mystery, Sherlock Holmes, maybe. The mist was an impenetrable wall of white to her car's headlights. The wipers swished and thunked as they swept the constantly accumulating moisture from the windshield.

In the distance foghorns bellowed out their low notes of warning on San Francisco Bay. Sheri felt tingly all over. She always felt that way at the beginning of an adventure, and the mystery added by the thick fog lent spice.

Adventure.

That was what she called them—adventures. It was the perfect term, for to her they were neither business arrangements nor immoral acts. She didn't need the money. She needed the excitement of doing something wicked and daring. And she got to meet all sorts of interesting people.

If she wasn't here, driving to the south side of Tres Cerros, she would be home, watching a program on the jumbo-screen stereo TV set. Or watching a movie from their extensive collection. Or reading a mystery. Not that those pastimes were unpleasant. It was just that she had done them again and again and again. Night after night. Read or watch TV.

True, the house was lovely, a big place on a hill with a marvelous view of the city with the bay in the background. It had an enclosed, heated pool, a tennis court, more rooms than the two of them could use. Sheri had heard Elena, the part-time housekeeper, tell a delivery man once that if she lived in a house like this she would never go out, not even for groceries, because the place was so fantastic she would never want to leave it.

But to Sheri it was a plush prison.

She'd married William Vanvleet five years ago. She'd been twenty-three. He'd been fifty-seven. She had been pursuing a foundering modeling career; he'd been a wealthy businessman.

He flew to Paris and London and the Middle East, making deals.

She stayed at home and watched the jumbo television set.

Her first attempt to escape the boredom was about a year into the marriage, when she started making it with Stan, the big, broad-shouldered gardener. Just like Lady Chatterley. Except that Stan proved to be an inept lover, not to mention a total bore as a conversationalist. It was a lot like making it with a Mack truck. Lots of mass, but no finesse, no refinement.

The gardener had threatened to blackmail her, and she'd put the barrel of her chrome-plated pistol between his eyes and told him she would use it if he ever came back. Apparently he'd believed her, because she'd heard nothing further from him.

She glanced at her purse, which was in the BMW's passenger seat. The same pistol was in it now. It was part of the game, part of the fun.

I should have been a spy, Sheri thought.

But that was just silliness. Spying could be dangerous. And what Sheri did was not. Sure, in LA or San Francisco it would be risky. But this was Tres Cerros. Expensive homes, luxury apartments, tennis courts, golf courses. The people who came here on business did so because of the Brockman Foundation, a think tank that provided extra income for a lot of professors from Stanford. She wasn't sure exactly what it did, except that people there were always making computer models of things.

And then there was Woodson-Wythe, which made electronic

stuff for the Pentagon. It was small potatoes as defense contractors went, and the think tank drew a lot more out-of-towners.

Staring into the fog, Sheri tried to see the road ahead of her. The fog was so thick she couldn't risk going over twenty miles an hour, and she was already late. Mentally she shrugged. She'd been late before. No one had ever complained.

Getting into the business had been simplicity itself. She'd given her number to a few desk clerks and bellman, promised them a commission on any business they sent her way. The phone had started ringing almost at once. She still had her model's figure and long legs, the thick blond hair, the smooth face with high cheekbones. She was in demand.

She wasn't worried that William would find out. His business kept him away so much that he'd never become part of the Tres Cerros social scene, although from what Sheri understood, the local upper crust was too snobbish to accept her anyway. She was from Cleveland, and she'd met William in New York. No one here knew her.

Although Peninsula Street was one of the city's major arteries, it was deserted tonight because of the fog. None of the community's residents wanted to risk their expensive machines in visibility of less than a car length. Sheri could see the white line, which was enough to keep her from driving into a parked car or a building. The lights of the city were invisible. Even the streetlamps were nothing but patches of brightness, floating above her in the impenetrable whiteness.

She nearly drove right through the intersection with Ocean Avenue. At the last possible moment, the traffic signal popped out of the mist, its bright, colorful lights seeming incongruous in this world of moisture and night.

Sheri suddenly felt very alone. Isolated by the fog and cocooned within her car, she seemed as cut off from the world as a castaway on a tiny island.

She shook the feeling off. This was her night for adventure and mystery, Mata Hari passing along secrets in a foggy alleyway.

She wondered what the man would be like. The last time it had been, for lack of a better term, a nerd. A computer expert visiting the Brockman Foundation. A thirty-eight-year-old man who'd never made it with any woman except his wife, if you could imagine such a thing. He'd taken the plunge, asked the bellman if he knew any women who'd like to have fun. The bellman had smiled and given him Sheri's number.

Another time it had been a salesman whose only sex life was with women he paid to come to his motel room. They had all been like that, men who in one way or another were lost, taking the sure path of paying for sex rather than risking rejection—or whatever it was they feared.

Sheri had done her best to show them a good time.

And she found the naughtiness of it sexually stimulating. Sheri enjoyed her work.

It had occurred to her that she, just like the men who paid her, was seeking something life had not given her. She almost always attributed it to boredom and tried to put the matter out of her mind. Sheri was not fond of self-analysis.

The entrance to the Seaward Hotel appeared out of the fog, and she pulled into the lot, found a parking space. Her BMW fit right in with all the other expensive cars. Before getting out, she removed all the identification, credit cards, and money from her purse. She put these things in the glove compartment and locked it. All she ever took with her were things like comb and makeup and tissues. And prophylactics. She had no intention of getting AIDS.

And of course, she had the gun.

She walked toward the hotel, the fog clinging to her like the icy fingers of ghosts.

The customer was in room 317. She walked past the desk, stepped into the waiting elevator. She wore a conservative blue dress, low heels. The men she visited did not want someone who looked like a street hooker coming to their rooms.

Of course, underneath the ordinary garb she wore skimpy black underwear.

No one noticed her as she left the elevator, walked to the door of room 317, and knocked gently. A tall, dark-haired man opened the door. Sheri was surprised. Usually her clients were on the homely side—drab, nerdy-looking guys. This man was a hunk. As her brother in Cleveland would have said, *The dude should have more pussy than you can shake a stick at.*

"Hi," she said, smiling. "I'm Mindy." Mindy was her professional name.

He returned the smile. "Hi, I'm Rex." Which was probably his name just for the evening as well. "Come in," he said, stepping back out of the doorway.

At this point she usually waited to see what a client would do. Some were so nervous she had to step in and guide the conversation. Others just took over.

"Drink?" Rex asked, and the confidence in that single word told her that he wasn't going to need any help from her to get through the evening. It also made her wonder again why this guy had called her. He could go down to the bar, mingle a few minutes, save himself three hundred dollars.

"What are my options?" she asked, sitting down on the couch.

"I've got some nice Scotch, and I make a mean martini."

Neither of which she had ever been able to acquire a taste for, but she was here to please, not to insist on drinks of her choice. "I'll have whatever you're having," she said.

He had one of those suitcases that was really a portable bar open on the dresser. As he assembled the drinks with his back to her, Sheri noticed that he was doing something odd. It took her a moment to realize what. He did everything with his right hand, the left one just sort of resting on the edge of the dresser, not really contributing. She wondered whether that was why he was paying for sex. Maybe he had a fake arm, and he was embarrassed about it. Showing it to a prostitute would be sort of like showing it to a doctor. The relationship was professional.

He brought her a drink—a martini—then returned for his own, carrying the glasses in his right hand, his left arm hanging at his side. He sat down beside her. As they sipped their drinks, he studied her, a bemused expression on his face. He had the features of someone trustworthy, the look of a person you'd confide in, a person who would offer help if you needed it. Sheri wasn't certain what it was about the face that gave it that look; it was just there.

Except for his blue eyes, in which Sheri saw something vaguely disquieting. Something akin to smugness.

He had a dimple in the center of his chin.

He smiled, and it was a warm, reassuring smile, an aw-shucks smile. And yet there was something vaguely disconcerting about that grin, for it was too confident, almost contemptuous, arrogant. The smirk of the inquisitor looking upon an accused heretic.

Sheri banished that image from her consciousness. She gulped some of her martini. It wasn't as bad as she'd thought it would be.

"Here on business?" she asked, surprised by the nervousness in her voice. Some men liked to talk about themselves and some didn't. Sheri usually tested the waters, then went with what it appeared the client wanted.

"Business?" he said thoughtfully. "Yes, I guess you could say that."

"What business are you in?"

"Collections."

"You mean, like getting people to pay their bills?"

"Sort of."

Sheri wasn't sure whether he wanted to talk about himself or not. No one had ever responded quite like this before. She took another swallow of her drink and said, "How do you get them to pay up?"

"I simply take what's owed."

"How . . ." The question couldn't quite seem to form itself in her mind. She felt strange, as if her brain was one of those snow scenes in a transparent plastic ball and someone had just shaken it.

And then it hit her: he'd put something in her drink. The no-good son-of-a-bitch had put something in her drink. He was smiling at her, and suddenly it seemed that grin was floating there all by itself, detached, like something from *Alice in Wonderland*.

And from the swirling tangle of thoughts in her head, one suddenly clamored urgently for her attention. *What's he going to do?*

And that was followed by an even more urgent thought: *Get out of here! Now!*

She picked up her purse and stood, swaying, the room spinning. "I'm leaving," she said, her words distant, muddled.

The man just watched her.

Sheri moved toward the door, which seemed a football field's length away, unreachable. Forgetting everything else, she concentrated on that door, put one foot in front of the other. Perspiration had formed on her forehead; a drop trickled into her eye. She ignored it.

The room tilted as if it had just been heaved up on one side by the mother of all earthquakes. Sheri managed to keep her balance, keep moving toward that door. Finally, she reached out for the knob, and her fingers found it.

"I'm afraid I can't let you leave," the man said behind her. *Right* behind her.

Sheri whirled, struggling to maintain her balance, to make her brain function. *The gun,* something in her head whispered. *Use the gun.* Her hand obeyed the command, found the butt of the pistol, pulled it out of her purse.

The man stood about four feet from her, grinning.

"Geh back," she said, her speech slurred. "Geh back er I'll blow your fluckin' head off."

"Nothing personal," he said, "but you have to die today."

"Keep away f' me, you cwazy fuckin'—"

Seeming to come from nowhere, his foot knocked her gun from her hand. It fell on the floor between them, and the man picked it up. "I'm an expert," he said, matter-of-factly.

Then, before she could scream, he clamped a hand over her mouth, and moved her into the bathroom.

He pushed her into the shower.

It was then that she saw the knife.

It was the last thing she ever saw.

Seven

The man undressed, folding each item as he took it off and putting it into the plastic laundry basket. It wasn't truly necessary, he realized to fold garments that were going to the laundry, but he found a basket full of haphazardly arranged clothes unsightly.

When he was nude, he stood before the bathroom mirror, inspecting his body. Except for his bad arm, in which the muscles had atrophied, and which hung at a slightly odd angle, he was in perfect shape, his tummy flat, his body hard and sleek. Even in confinement, he had exercised daily, maintained his condition.

Blue eyes stared back at him from the mirror. They were deep and mysterious, twin tunnels that seemed to lead into his very core, and yet they revealed nothing about him. They were intelligent eyes, wily and shrewd.

His hair was short, not so short that it looked like something from the early fifties, but just long enough on top to part, just long enough around the ears and neck to be stylish. He winked at the image in the mirror, which winked back at him and smiled. Smiling, he noted, accentuated his chin dimple.

He didn't need to bathe tonight, for he had showered at the hotel. To wash the blood off.

Leaving the bathroom, he went to the small dresser and opened the middle drawer. Everything inside was neat, folded to the exact same size, stacked with the precision of a brick mason. He unfolded his pajamas, slipped them on. He put on a clean pair every night.

The room was spotless. He'd dusted every nook and cranny, scrubbed up every suspect bit of discoloration on the vinyl floor tiles, disinfected everything in the bathroom. It was a small room, its only furnishings a double bed, a dresser, a chair, a wastebasket, and a Korean TV set that was bolted to the wall. Home sweet home.

In the corner was the Adler typewriter he'd bought at a little shop near Palo Alto. When he typed, he had to use the bed as his seat and the chair as his desk. It wasn't the best arrangement in the world—the machine rocked on the chair's spongy upholstered seat—but then the letters he wrote were few and quite short.

He turned off the lights, climbed into bed. A warm tingle slithered through him as he recalled what had transpired that night. The first time he'd killed, it had been partially the result of anger, an annoyance that simmered and grew until it exploded into action. He considered the word "exploded" and decided it was wrong, for it implied sudden, uncontrolled rage, which was not his style. When the situation became intolerable, he had thought things through, planned his moves, then taken action. That was how he did things.

And when he'd killed his mother and father, he'd discovered that the taking of life had rewards beyond those envisioned. For a few moments he'd had total control over two other human beings. The ultimate power had been his. It was a heady feeling.

Pleasure had not been his objective in the slayings he'd committed in California. The whore, the convenience store clerk, and the bum in San Diego had been targets of opportunity, as the military would say. Nothing personal. He'd been looking for suitable victims, and those three people had been available. And the Hollingsworths had died simply because he could not let them live. The five killings had been carried out in pursuit of a larger goal.

Still the deaths had provided a subtle satisfaction, akin to sampling a fine wine or eating an exquisitely prepared meal.

Will you know how I did it, Cotter? he wondered. *Will you feel my presence when you stand in the hotel room where the whore died and sense what I did and why? Will you realize that it's all for you?*

Eight

As Cotter approached room 317, a uniformed cop hurried out, nearly knocking him over. The officer had a hand clasped over his mouth. Had his face been any greener, he could have passed for a Mutant Ninja Turtle. Cotter stepped into the room.

Thompson from the medical examiner's office was there, looking at the nude body of a woman that was stretched out on the bed. Her blond hair was a tangled mess on the pillow, and the pillow itself was damp, as if she'd washed her hair without bothering to dry it. Her eyes were open, staring lifelessly at the ceiling, her expression blank, showing none of the horror of her death.

Thompson moved to the side, revealing the massive bloody hole in the woman's midsection. Cotter's stomach constricted as though something cold and clammy had reached into him and touched it. He knew of only one killer who disemboweled his victims. But then, that psychopath was locked away in a maximum-security facility in Texas, wasn't he?

"She's been eviscerated," Thompson said.

"Where are her organs?" Cotter asked.

"There," Thompson said, inclining his head toward the yellow plastic bucket at the foot of the bed.

Cotter started to step over for a closer look, then changed his mind. "What'd he remove?"

"Everything. Bladder, liver, intestines, you name it. Cleaned her out."

"Did he know what hc was doing?"

"You mean, did he have medical skill? No. But he had a very sharp knife of some sort, and a lot of patience."

There was no blood on the bed. Cotter said, "Looks like it was done in the bathtub or shower, and then she was put there afterward."

Thompson nodded. "There's something else here you should see. On her thigh."

Cotter stepped over to the bed. Emblazoned on her right thigh in red was the letter *W*.

"Whore?" Thompson said.

"Witch, wicked, wretched, wild." Cotter sighed. "Whore seems most likely, doesn't it? I'll have to find out whether it fits. How long ago did she die?"

"Last night sometime. That's as close as I can get at the moment."

The maid had come in to clean the room around ten-thirty that morning, and people in rooms at the other end of the hall had heard her scream.

Turning around, Cotter found Sergeant Abbott of the patrol division standing by the door. Abbott ran his fingers through his thinning brown hair. "We got a serial killer here, Mike?"

"I don't know yet," Cotter said.

But he did know. This was the work of the same person who'd killed Wanda Grant. It would be too much of a coincidence for two knife-wielding killers using the same signature to go to work at the same time in the same place. But his certainty that the same person had killed both women had nothing to do with coincidence. Cotter could feel the killer, sense his essence, as if it were a scent left in the room like a trace of perfume.

Inwardly he shivered, for it was the odor of madness, and he knew what it was capable of, knew it intimately.

Cotter said, "Anyone call the lab?"

"Cheech and Chong are on the way."

"Any ID on the victim?"

"Nobody I've talked to knows who she is. There's a purse there." He pointed to the small black bag by the couch. "But I didn't let any of my guys touch it. Her clothes are in the bathroom. We didn't touch those either."

Cotter nodded his approval. The lab guys were always complaining about how the uniformed officers—and sometimes even detectives—messed up crime scenes. "You check to see who the room's registered to?"

"Nobody. It's supposed to be vacant. It's one of the rooms the hotel holds back, just in case they need it for some reason, like if an important customer shows up unexpectedly or something."

Cotter made a mental note: Find out who would know which rooms were kept for that purpose.

"You make sure the staff and the guests on this floor will stick around so we can talk to them?"

"All taken care of. I've also got a list of names in case anyone decides to disappear."

"Good. Thanks." Noting the portable two-way radio in the sergeant's hand, Cotter said, "Call in and ask for whoever's available in detectives. I'm going to need some help."

Gonzales and Wu arrived, began taking pictures, lifting prints, vacuuming for potential evidence. Thompson left. Kozlovski, wearing a canary yellow sports jacket, showed up to assist, and Cotter had him start talking to the staff and guests.

Wu said, "Hey, look what I found under the couch."

Wearing the surgical gloves he'd donned the moment he'd arrived at the crime scene, he was holding up a plastic bag containing a chrome-plated automatic. "Twenty-five caliber," he said.

"As soon as you get back, run the serial number," Cotter said.

"You think I'd forget?" Wu asked, a little miffed.

"No. Sorry. I guess I've got a lot on my mind."

"I can see where you would," Wu said, "what with a serial killer on your hands."

"The serial killer's only a maybe at this point," Cotter said. "Before that's official, you've got to find me something to prove it."

"No problem," Wu said. "The same guy was in both places, he had to leave something. A hair, some blood, some fibers, something we can match. Nobody fails to leave something." He grinned. "Well, not very often, anyway."

Gonzales handed Cotter the black purse. "I'm done with this for the moment, but I'd appreciate it if you didn't dump out the contents the way some guys do. They forget that we deal in tiny particles, some of which can easily get lost and some of which can easily get added if you're not careful. Defense attorneys can have a field day, they find that we weren't careful with the evidence." He smiled. "If you know what I mean."

Cotter promised to be careful.

Small, with a thin strap, it was the sort of purse a woman carried when she went out in the evening if she wasn't going anyplace too formal. Inside Cotter found a comb, makeup, hairbrush, a package of condoms, and the key to a BMW. No identification.

"I need this key," Cotter said.

Gonzales shrugged. He'd given his little lecture for the day. The rest was up to Cotter.

Sergeant Abbott was gone, but the uniformed officer who'd been a little green around the gills earlier was stationed outside the door. Cotter gave him the key. "Go down to the parking lot and find the BMW this fits."

The cop returned about ten minutes later. Handing Cotter the key, he said, "Blue one in the side lot. I didn't go inside, but I ran the license plate." He glanced down at a small notebook. "It's registered to William and Sheri Vanvleet, 1616 Hillcrest, Tres Cerros."

"Get Dispatch to send someone over to that address, see if there's anyone there who can tell us whether this woman is Sheri Vanvleet."

The cop disappeared into the hallway, and Cotter just stood there, feeling apprehensive. This woman had a *W* on her body — for *whore?* Wanda Grant had a *C*.

C is for cheat.

The two killings were different. Not the work of two killers — he didn't believe that — but done for different reasons. If someone cheats you, you get even. Simple, direct. But killing a prostitute wasn't like that. The motivations were more complicated.

Why did I kill them? Robert Heckly had said, referring to his first victims. *Because they pissed me off.*

Cotter pushed the memory away. Heckly was in Texas, in a place no one had ever escaped from.

Wu emerged from the bathroom with the victim's clothes. A plain blue dress and black shoes, things you would wear to go to a medium-priced restaurant, not the customary attire of a hooker. The skimpy black underwear was the only thing that seemed appropriate for a lady of the evening.

What were you doing here in your conservative clothes and

sexy underwear? Cotter wondered, looking at the woman who lay on the bed, her insides in a plastic bucket. *Are you Sheri Vanvleet who drives a BMW? How did this thing happen to you?*

"Mike," Kozlovski said. He was standing in the doorway. "Can I see you out here a moment?"

Cotter joined him in the hall. A thin young man in a cheap suit stood beside him, nervously shifting his weight from foot to foot. The suit didn't fit him very well. Its collar stood out from the back of his neck as if he were hanging from a peg.

"This is Christopher Burns," Kozlovski said. "He's one of the desk clerks. Christopher, why don't you tell Detective Cotter what you told me."

"The woman," Burns said, inclining his head toward the room, "I think it might be Mindy—at least, that's the name she uses. We have a number, and we're supposed to give it to guys who are . . . well, you know, looking for a good time. I tell them to ask for Mindy and say Chris said to call."

"What do you get?" Cotter asked.

"Twenty."

"What's her real name?"

"Mindy's the only name I've got."

"You set her up with that room?" Cotter asked.

"No. Nobody's supposed to be in that room. I just give her number to guys who already have a room."

"What makes you think the woman in this room is Mindy?"

"She was here last night. I saw her. But she never gave me my twenty. I . . . I was wondering about it, because she always pays up right away. Then I heard about the blond woman in 317 . . ."

"How'd she get into 317?"

"I don't know."

"Who'd you give her number to?"

"Nobody. Not last night. But she still owed me the twenty. That was our deal. Otherwise she could make an appointment for a day or two later and cut me out—even if it was me that got her the business. You know, I mean, I'd have no way of knowing, would I?"

"Could someone else have given it out—another clerk, a bellman?"

66

"I was on the desk last night," Burns said. "I guess Ignacio could have given someone her number, but I didn't."

"Who's Ignacio?" Cotter asked.

"Bellboy," Kozlovski said. "He says nobody asked him for a hooker last night."

"Take a look," Cotter said, pushing the door open.

The desk clerk hesitated, then stepped into the room, his eyes fixing on the bed. He sucked in his breath, then turned and stumbled back into the hallway, saying, "Shit, shit, shit," repeating it quietly to himself, all the color gone from his face.

"That her?" Cotter asked.

Burns stared at him as if he hadn't understood the question.

"That Mindy?" Cotter asked.

The young man nodded. "Yeah, that's her." He shivered. "Who would do something like . . . like *that?*"

"That's the sixty-four-dollar question," Kozlovski said.

Kozlovski led the desk clerk away, and for a moment Cotter just stood there in hallway, wondering how many people could have known Mindy's telephone number. The staff at the hotel knew, at least those in a position to profit from knowing it. And all Mindy's customers knew it. The latter would be next to impossible to identify. The desk clerk might remember a few names, but there were many he wouldn't. How many lone men had checked into the hotel over the past few months, all of them from out of town? Cotter sighed.

As he stepped back into the room, Wu looked up from the equipment case that lay open on the floor in front of him. "Found diluted blood in the drain of the shower," he said. "Also a small smear on the jamb of the bathroom door and a couple places on the carpet, probably from when he carried her to the bed."

Cotter tried to picture what happened here. The killer had probably drugged her or knocked her out, carried her into the bathroom, removed her clothes and his, too, then put her into the shower and gone to work with the knife. When he was done, he'd washed away most of the blood, carried her to the bed. Then he'd washed any remaining blood off himself dressed, and left.

After Wu and Gonzales were through with it, Cotter checked out the bathroom. He found himself staring at the shower. It was ordinary looking, with a glass door and white ceramic tiles. Barely room enough for two people, and yet somehow the killer had hollowed out a woman in that small space, putting her insides in a plastic bucket. She probably had her back propped up against the wall, the killer straddling her. Or maybe he leaned in. Why'd the guy do it like that? Why not just do it on the bed? What did he care if he got the sheets all messy?

Cotter had the feeling it was done that way just to make the cops wonder. Someone who left one-letter messages on his victims probably considered himself clever, liked to think he was messing with the cops' heads.

Is that what you're doing? he asked, still sensing a mental link with the killer. It was like getting one of those phone calls when the person on the other end of the line doesn't say anything, but you still know someone's there. Someone was there now. In his head.

If the killer was listening, he wasn't answering.

When he left the bathroom, the lab guys were discussing the contents of a plastic bag. From where Cotter stood, he was unable to tell what was in it. He stopped and studied the victim, keeping his eyes away from the gaping hole in her midsection. She had a pretty face, an actress's face, with smooth skin and thick blond hair, and her legs were long and shapely. Mindy. And maybe Sheri Vanvleet of Hillcrest Drive, where all the homes had a wonderful view and sold for "one" or "two."

W is for whore.

But why would someone who lived on Hillcrest Drive be a call girl? It didn't make any sense.

He told the lab guys to check out the blue BMW when they were done here. He'd wait to go through it until they were finished with it.

"It's so frightening," Cindy said. "It's hard to believe there are really people out there who do things like that. It makes me want to lock myself inside and never come out."

They were sitting on Cindy's couch, reading, stopping from time to time to talk. Cindy didn't care much for television. That

68

was okay with Cotter; watching TV was what he did when he had nothing to do.

"Do you have any suspects?" Cindy asked.

"No."

"Will he kill again?"

"Yes."

"You can still feel him, can't you?"

"Yes. Do you believe that, that I can feel him?"

She hesitated, then said, "I can't picture myself doing it, but I believe you can. Does that make any sense?"

Cotter said it did. "The captain's assigned Kozlovski and Tuffle to work with me full-time. I can have more guys if I need them."

"Will you get him?"

"I hope so."

"How are you going about it? I mean, what exactly do you do?"

"Today we talked to the staff and guests at the hotel to see if any of them saw the guy. None of them did. We found Sheri Vanvleet's purse in the glove compartment of her car. The photo on her driver's license matched, and later one of her neighbors identified her. So we're sure it's her. Had a hard time locating her husband. We finally found him in Egypt. He's on his way back.

"I got the names of all the staff, everyone who's worked there in the last six months. We also got the names of all the lone men who registered at the hotel in the last six months. The staff pointed out the ones they were pretty sure they'd given Sheri's name to. I put all the names into the computer—staff, guests, everybody."

"And?"

"And a name's not much for the computer to go on. It likes a social security number, date of birth, something solid. Take Ignacio Chavez—the computer came back with thirteen of them. Offenses ranging from rape to reckless driving."

"Rape . . . that's a violent crime."

"This killer's not a rapist—at least, he hasn't raped any of his victims. He may not even have a record. There are lots of very scary people out there who don't."

"What do you do now?"

"Keep plugging away. We find out everything we can about

Sheri Vanvleet. You never know what will lead you somewhere. We check out the people on our list, starting with the staff, because they're the ones who knew about both the vacant room and Sheri Vanvleet."

"Why would someone do something like . . . that?"

Cindy was looking at him as though the murder had hurt her in some way, betrayed a trust, maybe destroyed her faith in something she'd always believed in. It was a little-girl look, pleading, asking Cotter to explain this terrible thing, make the world right again.

"Madness," Cotter said.

He gathered her in his arms and held her. He understood where she was coming from. He knew better than anyone how madness could demolish the foundations you'd built your life on and leave you with nothing solid to cling to.

"I don't want to talk about this anymore," Cindy said. "I know that ignoring it won't make it go away, but what he did to that woman . . . I just don't know how to deal with it."

"It's okay," Cotter said softly.

Cindy was reacting this way because it had happened here, where she lived. Similar crimes in Maine—or Texas—she could handle. But when it happened this close, you could see yourself as the next victim.

And it bothered her because of her relationship with the investigating officer. She knew someone who was involved, someone who had been there, had looked upon Sheri Vanvleet's disemboweled corpse. Someone who, if he did his job well, would come face-to-face with the killer.

They went back to reading. The true professional, Cindy usually read about advertising and marketing, although sometimes she'd opt for a mystery and occasionally something a little more literary, like Thomas Hardy. Cotter wasn't fussy. He'd read whatever was handy, even the tattered magazines in doctors' offices. He didn't like mysteries, though. They reminded him of work, and the writers always made a lot of mistakes, showed they'd never been cops and were just guessing about what it was like.

Cindy put down her *Advertising Age* and said, "I . . . I just can't stop thinking about it, about what happened to that woman.

I keep imagining what it must have been like for her."

He hugged her gently, wishing he could tell her that he'd protect her, and not to worry, not about anything. But he couldn't say that, for the last time someone had needed him, he hadn't been there.

For years he'd been tormented by that single thought. *If he'd been there. If only he'd been there.*

The way Cindy was curled against him he looked down on the part in her brown hair. She dyed it, he knew, to keep the gray from showing. She pretended not to care about that sort of thing. If he pressed her on it, she'd say it was for business. In advertising you had to look good. It wasn't vanity. In truth, she hated the gray sneaking in when she was only thirty-five.

Cotter smiled, thinking that the attitude was her, part of what she was. And he liked what she was.

But I can't protect you, he thought.

The last people who needed me found that out the hard way.

His eyes grew moist, and for a moment he thought their moisture would spill out and roll down his cheeks, but he held it back.

By the time Cindy looked up, his eyes were dry.

Nine

The first thing Cotter did when he got to the station the next morning was dial a number in Texas. It was pointless, making this call. He knew that. And yet it was the only way to rid himself of the icy nugget of apprehension churning in his belly.

"Southwestern State Hospital," a woman said in a West Texas drawl.

State Hospital was a euphemism. The place was a warehouse for the most dangerous criminally insane patients. Located in the hot, desolate country of southwest Texas, the facility was a hundred miles from anywhere. Where an escapee would have nowhere to go except into barren and inhospitable country in which the chances of survival would be slim. Where there were no neighbors to object. And where land was cheap.

The facility was the constant target of budget cuts in these lean times in the oil patch. Its only function was to relieve the overcrowding at the state's other mental institutions, and politicians, faced with a shrinking budget, didn't care much about the conditions in which the criminally insane lived. The only thing that kept the place open was the knowledge that the patients at Southwestern were all extremely dangerous, and the institution was considered escape-proof. Cotter thought closing the facility would be a grave mistake.

He asked for Keith Stiller, the administrator.

"Detective Cotter," Stiller said cheerfully in his Upper Midwestern accent. "What can I do for you?"

Stiller knew what he could do for him. Cotter only called for one reason. "Is he still there?" Cotter asked. He heard a click in the background. How far away was *he* from the phone? Had *he* heard the same click? Was *he* standing at Stiller's side? Was it *him* on the phone, mimicking Stiller's voice?

Forcing himself to stop thinking such nonsense, Cotter said, "I just want to know that he's still there."

"He's still here."

"When's the last time you checked?"

"An hour or two ago."

"You saw him personally?"

"Yes." He paused, then said, "Believe me, Mr. Cotter, when I tell you that no one escapes from here. No one has. And no one will."

"There's no place that can't be escaped from—by someone, sooner or later."

"This institution is surrounded by three fences, Mr. Cotter. The middle one is electrified. We've got a state-of-the-art electronic security system. And we're in the middle of nowhere, over a hundred miles from El Paso. There are no towns, not even any isolated ranch houses, that can be reached on foot."

Cotter said he was aware of all that.

"And in the unlikely event that Heckly did get away, you'd be notified immediately," Stiller added. In other words, no need to call us, we'll call you. Or more succinctly, stop bugging us.

Cotter thanked Stiller for his time and ended the conversation, relieved both by what he'd been told and by no longer being electronically linked to the place.

He met with Tuffle and Kozlovski in an unoccupied interrogation room, which offered more space and privacy than his cubicle. They decided they should check out William Vanvleet. Although he could hardly have murdered his wife personally if he was in Egypt at the time she died, he could still be involved. They needed to know about his business and financial affairs, whether he had anything to gain by his wife's death, whether he had any enemies. It would most likely turn out to be boring work, but it had to be done. Tuffle, the junior detective, got the assignment.

Kozlovski would finish checking out the employees of the Seaward Hotel, along with any guests thought to be among Sheri Vanvleet's customers. Cotter would see what he could learn from the Vanvleets' neighbors and talk to her husband when returned later that day. They left the room, going in separate directions.

Wu intercepted Cotter in the hallway. "Just the guy I'm looking for," the lab man said. "We got a human scalp hair from the hotel that appears to match one from the convenience store. Not proof positive at this stage, but I'd say it's most likely from the same person. Both hairs are from a male Caucasian."

"Color?" Cotter asked.

"Dark brown."

Cotter said, "Thanks, Tommy. Anything else I should know?"

Wu shook his head. "Your perp doesn't leave many clues."

"Only the ones he wants us to have," Cotter said grimly.

None of Sheri Vanvleet's neighbors knew anything about her—except that they didn't like her. "She was pretty," one gray-haired lady sniffed, "which was why he married her, I suppose." Another summed Sheri up thusly: "You'd see her drive past from time to time, but no one in the neighborhood really knew her. She kept to herself. I guess she didn't feel she'd fit in." Translation: She was an outsider, not one of them, not welcome in a neighborhood where maids from Colmer did the housework, eighty-thousand-dollar cars filled the garages and the contents of women's closets represented an animal-rights activist's worst nightmare. It was a matter of blue and green: one was absent from Sheri's blood; the other was what she was after.

Her husband returned that afternoon. Jet lag and the news of his wife's death had left him befuddled, unable to grasp what had happened or come to terms with the way Sheri amused herself in his absence. He shook his head a lot and looked at Cotter as if pleading for an explanation that would turn the pain and confusion into something he could understand. But that was beyond Cotter's ability. William Vanvleet needed a psychologist, not a cop.

Cotter used his car's two-way radio to check with Tuffle, who had learned that William Vanvleet's business dealings were concentrated in Asia and the Middle East, and involved everything from computers to tool steel, all made in places where labor costs were low, law enforcement lax. He was worth millions, his businesses were all healthy, and his contractual marriage to Sheri stated that in the event of a divorce, she left with what she came with. Cotter suspected that was nothing. He told Tuffle to keep at it.

He met Kozlovski at a small restaurant on the edge of town. Both men ordered coffee. Cotter told him what he'd learned so far; then it was Kozlovski's turn.

"One present and two past employees of the hotel have records," Kozlovski said, "but all three claim to have alibis for at least one of the murders. I'm still verifying them." He pulled out a notebook, flipped it open. "That hotel's like all places that pay rock-bottom wages. Lots of turnover. I must have a dozen former employees I haven't even talked to yet. I haven't even started on the guests."

"Let's divide up the employees," Cotter said. "We'll worry about the guests afterward."

"Hey, I won't pass up a deal like that."

The restaurant was one of those squeaky clean places that sold ordinary American fare—hotcakes and burgers and salads—unexcitingly prepared. Bring the kids. Family dining at reasonable prices. A teenage girl in a blue-and-gold uniform refilled their cups. She looked more like a cheerleader than a waitress.

"You think this guy just does women?" Kozlovski asked.

Cotter considered that. "I think he prefers women."

"But he'd do a guy if the circumstance arose."

"Yeah, I believe he'd do a guy if it suited him." He thought of the San Diego man whose body had been labeled as garbage and left in a dumpster.

Kozlovski sighed. "We going to get this guy? So far, all we know is that he's probably a white guy with brown hair. What's that leave us with? Twenty-five per cent of the population? Thirty per cent?"

"Do you have to be so encouraging?" Cotter asked.

"Hey," Kozlovski said, "I'm a realist." He tore a page from his notebook and copied six names and addresses on it, then handed it to Cotter. "Six for you, six for me," he said.

For a few moments, neither of them spoke. Finally Kozlovski broke the silence. "Remember Thornton Hollingsworth?"

"Who?" And then the name registered. "Wasn't he that computer hacker who broke into the systems at the naval air station and all those other places?"

"That's the one. Rosenbloom told me they found Hollingsworth and his wife dead a little while ago. Murder-suicide, looks like. Shot her twice, then himself. Apparently they'd been there a while before anyone found them. They were pretty ripe."

A twinge of something—uncertainty? intuition?—crawled into Cotter's consciousness. "They didn't find any red letters on the bodies, did they?"

The question surprised Kozlovski. "No, I told you; it was a murder-suicide."

Ill-defined doubts circled in Cotter's head, and he tried to push them away. It was an apparent murder-suicide; there was really nothing to tie the deaths of the Hollingsworths to the killings he was investigating—only a vague, inexplicable hunch. The two detectives finished their coffee and left the restaurant.

Two of the addresses on Cotter's list were in Colmer. He decided to start with them. The first one turned out to be a two-story stucco apartment building in the kind of neighborhood where you parked your car on the street knowing you might never see it again, at least not intact. He was looking for Elton McDivit, a former part-time clerk at the Seaward.

McDivit's apartment was on the second floor. The odor of grease seemed to have permeated the stairway. Though low-rent housing, the building hadn't deteriorated as much as many Cotter had seen. There were crayon marks on the stairway walls, low down, at a child's level, but no gang graffiti. No liquor bottles. No suspicious stains on the floor. No discarded syringes.

Suddenly a large man was blocking the way. He was about twenty-two, with thick dark hair pulled back in a short ponytail. The way his upper body muscles bulged said he worked out with weights. He was looking at Cotter through narrowed eyes. Why was it every time Cotter came to Colmer he ran into young guys who wanted to act tough?

"Would you mind stating your business?" the man said.

Cotter displayed his shield.

The guy studied it as if uncertain whether it was genuine. "I'm building security," he said.

"Can I see your company ID?"

"The security force is made up of volunteers from the building. We live here."

Putting his ID case away, Cotter said, "From the look of things, you're doing a good job."

The man seemed to relax a little. "They used to sell crack in the hallway. Everyplace in the building was broken into at least once a month. We got together and put a stop to all that."

"I'm looking for Elton McDivit."

"He's not here anymore."

"Know where he went?"

"Hospital. Six weeks ago."

"What's wrong with him."

"AIDS."

"He gay?"

"None of my business. I'm only worried about the slime that shoot up in the hallway and rob people. What the tenants do in bed is their own business."

Cotter got the name of the hospital and left. Although he understood and applauded the efforts of the building's residents to protect themselves, it also made him uneasy, for it was only half a step away from vigilantism. He wouldn't be surprised if the volunteer guards illegally carried weapons. Which meant the situation was ripe for a confrontation with pushers or street gangs, who were also armed. *Too many guns out there,* Cotter thought. He wondered whether the politicians would ever get the courage to do something about it.

The address given by Jethro Grandville when he'd gone to work at the hotel as a maintenance man was now a pile of rubble. A sign stated this was the future home of the Bay Plaza Shopping Center. None of the neighbors had known Grandville, and none of them knew where he'd gone.

The next name on the list took him back to Tres Cerros, to an address on Sandy Way, which turned out to be a street on which houses probably sold for a minimum of three-quarters of a million dollars. Seven-fifty, in real estate parlance. The address Rocky Hebert had listed on his employment application was a big two-story house, brick with white trim, probably five or six bedrooms, and had a lawn too weed-free to be the result of a homeowner's weekend efforts. Although he couldn't see the rear, Cotter presumed it contained a pool or a tennis court—or both.

The dark-haired woman with a Spanish accent who opened the door informed him that the Maddens lived here, that they had owned the place for years, and that she had never heard of anyone named Hebert. Mrs. Madden would be back in an hour or two, if he wanted to ask her about it.

Cotter pulled away from the house, knowing that Rocky Hebert, substitute night bellman at the Seaward Hotel, had most likely never even seen this expensive home on Sandy Way. Allowing his mind to reach out for the killer's, Cotter was suddenly sure that "Rocky Hebert" was an alias—and that the man who'd used it was the murderer.

R.H.—the same initials as Robert Heckly.

A chill slid down his spine, going around and around like the stripes on a barber pole.

But then, lots of people had the initials R.H. Robert A. Heinlein. Rutherford B. Hays. Rogers Hornsby. It was probably safe to assume that most people with those initials weren't homicidal maniacs.

And the man with the initials R.H. who was unquestionably a homicidal maniac was safely locked away in a maximum-security facility in Texas.

Was someone playing games with him? Did someone know who he really was, and was that person using Heckly's initials and style of killing?

The disturbing notion tumbled in his head as he drove.

Ten

He jogged through the same familiar neighborhood, ignoring the children who eyed him with expressions that ranged from suspicion to open hostility. The first few times he'd run here, he'd been regarded as an oddity. He'd assumed that would pass, but it hadn't. The looks he received seemed to grow ever more suspicious. Apparently strangers didn't often come here. And they absolutely never jogged here.

Maybe they thought he was a cop, on the lookout for illegal drugs or something. He chuckled. Him, a cop.

But the notion wasn't without its appeal, he realized. When he was done here, maybe he should try it. Put together a fake background and apply for a job on a police force somewhere. The irony of it would be marvelous.

Suddenly he was sure someone was watching him. The feeling was so intense he came to an abrupt halt, his eyes taking in grassless and weedy front yards, runny-nosed children playing on the sidewalk, a rusty wheelless car held up by cement blocks. Suddenly the windows of the small, squalid homes were eyes, dozens of them, studying him, probing him. He felt like cringing, as if the windows were looking into his most private places with their unrelenting glassy stares.

What was going on here?

Ever since coming to this part of California, he'd had the feeling that somehow he wasn't alone. He'd never felt that way before. He was an individual of supreme self-confidence, the master of any situation. Feelings of insecurity were new to him, and he didn't like them.

They were constant, always there, in his head.

As if something, some subtle presence, had moved in, taken over a dark corner of his brain. Which was ridiculous. He was a person of reason and logic, a truster of hard, cold facts. He knew there was no presence in his head, for that was impossible. Period.

If anyone was observing him, it was someone in one of the houses, a curious resident who thought he had to be either a cop or a crazy person to be jogging in this neighborhood.

He started running again, trotting leisurely along the sidewalk.

It was an overcast day, the gray sky combining with the neighborhood to make everything seem dull and grimy. Ahead of him two young boys were sitting in the middle of the sidewalk. As he drew near, he saw that one had an old claw-hammer and the other a large rock. They were pounding on the sidewalk, chipping pieces of it away. So far they'd created what amounted to a small pothole, a good bounce for someone's tricycle.

They didn't move, and he had to go around them. Once past them, he could feel their eyes on his back, feel the mistrust and loathing.

And he felt that other presence, inside his head, keeping him company. He ignored the feeling. It was just the neighborhood. And his imagination.

Twelve

"The travel agency said I could pick up my ticket here at the counter," he said to the sleepy-looking young airline agent.

"Your name, please," she asked. She had curly red hair, freckles, a pretty smile.

"Lee Heck."

Her fingers danced over the keys of her computer terminal. "Here we are. You're on flight eight-oh-nine, which leaves at six-fifteen for Albuquerque, and you'll change there for San Antonio. Is that right?"

"Completely." With his good arm he adjusted his bad one. The ticket agent's blue eyes flicked to the arm, then instantly darted away.

"You're very pretty," he said.

She hesitated, looking uncomfortable. "Thank you—although no one could be very pretty at this hour of the morning."

"You are."

"Any luggage?"

"Just the one bag," he said, indicating the small suitcase he'd placed on the scale. He would not be in Texas long enough to need any additional luggage. Before coming to California, he'd spent several weeks there, observing, making plans. He knew precisely what he had to do. He might not even need to spend the night there. He'd have to see.

The ticket agent put a tag on the suitcase, then lifted it onto the moving conveyor belt behind her.

He said, "Would you be offended if I were so bold as to ask you to have dinner with me when I return?"

She blushed. "I'm afraid I couldn't do that."

"Company policy?"

She nodded.

"No one would know."

"I'm also married," she said, displaying her wedding band.

He sighed. "Ah, well."

She handed him his ticket and boarding pass. "Gate C-9," she said.

He smiled and headed for the gate, satisfied that the young woman would have no trouble remembering Lee Heck when Cotter questioned her.

Thirteen

"They don't make them anymore, you know," the man said. He was a frail-looking old fellow, with that pale, seemingly transparent skin elderly people often have. His veins showed through like the blue highways on a road map.

"So I've discovered," Cotter replied.

The old man rested his arms on the scarred counter and surveyed his shop. He seemed saddened by what he saw. "A good manual typewriter was a solid, well-crafted machine, something that could take a lot of abuse. They don't make anything like that anymore."

Olivettis and Adlers and IBM were lined up on the tables. The one price tag Cotter could read from where he stood was $39.95.

"They were all replaced by the IBM Selectric, and now they don't even make that anymore. The only new machines you can buy are what they call 'electronic.' The big thing is computers. Even people who don't write anything more than a letter to Aunt Peggy twice a year figure they've got to have a computer to do it on."

"Have you sold any Adler manuals lately?" Cotter asked.

"Two of them." He smiled. "There are still a few people out there who like the old machines. Adler was one of the best."

"Do you remember who you sold them to?"

He hesitated, frowning. "Let me think about that."

"Would it be in your records?"

"What records?"

"You don't keep the names of your customers?"

"What for?"

He had a point, Cotter supposed. This wasn't the sort of business that needed to maintain a mailing list.

"One of these days there won't be any more manual typewriters — even at places like this. No parts. I have to cannibalize machines to fix other machines all the time."

89

"About the two Adlers," Cotter prompted.

"Hmmm," the man behind the counter said, staring off into the corner as if the answer were written there. He was about seventy-five, Cotter guessed, with a full head of sheet-white hair.

The investigation of the Wanda Grant and Sheri Vanvleet murders seemed to be going nowhere. Rocky Hebert remained a mystery. Employees of the Seaward Hotel who remembered him said he was a quiet man who kept to himself. They described him as tall and lithe, with a night worker's pale complexion. The only thing particularly memorable about him was his thick blond hair, which he wore in a curly mass reminiscent of Harpo Marx's.

The matching hairs from the two murder scenes were brown. But then, hair color was easily changed, and this was a killer who liked to play head games.

There was nothing to connect any of the Seaward's other employees, present or former, to either murder. Nor, so far, was there anything to implicate any of the guests believed to have used Sheri Vanvleet's services. Ditto for William Vanvleet. Tuffle had spent two days checking out Vanvleet's business affairs, learning nothing suspicious.

"Ah," the owner of Ted's Typewriters said, snapping his fingers. "I sold one of the Adler's to a woman. She said she was a writer, that she didn't like the electric or electronic machines."

"You catch her name?"

"I don't think she said."

"What she look like?"

"Short, brown hair, a plaid skirt sort of like the ones they used to wear at Catholic girls' schools — or maybe they still do, for all I know. Ah, and she wore glasses. I remember thinking that she looked like a librarian."

"Why?"

"The glasses. They made me think of a librarian."

Cotter got what more he could in the way of a description, then said, "How about the other machine? Do you recall who bought it?"

"No. I don't have any idea."

Cotter thanked him and left. As soon as he started the car, the dispatcher's voice came over the radio. She was calling his number.

"Three-thirty-eight," Cotter answered. "Go ahead."

"Ten-nineteen, see Captain Zinn." Which meant the captain wanted him back at the station.

"Ten-four," he said. "En route."

The typewriter store was in a strip mall on Tres Cerros's north side. The other occupants of the small shopping center included a paperback book exchange, a shop that sold baseball cards, and a movie rental place. The houses were smaller than most of the homes in Tres Cerros, two- and three-bedroom places that sold for a hundred and a half or so. In some yards the green was dotted by the yellow heads of dandelions. It wasn't Colmer, but it wasn't what most people thought of as Tres Cerros, either.

At the station, he went directly to the captain's office.

"This was in the morning mail," Zinn said, handing a plastic bag to Cotter. It contained a letter and an envelope. The envelope was addressed simply to the police department, and it had a local postmark. The letter's message was a single line:

W is for whore. But then, you already knew that, didn't you?

Two hours later, the lab confirmed that it had been typed on the same manual Adler as the last message. Half an hour after that, the lab reported finding numerous prints on the envelope but none on the letter itself.

Mid-afternoon found Cotter catching up on his paperwork. As the officer in charge of the investigation, he had to submit a weekly report. Kozlovski was finishing up the list of hotel guests thought to have been customers of Sheri Vanvleet. He was running up the department's phone bill, talking to police departments in places like Raleigh, North Carolina, and Tacoma, Washington, and learning nothing particularly useful. Tuffle was checking out more typewriter stores, but the task seemed hopeless. In a word, the investigation was just about at a standstill.

A sunny day was displaying itself brightly outside Cotter's window. Although Tres Cerros's climate would never inspire anyone to go surfing or sunbathing, it offered the occasional pretty day, most commonly in the spring and fall. The nice weather had brought the squirrels out en masse. At least a dozen of them were scampering about in the small park that separated the police station from City Hall.

Cotter shifted his gaze back to the papers in front of him. Among them was the coroner's report on Sheri Vanvleet, which showed that she'd been drugged prior to her death. The autopsy had found both chloral hydrate and alcohol in her system. The pathologist who'd performed the autopsy noted that she was probably out cold when she died. Which was good, considering the manner of her death. No glasses or liquor bottles had been found in the hotel room, which meant that if the killer had spiked Sheri's drink there, he had taken the evidence with him, not wanting to leave behind such a handy source of fingerprints.

No prints that could definitely be said to be the perpetrator's were found in the room, not even in the shower, where the cutting had been done. Had the killer worn surgical gloves for his brand of surgery?

Cotter felt that he had.

No, he *knew* it, knew it the way he perceived other things about the murderer, as if there were a signal passing between them. Not the sort of signal that gave you clear color pictures and high-fidelity sound, but rather a static-laden transmission that faded in and out. Sensations came through, hints of things. Vague, often distorted, and yet quite disturbing.

I'm going to get you, Cotter thought.

And he wondered whether it was bravado, for in truth, he was nowhere near catching the madman. No one had seen who was in the room with Sheri Vanvleet. No one had seen the person who'd slit Wanda Grant's throat. Cotter had no fingerprints, no useful trace evidence except for one blue-and-white thread and two brown hairs. The lab had reported that the red felt-tip used to mark the victims was a common item, available almost everywhere, just like the paper on which the killer's messages were typed.

The typewriter was identifiable.

If they could find it.

If.

Cotter slipped a standard report form into his IBM Selectric – though it wasn't a manual, Cotter suspected the old man at Ted's Typewriters would approve – and x-ed in the little box indicating that this was a status report on an ongoing investigation. When he reached the part where he was supposed to describe his progress, he hesitated, trying to think of an official-sounding way to say, Well, no, we don't have any suspects, but we're really busting our buns on this thing.

That the required weekly progress reports were a waste of time was a universally held opinion in the detective division. When guys had nothing to say they simply made things up. The requirement was probably the doing of faceless accountants somewhere in the city bureaucracy. *If we don't know how they spend their time, how will we know whether the expense is justified?* That sort of mentality. It would never occur to them that half the stuff the detectives put down was pure bullshit.

"Mike, I got something here you should see."

Cotter looked up to find Captain Zinn, who was clearly displeased about something. He was holding another plastic bag with a letter and envelope inside.

"The people in clerical must be political appointees," the captain said. "They couldn't possibly have passed the civil service test."

"I always heard that test was set up so the average moron could pass it," Cotter said.

"The average moron would have known better than to do what they did. Here, look at this."

Cotter took the plastic bag. The letter, plainly visible through the plastic, read:

> *I struggled through the alphabet as if it had been a bramble-bush, getting considerably worried and scratched by every letter.*

"What the hell," Cotter said.

"It arrived two and a half weeks ago. The geniuses in clerical filed it away and forgot about it."

Cotter already knew it was from the killer. Though encased in plastic, the paper reeked of the killer, gave off his essence like a cloying musk.

"It's an announcement," Cotter said. "He's telling us ahead of time what he's going to do. Playing with us, messing with our heads."

"What do you think the part about getting worried and scratched by every letter means?"

"I don't think it means anything. I think he does things just to confuse us."

"But sometimes these guys make up elaborate puzzles. You know, bramble-bush turns out be about the raspberry bushes in his yard or a reference to someone named Thorn – some other weird connection."

Cotter didn't think so, but it was based entirely on the weird link he seemed to have with the killer. He said, "That sounds like a quote from something."

"You mean like from Shakespeare, somebody like that?"

"More recent than Shakespeare, but yeah, it's from literature. At least, I think it is."

"Track it down, see if there's any meaning we can attach to whatever work it comes from. In the meantime, I'll get this down to the lab, make sure it's the same typewriter, see if the guy decided to cover it with fingerprints this time."

Before returning the plastic bag to Zinn, Cotter copied the message. Then he phoned the English department at the University of California's Tres Cerros campus and asked for Professor Nettleton. Cotter had met the professor about two years before, when Nettleton's house was trashed by someone who'd left hate messages on the wall, most of them alleging the professor was gay. Cotter had no idea whether there was any truth in the allegation, although Nettleton lived alone and had never married. The professor had been terrified until Cotter had discovered it was the work of a student upset about a bad grade, not a group of gay-hating white supremacists. The kid had been kicked out of school and sent home to face angry parents in Illinois.

"Detective Cotter," Nettleton said. "Sure I remember you. How can I be of service?"

"How are you at literary quotes?"

"At identifying them? Only fair, but I've got a dozen reference books at my fingertips. What's the quote?"

Cotter read it to him.

"Definitely something well known," the professor said.

"Can you be a little more specific?"

"Hang on." The receiver was put down, and Cotter heard the thump of a book, the turning of pages. And a moment later, "Ah, here it is – in *The Oxford Dictionary of Quotations*. It's from Dickens. *Great Expectations*."

"Wasn't one I read in college."

"Oh. Well, it's about the life of a man named Philip Pirrip—his nickname was Pip. Anyway, he's raised by his sister and her husband, who's a blacksmith. He's influenced by an eccentric woman named Miss Havisham . . ." When Nettleton finished relating the details of the story, Cotter could see no relevance to the murders he was investigating.

"What was the significance of the bramble-bush reference?" he asked.

"To tell you the truth, I don't remember. It's been years since I taught any courses that used that particular work."

"Thanks for the help. I appreciate it."

"Uh, you certainly have piqued my curiosity. What does Dickens have to do with police work?"

Under ordinary circumstances, Cotter probably would have told him. But the red letters on the bodies of Wanda Grant and Sheri Vanvleet were a closely-held secret, known only to the authorities and the killer. He said, "There are aspects of it I'm not at liberty to disclose, but it involves a murder investigation."

"You mean the grisly one—the woman who was disemboweled?"

Although Cotter didn't recall having seen a murder that wasn't grisly, he said, "Yes, that one. And that's all I can tell you."

"Wow," Nettleton said. "I can't imagine what connection there could be with *Great Expectations*."

"Me neither," Cotter said.

It took the lab only an hour to report that the same typewriter had been used on the bramble-bush note as had been used on the other two messages, and that there were no prints on the letter itself. None of which came as a surprise.

"Dickens?" Cindy said, looking at the book in Cotter's hand.

"Picked it up at the library on the way here."

They were standing by the door. She'd met him as he'd come in, greeted him with a hug and a kiss. It reminded him of another woman who'd hugged and kissed him as he'd stepped through the door. A part of him wondered whether he was forsaking her, betraying her memory. His rational mind said no. His emotions weren't sure.

Cindy wore jeans and a checked shirt. Her hair was pulled back in a ponytail held in place with a rubber band. She looked like a teenager.

She said, "You never cease to amaze me, Mike. A cop from Texas who likes Vivaldi and *Swan Lake*, and now it turns out you're into Dickens. You have single-handedly ruined some major stereotypes, do you know that?"

"My interests aren't literary. We got another letter from the killer, and it contained a quote from Dickens." He'd written the passage on a sheet of paper, which he'd slipped into the book. He pulled it out and read it to her.

"The alphabet," Cindy said. "Getting worried and scratched by every letter."

"Mean anything to you?"

She cocked her head, thinking. "Could you be the one getting worried and scratched by every letter?"

"I don't know. Maybe after I read the book I'll have a better idea."

"Mike . . ."

"What?"

"Nothing."

"Say it."

"I'm worried about you, Mike. I mean, this . . . this whole thing, it's scary. I was prepared to live my whole life alone, never give up my independence, never have to put up with the demands of a truly intimate relationship. And then you came along and showed me how wrong I'd been. It was terrible living alone. I just didn't know it. And now that I've found you, I'm afraid I could lose you. This whole thing is so . . . so dangerous."

"My job is always dangerous," he said softly.

Cindy shook her head. "I'm sorry. I promised myself I wouldn't do this. Being a cop's part of what you are, and I wouldn't change that. I'm sounding like the possessive little woman, always worrying. I don't mean to be like that."

"It shows you care," he said. "And it makes me feel good to know you care that much."

"Mike . . ." Her words trailed off.

Their eyes met, and a silent communication passed between them. It was a powerful instance of shared tenderness and feeling, and Cotter found himself held by it as if he were in the grip of a mighty unseen hand. They stood there, looking at each other, loving each other. When, on some unspoken signal, they broke off the eye contact, neither of them spoke about what had transpired, for words seemed a lesser form of communication than the one they'd just used. Cotter almost felt giddy.

"What's for dinner?" he asked, finally breaking the silence.

"Broiled fish with herbed butter, fettucini Alfredo, and steamed broccoli."

"Wow."

"You're not the only one who can cook."

"How long?"

"Give me twenty minutes. All the preliminary stuff's done. It's just a matter of shoving things into the oven and putting them on the stove."

"I'll read until then," Cotter said.

Good to her word, Cindy called him twenty minutes later. The meal was delicious. After dinner Cindy told him to skip helping with the dishes and get back to reading. Cotter accepted the offer. Sitting on the couch, he read as quickly as he was able, skimming some sections.

Being careful not to disturb him, Cindy joined him, slipping into an easy chair and picking up a magazine. He found the bramble-bush reference around ten o'clock, on page forty-seven. He continued reading until a snore woke him up.

"I think it's time for you to go to bed," Cindy said.

"Was that me – the snore?"

"That was you."

When they were lying in bed, Cotter said, "Have you read *Great Expectations?*"

"Not since college, but I remember it. A young man – I've forgotten his name –"

"Pip."

"Yeah, Pip. It's the story of his growing up. He has an unknown benefactor who turns out to be a convict who was transported to Australia. Uh, let's see, I think the title refers to Pip's great expectations when he goes off to London to become a gentleman."

"You've got a good memory."

"Thanks. Have you figured out the significance of the bramble-bush passage?"

"In the book it has to do with Pip's learning to 'read, write, and cipher' — those are the exact words, 'read, write, and cipher.' I don't see where that has anything to do with the case I'm working on, except for the reference to the alphabet. If there are any messages or clues, they're so cleverly disguised or so thoroughly convoluted I'll never get them."

"Could the killer be comparing himself to Pip?" Cindy asked.

"A young man finding out about life?"

"Maybe that's how he sees himself. Maybe he has great expectations. Or maybe had them, and they were somehow dashed."

"That's possible," Cotter said. "But it's not what I feel."

"Pip had a benefactor. Maybe the killer's got one, too — in the sense that there's someone behind him, backing him in some way."

Cotter considered that. "Someone put him up to it?"

"It's possible, isn't it?"

"It's very possible, but . . ."

"But it doesn't feel right."

"No."

"Okay," Cindy said, "what does feel right?"

"I think we're doing exactly what he wants us to do. We're trying to figure it out. We're looking for hidden meanings, disguised clues. He's playing with us. It's one big head game."

"You're saying he sent you the quote because the reference to the alphabet would tantalize you, make you think there was a deeper meaning when there really wasn't?"

"Exactly. And he was also announcing his intentions, knowing it would be meaningless at the time, and that the letter would probably get lost in the shuffle for a while before someone realized its significance in light of what was happening."

"Can he really plan things out that well? That's a lot of thinking ahead, a lot of scheming. Why? Why is he doing this?"

"It's an ego trip. He's proving how superior he is, how he can confuse us, manipulate us."

"A person like that is . . ."

She seemed to be groping for the right word. Before she found it, the phone rang. Cindy answered it, listened a moment, then said, "For you," and handed him the phone.

"Cotter," he said, sitting up.

"This is Beverly in Dispatch. A long-distance phone call came in for you from San Antonio. I told them I couldn't give out your number, but they said it was extremely urgent, so I told them I'd have you call them back." Cotter's grip had tightened on the phone. Something cold had just stabbed him painfully in the gut, as if he'd been run through with an icicle.

"It was from a Dr. Philippa Lockwood. You need her number?"

The cold seemed to have seeped into Cotter's throat, freezing his vocal cords.

"Detective Cotter?"

"I . . . I'm here, Bev." He switched on the bedside lamp, then nudged Cindy and pointed at the pad and pen on her bed table. She handed them to him. "You'd better give me the number," Cotter said.

After he had it, he broke the connection, then dialed the numbers. He was put through to Dr. Lockwood immediately. As he listened to what she had to say, the chilly, numbing fingers of shock caressed his belly, nuzzled his neck, stroked his limbs. He felt light, unreal, immobilized—except for the hand that was squeezing the phone so tightly it was a wonder he didn't crush it.

When he hung up, he realized that Cindy was staring at him pale and wide-eyed. "What's wrong?" she asked, her voice a frightened whisper.

"She's dead," Cotter said.

"Who, Mike? Who's dead?"

"My daughter."

Fourteen

"If you'd like to have a seat, security will let Dr. Lockwood know you're here," the woman said. She was small and round-faced and wore her hair in one of those short, frizzy styles that resembled a cheerleader's pompon. The small plaque on her desk said GRACE MEADOWS in white letters on a black background. Although Cotter had spoken to her many times on the phone, this was the first time he'd met her. The same was true of Dr. Lockwood.

Cotter sat down, and Grace busied herself at her desk, moving papers around, carefully aligning the edges in a short stack of file folders. She seemed reluctant to let her eyes meet his. Cotter attributed her nervousness to being in the presence of someone whose daughter had just died.

He didn't know yet why she had died. Over the phone Dr. Lockwood had told him that she'd been found in bed, looking as though she were asleep, but cold and not breathing. The coroner would have to establish the cause. On the flight here, as the land below changed from mountains to desert to the huge brown and green quilt of farm fields that stretched across the Texas plains, he'd told himself that it was for the best, that Jennifer's ordeal was over now. And he'd tried not to think about the reason his little girl had been brought to this place, sound of body and yet lost to him forever.

"Mr. Cotter," a middle-aged woman with a white smock and plastic ID badge said, hurrying into the office, "I'm Dr. Lockwood. Sorry to keep you waiting, but I didn't know exactly when you'd get here, and I was in another part of the complex." She patted her blond hair absently, apparently unaware she was doing so.

Even in these tense circumstances, some remote corner of the policeman's mind routinely noted Dr. Lockwood's description and filed it away for future reference. White female, about forty, blond hair and hazel eyes, five-eight, a hundred twenty-five pounds.

"If you'd told us when you were arriving, we could have had someone meet you," she said. She patted her hair again. She was emitting big waves of anxiety.

"I rented a car," Cotter replied.

"I think we should go into my office, where we can be more comfortable," the psychiatrist said.

She showed Cotter into a blue-carpeted room with a shiny black desk. The last time he'd been in this office, the carpet had been brown and the person to whom it belonged had told him to stop coming here, to get away before he drove himself mad.

"Has the cause of death been determined?" Cotter asked when they were seated.

"Yes," the psychiatrist replied. She hesitated, as if reluctant to go on. She took a slow breath and said, "Dawn — I mean Jennifer — was murdered."

"Murdered?" It was all he could think of to say. A cold lump of apprehension had formed in his gut.

"It had been getting harder and harder to keep her weight up — as if . . . well, as if she wanted to die. So when they found her, I assumed natural causes, but—"

"How was she murdered?"

"She was suffocated."

"Any suspects?"

"No. At least, I don't think so. You'll have to ask Detective Harris. He's in charge of the investigation."

"Could another patient have done it?"

"No. At least, it's extremely unlikely. Any of them who tend to be violent or hard to manage are on medication. If they're deemed dangerous to themselves or others, they're in a special security section."

"If not a patient, who?"

"I . . . I don't know. The whole hospital is secure. It's not a prison, but no one gets in or out without . . . without clearance."

"I want to see where it happened," Cotter said.

She nodded, touched her hair. "Oh, before we do that, does the letter *D* mean anything to you?"

"No. Why?" He felt as if his inner workings had just seized up like an engine that had lost its oil pressure, all the moving parts coming to a sudden grinding stop.

"It was written on her flesh, under her clothes, where we couldn't see it. The coroner found it."

"What color was it?" Cotter asked. His voice seemed hollow and distant, like an echo.

"Red."

"Red," he repeated.

"Yes. Is there some . . . some significance to that?"

He told her what had been happening in Tres Cerros.

"My God," she said. "You mean, someone's been . . ."

"All the killings in Tres Cerros have been directed at me. I didn't know it until this moment."

"But how could the killer have found out about your daughter? No one knew she was here. And no one here knew her as anything other than Dawn. Only I knew her actual identity."

"Who has access to your records?"

"That part of your daughter's records is in my safe. Only I know the combination."

"No one else?"

"No. No one."

"Not even Grace?"

"Not even Grace."

"She's spoken to me on the phone. Could she have put it together, a piece here, a piece there?"

"I . . ." Dr. Lockwood shook her head. "I don't know, not for sure. But even if she figured out you were Dawn's father, the name Cotter wouldn't mean anything to her. Besides, who would she tell? And why would she bother?"

All valid points. And yet someone knew who he was. And where to find his daughter. He'd sensed the killer in Tres Cerros, felt a link with him. And now he knew why. It was personal. The killings, the red letters, the bramble-bush note: all for his benefit.

"I . . . I'm sorry," Dr. Lockwood said. "If there's anything I can do . . ."

"Thank you."

"Nothing like this has happened here before. We're all in a state of shock."

"I want to see where it happened," Cotter said.

"Yes. Of course."

The psychiatrist took him to another wing of the building. As soon as Cotter entered it, he knew he'd stepped into another world. There was an odd dampness here the administrative part of the complex didn't have, along with an odor that seemed a mixture of medicinal and animal scents. And other, less tangible things seemed to waft along the corridors as well. Cotter thought he sensed despair, loneliness, hopelessness, and the electric tingle of fear.

Following Dr. Lockwood along a corridor with beige walls and brown-and-white floor tiles, he thought about this place having been where his daughter had grown from a child to a young woman. *I'm so sorry, Jennifer,* he thought. *So very, very sorry.*

But then, Jennifer Richland hadn't known about the despair and fear that permeated this place, for she hadn't known she was here. At least, that's what the doctors had said, and he hoped to God they were right.

He recalled a mop-headed little girl staring up at him in the kitchen with a frown on her face, saying, "How come they named them after us, Daddy?"

"They didn't. Your mom couldn't remember what the dish was really called, so she made up a name."

"Richland burgers."

"Right."

She laughed.

"What's so funny?"

"There's no bun. How can you have a burger without a bun?"

Cotter pushed the memory away; it was too painful.

The patients all wore what looked like pajamas. Cotter passed the TV room, in which half a dozen of them sat staring at the TV set, not moving. It was like being in the House of Wax. *And here, ladies and gentlemen, is our display of patients watching television in a hospital for the hopelessly lost.*

From somewhere in the building came a scream, a primal shriek that contained very little that was human. Cotter shivered; he couldn't help himself.

"You get used to it," Dr. Lockwood said.

Cotter didn't want to get used to it.

Though small and spartan, the rooms were clean. They had neither the medical ambience of hospital rooms nor the restrictiveness of prison cells. They were storage lockers, places to keep those whom society had no real idea what to do with.

Dr. Lockwood stopped at room 110. Through the open door, Cotter could see a middle-aged man, sitting on a chair, staring at the floor. His thick dark hair was disheveled, clumps sticking out in odd directions, as if he'd tried to spike it without a mirror.

"This is Carl," the psychiatrist said. "If we try to comb his hair, he'll leap into a corner, where he'll cower and whimper, even though he's on medication. In fact, without the medication, he masturbates uncontrollably, until his penis is bloody. Jennifer was next door, in number 112. Carl's the only witness to what happened to her."

"Can he talk?"

"Unlike some of our patients, he can feed himself, but other than that, he sits and stares. That's it."

"Never speaks?"

"Not very often."

"How often is not very often?"

"Last time was a year and a half ago."

Cotter realized that Carl was slowly moving from side to side, almost imperceptibly. "Why does he do that—the moving?"

"Because he wants to," the psychiatrist said.

They moved on to room 112. Jennifer's room. It was empty now, just a bed and a chair, the same brown and white as in the hall. This was where Cotter's daughter had died—where she had been murdered. She was gone now, the mop-headed little girl with dark eyes. Cotter stared at the cubicle, feeling his eyes grow moist. A tear trickled down his cheek. The young woman who'd died here had been a shell, nothing more; Cotter knew that. For all practical purposes, Jennifer Richland had been murdered fifteen years ago, and it was impossible to kill someone twice.

But realizing that didn't help.

The mop-headed little girl was really dead now, truly gone, and Cotter was overwhelmed with grief. Another tear dislodged itself from his eye, slithered downward. He wasn't just crying for his daughter. He was trying to deal with fifteen years of living the memory of one warm night in Houston.

A thump and a clatter came from Carl's room. Both Cotter and Dr. Lockwood moved to the open door. Carl was standing, the chair on its side. He stared at the policeman and the psychiatrist, his eyes wide, filled with horror and astonishment and things Cotter couldn't even imagine.

"Devil!" Carl screamed. "The devil!"

Dr. Lockwood stepped back from the door.

"The devil was here," Carl said, drool spilling from the corner of his mouth. "I saw him. I saw him. He killed her."

"Killed who, Carl?" Cotter asked.

"Deeeeeevvvvvil."

"Who'd the devil kill?"

"Her. Killed her. But not me. I'm not here. Devil can't get me because I'm not here."

"Carl, what did the devil look like?"

"Devil looks like the devil. Don't speak his name. He might come back."

"Was he tall?"

Carl giggled.

"Answer me," Cotter said. "Was he short?"

"Short-snort. I seen him, and I don't dare tell."

"Why, Carl, why don't you dare tell?"

"Devil'll get me."

"We'll protect you, Carl. We won't let him get you."

"Got her."

"Tell us what he looked like, and we'll get him."

Carl's eyes opened wide, filling with terror. He shook his head. "Devil, devil, devil, devil, devil." And then his eyes seemed to focus, as if Carl were seeing Cotter and Dr. Lockwood for the first time, and they were normal eyes, vaguely puzzled, but normal, as if he had been given a momentary reprieve from madness.

"Tell on the devil?" Carl said softly. "You must think I'm out of my fucking mind."

"Carl, it's okay," Cotter said. "You don't have to worry about the devil getting you, because . . ."

Cotter let his words trail off because Carl had just hurled himself at the wall. Screaming, he bounced off it and flew across the cubicle, slamming into the wall on the other side. Then he was sailing back toward the other wall again, bouncing back and forth like a handball in a particularly furious match.

"I'd better get some help," Dr. Lockwood said, reaching into the pocket of her smock. "Shit! I left my two-way radio in the office. Keep an eye on him. I'll be right back." She hurried down the corridor.

Carl continued bouncing back and forth. The walls were padded, so he didn't seem to be hurting himself too much, but the scene was bizarre. Every time he hit the padding, there was a loud smack, and the spots on both sides were marked with big circles of spittle that dribbled down the wall.

"Carl," Cotter said, "stop it."

Carl bounced from wall to wall, the saliva splattering as he hit.

"Talk to me," Cotter said. "Tell me about the devil, and I'll make sure he never bothers you again."

Carl stopped as if he'd been switched off. He stood there in the center of his cell, staring at Cotter with eyes that were looking into that other dimension known as madness. Abruptly he dropped to the floor as if he'd been poleaxed. He curled into the fetal position, moaning.

When Dr. Lockwood returned, accompanied by a uniformed nurse and an orderly, Carl was still on the floor, curled into a question mark, withdrawn into his own private sanctuary. They gave Carl an injection, then lifted him onto the bed and began strapping him to it.

Getting out of their way, Cotter moved back to the cubicle that had been his daughter's. He could feel the killer, but it was only a trace, like an old scent. Fragmented images came to him.

A shadowy shape slipping down the corridor, passing Carl's room . . .

Hands pressing a pillow over his daughter's face, Jennifer not resisting, not even knowing that her life-giving air was being withheld . . .

Cotter made the images go away. He didn't even know whether they were real or creations of his imagination.

Cotter tried to link with the madman, but it was like reaching into a mental mineshaft, for he found nothing but bottomless blackness. The killer was no longer in the vicinity.

He was still stunned by the discovery that all this was personal, an attack aimed at him. He'd felt safe, protected by time and a new name. Robert Heckly was safely locked away, a few hundred miles from here. And yet the madness he represented was still loose.

Someone had learned who he was. Cotter could see how that might have happened, someone recognizing him from an old newspaper photo, for instance. But how could anyone have known Jennifer was a patient here when she was known only as Dawn, her true identity a closely held secret?

A red *D*.

For Dawn? A way of telling him that he knew her secret name? Who was this guy? What did he want?

Cotter realized that Dr. Lockwood was standing beside him. The two staff members who'd sedated Carl and strapped him to the bed were gone.

"Shall we go back to my office?" the psychiatrist said.

As they headed in that direction, Cotter said, "Is there any chance Carl will be able to give us a description of the man he saw?"

"He may not have seen anyone."

"But—"

"He has absolutely no link with reality. As a witness he's useless."

"He saw something, but he was afraid to tell us about it."

"Maybe."

"He said, 'I saw him. He killed her.' "

She stopped, turned to face him. "I'm not trying to snatch hope away from you, Mr. Cotter. But you have to understand that anything Carl says is drawn from his own private fantasy version of reality. It's hard for us to know what to make of what Carl or any patient here says, because we don't know the rules; we don't know where they're coming from."

"Can I try talking to him again when he's better?"

"No one here gets better. Carl may spend the rest of his life curled up and moaning. The very best we can hope for is that he'll uncurl and go back to sitting and staring silently. Even if that were to happen, you have to remember that until today he hadn't spoken for a year and a half. He could go another year and a half. He might never speak again—ever."

Cotter nodded.

"I'm sorry, but I just don't think it's likely that Carl can help you."

"If he should start talking—"

"I'll be in touch. Immediately."

"I need to talk to the officer who's investigating this," Cotter said.

"Detective Harris. I've got one of his cards in my desk."

When they got back to her office, Grace said, "Mr. Cotter, you just got a call from California." She checked her notes. "Captain Zinn in Tres Cerros wants you to call him right away. He said you'd know the number."

"You can use my office," Dr. Lockwood said.

Cotter, filled with trepidation, placed the call. Zinn wouldn't have called unless it was urgent. The captain answered on the second ring.

"We got another letter," he said. "I thought you'd want to know about it right away because it might relate to what happened out there. It says, 'D is for daughter.'"

"She was murdered," Cotter said. "They found a red D on her body."

"Jesus. How . . . how the hell did he find her?"

"I don't know. The only witness is a patient who claimed he saw the devil. Last time I saw him he was curled up on the floor, moaning."

"What the hell have we got here, Mike?"

"I don't know that either."

After telling Zinn he'd be back late tomorrow, Cotter hung up, overwhelmed with a sense of déjà-vu. The circumstances were different, but he had met this madness before. The thought sent terror swirling through his belly like a winter storm. He shivered.

Fifteen

As he flew back to California, the man who'd killed Cotter's daughter looked out the window, seeing nothing but the night. Nevada was down there, he believed. Arid, sparsely populated. A solar-heated hell of scorpions and snakes and sand. Like another place he knew.

He had made this a challenge to himself. He'd mailed the letter to the Tres Cerros police before leaving town. He'd dropped it in a mailbox whose contents wouldn't be collected until the next day, which meant it wouldn't be delivered until the following day. That was his self-imposed time limit for killing Cotter's daughter. She had to be dead before the letter reached the Tres Cerros police.

And he had succeeded.

But then, he'd known he would.

"Get you anything?" the stewardess asked. She was a thin, middle-aged woman with hair showing the first signs of gray.

"Another," the chubby bald man in the aisle seat said, holding up his empty drink glass. He'd been guzzling booze ever since the plane left Albuquerque. The stewardess looked as though she were about to tell him he'd had enough and then thought better of it. He wasn't bothering anyone and thus wasn't really her problem.

When the stewardess shifted her gaze to the man by the window, he said, "A Coke, please." The seat between the two men was empty.

The stewardess delivered their orders. The man by the window took a couple of sips of Coke and resumed looking out on the night. He recalled that other hot, barren place, and he started remembering some of the things that had happened there.

"I've got it," he'd said.

"How do I know I can believe you?" Leo Duver had asked. He was a big redneck with flabby arms who thought he was tough and had no idea how dumb he was. To count to twenty he'd probably have to use his fingers and toes.

"It's in an account under the name of — under another name. I can draw it all out anytime."

"And just how did you come by all this money?"

"Illegally."

"Who'd you steal it from?"

"Lots of places, but mainly the telephone company."

"You stole two million dollars from the phone company."

"Yes — most of it anyway."

"How?"

"With a computer."

Duver hesitated, working the idea around, getting the feel of it. To Duver, computers were probably a mystery, some sort of electronic witchcraft. "So," the redneck said slowly, "how do you rob the phone company with a computer?"

"Money is nothing but electronic impulses these days. All you need is the skill to manipulate those impulses."

"You mean I can just sit down at the computer in the front office and rob the phone company?"

"If the computer has a modem and if you know what you're doing, yes."

"Then why doesn't everybody do it, if it's that easy?"

"Most people don't know how."

"But you do."

"I knew a man who did, a computer expert."

Duver gave him a smug look that said, *Aha, I just caught you, didn't I?* "I can see this computer expert getting money for himself, but why would he do it for you?"

"Because I was holding a gun to his head."

Duver nodded. That was a good enough reason. After a moment's reflection, he said, "Why rob the phone company? Why not rob a bank?"

"We did. The money came from the phone company's account."

"I see," Duver said. "Have other people stolen money this way?"

"Of course. There are a few others who know how to do it."

"How come I've never heard of it?"

"Do you think the banks want it to get out?"

Duver frowned. "It stands to reason, doesn't it?" Duver said. "I mean that if you could get into a bank's computer . . . well, you could do just about anything with those numbers you wanted to." He was grinning. He was hooked.

It was a good idea, which had later born fruit in the form of Thornton Hollingsworth. And Leo Duver, who abandoned his job and family in pursuit of a lie, was dead, his bones being picked over by coyotes and buzzards and lizards.

The woman had died first.

Then Duver.

Having served their purposes, they had become encumbrances. He'd left their bodies in separate places.

Staring into the darkness outside the jetliner, the man was completely relaxed, his thoughts drifting where they pleased. The feeling of being watched was gone. It had vanished as soon as he'd left California, as if his unseen observer were unwilling or unable to exit the state. The notion was ridiculous, he knew, but that was how it seemed. As if he'd left his watcher behind.

For just an instant he'd thought he'd felt that subtle presence while he was in Texas. But the sensation had disappeared as quickly as it had arrived, and he now wondered whether he'd imagined it.

It was probably some form of mental fatigue, he concluded. Since putting his plan into effect, he'd thought of nothing else. So consumed was he with every move and countermove that he'd lain awake night after night, planning, reviewing, weighing possibilities, evaluating each nuance.

From now on he was going to take it easy. The plan was working flawlessly. He should relax and enjoy the fruits of his labors.

He drifted off to sleep.

He got off the plane in San Francisco, wondering whether the sensation of being watched would reappear with his return to California. It didn't. No one was observing him as he collected his suitcase; no one spied on him from the shadows of his consciousness as he strolled from the terminal building and disappeared into the night.

Sixteen

Cotter spent the night in a San Antonio motel. In the morning, he made the final arrangements for Jennifer. There seemed little point in having a funeral, since there was really no one to attend it except him. Jennifer's grandparents, siblings, and mother were all dead. She hadn't had any friends for fifteen years, and they had all been little girls at the time. Jennifer had never worked, never dated, never joined a single organization. No one but the staff at the hospital, the coroner, and a handful of police officers knew she had died.

And the killer.

He decided on cremation. He did not want the ashes.

That afternoon he met with Detective Clint Harris of the Bexar County Sheriff's Office, who said, "Jesus. You're the guy from Houston. To have your family killed like that . . ." He shook his head.

Harris was a thickset man who looked a lot like the Texas cops in the pictures of Jack Ruby shooting Lee Harvey Oswald. He wore a nondescript dark suit and a felt Western hat that probably cost a good deal more than the suit had. He said he preferred conducting his business away from the station, the place being so noisy and all, so they were talking over coffee in a small restaurant. The deputy took notes.

"Getting into that hospital wouldn't be too hard," Harris said in his Texas drawl. "It's not exactly a maximum-security operation. The patients arc all sort of in Never-Never-Land, so they're not trying real hard to get out. And I'm sure no one ever figured on somebody trying to break *in*."

"Got any idea how entry was gained?"

Harris swallowed some coffee. "Nope. There were two deliveries late that day, one by a laundry, the other by an outfit that supplies food to places like that. I'll check them out, but I don't expect to learn much. To tell the truth, I don't think we'll ever know how he got in. The nurse at the front desk goes for coffee, and half the time no one replaces her. Somebody could just walk in. And there are doors in that place that open to the outside and that have locks so rinky-dink my five-year-old boy could probably 'loid them."

"If he had a credit card," Cotter said.

"Thank goodness he doesn't. He'd head for the nearest toy store and run up a bill it would take the rest of my life to pay off." Taking another swallow of coffee, Harris frowned. "How do you figure this guy found out about your daughter?"

"I don't know. Her identity was kept secret. Officially she was known as Dawn."

"Who knew she was there?"

"Dr. Logan."

Harris frowned. "No one else?"

"Not that I know of. I put Jennifer there myself fifteen years ago. The deal was that she would be known by another name, and that only the director would be allowed to know her true identity."

"But you have no way of knowing whether this was a closely held thing or more of an open secret, with most of the staff in on it."

"I was assured that our agreement was being honored, but when you get right down to it, all I have is their word."

Harris slowly turned the sugar container. It was one of those bullet-shaped glass things that had a metal top with a little flap in it. "What was the name of the guy who . . . who did those things to your family?"

"Robert Heckly."

"Where is he now?"

"Southwestern State Hospital."

"The place by El Paso? Any chance he got out somehow?"

"I've checked. He's still there."

Harris nodded. "From what I hear, there's no way anyone could get out of that place."

"No one ever has," Cotter said.

The deputy sheriff signaled the waitress for more coffee. Cotter declined a refill. He decided that Harris must have developed a Texas-sized bladder over the years, considering how much liquid the man consumed.

Harris said, "You figure the guy who killed your daughter has to

113

be the same one who's been killing people in California and sending you these letters." It was a statement, not a question, so Cotter didn't respond. Harris said, "You think this guy targeted you just because he found out who you are? Some sicko who feels he just had to add to your grief?"

"It's as good an explanation as any," Cotter said. But in truth, he thought that interpretation of what had happened was too apparent, too easy. There was more to it than that.

The deputy sheriff looked at his notes and sighed. "I don't have much to go on here."

"I know the feeling," Cotter replied.

"When you going back to California?"

"This evening."

Harris stared into his coffee cup a moment, then said, "I don't think there's much chance I'll get this guy. For one thing, if he isn't there already, he'll be getting back to California shortly, because that's where you're going."

"I agree," Cotter said.

"Which means it's going to be up to you."

But then, Cotter had known that all along. The two cops agreed to keep each other posted on any significant developments.

Cindy met him at San Francisco International. Dressed in jeans and a cream-colored sweater, she looked more like a college girl than a successful businessperson. She rushed up to him and hugged him.

"I missed you terribly," she said.

"Does that mean you did a terrible job of missing me?"

"No, it means being away from you all this time was terrible."

"It was only two days."

"Felt like two years."

"Did, didn't it?"

They stood there hugging, a small island in a river of moving people.

"You okay?" Cindy asked.

"Alive and kicking."

"I mean emotionally."

He took a slow breath. "I'm coping."

Releasing him, she stepped back half a pace, searching his face, her eyes saying she was worried about him, that she was available if he needed someone to lean on.

Cotter said, "We'd better find out whether my luggage made the change of planes in Albuquerque."

Although it took about twenty minutes for it to get there, his big gray suitcase finally arrived from the depths of the terminal building and tumbled onto the big stainless steel merry-go-round. Cotter grabbed his bag, and they headed for Cindy's car.

As they drove toward Tres Cerros, Cindy said, "Do you have any idea who killed your daughter?"

When he'd phoned from Texas to let her know when he'd be coming home, Cotter had informed her that Jennifer's death was a homicide, but he'd held off on the rest of the story, saying he'd talk to her when he got back.

Cotter said, "Her name was Jennifer. Something happened to her a long time ago. It drove her into herself so deeply that she could never come back from the place she'd fled to. She was . . . a vegetable. People in that place . . . it's just storage for the hopelessly lost. No one ever gets better there."

"Mike, I'm so sorry," Cindy said, her voice brimming with emotion. "How . . . how was she killed?"

"She was suffocated."

"Poor, helpless thing," Cindy said. "Why would anyone do something like that?"

"Captain Zinn called while I was in Texas. He'd just received a letter that said, 'D is for daughter.'"

Cindy sucked in her breath.

"This same person who's been killing people here went to San Antonio and murdered Jennifer," Cotter said.

"Mike, what the hell's going on here?"

"It's all personal, against me."

"But who would hate you that much? I mean . . ." She shook her head.

"I don't know how the killer found Jennifer," he said. "She was there under another name. No one was supposed to know her true identity, not even the staff."

Cindy stared into the night. Even at this late hour, the freeway was crowded, the darkness full of shifting, winking red and white lights.

"Mike, tell me what this is all about."

"I don't know what it's about."

"You have no idea who is doing this?"

"I have no idea."

"There are things you haven't told me, things that might relate to what's happening now."

"They're in the past."

And telling her about that past was going to be tough. It had been easy with Harris. He was a Texas cop; he knew the story. All Cotter had to do was reveal who he really was. Harris filled in the rest. But talking to Cindy about it was going to be painful, because it was going to force him to relive it. And that was going to tear him apart.

"Mike, I don't want to pry into places you don't want me to go. But I truly, truly care about you. I mean, you're . . . important, special. No, it goes beyond that. You're everything to me, okay? The number one thing in my life."

"You're number one in mine too," he said gently.

"I think you're a little afraid of the word, but we love each other."

Yes, he was afraid. Because bad things happened to the people he loved. He searched for the right words, didn't find them, and said, "Certain things are just hard for me."

"What affects one of us affects the other," Cindy said, her voice soft but earnest. "And if someone's murdering the members of your family, I think I need to know what's going on."

"I have no more family members to murder," he said. "Jennifer was the last." He watched the traffic for a moment, then said, "You have a right to know."

"It's going to be awful for you, isn't it, reliving the things that happened to you?"

"Yes."

"I'm sorry I'm asking you to do something that's going to be so painful. I don't want to cause you pain, not any, not ever."

"Just give me a day or two to collect my thoughts," Cotter said. And he thought, *Oh, Cindy, I hope I haven't unwittingly put you in danger.*

That night in bed they neither talked nor made love; they simply held each other. In part because they were happy to be together again. But also, Cotter thought, because they were a little afraid.

***

In the morning, Cotter walked Cindy to her car. She unlocked it, then turned to face him.

"You don't usually do this," she said.

"Do what?" From the other side of the underground parking area came the sound of a car door slamming, an engine starting.

"Accompany me to the car."

"Shows how much I missed you."

Cindy studied him, her eyes warm, loving. "You're doing your silver-tongued bit again."

"*Moi?*"

"Yeah, you. And don't think speaking French will enable you to change the subject."

"I couldn't possibly speak French. The only words I know are *moi* and Chevrolet. And Paris, of course."

"Except they don't pronounce it that way. And stop changing the subject. I want to know whether accompanying me to my car like this is an indication that you're worried about my safety."

"Let's just say I'm being careful. And I want you to do the same thing."

"You think this person might try to get to you through me?"

"I think we have to consider that possibility," Cotter said. "It's the one thing he could do that would really hurt me."

"I . . ." She smiled a smile that would have charmed a statue. "I think that means you care more about me than you do about yourself."

"That's what it means."

"The feeling's mutual, big guy."

They hugged, gently, so as not to wrinkle Cindy's stunning brown suit. She said, "One thing."

"Yes."

"In the future, don't try to protect me without worrying me. My best protection is knowing what's going on, so I can be prepared to deal with it."

"I only wish I knew what was going on," he said. "But you're right. And I promise."

She kissed him. "See you tonight."

He watched her silver Mercedes drive away, feeling empty and alone. *Don't even think about it*, he warned the killer, sending the words over the mental channel that seemed to connect the two of them. He had no way of telling whether the message had been received.

"I'm sorry about your daughter," Captain Zinn said, as soon as Cotter stepped into his office.

"I think she died fifteen years ago," Cotter said as he sat down. "Now it's official is all."

"If you need some time . . ."

"I don't. It's better that I keep busy."

Zinn nodded. "Kozlovski and Tuffle are checking the airline passenger lists, seeing who's been traveling between here and San Antonio."

Cotter said, "I talked to them just now. They're still missing the data from two airlines."

"Probably won't tell us anything. If I was this guy, I'd fly there under one fake name, fly back using another."

Cotter considered that. "I don't think that's what he'll do. He knows we'll check, so he'll leave us a message of some sort."

The captain studied him. "You too close to this, Mike?"

"You mean because it's personal, because it's directed at me? What good would it do to have me sitting on the sidelines?"

Zinn hesitated, then said, "None, I guess. Why is this guy after you, Mike?"

"I don't know."

"Is this just some loony wants to pick up where Heckly left off?"

"I don't know that either. But it involves Heckly, somehow."

"You mean some aspiring junior psycho decides he wants to grow up to be just like good old Rob?"

"I think there's more to it than that."

"You mean Heckly is somehow manipulating all this from behind the scenes? How could that be? Guy's isolated, no contact with anyone."

"No contact with anyone on the outside, you mean. He can talk to the other inmates and the staff."

"How could he possibly influence the staff?"

"I don't know," Cotter said. But he did know that when it came to madness, nothing, no matter how unthinkable, was impossible.

***

By mid-morning the missing passenger lists had been obtained. They had asked not only for San Antonio-bound passengers, but also for the names of travelers heading for any location from which one could connect with flights to San Antonio. The most likely transfer points seemed to be Los Angeles, San Diego, Las Vegas, Denver, Phoenix, Tucson, and Albuquerque. A lot of people flew to those places from San Francisco. And the number got bigger when you included flights from Oakland, San Jose, and Sacramento.

"What are we going to do with all this stuff?" Kozlovski asked. He and Tuffle and Cotter were in the conference room with a foot-high stack of computer printouts in front of them on the table.

"There's hundreds of names here," Kozlovski said.

"Thousands," Tuffle said. The young cop had light brown hair just long enough to part and a smattering of freckles around his nose. Had he been a girl, he'd have looked like Doris Day.

"Let's see if we can figure out who made quickie round-trip visits to San Antonio within the past few days." Cotter said.

"You mean that he made no attempt to hide his destination, used his own name?" Tuffle asked, obviously not believing that could possibly be the case.

"But this guy's not trying to get away with knocking off some rich aunt so he can collect his inheritance or anything like that," Kozlovski said. "This is a psycho. He's thinks he's superior to us dumb cops. He's playing a game with us."

Cotter nodded. "He's communicating with us, taunting us."

Surprisingly, only three people had made quickie round trips to San Antonio in the past few days. Their names were A. J. Covington, Lee Heck, and Bernadette McCallister.

"What kind of a name is Heck?" Tuffle asked. "You believe that's a real name?"

"Maybe he changed it from Hell," Kozlovski suggested.

"Who the heck ever heard of anyone named Hell?" Tuffle said.

Realization hit Cotter like a blow to the gut. He stood there, dumbstruck, a part of his mind telling him it wasn't so, couldn't be so. Lee Heck. Turn it around and you had Heck Lee.

Or *Heckly*.

"Mike," Kozlovski said, "uh, you okay?"

Cotter didn't answer. He pulled out his notebook, flipped through pages covered with his hard-to-read scrawl. He stopped when he came to a list of names. One of them was Rocky L. Hebert.

He stared at it, knowing it too was part of this bizarre game, although he didn't see it, not yet.

And then he understood what he should have realized before now. "It's a goddamned anagram," he said.

"What's an anagram?" Kozlovski asked.

"It's where you take words and rearrange all the letters," Tuffle said.

In his notebook Cotter rearranged the letters in Rocky L. Hebert. When he finished, he had spelled a new name.

Robert Heckly.

Cotter stared at it, feeling an Arctic coldness inside.

Reading Cotter's notebook from across the table, Tuffle said, "Who's Robert Heckly?"

Cotter told them all about Robert Heckly.

When he was done, Tuffle was pale.

Kozlovski whispered, "Jesus H. Christ."

In his cubicle, Cotter picked up the phone, dialed the number of the Southwestern State Hospital, and asked for Keith Stiller. While he waited for the administrator to come on the line, he reminded himself to be calm and in control, and not to let his puzzlement and anxiety show.

"Detective Cotter," the administrator said. "How are things in California?"

"Cool and foggy. I want to talk to you about Heckly."

"He's still here. You have my word on it."

Cotter thought he'd detected . . . *something* in Stiller's voice. A hesitation? A subtle tightness? Or was he just looking for those things? He said, "What does Heckly do during the course of a day?"

"Do? He watches television, exercises, writes letters, eats, reads. That's all there is to do here. That's what everyone does."

"He writes letters?" Whatever Cotter thought he'd noticed in Stiller's voice was gone.

"Yes."

"Who does he write them to?"

"*Newsweek*, the *El Paso Times*, other newspapers and magazines."

"Is his mail censored?"

"Of course."

"Both incoming and outgoing?"

"There is no incoming mail for Heckly."

"No one writes to him?"

"No."

"What does he say to the newspapers and magazines?"

"They're letters to the editor. They usually deal with social issues or defense spending."

"Defense spending?"

"Yes. Heckly is worried that we don't spend enough on defense. He thinks social programs should be cut and the money should be rechanneled to the Pentagon."

"Why?"

"He has conservative views. He hates environmentalists, labor unions, and abortionists."

"A serial murderer who's a right-to-lifer?" Cotter said.

"Ironic, isn't it?"

"Do any of these letters get published?"

"Occasionally."

"Does he ever mail any personal letters?"

"No. Why are you asking me all this? What's going on?"

Cotter told him, and when he was finished, a couple of silent beats passed before the administrator replied. "Someone knows who you are," he said. "Whoever it is is pretending to be Heckly for some reason."

"Why would anyone do this?"

"If we understood the why—really understood it—maybe we could do more than just warehouse people like Heckly in places like this. But that doesn't address your question, does it? Uh . . ." He paused, presumably considering his response. "Well, it's possible that this is someone looking for recognition, fame—like the guys who confess to high-profile crimes they didn't commit.

"It's also possible that there's a Heckly fan out there. People pick some unlikely role models. Hitler has a huge following—people who admire him, grow the moustache, wear the uniform. Pick any famous scoundrel; they all have their admirers. I'm sure there are Charles Manson imitators out there, people who would love to be just like him, carry on where he left off."

Cotter considered that. It was not a pleasant thought. "Can Heckly be involved in this somehow?" he asked.

"Involved? How could he be?"

"Can he be masterminding this whole thing from there? Now, before you answer—"

"The suggestion is ridiculous."

"—I want you to think about it carefully. Is there any way Heckly can be communicating with the outside world? Maybe these letters to the editor contain some kind of a code—whatever."

"Impossible."

"Why is it impossible?"

"He doesn't write to any given individual. The letters are always addressed to the editor. You think the editor of *Newsweek* is in cahoots with Heckly?"

"Can he make phone calls?"

"It's permitted for patients to make phone calls, but Heckly has never asked for permission. I doubt he'd get it, and if he did, we'd monitor the call."

"What if he said it was to his attorney?"

"Then we couldn't monitor it, but Heckly doesn't have an attorney."

Cotter heard it again, the shakiness in Stiller's voice. Softly but firmly, he said, "Is there anything you're not telling me?"

"No," Stiller replied angrily. "There's absolutely nothing I'm not telling you. I regret what's happening to you there, and if there's anything I can do to help, I will gladly do it, but please don't accuse me of withholding information from you. Why on earth would I?"

For that Cotter had no answer. He asked the administrator to call him if he thought of anything—anything at all.

Seventeen

It was back.

The feeling of being watched.

He sat on the edge of the bed, his eyes darting around the motel room, looking for . . . for what? Did he expect to find a surveillance camera mounted in the corner, an electronic eye that watched his every move? He took in the cheap TV set that was chained to the wall, the shabby chair, the dresser whose fake wood veneer was starting to peel, the worn blue carpet, the grimy beige paint on the walls. Clearly he was alone in the room. How could anyone be watching him?

And yet the feeling persisted.

As if the watcher were somewhere nearby and at the same time actually within him, in his head. What the hell was causing this? He shook his head as if to dislodge the culprit and fling him away, like a dog shaking off water.

But the unseen presence was still there.

"Go away," he said. "Get away from me before I . . ."

Before he what? How was he supposed to harm something he could neither see nor touch?

"There's nothing here," he said to the empty room. "I'm in control of this situation, and I know there is nothing here."

But there was something there. Unseen. Untouchable. And it poked into his mind, pried the lid off his inner being, sampled his secrets.

"Ridiculous."

The word could not exorcise his personal demon, which tormented him by being present but not present, in his head but not in his head, delving into his deepest secrets one day and vanishing into oblivion the next.

"Imagination," he said. But that word had no more power than the last one he'd tried.

Abruptly he got up, changed into his jogging clothes, and dashed out of the room. He ran hard, forcing his legs to work harder, his breath coming in deep gulps, sweat trickling down his back.

Slovenly yards, peeling paint, the usual collection of street urchins. He ran so fast these things became a blur. And then he ran still faster, until the ugliness that was Colmer seemed to vanish, until his muscles and joints were being pushed to their absolute limit. He raced along the sidewalk like a jet accelerating to take off speed. Powerful. Unstoppable. Cutting around a tricycle. Leaping over a discarded beer bottle. Flying over a hopscotch diagram chalked in white.

As he used up the last of his energy, his movements became uncoordinated, and he was stumbling, his arms windmilling as he fought to maintain balance, and then he was standing beside a broken picket fence, his lungs desperately sucking in air. Suddenly unable to remain upright, he sat down on the sidewalk.

The sensation was still there. His mad expenditure of energy had not expelled the demon.

He was still being watched.

Finally he got his breath back and headed toward the motel, walking slowly. The sensation, be it real or imaginary, could not be allowed to interfere with his plan. If there was no other way to deal with it, he would simply have to live with it. He could not allow himself to repeat the sort of madness he had just indulged in.

It was time to find another motel, time for the next phase of the plan. He concentrated on these matters, and the watcher watched. It didn't matter. He would not let it matter.

Eighteen

"Travel agent says the ticket order came in over the phone," Kozlovski told Cotter over the radio. "Paid with a credit card number. We're checking on that now."

"Ten-four," Cotter said. "I'm ten-ninety-seven at the airport."

Parking in front of the terminal building, next to a no-parking sign that warned of fines and tow trucks should the prohibition be violated, he flipped down his visor, displaying a police department decal, and hurried inside. The airline had already determined that the ticket agent who'd dealt with the traveler named Heck was a woman named Nancee Kray. He met her in a small room that contained a Formica-topped table, a wastebasket, and a soft drink machine.

"Want a Coke?" Cotter asked as they sat down at the table.

"Machine doesn't have Coke," Nancee Kray said. "Only Pepsi."

"Want a Pepsi?"

"Sure."

Cotter got her one and returned to the table. Nancee Kray was in her mid-twenties, with curly red hair, freckles, bright blue eyes, and a smile that was both shy and captivating.

"What's this all about?" she asked.

"You sold a ticket a few days ago to a man named Heck."

"He bought it through a travel agency. I didn't sell it to him here."

"You remember him."

"Yes."

"You must deal with a lot of people. Why do you remember this particular one?"

"Because the name's so unusual. I remember looking to see whether his initials were A.W."

"A.W.?"

"Yeah, that would have made his name Aw Heck. Get it?"

"I get it. Is that the only reason you remember him, his name?"

"He made a pass at me. He asked me out. It was kind of embarrassing, really. I had to tell him that it's against company policy, and besides, I'm married." She held up her left hand, displaying the silver-colored band.

"Describe him."

"Tall, brown hair, athletic build, and he wore an expensive suit. I guess I should say expensive-*looking* suit. I don't really know enough about men's clothes to say it was actually an expensive suit."

They'd have to go back over this, nail down things like how tall was tall, what color eyes, whether she could recognize him if she saw him again. It was clear that the man calling himself Lee Heck had intended for Nancee to remember him. No one trying to cover his tracks made a pass at a ticket agent.

Apprehension, cold and clammy, settled over him. The man calling himself Lee Heck wanted Cotter to learn what he looked like. The description was general. There were lots of tall, brown-haired guys out there. And yet . . .

"Is there anything else you can tell me about him?" Cotter asked.

Nancee Kray thought it over for a second or two, frowning, her head cocked slightly. She wrinkled her nose. "That's all I can think of," she said.

"No accent, no unusual mannerisms?"

"Nnnnno," she said slowly. "Oh, wait. I think he had a bad arm."

"A bad arm," Cotter said, the cold, clammy feeling abruptly surging through his system with such force that he nearly gasped.

"Yeah, he didn't use his left arm. In fact, I remember that he sort of adjusted it with his right one, so it hung a little differently, like it couldn't move at all by itself." She snapped her fingers. "Oh, and he had one of those dents in his chin. What do you call them. A dimple, that's it. He had a dimple in his chin."

Cotter stared at her, stunned.

"Are . . . uh, are you okay?" Nancee Kray asked, her eyes exploring his face.

"Oh, yes, sorry," Cotter said, collecting his wits.

He went over everything with Nancee Kray again, getting more details, confirming others, his fingers feeling numb, barely able to write the notes he was taking.

When he'd learned everything the ticket agent had to tell him, he phoned the police station. Tuffle said, "The credit card number doesn't help us any. Belongs to an elderly woman in San Rafael. She says she has her card, hasn't lent it to anyone, and definitely hasn't bought any airline tickets to Texas lately. Apparently someone got ahold of her number."

"Apparently," Cotter said, not really listening.

"How'd it go at the airport?"

Cotter told him.

"Holy shit," Tuffle said, his voice barely above a whisper. "The description fits exactly."

"Yes," Cotter said. "Exactly."

"It's gotta be someone playing with your head, right? I mean, the real guy's locked up in that escape-proof place in Texas, isn't he?"

Exactly the same question Cotter had asked himself. He's locked away in that escape-proof place . . . *isn't he?*

"You on your way back here?" Tuffle asked.

"No. I'm leaving for El Paso in half an hour. Tell Koz and Captain Zinn. And send someone for my car."

Tuffle said he'd take care of everything.

"One more thing," Cotter said.

"What?"

"Keep an eye on Cindy."

"You think she might be in danger?"

"It's possible," Cotter said. "She's in San Francisco all day, at her advertising agency—Brekke and Associates. Call Detective Lieutenant Thomas Cone at SFPD. Tell him I need a favor."

"I'll do it as soon you hang up," Tuffle promised.

Cotter phoned Cindy at work.

"El Paso?" she said.

"I don't have time to explain right now. Cindy, listen to me. I want you to be very careful. Keep your car doors locked. Don't go anywhere alone where you might be vulnerable. Promise me that, okay?"

"Mike, you're scaring me. I hope you know that."

"Promise me you'll be careful."

"Yes, I promise. What's going on?"

"I don't know what's going on. Maybe I'll find out in El Paso. When I get back I'll tell you what happened fifteen years ago."

"Mike, I . . ."

One of the things he would have to tell her was that his name wasn't Mike. "I've got to go, or I'll miss my plane."

"You be careful, too," she said.

"I will."

"Promise?"

"Yes, I promise."

He did not phone Southwestern State Hospital in West Texas. He didn't want Keith Stiller to know he was coming.

Accompanied by a few high wisps of clouds, the jetliner sped eastward, heading for El Paso. Cotter had a window seat. He stared out at the view, not seeing the clouds or sun-baked mountains and deserts of Arizona, but the flat, humid country of east Texas. Fifteen years ago. A young Texas state cop on routine patrol.

"Houston to all units," the dispatcher said over the radio. "Stand by for a rebroadcast of an earlier BOLO." A BOLO was a be-on-the-lookout bulletin.

"BOLO is on a Robert Heckly; DOB five, two; forty-eight; brown over brown; six feet, two inches tall; a hundred ninety pounds; athletic build.

"Subject is wanted for the murder of two people at a farm near Lufkin. Believed to be driving a white '77 Chevrolet four-door taken from that farm. Texas license H3C-3A8.

"Subject is also wanted for five homicides in New Jersey.

"Subject was last seen near Lufkin at approximately fifteen hundred last date, headed south.

"Extreme ten-forty-eight is urged with this subject. He is a martial arts expert. Unknown whether he possesses any weapons."

Ten-forty-eight meant use caution.

Officer William Michael Richland drove along the two-lane

highway, enjoying the first crisp fall day. It was a lovely morning, sunny but with a cool northerly breeze that had dropped temperatures from the low nineties to the upper seventies. Summers in southeast Texas were stifling, the air clinging wetly to your body, mildew thriving in every dank cranny, mosquitoes rising from the lawn in hungry clouds. It made a day like this a thing to be treasured.

The area in which he was driving was dotted with farms. A few grew vegetables for the Houston grocery stores, but most of the farmers here raised cattle or hogs or poultry. He passed a field with cows and half a dozen oil wells in it, the pump mechanisms going up and down, up and down. The commonest of sights in Texas, where people used miniature drilling towers to decorate their lawns.

Ahead was a white Chevrolet. Richland slowly overtook it and noted the license number. It didn't match the one given out in the BOLO, and the car was being driven by an elderly couple. The car had two bumper stickers. One said JESUS LOVES YOU, and the other said THANK GOD FOR AMERICA. As he pulled around the car, the man smiled and waved. Richland waved back.

Half an hour later, the Houston dispatcher repeated the BOLO on Robert Heckly. Richland had read newspaper and magazine stories about Heckly. He'd been a lawyer back in New Jersey, a member of the town council, an up-and-comer in the Republican Party who was often mentioned as a possible candidate for higher office. Everyone liked him. A few still refused to believe he was a killer.

Heckly was a sociopath, a person who could kill without compunction. The people he murdered had simply been in his way. One victim consistently opposed him on the town council. Another had gotten up a petition to fight a bridge he favored. Another was a troublesome relative. To Heckly, murder seemed to be a useful tool. So efficient was it, so quick and reliable, that he began to think of it as his solution of choice for any sticky problems that might arise. At least, that's what the psychiatrists were saying.

Of course, there were other reasons Heckly did what he did—darker, more complex reasons possibly not fathomed even by Heckly himself. In the case of the council member who opposed him, for example, Heckly had waited for the man's wife to get home so he could kill her as well, although she was uninvolved with town government. He'd disemboweled her.

New Jersey authorities eventually figured out that Heckly was the murderer. And when that happened, he disappeared.

Heckly had murdered the five people over a period of three years. The psychiatrists said he would probably continue killing, the time separating the incidents decreasing. Apparently the shrinks were right. He had already killed two people in Texas.

The farm couple near Lufkin had died because the car Heckly was driving had broken down. He'd needed a new one. The couple's farm had been the closest place. Lufkin authorities said he'd had no reason to slay the couple. They always left the keys in the car. He could simply have taken it.

He'd killed the man by bashing his head in with a pipe. He'd slit the woman's throat.

Richland cut over to highway 90, where he checked out two more white Chevys, neither of which turned out to be the one Heckly had stolen. He wrote two tickets for speeding, one to a white-haired woman who must have been in her eighties. Glaring at him, she said she didn't believe in speed limits and thought they were an infringement on her rights as an American citizen.

Shortly before noon, Richland pulled into a rest area on the outskirts of Houston. He liked to keep an eye on the rest areas. Occasionally people were robbed at them, and vandalism was an increasing problem. He'd spotted two stolen cars at rest areas, and recently a sheriff's deputy had found a van full of cocaine at one on this same highway.

This one was nothing fancy, just a parking area, a couple of picnic tables, and a brick rest room. The only car there was a gray Lincoln, its driver nowhere in sight. Richland routinely ran a check on the license plate. It came back negative, which meant the Lincoln hadn't been reported stolen. Getting out of his cruiser, Richland headed for the rest room—and not just to check it out. His bladder was reminding him of the two cups of coffee he'd had at a truck stop near Baytown. Inside he found a man at the sink, using the mirror to shave.

"Morning," the man said, glancing in Richland's direction. He had on jeans and a Western shirt. His face was covered with shaving cream.

"Morning," the policeman replied, stepping up to the urinal and unzipping. "Your Lincoln?" he asked conversationally.

"Um-hum."

"Nice car."

"Thanks."

"That gray color show the dirt?"

"Not too bad."

Slowly the realization settled over Richland that something was not quite right here. Police officers learned to spot things like that, to notice when a light that should be on was off, when a door that should be closed was open. But nothing like that was wrong here. And yet the feeling that something was amiss persisted.

He was zipping his fly when it came to him. The Lincoln outside was brand-new, one of the most costly models. People who drove cars like that usually had enough money to dress nicely and stay in the better motels. Why was a guy who wore an old cowboy shirt and shaved in a public rest room driving such an expensive car?

There were explanations, of course. The guy was one of those oddball millionaires you heard about. Or he was simply driving the car across the country for somebody. Or—

Or he'd stolen it, and it hadn't been reported yet.

"You mind if I check the registration on your car?" Richland said.

"Why?" the guy asked, still looking in the mirror. "Something wrong?"

"No sir," Richland said, sounding like cops everywhere. "Just a routine check."

"Okay," the man replied, "give me a second, and I'll be right with you."

Using a paper towel from the dispenser, he'd wiped off the shaving cream, and suddenly Richland was hearing the Houston dispatcher's voice:

. . . brown over brown; six feet, two inches tall; a hundred ninety pounds; athletic build . . .

Richland was looking at someone who matched that description exactly. A lot of guys fit the description; he knew that. And yet there was something was telling him that this wasn't just some similar-looking man. This was Robert Heckly.

Extreme ten-forty-eight is urged with this subject.

"Would you mind showing me some identification?" Richland said, his hand creeping closer to his holster.

The man smiled, looking a little embarrassed. His eyes seemed full of puzzlement, but they studied Richland with a calculating wariness. "Uh, this has never happened to me before."

"Some identification, please," Richland said.

"My wallet's in the car."

Richland put his hand on the butt of his service revolver. "Turn around and put your hands against the wall."

"Why? What . . . what's happening here?"

"Move!"

"Hey, yeah, sure. I mean, don't get too excited."

He assumed the position. Richland moved up behind him, patted him down. He had lied about his wallet being in the car. It was in his left rear pocket. Richland pulled it out, found a driver's license. The photo showed a suntanned man in his sixties, wearing a John Deere cap. The license had been issued to Joe Bob Denner, Rural Route 6, Homer. Homer was near Lufkin. This had to be the license of the farmer who'd been killed by Heckly.

Richland still held his gun ready. Reaching behind him with his free hand, he got his handcuffs. "I'm placing you under arrest," he said. "You have the right to remain silent. You have the right—"

Heckly dropped to the floor, his movement so fast Richland wasn't sure what had happened. Instantly, the man slipped through Richland's legs and was behind him. The policeman started to turn, and a powerful blow slammed him into the wall. The gun flew from his hand.

Extreme ten-forty-eight is urged with this subject. He is a martial arts expert.

Knowing another blow was coming, Richland moved to his right, turning so he could defend himself. A karate kick grazed his side, and then he was face-to-face with his opponent. They assessed each other, their eyes meeting, and in that moment Richland knew he had met madness as he had never known it before.

He'd looked into the eyes of a father who had just murdered his wife and children, seeing bewilderment and torment. He'd looked into the brutal, pitiless eyes of a robber who'd shot and killed a convenience store clerk. But nothing had prepared him for the eyes into which he stared now.

In their brown depths danced and twirled things that were incomprehensible to him, desires and delights drawn from a totally alien frame of reference. His eyes seemed aglow with these things, like two holes in the side of a roaring furnace, and yet, strangely, they also seemed to be twin tunnels into a bottomless blackness, a cold and lifeless void. It was all Richland could do to keep from looking away.

Tall and lean and muscular, Heckly would have been a formidable opponent even if he hadn't been skilled in the martial arts. Richland was in excellent condition, a large man who had managed to be both muscular and agile, in the way a stallion combines fluid motion and raw strength. He wasn't easily intimidated. But standing there in that rest room, staring into Robert Heckly's eyes, William Michael Richland knew he was in serious trouble.

He thought his gun had slid into one of the toilet stalls, but he wasn't sure. He dared not look for it, because it would mean taking his eyes off his opponent. Besides, even if he knew for sure where the weapon was, Heckly would never let him get to it.

Heckly made his move, launching another karate kick at Richland's face. He ducked and moved left to avoid the follow-up kick he knew was coming. The second blow caught the side of his face, but not hard enough to injure him. Knowing Heckly would be off balance, having just launched blows that failed to solidly connect, Richland moved in, hurling a blow of his own, his fist catching Heckly in the jaw, but before he could throw another punch, a karate jab caught him in the upper chest. It had been aimed at his throat. Even though it missed its target, it was a lot like being smacked with a hammer. Richland knew that if he didn't do something quickly, he was going to lose this battle, which almost certainly meant he would die here.

Ducking and weaving, he backed away from a series of chops and kicks. A small smile appeared on Heckly's face. He knew he had won.

Heckly was fast. He kicked and missed, and maintaining his balance flawlessly, moved in close enough to land a solid punch in Richland's gut, doubling him over. A kick to his upper body knocked him against the wall.

Groaning, Richland tried to remain focused on his opponent. Heckly's smile was a victory smile now, a self-satisfied grin. He stepped in to finish his opponent off, coming with a series of kicks and chops and jabs that hit with the rapidity of a fast drumbeat. Punishment rained on him mercilessly. Richland fought to resist the darkness closing in around him, for it was the blackness of death. Slipping down the wall to the floor, he forced himself to ignore the pain, and concentrate on staying alive.

Apparently satisfied that Richland was too groggy to be any further threat, Heckly stopped administering the pounding. Looking down at Richland, he said, "You're a hell of a lot less tough than you thought, huh?"

Richland just stared at him.

"I'm going to kill you now," Heckly said.

Still convinced Richland was beyond offering any resistance, he reached for him. As Richland was pulled to his feet, he grabbed Heckly's arm. There was nothing sophisticated about it. No trickery, no skillfully applied leverage. He simply latched onto the arm and, using his considerable strength, started forcing it into a position inconsistent with its construction. Heckly hollered.

Richland fought the dizziness that kept trying to wash over him and concentrated on the arm. Heckly screamed again, used his other arm to kidney-punch him, then kicked him in the shins. Their motion carried them across the room in stumbles and lunges, as if they were doing some bizarre dance. The men's room boogie shuffle.

Richland felt as if he were floating, darkness settling over him as if he were having his own personal nightfall. He fought its lure, for to yield to it would be to die. He was hanging on to Heckly's arm as if it were a life preserver and he would surely drown the moment he let go. Heckly landed a blow on the side of Richland's head, tried to spin out of his grasp. Richland hung on and, from somewhere deep within himself, called forth a last reserve of strength, channeled it to the pressure he was applying to Heckly's arm.

Heckly screamed in agony.

And there was a loud snap.

Richland, too groggy to fully understand what was happening, kept the pressure on the object in his hands. There were a number of strange sounds, pops like snaps being unfastened, a tearing noise like strips of Velcro being separated. And more screams.

Abruptly Richland found he was unable to hold off the darkness any longer. Letting go of the arm, he sank to the floor. The room seemed to swirl around him, as if he were at the stationary hub of a carousel. Forcing his eyes to focus, he saw Heckly crawling toward the door. And he saw his gun. It was inside one of the stalls, against the base of a toilet. Fighting the blackness and dizziness, he crawled toward the revolver. He heard some grunts and thunks. Heckly was at the door, trying to stand, one arm hanging at an odd angle. His eyes found Richland, and they instantly filled with hate, gleaming with a searing intensity.

Richland made it to the stall, reached under the door, and retrieved his service revolver. He sat up, his back against the stall, raising the gun. The rest room door closed. A moment later Cotter heard an engine roar, tires squeal.

Then he passed out.

Nineteen

Cotter rented a Ford Tempo in El Paso and drove east into mountains that seemed to be made of sun-baked rock, with little or no vegetation. To the north was Fort Bliss and the White Sands Missile Range in New Mexico, country so desolate it was used for missile testing and target practice. The sun beat down incessantly, as if trying to bake everything into dust, so the spring winds could blow it away.

Cotter had been driving about an hour when he turned south on a narrow state road that headed, straight as a ruler-drawn line, into country that was all sand and rocks and gullies. It was a place naturally inhabited only by snakes and jackrabbits and scorpions. There were no cows, no windmills, no side roads, not even fences. The vegetation was limited to cactus and an occasional squat bush. As he drove, even those things became fewer.

Somewhere ahead were the area's only human inhabitants, who lived behind razor wire and electrified fences. It took him another hour to reach the place, and when he saw it he realized why it was said to be escape-proof. Even Desert Pete could not survive here on foot.

Signs informed him that he had to park his car because no private vehicles were permitted to enter the facility. All the cars in the lot had their windshields and rear windows covered from the inside with cardboard, to keep the intense sun from fading their upholstery and cracking their dash panels. He walked to the pumice-block gatehouse, where a uniformed guard kept him waiting for ten minutes, before he was finally cleared to enter the place.

He had to pass through three gates, each one closing before the next one opened. The middle fence was covered with warnings like, EXTREME DANGER, HIGH VOLTAGE IN FENCE. One of them said simply, LETHAL ELECTRIC CHARGE. The innermost fence had razor wire coiled along its top. As he passed through the last gate, a brown-uniformed guard met him.

"I'll escort you to the administrator's office," he said.

Southwestern State Hospital was a low, sprawling complex of cream-colored block buildings, the majority of them with bars on the windows. Enclosed within its own protective chain-link fence was a satellite dish. To Cotter's left, outside the fences, were a number of small, flat-roofed houses, presumably the homes of the facility's employees and their families. Cotter wondered how you could pay anyone enough to work here.

The guard led him to a building with a sign out front that said ADMINISTRATION. Cotter stepped into its air-conditioned coolness, happy to have escaped the heat and glaring sunlight. A man in a light blue tropical-weight suit greeted him.

"Mr. Cotter, I'm Keith Stiller. After all those phone conversations, we finally meet face-to-face."

Lately, Cotter had been meeting all sorts of people he'd only spoken to over the phone. And he'd been traveling back in time, revisiting things he'd vowed to put behind him forever. The two men shook hands; then Stiller led Cotter into his office. It was a place for working, not showing off the trappings of power. One wall was lined with bookcases, their shelves loaded with serious-looking volumes many of which appeared worn from use. To the left was a library table on which papers had been spread out. On the wall were maps of West Texas and of the facility itself. In one corner were the obligatory Texas and United States flags, their brass holders in need of dusting. On Stiller's desk were a number of pictures. Although they were turned so he couldn't see them, Cotter assumed they showed the wife and kids and maybe even the dog.

"If you'd let us know you were coming, you could have saved yourself that delay at the gate," Stiller said.

A pale, balding man with a round face, he looked more like some faceless mid-level bureaucrat than a psychiatrist. Of course, that's what he was: a state employee, chief paper-pusher in an isolated and largely ignored part of the Texas criminal justice system. It was not a job one took if one was on the fast track.

"Is he still here?" Cotter asked.

"You mean—of course he's still here. You didn't have to come all the way out here to the boonies to find that out. You could have called. Actually, you didn't even need to call. I mean, no one escapes from here. It's never happened. It never will."

Stiller had been fidgeting ever since he'd sat down at his desk. He laced and unlaced his fingers, aligned papers, checked his nails. His eyes were puffy and had the distant, haunted look of someone with heavy-duty troubles.

"My daughter's been murdered," Cotter said.

"Murdered? Your daughter? But I thought she was—"

"By a man who likes to leave clues suggesting that he's Robert Heckly."

"Clues? What clues?"

Cotter told him, and he paled.

"How terrible," Stiller said. "Obviously someone is pretending to be Heckly."

"Because the real Heckly's here."

"Of course."

"Prove it."

"Prove it? I don't understand."

"Show me Heckly."

"All right." He picked up the phone. "Leon, switch the picture of Heckly in here, will you."

Stiller moved to the TV set that stood on a roll-away stand by the bookcases and switched it on. A color picture of a man lying in a hospital bed filled the screen. He was on his back, his eyes closed, an IV taped to his arm. Recognizing him instantly, Cotter experienced a mixture of powerful emotions. The first was just tingly shock, followed rapidly by revulsion, hate, and terror.

He was looking at something he had hoped to never see again.

A monster.

Madness and evil personified.

For a long moment Cotter simply sat there and stared, afraid his voice would crack if he tried to speak.

"You see," Stiller said. "He's still here."

"Why is he in a hospital bed?"

"He has the plague."

"What plague?"

"The bubonic plague."

"The black death?"

"Yes. There are rodents out in the desert, and some of them are carriers. Sometimes they get into the compound. They're drawn here because there's water and kitchen garbage. The plague is transmitted by fleas the rodents bring with them."

"I've heard that."

Stiller nodded vigorously. "It's a serious problem throughout the West, anywhere isolated enough to have wild rodents."

"I'm surprised they can live in a place this arid."

"Rodents can live anywhere."

"It's possible that everything you've told me is true."

"Of course it's true. Look here, Mr. Cotter—"

"It's also possible that the picture you're showing me is a videotape. Let's face it, I wouldn't know the difference, would I? But then, this is easily cleared up. Just show me Heckly in the flesh."

Cotter had come here to lay his doubts to rest. Stiller would show him Heckly, and that would be that. The man who drew letters on Jennifer and his other victims would be proved a fake, someone who for some warped reason was pretending to be Heckly. Now Cotter didn't know what to believe. He was afraid he was on the verge of learning something horrendous. A huge mass of terror began to undulate in his midsection.

"Heckly's been quarantined," Stiller said. "He's got an extremely communicable disease, and the state health authorities won't let anyone have contact with him except medical personnel."

"Uh-huh, and if I buy that, maybe you can sell me a bridge or two."

"A bridge? Oh, I see. I . . . I resent the suggestion that I might be trying to deceive you, Mr. Cotter. Why on earth would I do such a thing?"

"That's exactly what I'm wondering. Show me Heckly."

"I . . . I told you—"

"Show him to me through a sealed glass window."

"We . . . we don't have any facilities like that. We do everything with TV cameras."

"So all I have is your word that this isn't a videotape."

Stiller looked indignant. "I can assure you, I would not stoop to such behavior. For goodness' sake, why would I? What possible purpose could it serve?"

And that was the question, wasn't it? There seemed to be only one answer, and it scared the hell out of Cotter.

"Where's Heckly?" Cotter asked softly.

"I told you—"

"Stop it. It won't wash."

"Really, Mr. Cotter, I must say—"

"Do you want me to contact the Department of Public Safety and tell them I have reason to believe that something's happened here and that you're covering it up?"

Stiller stood by the TV set, staring at him. He was trembling. "No," he said, his voice barely above a whisper. "I don't want you to do that."

"Tell me," Cotter said, trying to display a calmness he didn't feel at all. He knew what was coming, and he braced himself for it.

Stiller looked as though he might faint. "He . . . he's gone."

Even though, deep down inside where it counted, Cotter had known that was what Stiller would say, the words tore through him like bullets. Heckly loose. *Uh-uh*, a part of him was insisting. *Unacceptable. No, no, no.*

And then anger, hot and unstoppable, overwhelmed everything else. "What do you mean, 'He's gone'? How could he be gone? Don't you realize what he is, what he's capable of—what he did to my family?"

"I know," Stiller said weakly. "I'm sorry."

Stiller was only about five-four. Cotter had to resist the urge to grab him and shake him. "Why the hell didn't you tell me?"

"He . . . he has Willie."

"Who's Willie?"

"Willa. My wife."

"Heckly has her?"

"Yes."

Stiller stood before him, stricken. He shifted his weight from side to side as if he wanted to collapse but was uncertain which way to fall. Cotter waited, letting the administrator proceed at his own rate.

"Oh, God," Stiller said. "What will happen to Willie now?" He

140

shuddered. "I . . . I got home, and there he was . . . with Willie. I don't know how he got out of the facility and into the residential compound. Willie probably knows, but . . . but she never had the chance to tell me."

He shook his head. "The law says we have to let him exercise. We can't just keep him locked up. If he proves a danger to himself or the other patients, then we can isolate him, but he never did that."

"You should have kept him in a special cage," Cotter said.

"Everyone confined here is dangerous. The idea isn't to keep them from mingling with each other. It's to keep them out of society. That's what the fences are for."

"The fences he got through to reach your house."

"Yes," Stiller said sadly. "Those fences."

"When did all this happen?"

Stiller looked away, unwilling to meet Cotter's eyes. "Months ago."

"How many months?"

"Three." He said it weakly, like a child mumbling a confession.

"Why the hell didn't you go to the police?" Cotter demanded. "Don't you have any sense at all?"

"He took Willie with him. He said he'd eventually let her go if I didn't contact the authorities."

"How did you manage to keep this from getting out?" Cotter asked, incredulous. "You've got staff here, other inmates. You're not in a vacuum. How could you cover something like this?"

"It only involved a couple of staff members. Everyone else was told that he was in the hospital in El Paso, that he had a heart attack and that it had happened overnight while he was asleep."

"And everyone believed this?"

"Why wouldn't they? Night staff's very small, just a few guards and a duty orderly. Everyone else is gone. And the patients are locked in at night. The two people I asked to go along with the story talked it over and agreed. You see, this place is sort of the end of the line for them. This is probably the only job they could get. We're fighting for our lives with the legislature now. An escape might be all it'd take to close us down. I told them I'd take all the blame, that they could say they kept silent out of fear for Willie's safety."

"Aren't there any other administrators here besides you? Surely someone would have found out."

"I don't have an assistant. The budget won't allow for one. If I'm away for any reason, one of the staff psychiatrists takes over—Dr. Bruhl."

"And he believed Heckly was in the hospital?"

"Yes. He'd have no reason to doubt it. He'd have no reason to even be interested. Heckly wasn't on his patient list."

"Who's list was he on?"

"Mine."

"Get back to the day of the escape. What happened?"

"I got home, and there he was, in my living room with Willie. You know what happened after that."

"No, I don't. How did he get away from your house?"

"He took Willie's car. It was about ten o'clock that night. He was holding a knife to her throat. He forced her into the garage, then into the car, and then . . . and then he drove away."

Cotter was having trouble believing this had worked. There were too many possibilities for things to go wrong. But then he sensed that Heckly's escape had been carefully planned, the weaknesses of his adversaries carefully analyzed.

Cotter said, "Have you at least made an effort to find out how Heckly got out of the maximum security part of the facility and into the employee housing part? If someone helped him, we need to find out who and talk to that person."

"How . . . how could I investigate something that wasn't supposed to have happened?"

Cotter started to tell him that there were ways to do these things quietly, then decided he'd be wasting his breath. He suspected the less-than-top-notch staff was one of the reasons Heckly had been able to get through the three fences to freedom. What a place. Society's most dangerous lunatics guarded by society's dregs. The minders no more trustworthy and upstanding than the inmates.

"How did you account for your wife's absence?"

"I said her mother was very ill, and Willa had gone to be with her."

"For three months?"

"That was what I said at first. When too much time had passed without her coming back, I said we were experimenting with a trial separation."

"Didn't it ever occur to you that you should drop this foolishness and go to the police?"

"Willa and I are very close. She's.. she's very special. I couldn't report what had happened. I just couldn't. If anything happened to her . . ." A tear trickled down his cheek.

Willa Stiller was dead, probably buried somewhere out in the vast isolation surrounding this place, or maybe just left for the coyotes and buzzards to finish off. Cotter suspected that deep down where reality resided, Stiller knew this. But to admit it to himself would be to give up hope, and hope was all he had.

"The videotape," Stiller said. "It's about a year and a half old. He had pneumonia. Developed out of a severe case of the flu."

Too bad he didn't die, Cotter thought. "You didn't tell me he was sick."

"All you ever asked was whether he was here. You didn't seem too concerned about his health."

"I'm going to have to notify the authorities," Cotter said.

Stiller nodded. "I know. What will happen to Willie?"

Cotter didn't know how to respond to that.

"Will I have to name the two staff people who went along with me? I think they did it out of loyalty to me," Stiller said. "It wasn't just to keep their jobs—or even the money."

"Money?" Cotter said. "What money?"

"I gave them a thousand dollars each. They deserved it. I mean, they were risking a lot to help me save Willie." His eyes pleaded for understanding, but at that moment Cotter had none to offer.

"Willie," Stiller said. "Oh, my God, poor Willie."

"Did you tell Heckly where to find Jennifer?"

"Jennifer?"

"My daughter."

"No." He shook his head almost violently. "I couldn't have told him that. I didn't know where she was."

"Did you tell him my name and where to find me?"

Looking totally miserable, Stiller nodded. "I had to. He had the

143

knife, and he was holding Willie, and he said . . . he said . . ."

"He said what?"

"He'd cut her up like . . ."

"Like what?"

"Like he did your wife."

Stiller shuddered. And then he began to cry.

Cotter called the police.

"Wow," said Sergeant Joseph Sanchez of the Hudspeth County Sheriff's Office, after Cotter had explained who he was and what had been happening. "This Heckly sounds like he was made by taking all the worst parts of the scariest people you can name and combining them all in one guy. Compared to him, Manson and Son of Sam and the Hillside Strangler and some of these guys come off as a bunch of feebs."

Cotter said he couldn't disagree with that.

He and Cotter were alone in the employees' lounge at Southwestern State Hospital. It had a coffeepot, soft drink and candy machines, and four small tables with chipped Formica tops. An assortment of stained cups was haphazardly arranged on the table that held the coffeepot. Taped to the wall was a sheet of paper on which the following admonition had been written in felt-tip: COFFEE 50¢, NO CREDIT.

"You see any chance that Mrs. Stiller's still alive?" Sanchez asked.

"I doubt she was alive twelve hours after he abducted her."

"Same here," Sanchez said. "How do you figure on Stiller not calling us in, even after three months had gone by?"

"Under stress, people do some strange things."

"Would have been nice if he'd let you know that this guy was loose. There couldn't be much doubt he'd come after you. Guy like that, after you ruined his arm . . . hell, he probably spent the last fifteen years dreaming about getting even."

Cotter didn't know what to say to that. He'd spent the past fifteen years trying to escape from a nightmare.

"I've been running computer checks on the employees," Sanchez said. "So far I've come up with one out-of-state felony warrant, a guy who served time in Huntsville for drug trafficking, a former prostitute, and three fathers who slipped out on the child support payments. One of them owes over ten grand in back payments." He shook his head. "This place is a regular sleaze city. Don't they ever check any of these people out?"

Cotter said, "I guess living in the middle of nowhere with scorpions and psychos doesn't attract your highest class of applicants."

"I can see that. I don't think they could pay me enough to work in this place."

"Apparently they've got to take whoever they can get," Cotter said.

"But hiring felons at a correctional institution? Gotta be a violation of state law."

Sanchez rubbed his brow. He had on a summer-weight gray sportcoat, which he wore over an open-collared green shirt. Though only about five-six, he was trim and athletic looking, and he had a face that seemed too fresh and smooth to belong to anyone who'd been a cop long enough to make detective sergeant. He studied Cotter with eyes that seemed full of good humor and intelligence.

"Speaking of the state," he said, "I've called them in, since this is a state correctional institution. I'm not sure how jurisdiction will be handled. I'd guess the kidnapping will be mine and the improprieties here at the facility will be theirs."

"What will happen to Stiller?"

Sanchez shrugged. "State cops will file a report with Austin, and paperwork people will grind out their decision. Probably depends on how much political clout he's got. Not much, I'd say, if he's working in this place. Top-notch shrink ought to have an office in Dallas and be driving a Rolls, wouldn't you think?"

Cotter nodded. "You learn anything from the staff?"

"Nobody's saying any more than they have to. They're a real see-no-evil, hear-no-evil bunch. They all believed Heckly was in the hospital. They all believed Mrs. Stiller was off somewhere, considering a divorce. At least, that's what they say. As for the patients, half of them are so drugged to the gills they couldn't tell you what planet this is. The other half know the same fate awaits them if they don't behave, and part of behaving is seeing no evil and hearing no evil. You want a Coke?"

"Sure."

Sanchez got two colas from the machine, sliding one across to Cotter as he returned to the table.

"You hear reports about this place," the Texas detective said. "Sex with female patients, physical abuse of patients, staff members selling drugs, the institution's supplies disappearing without a trace. But it's all rumors. No complaints are ever filed, and if you come out and ask around, you get the same old see-no-evil, hear-no-evil bullshit, so nothing ever gets investigated. That's probably one reason why nobody saw anything wrong when Heckly and Mrs. Stiller disappeared. None of them want the cops coming around, because damn near everyone on the staff has something to hide."

"Stiller in on any of this?" Cotter asked.

"What I hear about Stiller is that he's basically honest, but he's also too dumb to know what's happening right under his nose."

Cotter said, "Got any idea how Heckly got out?"

"Someone had to help him. I've got no idea who it was. The state guys will probably have the job of finding that out. If they apply enough pressure, someone will eventually decide to talk."

The Texas officer took a swallow of Coke, his eyes meeting Cotter's. "At least we don't have to try to pick Heckly's trail," Sanchez said. "We know where he went."

"Yes," Cotter replied softly. "We know where he went."

Twenty

Robert Heckly surveyed his new motel room. It was classier than the old one. Better TV set, and this one wasn't chained to the wall. Though not expensive, the brown carpet was fairly new. This was the first of many moves he would be making. Sometimes he would leave a message for Cotter, sometimes not, depending on the timing and how he felt.

The typewriter stood in the corner, with a package of cheap typing paper on top of it. It was possible he wouldn't need the machine too much longer, depending on how things went. The plan was quite fluid from this point onward. Instead of a precise line of attack, it was going to be more like a chess match, with moves and countermoves, each player responding to events, many of which would be unpredictable.

He was hungry, he realized. It was after nine and he hadn't eaten since lunch. There was a small restaurant down the street. Making sure the room was locked, he headed for it, walking casually, enjoying the evening.

His watcher was gone.

Not that it mattered. He had seen the sensation for what it was, an hallucination brought on by the excitement of the game he was playing with Cotter. He could not afford to be distracted by such things, and he had the willpower to shunt them aside, consign them to mental oblivion.

At the restaurant, he ordered a hot roast beef sandwich, which came with fries and gravy that tasted like wet bouillon cubes. Not the fare he would have preferred, but then, when you ate in cheap restaurants your choices were limited. When he got back to the motel, he went to bed.

Although he tried to empty his mind, it was a jumble of thoughts, instant replays of events both recent and remote. He found himself remembering an incident from his youth, a turning point in his life.

"No," his father had said.

"No?" Robert had replied, his voice filled with disbelief.

"Do you want me to repeat it?" his father had asked, looking at him through the center portion of his trifocals. A dumpy man who wore suits that always seemed to hang on him oddly, as if his frame made the cloth uncomfortable, Braden Heckly was extremely farsighted. The lenses in his plastic-framed glasses seemed thick enough to be miniature magnifying glasses.

Robert shifted his gaze to his mother, who sat beside her husband on the antique couch. Davina Heckly was an elegant-looking auburn-haired woman, who seemed entirely too graceful and sophisticated to be paired with her dowdy husband. Opposites attracted, he supposed.

"Mother—"

"If your father says no," she said, cutting him off, "then that's the answer."

"You have the money," Robert said. "It's not as though the lousy price of a car would prevent you from eating."

"I have the money," his father said, "because I'm careful with it. I save it, invest it, handle it wisely."

"But I've—"

"—already got a car."

"It's seven years old. It's the oldest, most decrepit one at my dorm. The other guys—"

"Have fathers who spoil them."

"Look—"

"Okay, you can have a new car."

"I can?" There had to be a catch. He waited for it.

"Certainly. All you have to do is earn the money. As long as you're using my money, the car you have is good enough."

He shifted his eyes to his mother again, hoping to find a hint of sympathy, something he could latch onto and build on, but she was giving him her stern mother look, the one she'd used since he was four. His father was giving him his own patented expression, the I'm-sure-you'll-straighten-up-and-become-responsible look.

He hated those looks.

Turning away from them, the young Robert Heckly had walked out of the living room. In the hall, he'd paused, collecting his thoughts. His was an upper middle-class family, and the house was typical for people of that income level. Two stories with four bedrooms, an eat-in kitchen plus a dining room, cedar shakes on the roof. It was in a neighborhood of similar homes, all with two-car garages, lovely lawns, console TV sets. The majority of the neighbors had new cars—Fords and Buicks seemed to dominate. Station wagons were quite popular.

He stood among the antiques in the hallway, his anger growing. The old furniture was his mother's passion. She constantly went to antique sales, returning with a dresser or chest or chair that looked like something any sensible person would have donated to Goodwill. But to Davina Heckly, they were treasures.

Robert didn't like them. His mother had given him an antique dresser, and whenever he opened any of its drawers the musty odor of having been forgotten for too many years in a damp basement wafted out. And the drawers, not equipped with proper glides, often stuck.

The anger was surging through his system now, making him hot all over, as if his veins were carrying steam. He turned and walked back into the living room. His parents were still sitting on the couch, a hideous thing of dark wood and flowered upholstery. He was reading *Time*, and she was studying one of her numerous antiques magazines.

"Why do you treat me like dirt?" Robert demanded.

"Dirt?" his father said.

"Making me drive that old wreck of a car when everyone else has a better one."

"Bobby," his father said, frowning. Robert hated being called that.

"Stanley Garland drives a BMW. Ashley Addington drives a Corvette. George—"

"I don't care about Stanley or Ashley or George," his father snapped. "You don't know how lucky you are to have what you've got. I had to get student loans to get through college, then spent years paying them off. For my first two years of college I didn't even have a car, and when I finally got one, it was basically a junker that I bought off a guy for—"

"That was then, and that was you. This is now, and this is me."

"And you deserve better than what I had?" his father asked.

Inside, Robert's rage churned and bubbled, but he kept it inside, for allowing oneself to explode accomplished nothing. Controlled, anger became a tool, a shot of adrenaline that got one thinking, planning, accomplishing.

"It's different now," he said. "What you've got, the car you drive, the clothes you wear, these things determine your status, and that determines who your friends are."

Braden Heckly shook his head. "If this is the criterion by which your friends judge you, then I'd say you need new friends."

"You simply don't understand."

"Yes, I do," his father said. "I understand quite well. When you were a boy, we got you an electric train if you wanted it, a tenspeed bike, a TV set in your room, a stereo, your own phone. You've always had everything you wanted, but you never had to earn a thing. Well, you're just about a grownup now, and you have to start learning that nothing is free in life. Someone has to earn the things you get." Braden Heckly sighed. "Look, son—"

"If you loved me, you wouldn't treat me like this."

"Robert!" his mother exclaimed. "How can you say something like that?"

His father said, "It's because I love you that I want you to start learning the—"

"Value of money," Robert said.

"Yes, the value of money. It would be easier to avoid the argument and let you have the new car. But it wouldn't be the right thing to do. It wouldn't be the action of a father who truly loved his son." His father's eyes met his, pleading for Robert to understand.

"That's the most upside down and backward reasoning I've ever heard," Robert said, and walked out of the room.

Although his anger still surged through him like waves driven by a hurricane, he controlled it, nurtured it, cherished its flame, for soon he would put it to use.

It was Sunday, the end of the weekend, so he drove back to Rutgers after dinner. Nothing further was said about his desire for a new car.

He lay in bed in the dorm that night, thinking about the situation. What infuriated him the most was his powerlessness. He was totally at the mercy of his father, who could stop paying his way through college anytime he felt like it. He could say no to new clothes, a new tennis racket, or a new car. His mother passed judgment on his friends, and he was encouraged to avoid those who didn't stack up. She knew how to make a child feel small and unworthy if his grades weren't up to snuff. Everything was their way, because that was how they wanted it. He was never consulted. His opinions were unimportant.

That night, lying in bed at Rutgers, he started putting together the plan that would allow him to take care of this problem.

He started going out with Kari Highler, a tall, almost gangly brunette who always made a point of talking to him as they left Psych 273. Although he'd realized she was sort of coming on to him, he'd never encouraged her. Girls didn't interest him too much. He was still a virgin, which didn't worry him. Sex, he had always suspected, received a lot of hype it didn't deserve.

He confirmed that supposition when he started sleeping with Kari, who had a small apartment off campus. He didn't mind having sex with her; he just wouldn't have gone out of his way to do it.

The night he drove home unannounced, he and Kari drank some wine. Hers was laced with the white powder he'd extracted from her prescription sleeping capsules—so she would not wake up and find him gone.

Because it was after midnight, he had the road to himself. The trip, ninety minutes by day, took only an hour, even though he carefully obeyed all the traffic laws.

He parked around the corner, out of sight from his parents' house and its immediate neighbors. Slipping through the shadows, he went home, using his key to get into the garage through the back door. The master bedroom was above the garage, which meant his parents slept only a few feet from where he now stood, holding the gas can that supplied the lawn mower and garden tiller. He began pouring the liquid onto the newspapers his father saved in the garage. The pile, as always, was huge, for he was always saving more than he needed for the odd paint job or carpentry project.

He spread the gasoline-soaked papers out, poured more fuel on them, splashed some on the wall. When the can was empty, he lit a match, tossed it onto the newspapers.

Fruuuuummmmmp!

The garage was full of flames.

Robert shut off the power to the house at the circuit-breaker box. Taking the three-foot two-by-four that had been on his father's workbench, Robert went inside. He used a penlight to find his way through the dark house. In the kitchen he took the phone off the hook, thereby disabling all the phones in the house. Then he went upstairs, positioned himself outside the door to his parents' room, and switched off the penlight. Enough illumination seeped in from the streetlight in front of the McCannons' house for him to dimly make out his surroundings.

The odor of smoke filled the house.

Then the smoke alarm went off.

"What the . . ." His father's sleepy voice.

"Oh, my God!" his mother shouted. "There's smoke. There's really a fire!"

"Call 911, and then let's get out of here."

The phone was lifted, its disconnect button rattled. "It's not working!" Davina Heckly screamed.

"The lights are out, too," Braden Heckly said, and then he coughed. The smoke was getting thicker.

Robert's mother was the first one out the door. She rushed right past him, unaware of his presence, and he swung the two-by-four, hitting her in the back. As she staggered forward, he stepped up behind her, giving her a shove. She took two out-of-balance steps, and then she was tumbling down the stairs.

"Davina!" her husband shouted, standing in the upstairs hall in striped pajamas, groping in the darkness with his hands.

He didn't have his glasses on, Robert realized. Even had the lights been on, his surroundings would have been a blur. In the dim, smoke-filled light of the burning house, he was blind.

"Hello, Father," Robert said.

"What? What . . . what are you doing here?"

"I set the house on fire."

"You . . . you . . . you want to burn the house down?" he said, bewildered.

"No, Father, I'd much prefer not to burn the house down."

"Then why—"

He swung the two-by-four.

About an hour later, Robert was back in Kari's apartment. She was deep in her drug-induced sleep; she didn't stir when he slipped in beside her.

Shortly before dawn, the authorities called with the bad news. There had been a fire at his parents' home in Issington. His mother and father had both died in the blaze.

Fire investigators suspected arson. Officers questioned him concerning his whereabouts on the night of the blaze, and he said he was in bed with Kari. Kari confirmed his story.

A few weeks later, he broke off the relationship with Kari and went back to living in the dorm.

After his parents' wills were probated and the company insuring the house had paid the claim, Robert bought a new Mustang. He'd considered one of the super-expensive European models, but people would have looked askance at him if he'd done that. No one questioned the Mustang.

Although they remained suspicious, the authorities had to suspend their investigation into the fire for lack of evidence.

Something totally unexpected had happened to Robert the night he'd killed his parents. He had tingled all the way back to Rutgers. Part of it was just plain adrenaline, he knew that, but part of it was something else, too. It took a few days for him to sort it out, but when he did, he realized that he had enjoyed the act of killing.

And he knew, somewhere in the depths of his consciousness, in that place where proscribed thoughts were hidden away, that he would do it again.

Twenty-one

It was after midnight when Cotter landed in San Francisco. Cindy met him at the airport. As they drove to Tres Cerros in her Mercedes, she said, "Whatever you found out, it's bad, isn't it?"

"It's that obvious, huh?"

"You haven't said a word since we left the airport. You're in your own world."

"I've got a lot of things to tell you. I'm trying to decide how to go about it."

"Mike—"

"One of the things I'll have to explain is that my name's not Mike."

After a long moment of silence, Cindy said, "You really are my enigma man, aren't you."

"I'm sorry. I hope when you hear what I have to say you'll understand why it was so hard for me to tell you."

"Mike, I—should I still call you that . . . Mike?"

"I've been Mike Cotter for fifteen years. There's no reason to change it now."

"Good. I don't want to learn a new name for you."

"On my birth certificate it says William Michael Richland."

"Did they call you Billy?"

He thought of Willie, Willa Stiller's nickname, pushed the thought away. "They called me W. M."

"Like J. R. on *Dallas?*"

"Except I was from a middle-class family, not a rich, powerful one. My dad started calling me that because the letters stood for both my initials and the abbreviation of William. My friends picked it up, and it just stuck."

They were southbound on the Bayshore Freeway. The evening

traffic was light by Bay Area standards, everybody getting where they were going without any serious hassles. A red Corvette zipped past them, weaving in and out of traffic and going a good twenty miles an hour over the limit.

"Jerk," Cindy said.

A California Highway Patrol cruiser sped past, its lights flashing. A moment later they came upon the Corvette, pulled to the side of the freeway with the patrol car behind it.

"Good," Cindy said.

"What's surprising," Cotter said, "is how often these guys have a jillion prior citations and are driving with no insurance and a suspended license. I don't know if they figure they won't get caught or the rules don't apply to them or what."

They drove the rest of the way to Cindy's apartment in silence. When they arrived, they sat down beside each other on the couch. They had decided by some unspoken consensus that this would be the moment of truth.

Cindy squeezed his hand, her eyes meeting his, urging him to tell her the things that had haunted him for so long.

"It was fifteen years ago," he said. "I—" And the words seemed to die in his throat. He wasn't just going to tell it; he was going to relive it.

"What happened fifteen years ago?" Cindy asked. Her eyes were saying, *Let it out, Mike. Please. Let me help you bear the pain.*

"My wife's name was Julie. The kids were Jennifer and Sean." A tear trickled down his cheek, and he wiped it away. "Julie and Sean have been dead for a long time. Jennifer—well, you know what happened to Jennifer.

"We lived in Houston. We had a little place in the suburbs. I was a rookie state cop. One day, I was on routine patrol, and there was a bulletin out on a man from New Jersey. Robert Heckly. He was wanted for killing several people in New Jersey, and now he was in Texas, where he'd killed a farmer and his wife. I stopped to check out a rest stop, and there he was, in the rest room. We were alone, just the two of us.

"It shouldn't have been much of a contest. I was armed, and I'm a big guy. But Heckly was a martial arts expert. I'd drawn my gun and was about to cuff him when he slipped out of my grasp. It was so quick I didn't know what had happened. All of a sudden I was slammed against a wall, and my service revolver flew out of my hand. After that it was purely a physical fight—my strength and speed against his martial arts skills. It was no contest. To use Texas terminology, he was stomping the shit out of me. I thought I was going to die. I truly did.

"He worked me over until I was on the floor, barely conscious. Then, knowing he had won, he got careless. He reached for me, and I managed to grab his left arm. I put all the strength I had into breaking it. It was my only chance to survive, and I hung on to that arm for all I was worth. I caused him so much pain that he had to give up the fight. I found out later that I'd completely mangled his arm. To this day he can't use it."

Cindy tightened her grip on his hand. She seemed to be offering her strength, reminding him that they were in this together now, that she could help him through it.

"Heckly went to ground at that point. He had to be in a lot of pain because of his arm. We alerted all the doctors and hospitals in the area to let us know at once if a guy with an injured left arm showed up. We got some reports, but none of them turned out to be Heckly. Heckly knew we'd be waiting for him if he sought medical help, so he didn't do it. It probably would have taken a series of operations to repair his arm, so he apparently just lived with the pain until it subsided enough for him to function again.

"Turns out that while a massive manhunt was under way throughout East Texas, he was in a shack outside Houston. A feeble-minded old man lived there, made his living as a picker. You know what a picker is?

"A picker is someone who pokes around in the dump, looking for anything of value—aluminum and copper, for instance. Along with anything that can be cleaned up and sold to a secondhand store. Anyway, that's what the old guy did. He was sort of a hermit, and he'd been known to take potshots at anyone who came around uninvited, so people stayed away. We found his body buried out back. The car Heckly had been driving at the rest stop was in the barn. Everything in the place had Heckly's fingerprints on it."

Cotter wasn't sure why he was telling her about the old man.

Maybe he was just putting off the next part. He said, "Heckly hid out there a month. His arm would still have been painful at that point, but not enough to prevent him from . . . from doing what he'd decided to do."

Cotter smelled the sickly coppery odor that had permeated his house on that terrible day. The scent enveloped him, seeping into his every pore, and he shuddered, suddenly cold, as if something were sucking the warmth from his body.

It was the odor of blood.

Julie's blood.

Sean's blood.

He forced himself to keep talking. "I was on patrol when I got a call informing me that . . . that . . ."

He felt his lower lip quivering, and he tried to get his emotions under control. He saw his house, the flashing lights; he smelled the coppery odor . . .

Cindy slipped her arms around him, held him.

"I was patrolling Interstate 45, between Houston and Galveston. I got a call that I had an emergency at home. When I asked what had happened, the dispatcher said there was no further information. You hear something like that, you start thinking the worst. Maybe there was a fire that gutted part of the house, or maybe one of the kids swallowed something and had to have his stomach pumped. You try not to think about the really horrible possibilities, like your whole family dying in a car accident.

"I couldn't have imagined what really took place. Even my worst nightmares couldn't equal that.

"My block was solid flashing lights. It was apparent that something really terrible had happened. The cop at the corner let me in, telling me to see a Houston lieutenant named Travers. I didn't bother with that. I headed straight for the house. Someone recognized me, and a couple of uniforms tried to stop me, but I wasn't about to be stopped."

Cotter took a deep breath. "At first, everything seemed normal. I mean, there was no blood in the living room, no broken furniture; everything looked okay. Then I realized there was this . . . this smell. It was faint, and yet . . . and yet . . ."

The odor was overwhelming now. And he could feel his gut

churning, the icy grip of fear, everything as intense as it had been on that day.

"Lieutenant Travers had found me by that time, and he was trying to lead me away, saying, 'You shouldn't go in there. Let's go somewhere so I can talk to you.' "

He shook his head. "I pulled away from him and ran into the bedroom, pushing two cops out of my way. I didn't know what I was seeing at first. The bed was covered with white bundles. Butcher paper, like the stuff they use at a meat market."

Cindy was staring at him, wide-eyed and pale, but he was barely aware of her presence. He was in the past, reliving the most horrible day of his life.

He heard himself speak, and the voice seemed strange and muffled, as if were overhearing a conversation drifting to him from some unseen, distant source.

"Julie and Sean were in the paper . . ."

Tears were streaming down his cheeks, dripping into his lap. He could feel Cindy holding him, could sense her warmth, her concern, her love, but even Cindy could not help him now. The only thing he could do was force the words out, get to the end of the story.

"They were cut up like . . . like roasts and steaks . . ."

"But there was no blood . . . not there . . ."

"He . . . he did it in the bathroom . . ."

"Their . . ."

The image was so vivid, so overpowering.

"Their heads . . ."

The coppery odor made him want to gag. He could feel his face contorting, as if it wanted to break itself.

"Their heads were in the tub."

He heard Cindy gasp, felt a tremor travel through her body.

Then the words came in a rush. "Travers and another cop were leading me back into the living room when it occurred to me that there were only two heads in the tub, that Jennifer's was missing. I started yelling, demanding to know where my daughter was. They said that she was next door, with Mrs. Haldane, that she was okay.

"Well, she wasn't okay. She had been made to watch the whole thing. It had been too much for her little girl's mind to handle, and when I tried to comfort her, she just stared at me, as if she didn't even know I was there. I thought it was shock, that she'd get better, but . . . she didn't. Not even a little. Not ever."

"Oh, Mike," Cindy whispered. She was crying.

"It was definitely Heckly. He made a point of leaving his fingerprints on just about everything, so I'd know who did it."

He fell silent, lost in his own private world of pain. He heard the *pat-pat-pat* of tears dripping on the sofa. He didn't know whether they were his or Cindy's.

"I'd go almost every day to the hospital to see Jennifer. She was all I had left. And every time I saw her, I relived seeing the white packages on the bed, and the two heads. Jennifer just . . . just stayed the same. Month after month. Finally the psychiatrist told me to stop coming. Jennifer didn't know I was there, would never improve, and the visits were killing me. I finally did it. I changed my name, because the case had received so much publicity. And because Heckly was still out there."

He shuddered, unable to go on. He felt as if everything that was warm and human had been sucked out of him, leaving only a vast lifeless emptiness.

They were both still crying, so they simply held each other and sobbed.

Later, after their tears had subsided, Cotter resumed his story. Suddenly he was overwhelmed with the need to get it all out, purge himself of every last detail.

"They caught him in Austin six months later," Cotter said. "He was picked up driving a stolen car. Surprised the hell out of the Austin cops when they found out who they had."

"He just went peacefully?" Cindy asked.

"No, he knew they'd figure out who he was, so he tried to use his martial arts. The Austin cops simply maced him." Cotter drew in a deep breath, let it out. "If I'd had mace with me in that rest room, maybe it would have all worked out differently." He shook his head. "And maybe not. I'll never know, will I?"

"Mike, you can't—"

"Blame myself? Of course I do. Some little voice inside keeps saying there must be something I could have done, some way I could have prevented what happened."

"Mike, you were a victim, just as innocent as Wanda Grant—as innocent as your family."

"I've told myself that a thousand times. On one level I know it's true, but . . ." He sighed. "Deep down there will always be this little nugget of blame. I've internalized it, and I'm afraid it's mine till death us do part."

"It's not your fault," Cindy said softly, studying him with eyes that were red from crying.

Cotter felt his own tears welling up again, and he held them back. He'd done enough crying.

He told her about Heckly's escape from Southwestern State Hospital. "Stiller must have known his wife was dead, and yet for the past three months he kept right on doing exactly what Heckly wanted him to do."

"He had to," Cindy said. "Otherwise he would have been forced to admit that his wife was dead, and he couldn't do that. This way he had a thread of hope to cling to."

Cotter nodded. "I guess that's what I did with Jennifer, clung desperately to a totally unrealistic hope, refused to admit the truth."

"We're all capable of getting into heavy denial," Cindy said. "Some things are just too unbearable to accept."

"Accepting is better. Because the fantasy always falls apart."

He told her all he knew about what Heckly had been doing since his departure from West Texas. "He's been taunting me right from the beginning. Everything that's happened has reminded me of him, and yet I was being told that he was still locked safely away. It was his way of having fun. He flew to San Antonio under the name Lee Heck, which is Heckly with the syllables in reverse order. When he worked at the Seaward Hotel, he used the name Rocky L. Hebert, an anagram of Robert Heckly."

"He's been in control from the beginning," Cindy said. "That's very frightening, that he could orchestrate everything like this."

"He's supposed to have a genius-level IQ."

"A bloodthirsty lunatic who also just happens to be a karate expert and a genius."

"Succinctly put."

They fell silent then, as if neither knew what to say next, and

Cotter felt his mind slipping from the room, expanding itself into the world, searching for Heckly. Almost immediately he sensed a presence, and although no direct communication was passing between them, Cotter could detect an aura of haughty superiority combined with an unwavering determination. And a strange dark void, as if something, some critical human characteristic, were missing. And yet from that emptiness oozed a malevolence so overpowering Cotter wanted to cringe.

He was linked to Robert Heckly.

Linked in a way that had not occurred before.

As if he had just reached into Robert Heckly's soul.

He could feel the evil. It seemed to be seeping into him, engulfing him, befouling him. He felt as if his innermost self were desperately wriggling to get free before everything within him that seemed wholesome and good and decent was defiled.

Cotter broke the connection.

Inside, where it didn't show, he was trembling. He had to use the link with Heckly cautiously, had to avoid letting himself sink too deeply into the madness on the other end of the connection.

Cotter's mind reeled. Could he really have slipped into the quicksand of Heckly's madness, nearly been sucked into its depths? Although a part of him refused to accept such a notion, there was a primal place somewhere deep within him that had been terrified by what had just occurred.

"Is there somewhere you could go until this is over?" he asked.

"You mean somewhere I could hide?"

"Have you got a friend or relative no one knows about who lives in another city, preferably in another state?"

"Mike, I can't just leave. You need me here. I need to be with you. Besides, I've got a business to run."

"But—"

"I won't, Mike. We've got to be together, lean on each other. This isn't the right time for either of us to be alone. We need each other too much right now."

"That might be a luxury we can't afford."

"And . . . I don't know how to put this part. I guess the best way to put it is to say I've got to show you that you can depend on me."

"Of course I know I can depend on you."

"I mean that this . . . this horror story won't scare me away—out of your life. If you're in danger, then I'll share that danger, because . . . well, because that's how it has to be."

"Cindy—"

"No, Mike, I know what you're going to say, and I can't; I just can't."

"You don't know what Heckly's like."

"I know what he did to you, to your family, and it scares the hell out of me—even just knowing that a person like that exists scares the hell out of me. But I can't leave. Not now." Her eyes filled with determination. "No way."

"Think about it," he said. "Please. I know what it's like to lose the people I care about. I don't want it to happen again."

"Mike," Cindy said gently, "I love you." She was looking at him with eyes that seemed full of hurt, as if they'd tried to siphon off some of his pain so she could ease his burden.

"I love you, too," Cotter whispered. The last time he had spoken those words was fifteen years ago, to a little girl who could not comprehend them.

Then they simply sat there, holding each other.

Confused and exhausted, his defenses down, Cotter suddenly found himself slipping back into the memories of that day fifteen years ago. He tried to push the images away, but they overwhelmed his defenses and filled his head.

The packages on the bed, like roasts and chops and steaks from the meat market . . .

The heads in the tub . . .

Twenty-two

Robert Heckly jogged in the early morning coolness, the thick fog caressing his cheeks like a ghostly touch. He was circling a small park a few blocks from the motel. He'd spotted another jogger, a man in a blue running suit, and fallen in behind him. This was where the man had been heading.

There were at least a dozen joggers here, all in running suits because of the chilly morning. The park covered an entire block, and the joggers trotted along its perimeter. In some places there was a sidewalk, and in others there was nothing but a path in the grass.

A man and woman in matching red running suits trotted past him and disappeared into the fog.

His watcher was back, that disquieting presence that somehow seemed to be observing him both from afar and from within his head. Once more it was lurking in the shadows of his consciousness, studying his behavior, prying into his private places.

It's not real, he reminded himself. It's lack of sleep, a chemical imbalance, an overdose of adrenaline. He ignored it, hoping it would go away.

But it persisted.

The light touch of another.

Inside his head.

And yet distant.

It was like a radio link that was periodically established even when no transmissions were intended. As if the channel were routinely opened just in case it was needed.

Nonsense, he thought. And he resolved to be stronger, to ignore the tricks his brain was playing on him. He jogged on, the white mist enveloping him in its moist grip.

His thoughts traveled backward in time, randomly presenting him with images of his high school, his first bicycle, the first time he drove a car, the day he learned the hard way about poison ivy. And then a single scene solidified.

He was about seven years old. Winnie London and he were playing on the floor of his room, making tracks in the soft blue carpet with toy cars and trucks and bulldozers and such. All around them, cartoonlike animals frolicked on the blue background of the wallpaper, along with the matching curtains and bedspread. It had been his mother's idea of what a boy's room should look like. Though fine for a seven-year-old, the room had become a terrible embarrassment when he was twelve, and it still looked the same.

Winnie's full name was Winfield Lloyd London, and when he grew up, he studied law at Yale. But that day in Robert's room, Winnie was a spoiled little boy who threw a temper tantrum when he didn't get his way. He was there because his mother was visiting with Robert's mother, and the youngsters had been admonished to go somewhere and play. It was raining, so "somewhere" meant Robert's room.

"Whreeeeeee!" Winnie said, providing the engine noises for the fire truck he was operating. A chubby kid with blond curls that adorned his head in a mass of fluffy yellow ringlets, he looked like a cherub.

Robert watched him, not at all pleased to have someone else playing with his things.

"Big fire on Merriweather Street," Winnie said, trying to sound like a two-way radio. Merriweather was the street on which he lived and probably the only one he could name.

"Rhuuum!" Robert said, making the sound of a diesel engine as he rolled his road grader forward. "Gonna have to stop. Road grader's in the way."

"You can't stop a fire engine!" Winnie protested.

"Sure you can. A road grader's too big. You have to stop."

Winnie swerved the fire engine around the grader, but Robert shoved the toy into the path of the one being propelled by the other boy, and there was a collision.

Then Winnie cheated. He used his hand to bat the grader out of the way.

Robert said, "Hey, you can't do that!"

"Fire engine knocked that stupid grader right out of the way."

Robert shook his head. "You'd wreck if you hit a road grader. You have to stop."

"Do not."

"Do too."

"Do not."

"It's my fire engine, and I say it's gotta stop."

Winnie continued on to the scene of the fire, ignoring him. He was on his knees now, crawling along beside the toy, which he seemed to be steering toward the bed, the apparent site of the fire.

Quickly getting up, Robert grabbed the grader and put it down directly in the fire engine's path. Winnie rammed it with his toy, knocking it aside. Robert grabbed the grader and slammed it into the fire engine, flipping it on its side.

"Hey!" Winnie shouted. "A road grader can't catch a fire engine! Nothing can catch a fire engine!"

"My road grader's faster than your fire engine. I just proved it."

"A road grader is not faster!"

"Is too."

"Is not."

"Well, mine is," Robert said, and the two boys stared at each other, each one's eyes filled with the certainty that the other guy was wrong.

"A fire engine's faster than a stupid road grader," Winnie said. "Anybody knows that."

"If you don't want to play right, give me my fire engine."

Winnie's eyes darkened, and then he grabbed the fire engine and hurled it at Robert. The toy hit his cheek, bounced across the room. Robert felt the spot. No blood, but it was sore. Winnie was eyeing him smugly, as if to say, *What you gonna do about it?*

Robert felt hot all over.

But he only stared.

The moment passed, and the boys were playing again. Winnie had a red racing car, Robert a blue bus. They avoided each other, each operating his vehicle independently, as if the other boy didn't exist.

Finally Winnie said, "Wanna play hide-and-seek?"

"Inside?"

"I've played it inside before."

"Where?"

"At my house. Wanna try it?"

"Okay. You're it."

Winnie ran to the corner by the door, leaned against the wall, and rested his head on his arm. "Ready?"

"Yeah."

"Okay. One . . . two . . ."

Moving as quietly as he could, Robert was heading for the door. He didn't know where he was going to hide, but he knew it had to be somewhere away from this room.

"Three . . . four . . ."

As he stepped into the hall, he noticed something sticking through the narrow space between the jamb and the hinged side of the door. Fingers. Four of them. White and chubby and vulnerable.

"Five . . . six . . ."

Robert grabbed the door and pulled.

Winnie screamed.

Robert could see the four fingers, trapped between the door and the jam; they were turning a lovely shade of purple, swelling. He pulled harder.

Winnie shrieked, an ear-splitting, primal wail of terror and pain.

Robert yanked on the door with all his strength, and Winnie's cry rose another octave.

He was getting ready to pull on the door one more time when his mother and Winnie's mom showed up, and the incident was over. He said he hadn't known Winnie's fingers were in the door; he'd just been pulling it closed to give him another second or two to hide. They were just playing a game, and Winnie was it, and he felt just terrible about what had happened.

Which, of course, was a lie.

He'd tried to cut Winnie's fingers off.

And the momentary power he'd had, the total control, had been a very heady thing.

Winnie's fingers were cut to the bone, but they healed. Winfield Lloyd London, who lost his pudginess by the time he was thirteen, played on his college tennis team, married a former high school cheerleader, and was presently a partner in a prestigious New York law firm.

Robert Heckly thought about those chubby fingers sticking through the crack of the door and wished he'd snapped them off.

He jogged another couple of laps around the park, then headed for the motel. It was time to send Cotter another message, and he had already decided exactly how he was going to do it.

Twenty-three

Dink Hawthorne stood in the shadowy mouth of the alley, waiting for an unsuspecting motorist to stop at the traffic light. It was mid-morning, foggy and cool, ships' horns carrying so loudly on the moisture-laden air that he half expected to see one of the steel monsters materialize out of the mist and come gliding down the street. At Dink's feet was a plastic bucket in which a sponge floated in brownish-gray water.

The traffic signal was at the intersection of Commerce and Enterprise Streets. To Dink the street names always sounded impressive, like something in the financial district. The reality was that this was the heart of skid row in Colmer, California, a shit heap of a town surrounded by yuppies, most of whom were too stupid to know that Colmer was a good place to stay away from.

Enterprise was a shortcut for people heading north from Tres Cerros. The way the yuppies figured it, you hit a couple of lights, but you avoided the snarl on Interstate 280, which saved ten minutes, not to mention the wear-and-tear on your nerves and on your shiny new Lexus.

Dink hated yuppies.

Maybe it was because they consumed so conspicuously while he literally didn't own a pot to piss in. Well, there was the plastic bucket, but then, that wasn't really a pot, was it? And it wasn't really his in the truest sense of the term, since it had never been paid for. He tried to recall where he'd stolen it, but remembering was a formidable task for brain cells that had been pickled as thoroughly as his had over the years.

Which reminded him of his problem. He had nothing to drink. Dink shook his head. He'd been in Alcoholics Anonymous once, trying to get his life back together. Hadn't worked. Most likely because he hadn't wanted it to work. Being drunk had just been so much nicer than coping with all the horseshit. He chuckled, which came out as a whispery, rasping sound. Street life and wine would kill him, he supposed. Not that he gave a shit.

In AA they'd told him to take it one day at a time, and that's exactly what he was doing: staying drunk, one day at a time.

The alley was littered with wine bottles, many left by Dink. Pushed up against a grimy cement wall was the large cardboard box he'd slept in, night before last. He was getting too old for that sort of thing. He'd wake up stiff and sore, his leg joints hurting and not working right. So mostly he slept at the rescue mission, which was where he'd acquired his *nom de rue*, as he called it. His street name. His real name was Ralph, although not too many people knew it.

At the rescue mission one night a few months ago—months? Could have been years. Hell, could have been decades, as good as his sense of time was. Anyway, one of those Australian movies had been on TV, and one of the characters had been named Dink. Dink had worn one of those Australian bush hats with the brim turned up on one side. And so had Ralph, who'd found the hat in a trash bin behind the Seaward Hotel. The hat was gone now, lost God knew where, but the name had stuck.

How'd you get like this, Dink? he asked himself. Vague images came to him. A boy playing with assorted toys on a tan carpet. A white dog chasing a Frisbee. A woman with curly blond hair, smiling warmly. But Dink wasn't sure whether these things were memories or just imaginings, bits and pieces of TV shows seen at the rescue mission, or maybe just fragments of pure fantasy.

Dink didn't know how he'd ended up like this. If he'd had a life before the street, it had been expunged from his memory long ago.

The alcohol was partly responsible, Dink was sure. It seemed to slowly wear away the memory, like a river carving out a canyon. It wasn't quick, but it got there. Besides, if there were recollections of a better life, they would be too painful to endure, and it was just as well they stayed out of reach.

A car was coming, a shiny red . . . something. Didn't matter what, actually. Just as long as it was expensive, and this one seemed to fit the bill. Change, he commanded the traffic signal, and as if obeying his wishes, it switched to amber, then red. The car stopped.

Dink grabbed his bucket and hurried up to driver's side of the car. "Clean your windshield?" he asked.

Before the startled driver could reply, Dink slapped a sopping sponge against the glass, and began smearing dirty water around.

"Hey!" the driver yelled, his voice muffled because all the windows were rolled up. "Hey, don't do that!"

Dink ignored him. He preferred women—a guy had climbed out and taken a swing at him once—but he'd successfully worked the window washing bit on both sexes.

"Hey!" the driver said, his voice getting louder as the window lowered. "What the hell are you doing?"

"Washing your windows."

"Well, stop it. That water's filthy."

"They'll look fine. Don't worry."

"Here." He was waving a bill out the window. "It's yours if you stop."

Dink reached for the bill. The light would change momentarily, and he wanted to get it before the car was free to simply speed away.

But as his fingers neared it, the man pulled it back into the car. "How'd you like to make about fifty dollars?" the man asked.

"Doing what?" Dink asked suspiciously. Experience had taught him that when other folks dealt with street people, they generally didn't have the street people's best interests in mind.

"Clearing away some weeds."

Fifty dollars would buy a lot of wine. He said, "Fifty bucks for how much work?"

"About five hours. Tell you what, I'll make it a straight ten bucks an hour with a guaranteed minimum of fifty bucks. How's that?"

Dink thought it over. He hated the idea of digging up weeds—or worse yet, pulling them up. He needed a drink, felt terrible, and the work would make him feel even worse than he already did. But the money was an irresistible lure. Having that much wine money in his pocket was like having financial security.

The light turned green. "Gotta go," the man said. "You want the work or not?"

No, he didn't want the work; he hated the very thought of the work.

But he did want the money.

"You give me an advance?" he asked.

"Sure." He held up the bill again. It was a ten. "Get in and I'll give it to you."

Dink emptied his bucket and got in the car. The driver gave him the money. He was wearing a blue blazer with gray trousers, a tie that had red and blue stripes on a gray background. Not trendy enough to be a yuppie. An aged preppie, Dink decided.

Glancing at Dink, the driver wrinkled his nose.

Hey, Dink thought, *you don't like the way I smell, get someone else to pull your goddamned weeds. See if I give a shit.*

Dink's wardrobe, the entirety of which he was wearing, consisted of an overly large plaid flannel shirt, a torn pair of khaki pants, and a battered pair of high-topped work shoes he'd been given at the rescue mission after his sneakers had been stolen. It had been about a month since he washed his garments, at least two weeks since he'd used the shower at the rescue mission. One might say he exuded the natural human fragrance.

"Nice car," Dink said, admiring the plush red interior.

The street on which they were driving was lined with abandoned brick buildings with windows that had been smashed, then boarded over, and others that had been smashed and simply left that way. Abandoned warehouses that now served mainly to provide shelter for rats and roaches. Alleyways where the street people roamed. A little chink in the California good life.

"My name's Robert," the driver said.

"Dink."

"What kind of a name is that?"

"That's what they call me—my friends."

As they drove, the view changed from warehouses to seedy low-income housing, then to small homes, and then they were out of Colmer altogether and into the cleaner, pricier environs of Tres Cerros. Dink noticed that Robert did all his driving with just one hand. Must be the way preppies do it, he supposed. Casual, too well-heeled to sweat the small stuff.

Robert seemed to be in good shape. He had the trim, healthy look of a someone who exercised. Probably played tennis and golf and all the other things rich people did. Probably jogged.

His expression was innocent, almost boyish. And yet there was something hard about him, something that didn't show, exactly, and yet you could feel it. Probably a financial shark, Dink decided.

Robert was driving past some expensive-looking high-rise apartment buildings. The people living in those places were so far removed from Dink's world they might as well reside on another planet. The Dink Hawthornes of the world weren't tolerated in Tres Cerros. Didn't fit with the city's image. Cops ran you off before you could soil the sidewalk.

Robert turned right at a stop sign, and after a few blocks, Dink found himself in a neighborhood of modestly priced homes. Robert pulled into the driveway of a brick house with a large shade tree and a For Sale sign in the front yard.

"House is for sale," Dink said.

"Yeah, there's nobody here. I work for the real estate company. We have to keep the place looking nice, keep the weeds cut down, or we won't be able to sell it."

"Where are the weeds?" Dink asked, puzzled.

"They're in the back. Come on, I'll show you."

Robert got rake and hoe from the trunk and, carrying them with one arm, led Dink through the high wooden gate at the side of the house and into the backyard. Tall board fences and shrubs gave the place privacy so complete one could sunbathe here. The yard was immaculate, the lawn weed-free, the shrubs trimmed, the borders along the flowerbeds ruler straight. The owners were apparently gardeners and yardwork enthusiasts.

Dink said, "There's no we—"

"You're right, Dink," Robert said. "No weeds."

All at once it became clear to Dink that something was wrong here. Very, very wrong. That maybe this guy was one of those devil worshipers looking for a human sacrifice—or maybe just someone mean who enjoyed hurting people. There were other explanations, Dink was sure, but he knew they were all bad.

"I think I'll be going now," Dink said.

Robert studied him, his eyes alight with strange, dark things Dink wanted no part of. Dink turned, took a step, and fear sizzled through him like a lightning bolt. He ran.

But not far.

For the blade of the hoe caught his left ankle, pulling his leg out from under him. Dink went face-first onto the immaculate lawn, his cheek sliding on the grass. Driven by sheer terror now, he scrambled to his feet and raced for the gate. He reached it, thinking he was okay, that the man could have grabbed him when he was down but didn't, so the fun was over, and Dink was free to go, ten dollars richer but a long way from familiar territory.

An arm grabbed him from behind, spun him around. Dink fought for equilibrium, lost the battle, and fell. He saw Robert standing over him, bending toward him. Then he saw the knife.

He tried to scream.

But he was too late.

Twenty-four

"Kozlovski found the store the typewriter came from," Cotter said. "Place down by Palo Alto. Owner recognized Heckly's photo."

"And?" Captain Zinn said.

"There is no and. The owner found the receipt, but it had no name and no address, not even the serial number of the typewriter. All it said was, 'One Adler manual, $36.95.' Date was about four weeks ago."

The two men were sitting in Zinn's office. It was two days since Cotter's return from El Paso.

Cotter said, "We got nowhere on Rocky L. Hebert. No trail at all. People at the hotel don't recognize Heckly's photo. He'd changed his appearance. Managed somehow to hide his bad arm."

Zinn frowned. "When he bought his ticket at the airport, he wanted to be recognized and remembered. Why be secretive one time, then make sure he's recognized the next?"

"It was too early in his plans when he was working at the hotel. He needed time to get everything set up."

"Then why use the anagram—Rocky L. Hebert?"

"He knew we wouldn't get it right away," Cotter said. "And we didn't. Not until he wanted us to."

He rubbed his cheek. He felt old and tired. The horror that had utterly destroyed his life was back for another go at him. The knowledge left him dazed, unsure of what to do—and unsure of himself. Fear undulated in his belly like a living thing.

"What have you got in mind?" Zinn asked.

"I'm getting a bunch of photos of Heckly. I'll see that every department in the area gets one. Then we're going to start checking out the motels, showing Heckly's photo, looking for names on the register that could mean something—more anagrams, whatever. He's here, and he's got to be staying somewhere."

"He could be staying with somebody," the captain suggested. "Maybe he's living with a woman he picked up in a bar—or a guy."

Cotter shook his head. "Doesn't feel right. Heckly's a loner. Never had much of a sex life that anyone knew about."

When he was linked with Heckly, the presence Cotter sensed seemed solitary by nature, preferring to be alone unless there was a good reason not to be. But he couldn't tell Zinn about that, for the captain would think he had two lunatics on his hands.

Cotter said, "I wanted to ask you if—"

The phone rang, cutting him off. Zinn answered it with his name, then listened. Cotter had been about to ask whether there was anything Zinn could do to get more protection for Cindy while she was at work in San Francisco. Lieutenant Cone, Cotter's friend in the SFPD, had only been able to arrange a catch-as-catch-can check of Cindy's office, which meant hours could go by between visits by an officer. Cotter wanted to see whether he could get anything better by going through official channels.

Zinn hung up, his eyes settling on Cotter. "We have another one—another letter from him. Wu's on his way up with it."

"I take it any mail that might be from him is being opened by the lab now."

"While you were gone I issued the orders. Any letters addressed to you and any typed envelopes with no return address."

"How was this one addressed?"

"To you, personally."

Wu arrived with the letter and envelope in a plastic bag, which he handed to the captain. "Same machine," he said. "Adler manual. No prints except on the outside of the envelope."

Zinn studied the letter through the clear plastic for a moment, then handed it to Cotter. It said:

V is for vagrant. You know who I am now, don't you? By the way, this one was just for the heck of it. Heck—get it?

175

"Man has a sense of humor," Wu said.

"But there hasn't been another murder," Zinn said.

"Yes, there has," Cotter said. "We just haven't found the victim yet." And as he said it he sensed that Heckly had intended it that way. More playing with their heads, showing his superiority.

"No hairs or fibers this time," Wu said.

Cotter wondered whether there were hairs and fibers only when Heckly wanted them to be there. Or could anyone be *that* thoroughly in control?

You're a lunatic, not a demon with supernatural powers.

Cotter sent the message down that long black tunnel that linked them. There was only silence at the other end of the connection.

Zinn's phone rang again. He put the receiver to his ear, listened a moment, then said, "You got a call from a Sergeant Joseph Sanchez of the Hudspeth County Sheriff's Office in Texas."

Sanchez was the officer who'd taken the report on Heckly's escape. Cotter had liked him. Sanchez was a good, hard-working cop. "I'll take it at my desk," he said, rising.

"Line three," the captain said.

Cotter slipped into his cubicle, pushed the flashing button on his phone, and said, "Joe, how you doing?"

"Good, and you?"

"Getting by. What you got for me?"

"A lot of things. First, we found Mrs. Stiller's body—or what was left of it. It was maybe a hundred miles from the hospital, in the Delaware Mountains. Scavengers had pretty well worked it over, but there was enough to be sure it was her." He grunted. "Stiller's a dumb son-of-a-bitch, you know that?"

"Yeah, I know that. On the other hand, you've got to know Heckly. Stiller didn't know for sure what would happen if he did what Heckly said, but he sure as hell knew what would happen if he didn't. And he loved his wife a lot."

"It happened to her anyway."

"Yeah." Cotter wondered what he'd do if it was Cindy. He

hoped he'd have enough sense to get help immediately, but he wasn't sure what he'd do. You love someone, you do unpredictable things.

"Stiller's been fired, by the way. There's a new guy running the place now, a Dr. Morganstern."

Cotter wondered what Dr. Morganstern had done to get sent to the psychiatrist's equivalent of Siberia. "I figured Stiller would get canned," he said.

"He's got more troubles than just that. They're going to review his license. He might lose it."

"I guess that figures, too," Cotter said.

"I know how Heckly escaped now," Sanchez said.

"How?"

"Basically, he talked his way out—if you can believe that. I'm told this guy could sell sand to an Arab, but I didn't think anyone was slick enough to talk his way out of a maximum-security facility like that."

"Should have kept him locked in a heavy-duty cage, and to hell with his rights," Cotter muttered.

"What's that?"

"Heckly can be extremely persuasive. Used to be a lawyer, a city council member, an up-and-coming Republican."

"Yeah, that's what I heard. Anyway, he apparently talked a guard named Leo Duver into letting him out. Duver's gone. Resigned. And wouldn't you know, his last day at work was the same day Heckly escaped? He left behind his wife and three kids, who are still living in the compound out there at the hospital because they've got nowhere else to go. I've been talking to his wife—her name is Donna Diane Duver, by the way. Lots of Ds. Anyway, she said Leo had been talking about all the money he was about to latch onto. Putting pieces together gets you the idea that maybe Heckly convinced Duver he had a lot of money stashed on the outside somewhere, and that he'd give him a sizable chunk of it if he was able to get to it. Even Duver wouldn't be dumb enough to trust Heckly to send it to him, so I assume they left together." He cleared his throat. "Think there's any chance Duver's alive?"

"No."

"Me neither."

Cotter said, "You'll probably find him somewhere near where Mrs. Stiller was discovered."

"That's what I think. I'll tell you, Cotter, I've been doing this job for fifteen years now, and I never cease to be amazed at how gullible people can be."

"Did Duver take his car?" Cotter asked.

"Yes. Along with everything else, he left his wife and kids with no wheels."

"Then there are two cars missing," Cotter said. "Duver's and Mrs. Stiller's."

"Nothing on either one of them. Of course, it's not hard to make a car disappear around here. We're pretty close to the border, and if a vehicle makes it into Mexico, it might as well have been shipped to Mars. It's gone for good."

"Could you get rid of a car that way, just leave it somewhere with the keys in it?"

"Chances are it would be somewhere in Chihuahua within twenty-four hours."

Cotter considered that. "He might have disposed of Duver's car that way, but he wouldn't have taken the chance with Mrs. Stiller's. He did something else with it."

"If neither one of them has turned up by now, we'll never know," Sanchez said. "What's the latest on your end?"

Cotter told him about the latest communication from Heckly.

"So now you're waiting for the body to show up," Sanchez said.

"I don't think we'll have to wait long."

The Texas deputy was silent a moment; then he said, "I don't mind telling you, Cotter, that this Heckly character is one scary son-of-a-bitch. He's smart, he's smooth, he's deadly, and he's . . . no, no he's not. I was going to say he's totally bug fuck, but that's not right. His mind . . . it works on some weird set of rules that the rest of us can't understand. I mean, he's crazy, but not bonkers crazy. He's not going to go berserk and start shooting up a school or something like that. I mean, people who do that are certainly frightening, but I think a guy who plans out his moves the way Heckly does is even scarier. That make any sense?"

Cotter said he understood it completely. He'd seen what Heckly's kind of crazy could do.

Cotter spent the rest of the day visiting motels. Kozlovski, Tuffle, and he split up, each taking a separate area. At each stop they checked the register for names that could have been derived from Robert Heckly—like Lee Heck or Rocky L. Hebert. And they left a photo of Heckly with the number of the Tres Cerros police department stamped on the back, along with the admonition to call at once should the escapee be spotted.

Cotter didn't think Heckly would be spotted.

Unless he wanted to be.

As he was heading north on Peninsula Street, Cotter used the radio to ask Kozlovski and Tuffle whether they'd had any luck. The reply from both was negative.

Peninsula Street was a divided thoroughfare with a landscaped island full of tulips. This early in the year they were just green fingers poking out of the earth, but soon they would blossom into a yellow-and-white celebration of spring. Ahead was the next motel, its sign proclaiming that one could find free cable TV and reasonable rates within. The place was called the Pacific Paradise. At night, when the sign was turned on, a grass-skirted native girl swayed back and forth, probably freezing her neon buns off in the Bay Area's cool, foggy climate.

"Control to 338," the dispatcher said, calling Cotter's unit number.

"Three-thirty-eight," Cotter replied.

"Ninety-one-eighteen Luminaria Lane. Your presence requested that ten-twenty, authority 551." Five fifty-one was Captain Zinn.

"Can you tell me the forty-nine at that twenty?" Cotter asked. In police radio parlance, it meant: How much can you tell me about what we've got there?

"This is reference a one-eighty-seven." A homicide. Which

was all Cotter needed to know. Robert Heckly's latest victim had been found.

"Ten-four," Cotter said.

"Five-fifty-one requests you ten-eighteen." Which meant the captain didn't want him to waste any time getting there.

The scene was typical of so many others Cotter had been to. Police cruisers, the lab's gray van, the plain white car with the inconspicuous black lettering on the door that said "Medical Examiner's Office." Red lights flashed. Onlookers ogled, some peeking from windows while others stood on their side of the yellow crime-scene tape, openly gawking.

It was a middle-class neighborhood, nice "Leave It to Beaver" sorts of houses, neither the castles of the rich nor the hovels of the poor. A uniformed cop directed him to the backyard of a home that had a For Sale sign out front. Stepping through the gate, Cotter saw Gonzales taking pictures, but there was no sign of Wu—Cheech but not Chong. A tall, thin medical examiner named Hamlin was talking to him. Captain Zinn was standing off to the side, observing. On the ground was a sheet-covered lump.

"The *V*-is-for-vagrant victim," Zinn said as Cotter joined him.

"That's what I figured," Cotter said. "What have you got?"

"Victim's a middle-aged male, no ID. Judging from appearance, I'd say he was definitely a vagrant."

"How'd he die?"

Zinn winced. "You'll have to see it."

The captain led him to the covered form on the grass. Bending down, he pulled back the cloth. The victim's shirt was unbuttoned, revealing his chest, from which a two-inch-wide strip of flesh had been removed. Cotter traced it with his eyes, from the left nipple to the belly button, then straight to the other nipple. It was a huge letter *V*.

"*V* is for vagrant," Cotter said, his voice barely audible.

Zinn said, "Unbelievable, isn't it?"

"No," Cotter replied. "For Heckly, it's perfectly believable."

Zinn nodded. No explanation was necessary.

"Where's the skin? It looks as though it was taken off in a continuous strip."

"As if the crazy son-of-a-bitch was making a belt," Zinn said. "I don't know where it is. Maybe he took it with him."

"No," Cotter said. "That's not his style. It's here somewhere." He looked around the yard, noting the tall wooden fence and thick bushes.

Zinn said, "You could throw an orgy here, and if you didn't make too much noise no one would notice."

"Maybe the owner made porno movies," the medical examiner said, joining them.

"What killed him?" Cotter asked.

"A very sick person with a very sharp knife," Hamlin said. He shuffled his feet. Hamlin was one of those people who was always burning off nervous energy, incapable of standing still. Which, Cotter figured, was why he was nearly as thin as a child's stick man drawing. Six-one or so, Hamlin probably weighed about one-thirty.

"Could cutting the *V* have killed him?" Zinn asked.

"Not the sort of wound that's usually fatal," Hamlin said, wiping his hands on a handkerchief.

"Then how'd he die?"

"Don't know yet."

"Could he have still been alive while . . . while this happened?" the captain asked.

"Not and be conscious," Hamlin said, rubbing his cheek. "He'd have kicked and screamed like crazy."

"Any indication he was tied?" Cotter asked.

"No."

"Drugged?"

"Who can tell at this point?" Hamlin said, shifting his weight from foot to foot. "That's what autopsies are for, to find out that kind of stuff. You guys are just going to have to wait."

A young uniformed cop hurried over. He hesitated, apparently uncertain who he should tell, then looked at Zinn, who was the highest ranking officer present. "Sir, uh, there's something here you'd better see."

The captain, Hamlin, and Cotter accompanied the officer to a rearmost portion of the yard, where a large shade tree stood. "There," the young cop said, pointing upward.

Just above eye level, tied around one of the tree's limbs like one of those yellow release-the-hostages ribbons, was a ghastly decoration. A long, roughly cut belt of human flesh.

Twenty-five

"Oh, no," Cindy said, wrapping her arms around herself as if she were cold. She and Cotter were sitting on the couch. He had just told her what happened.

"None of the neighbors heard anything," he said. "And they couldn't see anything because of the fence and shrubbery. It's the most private backyard I've ever seen. The place has been vacant for six weeks. The owner was transferred to Virginia."

Cindy shook her head as if trying to dislodge the image of a man with a large V carved in his chest. Then her expression became thoughtful. "Mike, something just occurred to me. Most people wouldn't know that house with the absolutely private backyard was there. And Heckly's a stranger; he's only been here a few months. Do you think he could be living nearby—in the neighborhood?"

Cindy was like that. No matter how unspeakable the things he dealt with, she would try to remain objective, to ask questions that would help him think logically about the situation. Even now, when the threat was getting very close to home.

"You're learning to think like a cop," Cotter said. "We came up with the same idea. Unfortunately, no one recognized Heckly's photo, and the only stranger in the neighborhood turned out to be someone's nephew who's visiting from Nebraska. He's about twenty, pimple-faced, short, and extremely plump. He's definitely not Heckly."

Cindy thought for a moment, then said, "So how did he find out about that secluded backyard?"

"It's possible Heckly was shown the property by a real estate agent—or he was working as a real estate agent. We're going to start checking on that first thing tomorrow."

"He's only been here three months," Cindy said. "He worked

at the Seaward Hotel. Could he have worked as a real estate agent, too, in such a short period of time?"

"He can usually talk his way into or out of whatever he wants to. He's Mr. Smooth. He knows how to win people's confidence."

Cindy stood up, walked to the window, and looked out on the night. A light fog softened the lights of Tres Cerros, giving the city a serene, dreamlike appearance that belied the presence of Robert Heckly.

"This . . . this man," Cindy said, still staring out the window, "he disembowels people, slits their throats, cuts a huge letter on someone's chest, travels to Texas to kill a poor creature who doesn't even know she's getting murdered." She shuddered. "And then there's what he did to the rest of your family. How . . . how do people get to be like that? What happens to them to make them that way? I wish I could understand."

Cotter said, "You'll have to get someone smarter than I am to answer that."

For several moments neither of them spoke; then Cindy said, "What do you know about his childhood?"

"Heckly's?"

"Yes. Did he play the tuba in the high school band? Did he date? Did he steal the lunch money from other kids? What was he like?"

"Pretty ordinary, from what I can gather. He was a Boy Scout, made passing but not exceptional grades in school, and didn't get into trouble. His only extracurricular school activity was the chess club."

"Go on."

"He did his undergraduate work and went to law school at Rutgers."

"Good grades?"

"Good enough to get what he wanted."

"No sports or anything like that?"

"No. He never showed any interest in things like that."

"When did he take up martial arts?"

"Later, after he was out of school."

"So he became an attorney."

"Yes, in New Jersey. Issington. His hometown. He got involved with the local Republicans, ran for the town council and won."

"When did he start killing?"

"The first deaths we can be sure about came after he was on the council. The people he killed were opposing him on various issues. If he ran into trouble with somebody, he simply eliminated the problem. For a long time no one suspected him because he was who he was."

"Wow. Heckly's the guy-next-door in some attractive upper-middle-class neighborhood."

"After he started killing, he discovered he liked it. One of the people he killed in Issington was a local businessman who opposed a zoning change Heckly was proposing. He went to the guy's house, killed him, then waited for the guy's wife to come home so he could kill her, too. Disemboweled her, just like Sheri Vanvleet."

Again Cindy shuddered. "You have any idea what caused him to . . . to change from being such an ordinary guy?"

"I think the other part of him was always there, just waiting for the chance to come out."

"How did it get there, this other side of him?"

"I only know things you can learn by looking at records or asking questions. I don't know what goes on inside Heckly. I doubt anyone does."

"What were his parents like?"

"Ordinary. His father was a successful accountant, and his mother didn't work. I guess I'd say they were comfortably upper-middle-class, but not wealthy. They were law-abiding people who went to church every Sunday, and their neighbors had nothing bad to say about them."

Cindy stared out the window for a few moments, then returned to the couch. "You learned everything you could about him, didn't you?"

"I wanted to stop him. I thought anything I could learn might help. And it gave me something to occupy my mind. It gave me a purpose."

"Oh, Mike, I wish there were something I could do, some

way I could take away the hurt. But pain like that . . . it can't be taken away, can it? I mean it's too great, too overwhelming."

"Yes. What happened is part of me. I can learn to function, to keep it from destroying me, but I can never just put it away and say enough time has passed to heal me and it's okay now."

She held him tightly for a few moments, not speaking. At last she said, "It must be horrible for them."

"Who?"

"Heckly's parents."

"They're dead. Died when their home caught fire while Heckly was in college. There was evidence that the fire had been intentionally set—in the garage, which was directly below the Hecklys' bedroom."

"You mean he killed his own . . ."

"He was supposedly away at college. But he had time to get home and back. The campus was only an hour's drive from the house at night. He had an alibi. A woman swore he spent the night with her. Maybe she was telling the truth; maybe she wasn't. We'll never know."

"You know, don't you?"

Cotter nodded. "At least, I think I do. It's a feeling, not anything I can prove."

"You're pretty sure he did it, aren't you?"

"I know he did it. It's more than a hunch. It's like . . . well, it's like this certainty settles into your head, and you know. You just know."

"This thing between you and Heckly, this mental connection, is it just with him, because of what happened, or do you have it with other people, too?"

"I'm not sure." He frowned, trying to look within himself and understand what he saw there. "It only started happening recently—after Heckly arrived here. But now that it's happened, I sort of know how to go about it. I might be able to do it again with someone else. Maybe. But so far, it hasn't happened. Am I making any sense?"

"Yes. Perfect sense."

"I don't really understand it, but I know it's there; I know it's real."

Cindy's eyes filled with excitement. "Mike, you can use this to catch him!"

"How?"

"You're in his head, you know what he's thinking. Maybe if you worked at it you could figure out where he's staying, what name he's using, what his plans are."

Mike shook his head. "I don't learn anything that specific. It's just suggestions of things, feelings."

"But if you worked on it, tried harder."

Cotter considered that. "I'm not sure I know how to try harder."

"When it happens, what do you do?"

"I . . ." He hesitated, considered his answer. "Well, I think of it as reaching out with my mind, but I'm not sure that's right. It's probably more accurate to say I just let it happen. Or maybe I turn off whatever prevents it from happening."

"Try it."

"Now?"

"Try to find out where he is."

"I . . ." He hesitated, remembering what had happened the last time he'd gone too far into Heckly's mind. He hadn't learned anything that would help him catch the madman, and it had been a terrifying experience.

"What's wrong?"

"It's a scary place to go."

"Anyone would be scared to go there," Cindy said gently. "I don't think I could do it."

"I've never really been able to tell things when I'm linked with him. I mean, I don't know where he is at that precise moment, or what he's wearing. I sense a presence, the same way you can sense a presence when someone's on the other end of the phone and not speaking. The things I sense about him just sort of float into my head. I just know them. And I know them with the same confidence I know where I work or how to drive a car. And yet . . ." Uncertain what he'd been intending to say, he stopped.

"What sort of things do you know about him?"

"That he's there, linked with me. That he's the killer."

"Have you ever tried to learn more?"

"There doesn't seem to be any way to go about it."

"Can you establish this link anytime you want to?"

"No, not every time. It might only happen when he's willing to participate. I don't know. I also don't know to what extent it's a two-way link. Maybe he can learn all sorts of things about me, even though I can't tell much about him."

"So there's a risk."

"There could be."

He started to tell her what happened on the one occasion he'd gone too deeply into that black hole at the other end of the connection, then changed his mind. He wasn't really sure what had happened. And he'd done it only once. It might be entirely different if he did it again.

"I think you're right," he said slowly. "I should try anything that might help."

"Mike . . ." Her eyes searched his. Apparently she realized there was more going on here than she knew. "Maybe I was wrong," she said. "Maybe it's not such a good idea."

"I want to catch him."

Cindy hesitated, then said, "Mike . . . if you do, if you catch him, what will you do?"

"You're asking if I'll kill him, aren't you?"

She nodded.

"I don't know. What do you think I'll do?"

"I don't know, either," she said.

"Does it worry you, what I might do?"

"Yes, but not because of Heckly. After what he's done, I can't make myself feel anything for him. But I do care about you. I don't want you to ruin your life."

"It's already been ruined."

"Not all of it."

Looking into her eyes, seeing the confusion and worry there, Cotter realized what she meant. There was still time to share what remained of his life with her, and she did not want him to throw it away.

She said, "I love you, you big lug. And I don't want to lose you."

"When we find Heckly, I'll remember that."

"Promise?"

"Promise."

And then Cotter reached out for the link with Heckly. Although he didn't know why he was doing it, he imagined an invisible wire with a plug on the end, floating on unseen currents, trying to find the receptacle into which it would slip, completing the connection.

Abruptly he sensed the presence, as if someone had lifted the receiver at the other end of the line and was now listening in silence.

"Mike . . ." Cindy's voice.

Cotter held up his hand, signaling her to be quiet so he could concentrate. He focused his mind on the presence, trying to become more in tune with it, to move closer to it. Nothing changed. The presence was just there, anonymous and seemingly unreachable.

Cotter tried harder, tried to will his senses to slide along the path of the connection and tell him useful things about the person on the other end. Abruptly he was surrounded by a roiling blackness that was closing in on him, engulfing him, and he felt . . . something.

Something . . . bad . . . ugly.

He tried to pull back from it, shut his mind to it, but it pierced his defenses with the ease of a scalpel gliding through flesh. Suddenly Cotter recognized what he was sensing: it was feeling, emotion. Not just one, but many emotions. A maelstrom of them.

Cotter was experiencing determination and hate and lust, and everything seemed all mixed up and turned upside down, for thoughts of death and suffering were pleasurable, while concepts like caring and warmth seemed not to exist here.

Either that, or they were twisted, unrecognizable.

Suddenly Cotter was falling. Using every ounce of willpower he possessed, he tried to resist, but he didn't know how. Powerful feelings swirled around him, and they were convoluted, corrupted. Love was no longer a deep caring for another; it was warped so that it was love of destroying. It was a tool, a means to an end. All that mattered was the self, its desires. Selfishness was good, cherished. Honesty and trust were weaknesses to be exploited.

Down he fell.

Faster.

And still faster.

And then he heard a voice, saying something about fog. Cotter tried to ignore the voice, for it was part of this upside-down place where destruction was love and everything was evil and wrong.

"People living near the ocean are going to be socked in all night."

The words seemed distant, dreamlike, unreal. And although they weren't threatening by themselves, they emanated from this place he was being drawn into, this place of evil where no sane person should ever attempt to go.

"No!" Cotter shouted. "I'm not going there."

"So it would be a good idea—"

"Mike?"

"—to stay home tonight unless—"

"Mike, are you all right?"

"—you absolutely have to go somewhere."

"Mike, you're scaring me. Snap out of it. Please."

And then he was sitting on the couch with Cindy, who was looking at him with wide, frightened eyes. "You were . . . gone, away. Are you all right?"

"I'm okay," he said.

"What happened?"

"I found Heckly." He realized he was shaking.

"Mike, I'm sorry I suggested that. It was as if you weren't here anymore, as if you had . . ."

"Had what?"

"Left your body. As if you were just a shell, with nothing inside." She was pale. "Don't do that again. Please. It scared the hell out of me. You were so cold. It was as if I'd lost you and I never want to lose you, not ever. Promise you'll never do it again. Please."

"I won't do it again," Cotter said. "I promise. I . . . think I stepped into Heckly's madness. It's a terrible, awful place, where everything is wrong. No normal person can survive there—not if he wants to stay sane."

Cindy held him, and the chill that had penetrated to the center of his being slowly began to disappear. "Someone was giving a warning about staying home tonight," he said.

"I don't understand," Cindy said.

"While I was there, in Heckly's mind, I heard this warning. Don't go out unless you have to."

"What does it mean?"

"I have no idea."

The impact of it nearly knocked Robert Heckly off the chair. He'd been sitting in the motel room, watching the news when . . . when what? He wasn't sure what had just transpired. It seemed as if someone had crawled into his head with a blowtorch and started melting portions of his brain. He put his hand on his forehead, as if checking for a fever, half expecting his flesh to be too hot to touch. It was only slightly warm, and yet he felt as though the inside of his head was a blast furnace.

He wanted to look at himself in the mirror, but he felt too weak to stand. And then he realized what he was feeling. It was the now familiar sensation of a presence. He'd been successfully ignoring it for days. He simply pushed it into a dark corner of his mind and closed the door on it. But suddenly it was back, with a vengeance. This wasn't like the prickly feeling of being watched. This was like someone stomping on your brain.

His eyes scanned the room, exploring the shadowy corners, lingering on the window, then shifting back to the television program he was watching. He was alone. No one was watching him.

And no one was in his head because it was impossible for anyone to be inside his head.

Heckly concentrated on the newscast. The weatherman was saying the fog would be getting really thick tonight all along the northern California coast.

"It would be a good idea to stay home tonight," the weatherman cautioned, "unless you absolutely have to go somewhere."

Abruptly the powerful feeling vanished.

He sat there, disquieted, trying to sort out what had just happened. Everything was back to normal now, the feeling of being watched still with him, but now just vaguely perceived, a hint, a suggestion.

Too much excitement, Heckly told himself. Not enough sleep.

And then a new thought occurred to him. Could it have been Cotter? Could the cop be doing something to him? Heckly considered that possibility and dismissed it. There was simply no way Cotter could be involved unless the cop was psychic. And even if he were, telepathy and psychokinesis were the stuff of science fiction. Heckly was a realist, a planner, with no interest in fairy tales.

He needed a rest, he concluded. That was all. He'd been pushing himself too hard.

Soon he would get all the relaxation he needed, for the end of the game with Cotter was near. Another few days and it would be over.

Twenty-six

"That's him," Oscar Wyrick said, studying the photo Cotter had given him. "R. H. Lee."

The two men were sitting in Wyrick's office, a surprisingly small and spartan room for the owner of Tres Cerros's largest real estate firm. The dark plywood paneling on the walls absorbed the light, making the office seem dingy. The desk was one of those utilitarian gray metal types used by civil servants the world over.

"Hired him a couple of months ago," Wyrick said. "He came across as a very personable, intelligent man, a good conversationalist, and when he smiled, it said, 'You can trust me.' Those things are exactly what you look for in this business, so I offered him an associate's position on the spot."

"Associate?" Cotter said.

"That's what we call our sales representatives." Wyrick was a short bald man with eyebrows so bushy and white they looked like part of a Santa Claus costume. The top of his head was such a bright pink it could have been rouged.

"Where can I find Mr. Lee?" Cotter asked.

"I don't know. He hasn't shown up for work in several days." Wyrick sighed. "Very disappointing. He seemed such a nice man, so dependable. You just never know, do you?"

"Do you have an address?"

"Yes." Wyrick got a folder from a gray metal file cabinet and returned to his desk. "It's 1048 West Twenty-Seventh Street, in Colmer. That was something about him that didn't fit, you know. Maybe it should have tipped me off."

Cotter wrote down the address. "What should have tipped you off?" he asked.

"His living in Colmer. Why would a nice man like that live in Colmer?"

Cotter knew lots of nice people who lived in Colmer. Belinda Grant, for example. He said, "May I see that file, please?"

Wyrick hesitated, apparently weighing his responsibility regarding the confidentiality of personnel matters against his obligation to help the authorities; then he handed the folder to Cotter. The file was skimpy, even for a new employee. It contained an application for employment, a signed tax withholding form indicating that R. H. Lee had only one dependent, himself, and a sheet signed by Lee that set out the terms of his employment.

"That's the standard form," Wyrick said. "It explains how the commissions are split between the company and the employee and states the obligations of each party."

"On the application, he lists experience with a real estate company in New Jersey. Did you check it out?"

"I tried, but the company's out of business. That happens a lot, I'm afraid."

"How about these other jobs? Manager of a hardware store, assistant manager at a convenience store."

"Those go too far back, so I didn't check. I mean, he said he'd been with the real estate firm for ten years. People at those other places might not have the records anymore. They might not even remember him."

Cotter nodded. "It doesn't say anything here about a real estate license. Don't you have to be licensed to sell real estate?"

"To be a broker, yes. That's what I am, a licensed real estate broker. But the people I hire as sales representatives don't have to be licensed brokers. It's sort of like saying you don't have to be an authorized Chevy dealer to work as a Chevy salesman."

"Do you know whether Lee ever showed the house at 9118 Luminaria Lane?"

Wyrick's eyes widened. "Where the body was found? Oh my god, you don't think Lee did . . . did *that*, do you?"

"Let's just say I want to talk to him about it."

"Jesus," Wyrick said, shaking his head. "I mean, I shook his hand, ate lunch with him. I even considered inviting him home for dinner with Yvonne and me."

"I'll need to borrow this file," Cotter said.

"Yes, of course."

"Did Lee say anything to you that might help us?"

The real estate man considered that. "No," he replied after a moment. "Now that I think about it, he was always quite talkative, but it was all small talk, nothing informative." He shook his head. He seemed dazed. "But then, that's what a person like that would do, isn't it? I can't believe he was right here in our midst, a person who would do something like that."

"Did you notice anything unusual about him?"

Wyrick frowned, thinking. "No."

"How about his left arm?"

"I didn't notice anything. Should I have?"

"The man we're looking for had a bad left arm, but he's quite adept at concealing it."

"I just don't remember an arm problem." The real estate broker shrugged. "But then he didn't do anything physical in my presence that I can recall. I'll tell you this. He was a very good salesman. He sold quite a few homes in the short time he was here. He had a good future in this business. His income would have been quite handsome."

"I see. Well, thank you for—"

"He doesn't have it all."

"Doesn't have what?"

"The money he earned. He still has several thousand dollars coming. You see, you don't get paid the instant you get a buyer's signature on the form. The owner may want to haggle. Work may have to be done on the property. The lender has to approve the loan, which will probably include a title search and all sorts of other details that have to be attended to. It usually takes at least a month to close formally—and that's only if there aren't any snags. Anyway, some of what Lee earned he hasn't collected." Wyrick leaned forward, his eyes suddenly filled with excitement. "Don't you see, this is your chance to catch him. He'll have to come back for the money we owe him."

"He won't be back," Cotter said.

"But . . . but we're talking thousands of dollars here. He earned it. It's his."

"He doesn't care about the money."

"How can he not care about the money?"

Closing the file folder, Cotter rose. "Thank you for your help, Mr. Wyrick."

"You mean he knows you've figured he's the one you're after, so he doesn't dare come back?"

"No, he was never interested in the money." It was one of those things Cotter just knew. Another tidbit somehow sensed because of the link between him and the madman.

The real estate office was on the north side of Tres Cerros. Cotter drove directly to the Colmer address Heckly had used on his employment application, fully expecting it to be a vacant lot or a juvenile detention facility or an abortion clinic. Whatever Heckly considered amusing.

But the address was a motel.

Not wanting to use the radio, since anyone with a scanner could monitor the police frequencies, he called Captain Zinn from a pay phone. Within an hour, the place was surrounded by police officers.

"Yes, that's him," said the owner of the Land's Edge Motel when Cotter showed him Heckly's photo. "Room sixteen."

Heckly had registered under the same name he'd used at the real estate company, R. H. Lee.

"Is he in?" Cotter asked.

"As far as I know. I haven't seen him leave."

This was one of those mom-and-pop motel operations that were disappearing as chains took over the business. The owner was thin and gray haired, and he wore a Hawaiian shirt with the top two buttons open, revealing a tangle of salt-and-pepper chest hair. He spoke with a Midwestern accent.

Cotter was accompanied by Sergeant Tucker of the Colmer force. Because this was in Tucker's jurisdiction it had to be a joint operation. The Colmer cop, a tall, broad-shouldered black man, was a natty dresser. At the moment he was decked out in a gray double-breasted suit with a burgundy-and-white patterned tie, the three points of a white linen pocket square poking out of his breast pocket. Cotter knew him. Tucker was a good cop.

"What about the other rooms?" Tucker asked. "How many are

occupied right now?"

"Most of the units are empty," the owner said. "People stay one night and go on. We've only got two kitchenettes, sixteen and seventeen."

"Anybody in seventeen?" Tucker asked.

"That would be the Nyquists. They just moved out from Minnesota and they're staying here until they can buy a house. But they both work, so neither of them should be here."

"Phone each room," Cotter said, "just to make sure."

"What's going to happen?" the owner asked nervously.

"Lee is a dangerous wanted criminal," Tucker said. "We just want to make sure nobody gets hurt."

The owner looked from Tucker to Cotter and back again. "Is there going to be any shooting?"

"We hope not," Tucker said.

"Will you use tear gas?"

"I don't know. It depends on him."

The owner smoothed the front of his colorful shirt. "This place is all we've got. I don't want it to get damaged."

"The city's got insurance," Tucker said.

The cynical look on the owner's face said he had a pretty good idea of what would happen if he filed a claim. He started phoning the rooms. Cotter considered phoning Heckly's room to confirm that he was there, but decided against it. The call would have to be made on a pretext, and if Heckly saw through it, the element of surprise would be lost.

Although he was outwardly calm, Cotter's emotions were a palpating mass in his gut, electric in their intensity, yet too confused to sort out. He wondered whether this could truly be it, whether he was moments away from coming face-to-face with the madness that had nearly destroyed his life. And hanging in the background, a dark and sinister presence, was the question he could not answer. What would he do when he *did* come face-to-face with the monster who had literally butchered his wife and son while his daughter watched?

His .38 was a noticeable lump beneath his left armpit, hanging there, reachable, ready.

There was an electricity in his fingers, as if they were letting him know that the gun was unnecessary, that his bare hands would be all that was required to make sure Robert Heckly never did to anyone else what he had done to William Michael Richland.

At the same time he knew that these thoughts were wrong, all wrong. His job was to arrest Heckly, see that he was charged with the murders of Wanda Grant and Sheri Vanvleet and Willa Stiller and the vagrant who was killed in the privacy of a secluded backyard.

And a helpless creature in Texas who as a little girl had been forced to witness a horror so unspeakable it could have destroyed even the most hardened of adults.

Only room seventeen answered. Mrs. Nyquist had the flu and had called in sick today. Tucker took the phone from the owner, whose voice was rapidly filling with panic.

"This is Detective Tucker, with the Colmer police. I want you to quietly leave the motel . . . No, no, you're in no danger at this time, but we're about to make an arrest here, and it would be better if you left the premises . . . Yes, right now, please."

They watched from the window of the office as a young blond woman emerged from room seventeen, got into a station wagon, and drove away from the motel. The owner called his wife, who until then had been unaware of what was happening, and officers escorted them to the safety of the police lines.

The motel was empty.

Except for Heckly.

Cotter's fingers tingled.

Kozlovski and Tuffle were there. So was Captain Zinn, along with some brass from the Colmer force. The Colmer SWAT unit was on hand, four guys dressed like ninjas, carrying assault rifles and exuding an air of superiority.

Cotter joined Kozlovski and Tuffle, who were standing behind an unmarked van that belonged to the Colmer Police Department. Kozlovski said, "Colmer honchos have decided to give him a chance to come out. If he doesn't, they'll use teargas; then the SWAT unit will go in."

"I guess it's their show," Cotter said. In a way he was relieved. If he wasn't among the first to get to Heckly, he would not have the chance to administer his own brand of summary justice.

"Colmer wants all the glory for themselves," Tuffle said.

Glory? Cotter thought. *Glory?* He pushed the thought away.

From their position behind the van, they had a clear view of the motel. The rooms were a white stucco *U* built around a separate structure housing the office and the owners' home. The sign out front proclaimed LAND'S EDGE MOTEL in big blue letters. Below them, much smaller, was the word "Vacancy."

Captain Zinn had been conferring with the Colmer brass. Joining the men from his own department, he said, "They're going to clear the entire area and block off the street. As soon as that's done, they're ready."

Cotter didn't like the delay. Heckly was extremely intelligent. If he caught even a hint of the activity, he might find some means of escape that they hadn't prepared for. But then it was out of his hands, so he simply nodded.

Do you know we're here, Heckly? he wondered. But there was no link at that moment. The lines were down.

It took half an hour to get everyone out of the businesses in the area and detour traffic. Cotter had to give the Colmer people credit. They got it done efficiently and quietly.

The SWAT unit moved in, ninjas in gas masks moving silently, keeping low. Two of them positioned themselves on each side of the door to room sixteen, while the remaining two moved to the rear.

"Attention room sixteen," a Colmer deputy chief said through a bullhorn. "This is the police. We know your name is Robert Heckly, and we know you're in there. Come out with your hands on your head, and you won't be harmed."

There was no response from the motel.

The deputy chief repeated his message.

Still no response.

The deputy chief warned Heckly that tear gas was coming in sixty seconds if he didn't give up. A minute later, tear gas was fired through the window. A moment later more canisters followed them. A white cloud billowed from the broken glass.

Still there was no response.

"He must have a mask," Tuffle said.

"Uh-uh," Kozlovski said. "He isn't in there."

And then the SWAT unit was at the door, unlocking it with the master key provided by the owner, pushing it open, white smoke pouring out, the ninjas going in with their assault rifles ready.

And then there was silence.

Gripping the butt of his .38, his heart pounding, Cotter kept telling himself that Heckly was there, overcome by tear gas, that he hadn't gotten away because it was unacceptable, because it would mean that the nightmare would go on.

And on.

And on.

Tucker appeared beside Cotter. "Think we just evacuated a neighborhood and tear gassed a motel for nothing?"

Before Cotter could respond, the radio clipped to Tucker's belt crackled into life. "Room's empty. We're going to check out the others."

The men in black moved from room to room, unlocking the doors and entering with weapons ready. Ten minutes later, they announced that the motel was empty.

They used fans to get the tear gas out of the room. When it was clear Cotter, Tucker, and Kozlovski went inside. Though spotlessly clean, these were economy accommodations. Cracks made intricate patterns in the plaster walls, the carpet was worn thin by the door, and the furniture looked like something from a garage sale.

There was nothing in the room. No clothes, no suitcases, no change on the dresser, no toothbrush in the bathroom.

Cotter sensed Heckly's presence here like a dog picking up a recent scent. The man had known they'd find this place, and he was long gone. He's smarter than we are, Cotter thought, and instantly shoved the thought from his consciousness, for it was unacceptable. Heckly would make a mistake. Heckly would be caught. For it had to be so. Absolutely had to be.

"He's out there watching all this," Cotter said.

"Laughing his ass off," Kozlovski said.

Abruptly Cotter ran from the room, ignoring the surprised reactions of Kozlovski and Tucker. He ran to the street, then turned right, hurried to the end of the block where the Colmer police had set up a barricade. A number of spectators had gathered, speaking to each other in low tones, trying to figure out what all the excitement was about. Cotter scanned the faces, looking for the one he would never forget. He took in round faces, long faces, fat ones, and thin ones. He looked into eyes that were blue and brown and hazel and gray. Heckly was not here.

Cotter hurried to the other end of the block, where another small crowd of the curious had gathered. Again he studied the faces. Heckly was not among them.

He started back toward the motel, and suddenly he was running as fast as he could, convinced that Heckly was still in the building somewhere, hiding, laughing at them. Faces, trees, parked cars flashed past, a blur. He forced his legs to pump harder. He would not let Heckly get away. Not, not, not.

Abruptly Cotter stopped. He was on the sidewalk in front of the motel. He stood there, panting, trying to collect his composure. Heckly was gone. He had given the real estate firm his correct address because he wanted Cotter to find it. He'd planned to be long gone from the beginning. He was hardly dumb enough to stay here and wait to be caught. This was just more of his games, some additional mocking, an extra serving of torment. Heckly's way of saying, *See how much smarter I am than you are.*

Cotter walked back to room sixteen. Captain Zinn and the Colmer deputy chief had joined Kozlovski and Tucker inside the room. All four of them studied Cotter appraisingly.

Zinn said, "We've agreed that our lab crew should handle it. Cheech and Chong are on the way."

Cotter nodded. Realizing his right hand was shaking, he slipped it into his pocket.

"You okay?" Zinn asked.

"Fine."

The lab guys arrived and went to work while Cotter and the others waited outside. The Colmer deputy chief left, along with Captain Zinn. Cotter realized he would have to be careful around the captain. Zinn was allowing him to stay on a case in which he had a personal interest. In part, Zinn was doing it because Cotter had been handling the case from the beginning, before his connection to the killer was known. But he was also doing it out of professional courtesy. How could he remove from the case someone who had gone through what Cotter had?

But these things would only count for so much. If Cotter started looking flaky around the edges, Zinn would do what he had to do.

An hour and fifteen minutes after the lab crew had arrived, Wu emerged from room sixteen with a magazine, which he handed to Cotter. "This is the only thing he left behind."

Cotter was holding a year-old issue of the *American Journal of Psychiatry*. He sensed Heckly's presence on it, emitted by the pages the way the aroma of expensive designer fragrances wafted from *GQ* and *Esquire*. But this was no creation of Christian Dior. It was madness, the essence of evil.

Cotter knew it had been left for him. A message from Heckly.

He flipped through the pages, searching for whatever Heckly had wanted him to find. He almost missed it. The article was entitled "Permanent Withdrawal as a Result of Psychological Shock."

The author was Dr. Philippa Lockwood.

It told of a patient referred to only as Dawn, related how the young woman had witnessed the ghastly deaths of her mother and brother, how she had withdrawn so deeply into herself she would remain there, hiding from the horror forever. Although Jennifer's name was never used, anyone familiar with the case could have figured Dawn was Cotter's daughter. Although no institution was named, it wouldn't have been too difficult to find out where Dr. Lockwood was employed.

Cotter stared at the journal, stunned. Lockwood, in her quest for professional recognition, had given Heckly the location of the sole surviving member of Cotter's family.

Twenty-seven

"I was so furious I could have picked her up and shaken her," Cotter said. He lay beside Cindy in bed, staring at the shadows on the ceiling. "If she'd been here instead of in Texas . . ." He let the thought trail off.

"You wouldn't have hurt her," Cindy said. "It's not you."

Cotter sighed. "I called her, and while her phone was ringing, I was sitting there trembling, I was so mad. But when she came on the line, it just vanished. I simply told her about it and let it go at that."

"What did she say?"

"She cried."

"Someone like that, a woman who's made it to a high supervisory position, hated having to cry in front of you. For her it was . . . well, she probably felt she disgraced herself."

"Am I supposed to feel sorry for her? I mean, she's at least partially responsible for Jennifer's death."

"I know. And so does she."

"So how am I supposed to feel?"

"There's no right way to feel, Mike. You feel how you feel."

"I feel confused."

"I can tell. Put it away, big guy. You've got a heart that's pure and instincts that are scrupulous."

"Scrupulous? It sounds like something you'd use to get the burnt-on stuff off the bottom of a pot. 'Can't get it clean. Use the miracle scrupulous.'" But his attempt at humor came off forced. There wasn't much to be cheerful about.

He watched the shadows on the ceiling for a while. They were fairly static this far above the street. No headlights shone in through the window like monster eyes; there were no tree branches to be stirred by the breeze and cause spooky shapes to slither around the room.

"He's still playing with me," Cotter said.

"You know he'll make a mistake."

"Will he?"

"He's been caught before. He's not supernatural. He's a man, an insane and dangerous one, but a man nonetheless. And being human, he'll screw it up. Just give him time."

"How many people will he kill while I'm waiting?"

"Don't take it out on yourself. No one else could do any better."

Cotter sighed. "It's just so damned frustrating to have Heckly manipulating me."

After a moment's silence, Cindy said, "Maybe you should be trying to manipulate him."

"And how do I do that?"

"Hey, we executives just deal in concepts. We have underlings to work out the details."

"You're idea people."

"Precisely."

"Do you have any ideas as to how I could put all this out of my mind for a little while, think about something else — anything else?"

"I have one."

"Yes?"

"It starts like this."

She pulled herself tightly against him, her body molding itself to his, proclaiming that it was a woman's body, firm where a woman should be firm, soft where she should be soft. Then she kissed him, her lips gently brushing his at first, then lingering, becoming more eager.

"It's starting to work," Cotter said.

"It gets better," she said.

And it did.

And Cotter pushed Heckly from his thoughts.

For a while.

"Are you all right?" Captain Zinn asked.

Cotter had been summoned to the captain's office as soon he'd arrived at work. Zinn had closed the door, something he rarely did. It indicated that he had things on his mind that he considered weighty and confidential.

"I'm fine," Cotter said.

"Yesterday you seemed a little . . ."

"Upset? Excited?"

"Let's say under a strain."

"Anybody handling this case would be under a strain. It's that kind of case."

"Look, Mike, we've known each other too long to have a little verbal contest where we dance all around the point. Be straight with me. Are you okay?"

"I freaked out a little yesterday when I realized he'd gotten away. I never expected him to be there, not in the beginning. Then the old guy who owns the motel told me Heckly was in his room, and I allowed myself to believe it." Cotter made a gesture of frustration with his hand. "Getting him means a lot to me. Obviously."

Zinn studied him, frowning. "I'm sort of out on a limb here. You know that."

"For keeping me on the case?"

"Of course for keeping you on the case. I doubt anyone's ever been more personally involved in a case in the whole history of police work."

"I'm involved in the case if I'm actively taking part in the investigation or not. There's no way I can become uninvolved."

The captain nodded. "I know."

"I won't go bonkers on you."

"I'll be watching, Mike. I have to. It has to be that way."

"If our roles were reversed, I'd do the same."

"What will you do if you find him, Mike?"

"Go by the book."

"Do I have your word on that?"

"Yes."

"If I have any reason to think otherwise . . ."

"You won't have."

"I'll accept that," Zinn said, but he looked pensive, as if not entirely satisfied with Cotter's answers.

"Cindy needs more protection," Cotter said, changing the subject.

"I've got someone watching her apartment every moment she's in it. What more can I do?"

"It's too little. Heckly is sharp. He'll spot the surveillance, move on her when she's at work—or when she's commuting."

"When she's at work, she's in San Francisco's jurisdiction; you know that."

"But San Francisco is just checking on her from time to time. There's no one on her full-time."

"I put in an official request you asked for, Mike. San Francisco's got manpower shortages just like everybody else."

Cotter's eyes found the captain's, held them. "It's not just that Cindy's my . . ." He hesitated because he'd never had to label the relationship before. "It's not just that she's my girlfriend. Watching her could turn out to be the way we catch him."

"You're certain he's going to move on her, aren't you?"

"No, I'm not certain. But it's likely. It's the sort of thing he'd do."

"Okay. Anyone in particular you want on it?"

"A woman with secretarial skills."

"You want to put her in the office with Cindy?"

"Best place. She'd be right on top of things, and at the same time she'd blend in; she'd be inconspicuous."

"Cindy would have to agree. Have you talked to her about this?"

"Not yet, but I'm pretty sure she'll go along."

"Okay, we're bound to have a woman with secretarial skills on the force."

"Seven sworn officers who were once secretaries. I checked."

"I get the impression you have a preference among the seven."

"Melanie Gunderson."

"Can't place her."

"Red hair, tall and thin, doesn't use makeup."

"Okay, I know who she is. Good cop. Just took the sergeant's examination."

"She's the one. Can you get her?"

"I can try."

"One other thing. I want a consult with a psychiatrist or a clinical psychologist."

Zinn frowned. "I thought . . ."

"Not because I want my head shrunk," Cotter said quickly. "I want to talk about Heckly. Basically, I want an expert whose brain I can tap."

"I'll arrange it. What do you have scheduled for today?"

"More of the same. Going from motel to motel with Heckly's picture, looking at the names of the guests, hoping to find a Lee Heck or some other derivative of his name."

"How long do you figure it will take to do them all?"

"A while. He could be staying anywhere in the Bay Area—Oakland, San Rafael, San Jose, you name it. We're talking a lot of hotels and motels, probably hundreds."

"You're about to ask for more manpower, right?"

"It wouldn't hurt to have a few more bodies on this. We could borrow some people from patrol."

"How many do you need exactly?"

"Four."

"Four?" the captain said, raising his eyebrows. "With Gunderson that's five."

"Except for her, I'll only need them for a few days. Until we get all the hotels and motels checked."

"Considering it's for you, for this, Captain Endu probably won't scream too loud—as long as I get his people back to him quickly."

"Does the whole department know—about me, about what happened?"

The captain studied him a moment. "Yes," he replied softly. "You know cops. A police department's a tight little group with a hell of a grapevine and damned few secrets." Zinn frowned. "Do you mind that it's out?"

"I guess, in the overall scheme of things, it doesn't matter that much, does it? I'd like to have a meeting this afternoon with everyone who's going to be checking motels. Can you do it?"

"What time?"

"Two."

"You want Gunderson there, too?"

"I'd like to meet with her at four-thirty, after I get things organized on the motel check."

"You know how many favors I'm going to owe Endu?" Zinn shook his head. "Never mind. I'll get it done."

Which he did. At two, Cotter met in the conference room with Kozlovski and Tuffle and the four officers on loan from patrol division—Anislov, Krone, Mackelson, and Vickers. They divided the Bay Area into seven sections, one for each. Beepers, already carried by the detectives, were issued to the patrol officers as well. If anyone located Heckly, the others would learn of it immediately.

Next Cotter met with Melanie Gunderson. She was thirty-five, an attractive redhead with intelligent blue eyes and an impish grin. On the sleeve of her navy blue uniform were three light blue slashes, hash marks in military parlance, which indicated she was a patrol officer first grade, the rank just below sergeant.

Cotter was one of the few officers who knew she was a lesbian. She maintained a monogamous relationship with a big blond woman named Leandra, whom she referred to as her "life partner." Cotter had joined her for a drink one night at Thad's, a cop bar near the station. He'd been down, and so had she, and he'd told her his secret, and she'd told him hers. Captain Zinn was wrong about there being no secrets within a police force. Melanie was firmly in the closet. She deflected the constant passes from male cops with aplomb, saying simply that she had no intention of getting involved with anyone on the job. She did it so well that no one looked beyond the explanation she offered.

"Sure I'll do it, Mike. Of course."

"If Heckly comes after her—"

"I'll handle it."

"Melanie, you don't know Heckly."

"I know what he did in Texas."

"I'm just saying you'll have to be on guard constantly. Heckly isn't your ordinary gun-toting gang member or knife-wielding addict. He's something else entirely."

"I can handle the assignment, Mike. I'm not inclined to risk my life or anyone else's if I don't have to." Her eyes were fixed on his, saying, *Trust me, you can count on me.*

"As long as you know what you're getting into."

She studied him silently.

Cotter said, "How sharp are your secretarial skills?"

"It's been a few years, but it's sort of like riding a bicycle. You never forget your shorthand squiggles or keyboarding, as they call it these days. I have a computer at home with a word processing program. As far as I can tell, I'm nearly up to speed right now, and with a day or two of practice, I'd be right back where I was."

"If Heckly watches you, I don't want him to see anything but an efficient office worker doing her job."

"I type seventy to eighty words a minute flawlessly, and I'm a good speller. I do WordPerfect 5.1, Lotus 1-2-3. I can make cantankerous copying machines work. Hey, I'm the businessman's best friend." She smiled. "Although I prefer businesswomen." Again her eyes found his. "Thank you for keeping my secret," she said.

"Thank you for keeping mine."

"I don't know what prompted me to tell you."

"Sometimes things just seem to come out."

"Yeah," Gunderson said softly, "sometimes they do. Maybe they need to—if you can find the right person to tell."

"I'd like you to meet Cindy this evening."

"What does she know about me?"

"Nothing. Not even your name."

"She doesn't know I'm going to be her new employee?"

"I wanted her to meet you before she decided."

"So this isn't a done deal yet?"

"Not if Cindy says no. I don't think she'll do that, but the final decision has to be hers. Any problem with that?"

"No," she said. "It's the right way to do it. What hours would I work?"

"Nine to five, just like any other employee."

"Do I follow her to work and back?"

"No, Heckly would spot it and know there's a cop in the office. Tuffle and Kozlovski are handling that. I'd do it myself, but I'm supposed to be the guy in charge of the investigation, so I've got to be here."

"Mike," she said, "it just tore me up when you told me what happened in Texas. I . . . well, I couldn't sleep for the next two nights. Every time I closed my eyes, I started imagining it— what happened. If there's anything I can do that will help, you've got it. Anything at all."

"Just be a secretary for a while."

She held up her fingers. "You ready to type, guys?" Shifting her gaze to Cotter, she said, "They're ready."

Twenty-eight

After meeting with Melanie Gunderson, Cotter went back to checking motels, wishing he could be with Cindy, who would get home about six and then be alone in the apartment. All the officers assigned to the Heckly case would be working late tonight—and probably for many nights to come. Cotter's area included the communities of Redwood City, Menlo Park, Atherton, and North Fair Oaks.

"Yeah, I know him," the young Hispanic desk clerk at a motel on Interstate 80 said, studying Heckly's photo.

Little prickles of excitement danced through Cotter's system. "What room's he in?"

"Room?"

"You said you recognized him."

"I do."

"Where is he?

"In Tucson."

"What are you talking about?"

"That's where I know him from. Tucson. I used to live there. Worked for this outfit that pumped out septic tanks. Real shitty job, you might say." He paused, waiting to see whether Cotter got the joke. "Uh, he was my boss. He owned the company."

"When was this?"

"Two years ago."

"Two years ago the guy I'm looking for was in Texas, locked up."

"Oh. Guess it's not the same guy, huh?"

"No."

"Sure looks like him."

It was as close as Cotter came to a lead all evening.

At seven-thirty he headed for Cindy's place. Melanie Gunderson was supposed to meet him there at half past eight. He drove once around the block in which her apartment building was located, just making sure nothing seemed amiss. Nothing did. He spotted the unmarked car across the street, a white Ford with two antennas that proclaimed *I am a cop* to any crook with an IQ that made it into double digits.

On impulse, Cotter reached out for Heckly's presence, trying to sense whether he was nearby. Suddenly Cotter was overwhelmed with the feeling Heckly was there.

It was like being within a few feet of someone in a totally dark room. You could tell the person was there, practically reach out and touch him, even if you could neither see him nor hear him nor smell him.

That's the way it was now. Heckly was here, nearby, right now. Unquestionably. As real as the street or the lampposts or the car Cotter was driving.

Cotter reminded himself not to probe too deeply. Never again did he want to slip into that part of Heckly's mind where the madness lived.

He drove around the block once more, his eyes taking in luxury apartment complexes, signs reminding the less well-off that the underground parking areas were for residents only and that others would be towed at their own expense. Parked at the curb were Infinities and Lexuses, BMWs and Porsches. A Jaguar sedan glided down the ramp into a restricted parking area.

No sign of Heckly.

But he was *here*, his presence so powerful he could be sitting in the car right beside Cotter.

Abruptly Cotter's eyes were drawn to the rearview mirror. Behind him, a green sports car had just emerged from the parking area of an apartment complex partway down the block from Cindy's. Something European and very expensive looking. And suddenly Cotter was absolutely certain that Heckly was driving it. The green car was heading in the opposite direction. It turned the corner and disappeared.

Cotter pulled into the entrance to an underground parking area, jammed on the brakes, shifted into reverse. Tires squealing, the Dodge roared backward. Someone honked angrily. Ignoring the irate driver, Cotter slapped the shift lever to drive and sped toward the end of the block. Cutting sharply in front of a Cadillac, he turned the corner where he'd last seen the green sports car. For a second, he thought he'd lost it, but then he spotted it, two blocks ahead of him.

Grabbing the microphone, Cotter pressed the transmit button and said, "Three-thirty-eight to Control. I'm in pursuit."

Instantly the woman dispatcher said, "All units, ten-three, we have a pursuit. Ten-twenty and direction of travel, three-thirty-eight."

"West on Half Moon from Greco. A green sports model, expensive, a Ferrari or one of those."

"Units to assist?" the dispatcher said.

"Three-thirteen's at San Pedro and Marshall," said an officer.

"Four Adam—from College and Perkins."

"Four Edward's rolling from Amador and Peninsula."

"Three-thirty-eight?" the dispatcher said.

"Still westbound on Half Moon. Be advised that subject Heckly may be in the vehicle."

Cotter was gaining on the green car rapidly. Apparently Heckly wasn't aware of his presence. Did this mean that the psychopath was unaware of the mental link between them? The sports car was no more than half a block ahead now. One occupant. Cotter could make out the silhouette of a head. Heckly's head.

A quarter of a block now.

Several car lengths.

"We sure it's him?" Kozlovski's voice.

"It's him," Cotter answered.

Three car lengths now. Cotter was gripping the wheel so hard his fingers ached. The neighborhood had changed from apartments to upper-middle-class homes. This was not a good place to make the stop. It should be done somewhere as unpopulated as possible.

"Subject doesn't seem to be aware that I'm behind him," Cotter said. "He's just moving at the same speed as the rest of the traffic, about thirty."

One car length.

He was close enough to Heckly to hit him with a stone. Close enough to kill him with a well-placed shot. Close enough to reach him in less than a dozen steps, crush his neck the way he was attempting to crush the steering wheel now.

And he wondered, if he were face-to-face with the monster, what would he do?

"I'm right behind him," Cotter said. He gave the license number.

Suddenly the green car cut to the right, its tires squealing as it passed between two joggers, narrowly missing them both. Its powerful engine roared, and the car was speeding away on a side street.

"North on Prosperity!" Cotter shouted into the microphone. "He's made me!"

"North on Prosperity from Half Moon," the dispatcher said. "Units?"

Officers responded with their locations.

One of the joggers was standing in the middle of the street shouting at the driver of the green car. Cotter had to maneuver around him, losing precious seconds.

The green sports car was already at the end of the block.

"Still northbound on Prosperity," Cotter said over the radio. "I'll never catch him, not with what he's driving."

Over the radio, units gave their locations. The dispatcher tried to move them into position to intercept Heckly.

Although he knew he shouldn't, not in a residential area, Cotter had floored the Dodge. Lawns and driveways and shade trees flew past in a blur. A block and a half ahead now, the sports car turned right.

"East on a cross street," Cotter said. "I've lost sight of him." When he reached the street, Cotter was going so fast he nearly failed to make the turn. He had enough presence of mind to note the street's name and gave it out over the air. Heckly was two and a half blocks ahead of him now.

The sports car turned left.

When Cotter slid through the same intersection, there was no sign of the green car. He gunned the Dodge, scanning every driveway, every alley, every garage, hoping against hope that Heckly had tried to hide somewhere. But it was a stupid notion, for Heckly had the faster car and a sizable lead. He had no reason to try subterfuge. He had already won the contest.

"Lost him," Cotter said over the radio.

There was a flurry of radio traffic, the dispatcher giving Heckly's last known location and direction of travel, the units trying to position themselves so that they might spot him before he made it out of the area.

Suddenly a station wagon backed out of a driveway, right into Cotter's path. He stomped on the brakes, spinning the wheel to the left. His Dodge sped into the opening of a driveway and bounced onto a lawn, mowing down dormant rosebushes. Suddenly a tree was in front of him, which he somehow managed to miss, and then he was back in the street, rolling at a nice, safe twenty miles an hour.

Cotter pulled to the side, made himself let go of the steering wheel. His hands were shaking. He'd been close enough to Heckly to hit him with a rock, and Heckly had gotten away in the super-powerful green car.

The dispatcher said, "The plate comes back to a Justin Seems, 1717 Sutton Place, Tres Cerros. License should be on a 1992 Maserati, green."

"Gotta be a five-oh-three," someone said over the radio, which meant a stolen car.

No kidding, Cotter thought. He rested his head against the steering wheel.

The station wagon pulled up alongside him, the gray-haired woman behind the wheel giving him a lecture he was unable to hear because both her windows and his were rolled up. Her lips moved venomously, her face filled with rage. Just before she drove off she shook her fist at him.

As soon as he calmed down enough to make his mind function properly, he reached out for Heckly, searching, scanning, groping. And finding nothing but silence. It was like turning the dial on a radio when all the stations were off the air.

He vaguely sensed that Heckly was out there. Somewhere. But no longer close.

The radio traffic confirmed what Cotter already knew. Heckly had gotten away.

***

Melanie Gunderson was already there when Cotter arrived at Cindy's apartment. The two women were sitting on the couch, smiling, engrossed in conversation.

"I see you've already met," Cotter said.

"We're already the best of friends," Cindy said.

It was a thing women could do that men usually couldn't, make an instant friendship. Cotter was glad they'd hit it off. It would make things easier.

"I do have a bone to pick with you," Cindy said. "You've been arranging things on your own, without consulting me—in this case without consulting me about the plans for my own protection."

"It was always your option to say no," Cotter said. "I just wanted to present it to you in a package that included the person who'd be working with you."

Cindy gave him a stern look, but it was half-hearted and quickly gave way to a smile. "I guess I can't complain too much. Help with Melanie's skills is hard to come by. I'm going to hate to see her leave."

"And," Cotter said, still defending his actions, "I was worried about your safety."

"Yes," Cindy said, "you were."

"And it turns out that I was right to be worried."

Both women were looking at him intently now. The warm mood had abruptly cooled.

"Heckly was here this evening. Down the block. I pursued him, but my Dodge was no match for his Maserati."

"He was here," Cindy said softly, concern evident in her eyes.

"Coming out of the parking area of that high-rise near the end of the block." He indicated the appropriate direction.

"You make a positive ID?" Gunderson asked. Which was cop talk for, You sure it was him?

"It's not a face I'd forget."

"No," the women agreed.

That would have to be his story, that he'd gotten a good enough look at the driver of the Maserati to be certain it was

Heckly. Later he could tell Cindy the truth, but his psychic link with the madman was a secret he was unwilling to share with anyone else, even Melanie Gunderson.

For a few moments the room was silent except for the sound of nervous breathing as the women digested Cotter's information. Finally Cindy said, "Melanie and I have discovered that we like a lot of the same things."

"Like ballet," Melanie said.

"She took lessons," Cindy said.

"We both wanted to be world-famous ballerinas," Melanie said.

"What went wrong?" Cindy asked.

"The world has a greater need for advertising and law enforcement than it does for dancing," Melanie said.

"No," Cotter said gently. "There's more of a demand for those things, but I think what the world needs is more dancing."

"You're such a romantic," Cindy said.

"Me? Hard-nosed, stalwart, enforcer-of-the-law Mike Cotter?"

The women chuckled, but it was a little too giggly, a little too loud. We're all trying not to think about Heckly, Cotter thought. We're pretending that everything's going to be just fine.

The cordless phone on the arm of the couch rang, and Cindy answered it, listened a moment, then handed it to Cotter.

"This is Colleen in Dispatch. They found the Maserati. It was abandoned beneath an overpass on 101, in a cement-lined storm channel."

"No sign of the driver, I take it."

"No."

"Give me the exact location. I'd better have a look at it."

Colleen told him where to find the car.

"Thanks for letting me know," Cotter said tiredly.

"Oh, one more thing," the dispatcher said. "They only found one thing in the car. A blond wig."

"A wig?"

"Yes, a man's hairpiece."

Cotter told the others what he'd learned.

"A wig?" Gunderson said. "Why do you figure he left it in the car?"

"For us to find," Cotter said. He remembered Rocky L. Hebert, the name—an anagram—Heckly had used when he'd worked as a bellman at the Seaward Hotel. Hebert had been blond.

In a voice filled with both worry and awe, Melanie Gunderson said, "He's telling us he's smarter than we are, that he can disguise himself so we won't recognize him, spy on us at will, and there's nothing we can do."

"Yes," Cotter said.

"He's just another asshole," Cindy snapped, suddenly looking defiant. "Maybe a little smarter, and a lot crazier than the others, but an asshole just the same."

"A very dangerous one," Cotter said.

And then there seemed to be nothing to say. The defiance faded from Cindy's face, proving it had been mostly bravado.

Cotter broke the silence. "I'm going to check with Dispatch to make sure someone's here to watch the place while I'm gone; then I've gotta check out the Maserati. I shouldn't be long."

"I'll stay until you get back," Gunderson said.

"You don't have to do that," Cindy said. But she seemed grateful for the company.

Twenty-nine

"I want Melanie to start tomorrow," Cotter said.

He and Cindy were in bed. Melanie Gunderson was home with Leandra. The Maserati had been towed to the police garage, where lab techs would give it a thorough going-over. An initial inspection had turned up nothing useful.

Cindy said, "I'll have to admit, I'll be more comfortable with her there."

"Melanie's good. She can blend in, and if something sticky should happen, she'll keep her cool, handle it correctly."

"Do . . . do you think something sticky is going to happen?"

"I don't know, but we've got to be prepared."

"This is scary, Mike."

"I know," he said, rolling over and taking her in his arms.

"He could show up in a blond wig and wearing some makeup and we'd never know. He could pretend to be a client. I could be sitting in my office with him—three feet from him, close enough for him to . . . to touch me." She shuddered.

"Melanie knows what to look for."

"A guy with a gimpy arm?"

"That's one thing, yes."

"He can hide that. He was a bellman, for goodness sake, carrying heavy luggage, and no one seemed to notice."

"He didn't really carry it very far. They use carts."

"If anyone rolls a cart into my office, I'll know it's him."

"The people at the Seaward weren't looking for a guy with a bad arm. We will be. It's the one thing he can't disguise. Melanie will watch for anyone who seems to rely on just his right arm. All Heckly can do is try not to call our attention to the arm. He can't hide the problem from someone who's looking for it."

"That's true," Cindy said. She felt small and delicate in his arms, terribly vulnerable.

"I've said all along that you should let us take you somewhere safe until all this is over."

"No," she said flatly. "I may be so scared that I'm constantly on the verge of wetting my pants, but I'll be damned if I'll let this . . . this creepy-crawly that slithered up from wherever he slithered up from run my life."

"I want you to be safe."

"Mike, I've got a business to run. I have to see people, go to meetings, make decisions about the fees we charge and the jobs we accept, which contracts we make a major push for and which are too iffy to be worth the expense. How can I do all that if I'm hiding?"

"Hiding you is the only way I can be sure you'll be okay."

"At night, where would you be?"

"My apartment, I suppose. I'm still paying the rent on the place. I should get some use out of it."

"And I'd be in the hideout, wherever it is."

"Of course."

"Sleeping alone."

"I couldn't stay with you. Heckly would be watching me, hoping I'd lead him to you."

"This is scary enough without sleeping by myself," Cindy said. All traces of the irate citizen who'd called Heckly a creepy-crawly were gone. This was the voice of someone who was afraid and uncertain, trying to figure out how to deal with a bad situation.

"There'd be police officers guarding you."

"Remember what I said about leaning on each other? I want to see you, hold you, know you're okay. I want us to be together, to be there for each other. If I'm in a hideout somewhere without you, I'll feel . . . well, lost."

"Me too," Cotter said. "But it's the only way I can be sure nothing will happen to you."

A few silent moments passed, and she said, "I'll do it if you go with me. That way we'd both be safe, and neither one of us would have to worry."

"You know I can't do that."

"I know," she said softly.

There seemed to be nothing more to say, so they simply lay there, not talking. Cotter thought Cindy had fallen asleep when she said, "I like Melanie Gunderson very much."

"Me too."

"She's very fond of you," Cindy said. "She says you're the only man on the force she can really talk to. Should I be jealous?"

Obviously Melanie Gunderson had not discussed her sexual preferences with Cindy. Cotter said, "You will never have reason to be jealous because of me."

"No," Cindy said after a moment. "I don't think I will."

"I'm loyal, trustworthy, reverent, and brave."

"Yes," Cindy replied, "I think you are."

"Not to mention—"

"You're pushing it, big guy."

They moved into the spoon position, Cindy's back to Cotter, who slipped his arms around her, holding her snugly against him. They fell asleep that way.

"The typical serial killer is a sociopath," the psychologist said. "He doesn't have any feelings of remorse about what he does. If it suits him, he does it. The pain and suffering he may inflict on others are of no concern, except to the extent he may find them enjoyable."

The psychologist's name was M. Covington King, which seemed somewhat snobbish to Cotter. His Stanford office was as cluttered as the room of the messiest child, except that instead of toys the chaos here was caused by books and papers, which were heaped and strewn just about everywhere.

Professor King was the epitome of the tweedy, casual academic. His sports jacket was nubby, his hair somewhat mussed, his unfashionably thin, solid gray tie loose at the neck. A profusion of pens poked from the breast pocket of his shirt. A pipe with a curving stem lay in a glass ashtray on his cluttered desk.

Noticing the direction of Cotter's gaze, the professor said, "I don't smoke it anymore, but I discovered I was used to having it there."

Captain Zinn had set up the appointment with King after learning that the psychologist had recently been involved in a major study of serial killers. Cotter would have preferred someone with experience in parapsychology, but he couldn't tell Zinn that.

"I remember your case quite well," King said. "Unfortunately, we weren't able to include it in the study. Because of budget considerations, we had to limit the number of killers we could examine. The examinations were very extensive. We traveled to various parts of the country and interviewed witnesses, police officers, friends, and families of both the victims and the killers. It took two years to get everything done."

"About Heckly," Cotter said, trying to move the professor along.

"Oh, yes. Uh, as I said, Heckly is a sociopath, a man without the usual conscience, the usual concept of right or wrong. Such people are solely concerned with self-gratification, which is often elusive. But the need for it drives them to do what they do. Heckly's need—not necessarily the only one, but one that's apparent from his behavior—is to feed his huge ego, which can never be fully satisfied. He's going after you because you hurt him, and that can't be allowed. He has to see himself as superior. Now he's showing how much smarter he is than you are, how he can kill at will and no one can stop him."

The professor picked up his pipe, studied it as if he were trying to discern its true meaning, then put it down. "All this goes on because, deep down, the sociopath is awash in suppressed feelings of inadequacy, impotency, insecurity. Because he truly sees himself as powerless, he kills, often in the most gruesome ways, to demonstrate his total control over his victims. He dominates the victim, dehumanizes him, makes him plead for mercy that is never granted. He's playing God, if you will."

"A power trip," Cotter said, struggling to avoid imagining what it must have been like for his wife and son—and the daughter who was forced to watch.

"Yes," the psychologist said. "A power trip."

"And now he has to prove himself superior to me," Cotter said.

"Yes, because of what you did to him in Texas."

"I should have killed him," Cotter muttered.

The psychologist's only response was to frown disapprovingly. He said, "The typical serial killer—any mass murderer, actually—is a white male, an adult, almost always a loner. Often he will have been abused as a child, and he may have abused animals or even other children when he was young."

The psychologist cleared his throat. "Serial killers are often meticulous planners. They may prepare for months, plotting every detail, right down to what the victim should be wearing. Sometimes they'll bring the clothing they envisioned with them and then make the victim put it on. It's not unusual for them to repeatedly rehearse a killing before committing it.

"We call that a rehearsal fantasy. Fantasy can play a major role in the behavior of a serial killer. Often it's sexual and sadistic. The fantasies stretch it out, enable the killer to turn the event into a major production. In some instances, the fantasies can be more satisfying than the actual act, but it's all tied together. Without a real murder to think about and work up to, the fantasies lose their meaning.

"Some serial killers keep souvenirs to help them remember, to relive the experience. These mementos can be rather gruesome, body parts and things like that. I understand one killer of small boys kept his victims' penises in a cigar box.

"Serial killers like to read about themselves—not just their own acts, but also the deeds of their counterparts. Sometimes they'll imitate other serial killers. But then, I suspect you already know most of this."

Cotter nodded. He had yet to learn anything he didn't already know. But then, these things weren't what he had come to talk about.

"You've probably also noticed that there are ways in which Heckly is atypical. For one thing, he was never a loner. He was a lawyer, involved in the community, a member of the city council. And there are no recorded incidents of things like animal abuse in his childhood. No indication that Heckly himself was an abused child."

"What do you make of these discrepancies?"

"For one thing, I don't call them discrepancies. The profile of the typical serial killer is just a compilation of traits that many of them have been found to share. No one claims that all serial killers will have all the traits. It would be rather shocking if they did."

"Do these places where Heckly doesn't fit the mold tell us anything we can use—anything at all?"

"There's one way that Heckly's being unusual is helping you. The typical serial killer is very hard to catch because he murders strangers, people with whom he has no connection. His victims are simply targets of opportunity. Heckly, on the other hand, is here for a purpose."

"Revenge."

"Exactly."

"Against me."

"And everything he does will revolve around you in some manner. The things he does will be part of a plan, not actions prompted strictly by opportunity."

"How can I use this to catch him?"

"That I can't tell you."

"What might he do next?"

The professor considered that. "I think he'll avoid any direct confrontation with you. He doesn't want to kill you. He wants to humiliate you, make you suffer." King hesitated, then said, "If his past actions are any indication, then anyone close to you is in danger. He'll try to make you suffer by harming those you care about."

"As if I haven't suffered enough," Cotter said.

"You haven't suffered enough to satisfy someone with Heckly's ego," the psychologist replied. "He's obsessed with you. He sees destroying you as the only way to prove to himself that he's in control. He has to show that he has the power to crush you. It's become a need, a driving force."

"Lucky me."

The psychologist studied him sadly. "We need much more research into this problem," he said. "What we've learned so far amounts to bits and pieces, a scratching of the surface, if you will. For instance, did you know that a significant percentage of serial killers seem to work in the food industry—often as cooks, bakers, or owners of the business? We have no explanation for that."

"One more thing," Cotter said, and this was what he had come to ask. "Do you have any experience with parapsychology?"

"It's not my field. Does this have anything to do with the matter at hand?"

"It might. I, uh, I realize I'm not here as a patient, but can I ask you to treat it as if I were?"

"You want me to guarantee confidentiality."

"Yes."

King smiled. "All right. You've certainly piqued my curiosity, and I suspect that promising confidentiality is the only way I'm going to find out what this is all about."

Cotter collected his thoughts, then told him about the apparent psychic link with Heckly.

After listening intently to Cotter's story, King said, "You realize you could be imagining this, don't you?"

"I could be, but I'm not."

"This . . . this thing between you and Heckly constantly occupies your thoughts. Heckly is what you're most concerned about. Nothing else comes close. In these circumstances, it would be understandable if your desire to find him led you to believe that you were somehow linked to him psychically."

Cotter rubbed his cheek. "I've thought about that. I'm not dismissing it out of hand. Everything you say makes sense. But what I feel goes beyond what I think I could imagine. I mean, there's a difference, isn't there, between actually doing something in hard, cold reality and just thinking you did? If you look at the situation objectively, with a lot of hard, cold logic, can't you tell when you're just fooling yourself?"

"Not always. Sometimes the fantasies our minds concoct for us seem more real than the truth does."

"Is that what you think is happening to me, that I'm imagining it?"

"I can't say that. It's just a possibility you have to consider. I'd be remiss if I didn't bring it up." He loosened his already slack tie. "On the other hand, we have to realize that these links with Heckly may actually be occurring. There is some evidence that such things happen. And it has certainly never been proved that they don't. When this link occurs, is it one-way, or is he aware of you, too?"

"As far as I can tell, it's one-way, but I can't be positive of that."

"Have you had any what you might think of as paranormal experiences prior to this?"

"No."

"Never sensed when anyone had died, knew an event was going to occur before it did?"

"No."

"No telekinesis or telepathy?"

"No. If I did, I'd just will him to come in and surrender. Or maybe I'd will him to practice the high dive from the Golden Gate Bridge."

"Would you?"

"Will him to kill himself? I don't know. I think I have adequate reason for doing it."

"Yes," King said. "I can see where you'd think that."

"So, can you tell me anything that will help?"

King leaned back in his chair. "About all I can suggest is that you see a colleague of mine here, Dr. Ventana. She's heavily involved in parapsychological research. I doubt she could give you any easy answers, but she could test you to see whether you have any unique talents." He glanced at his watch. "I think she's at a meeting right now, but you could call her for an appointment."

Cotter said he'd do that.

"How much faith do you put in these feelings of linkage?" King asked.

"I think they're real. I never saw the face of the person who was driving the Maserati. I'm positive of that. But the lab found Heckly's prints in it. Definite match."

"If you're going to use these links, I'd recommend you look at them as just another source of data, no more reliable than any other."

"That makes sense."

"And I guess I only have one more piece of advice for you. Never allow yourself to think of Heckly as a raving maniac. Serial killers are among the most controlled people you'll ever meet. They rarely lose touch with reality. They're highly organized, and they plan carefully. They make very dangerous adversaries."

"I know that better than anyone," Cotter said, rising.

"One more thing. I described them as being basically insecure. That's not the way they behave outwardly. They may not even be aware of the things that seethe in their unconscious minds. Outwardly they are often convinced that they're special, that they're even invincible. While this may not be the underlying driving force, it is the operative one. It may be possible for you to use this against him at some point."

"May I give you a call if I need some spur-of-the-moment advice?"

"Of course. I'd be delighted to help in any way I can."

Cotter thanked the professor for his help. As he was leaving King's office, the psychologist said, "If you get the chance, set up something with Dr. Ventana."

"First chance I get," Cotter promised.

He rounded a corner of the hallway, and directly in front of him was a wall plaque that said EMILIA VENTANA, DEPARTMENT OF PSYCHOLOGY. Next to it was an open door, through which Cotter could see an attractive dark-haired woman at a desk. She looked up, and their eyes met.

"Are you looking for anyone in particular?" she asked.

"Are you Dr. Ventana?"

"That's me. What can I do for you?"

Cotter stepped into her office. The psychologist had thick shoulder-length hair. Like her eyes, it was a shade of brown so dark as to be almost black, and it contrasted sharply with her fair skin. Unlike Dr. King's office, hers was fastidiously neat;

the only paper on the desk was the single sheet she had been examining before Cotter distracted her.

"Dr. King referred me to you," he said. "But he didn't think you'd be in. He said you were at a meeting."

"Faculty representative to the Academic Advisory Committee," she said. "It was canceled—thank goodness. You can't believe how boring the meetings are." She tilted her head slightly. "I didn't think Dr. King was doing any clinical work right now."

"I'm not a patient; I'm a police officer. I, uh, I put some questions to Dr. King, and he said you'd be the one to answer them for me."

"What questions?"

He told her, and she said, "Have you ever been tested for ESP?"

"No."

"I'd like to test you. Could you arrange for some free time next week?"

"I don't have much free time at the moment. Couldn't we do something now, while I'm here?"

She frowned. "Maybe a preliminary test."

"Let's do it."

She asked him the same questions Dr. King had, and he gave the same answers.

"All right," she said. Reaching into her desk, she produced a box from which she removed a deck of cards. "These are Zener cards. There are twenty-five of them, and they have five different symbols." She held up a star, a circle, a plus sign, a square, and three wavy lines.

"Come with me," she said, and he followed her to an office two doors down. The plaque on the wall read ZACHARY TITUS, DEPARTMENT OF PSYCHOLOGY. Dr. Ventana unlocked the door and let him in.

"Professor Titus won't mind if we use his office. Sit down at the desk, and when the phone rings, it will be me."

She closed the door and left. A moment later the phone rang.

"All right," she said, "now here's what we're going to do. I've got the Zener cards in front of me. I'll say 'now' every time I turn one of them over, and then I'll concentrate on it. I want you to name the card I'm thinking of. Got it?"

"Yes."

"All right, I'm shuffling the cards."

While he listened to the *zip-slap-flutter* of cards being shuffled, Cotter looked around the office. He was sitting at a nondescript wooden desk. The room seemed to occupy the middle ground between King's sloppiness and Ventana's neatness: a few papers and books piled here and there, but nothing that couldn't be straightened up in a few minutes.

"You ready?" the psychologist asked.

"I'm ready."

"Now."

Cotter concentrated. Images of the five cards floating through his brain, but none seemed any more significant than the other. Knowing he had to say something, he said, "Wavy lines."

"Now."

Again he tried to open his mind to Dr. Ventana's signals. All five of the card faces seemed to bob in his mind, gently rising and falling, slowly turning, converging, then separating in a gently undulating dance. Suddenly one of the symbols seemed larger, more distinct than the others. Swelling. Dominating the scene like the big *E* on an eye chart.

"Circle," he said.

"Now."

It occurred to him that he might be trying too hard, so he made himself relax, tried to let the telepathic message come to him.

"Star, " he said.

And it went on. Although he made no attempt to count, he was sure they'd gone through the deck several times before the psychologist said, "We're done. Come on back to my office, and I'll add up your score."

When he got there, the door was open, and Dr. Ventana was sitting at her desk, pushing the buttons on a pocket calculator.

"Sit down," she said without looking up.

He sat.

After a moment, she slipped the calculator into her desk and studied him appraisingly.

"We went through the deck four times," she said. "By chance, you should have made twenty correct responses, or an average of five for each run through the deck. That's how we state the result, based on the number of correct responses for twenty-five cards—no matter how many times we actually run through the deck. As few as seven or eight correct responses is considered statistically significant. You had nine."

"Does this mean I have ESP?"

"It means further testing is called for. I'd really like to get you into the lab, do some controlled experiments."

"I don't have time for controlled experiments."

"What we did today was barely better than fun and games. It shows that further study is indicated, but by itself it doesn't mean that much."

"Do you think I have ESP?"

"I don't know. Come in next week, and we'll find out."

"Will it help me catch a serial murderer?"

She sighed. "I'm tempted to say yes, just to get you in here for some thorough testing, but an honest answer is that I doubt it."

"Then it'll have to wait."

She nodded, resigned. "After your investigation is over, will you come in then?"

"Yes. I want to understand what's happening."

"Please don't forget." Her eyes dropped to the notes from which she'd been entering the numbers into her calculator.

Cotter said, "If I do have this link with the killer, is there anything I should know, anything that will help me deal with him?"

Still looking at the numbers, she thought it over, then shook her head. "Telepathy exists. I'm sure of that. I have a small ability as a sender—which is what I was doing with you, sending. But only you can decide how to use this link, because only you can experience it."

"Could it be two-way, him going into my head at the same time I go into his?"

"Does it seem that way to you?"

"No."

"Then it probably isn't." She held up her hand. "Let's not speculate. Let's test. In the laboratory. Under controlled conditions."

"After this is over," Cotter promised. He stood up. "Thank you for your trouble."

"Wait," she said. With a pencil, she began furiously marking the sheet of paper she'd been studying. She looked up at him, her expression full of puzzlement.

"I don't believe this," she said.

She yanked open a drawer and grabbed her calculator, punched a few keys, frowned.

"What's going on?" Cotter asked.

She was studying him intently, almost warily.

"What did I do?" Cotter asked.

"If you take out the circle, you made the chance score. But if we look at circles alone, you were correct on ninety percent of them."

"What does that mean?"

The psychologist stared at him. "I have no idea."

Before letting him leave, Professor Ventana made him promise again that he'd come back as soon as the murder investigation was over. As he was turning to go, his beeper went off. "May I use your phone?"

The psychologist nodded, politely stepping out of the office so he could have some privacy.

Cotter called Dispatch and identified himself.

"Officer Vickers wants you at The Best Motel on the Interstate—"

"The what?"

"That's the name of it, The Best Motel on the Interstate. It's on 101, about ten miles north of here. Vickers said to tell you that the manager has identified the subject from the photograph."

"I'm on my way."

Thirty

Melanie Gunderson had temporarily taken over one of the two desks in an office located to the left of the reception area as one entered the business. Through the open door she could see the receptionist, Dominique Long, a petite brunette with a dazzling smile who could probably nudge a scale to a hundred pounds only by wearing a heavy winter coat. The reception area was separated from the main seventh-floor hallway by glass, allowing Melanie to see people stepping off the elevator, as well as anyone entering the office.

The desk on the other side of the room belonged to Tyleen Windley, a tall, sleek black woman who was the firm's media buyer. As far as Melanie could tell, Tyleen was usually on the phone to people at magazines and TV networks or out dealing face-to-face with people in the Bay Area media. At the moment she was out.

The ad agency's employees had been told the truth—although not quite all of it. The official explanation of her unannounced arrival was that she was a police officer on official business and that her presence should not worry anyone at the agency. No one was suspected of any wrongdoing or anything like that. Cindy had personally asked everyone to keep Melanie's presence confidential, not to mention it to anyone outside the office.

Melanie got lots of curious stares as people passed the office, but no one spoke to her. They seemed leery of her, which under the circumstances was understandable, she supposed.

Melanie had never been inside an advertising agency before. This one seemed to employ mainly women, presumably because it was owned by a woman. The walls were a pinkish gray, which seemed to suggest that while this was a conservative place of business it was also up-to-date and unafraid of trying new approaches.

Melanie's eyes shifted from the reception area to her computer screen. She was typing letters for Cindy so she would seem busy to anyone spotting her—and so she would have something to do to pass the time. This one was to a client who hadn't paid his bill. It was the gentle approach, just a polite reminder. Presumably, sterner letters would follow if the payment wasn't received. It surprised Melanie that the letter was to a well-known regional chain of upscale women's boutiques. You didn't expect places like that to be deadbeats.

"I'm back," Tyleen said as she glided into the office, filling the room with the subtle scent of expensive perfume. She wore a slinky green outfit that made Melanie feel terribly unsophisticated in her blue polyester suit.

"How long you going to be with us?" Tyleen asked as she sat down at her desk.

"Don't know for sure," Melanie replied. "I, uh, I hope you don't mind my using your office."

"Hey, no problem. That desk was just sitting there. Someone might as well get some use out of it. How long you been a cop?"

"Ten years."

"Like it?"

"Usually."

"If you get tired of it, don't go into advertising. It's sort of like being in a beauty contest. You smile all the time. Even when the people you're dealing with are total assholes. You keep that damned smile pasted on until it hurts, until you think you'll have to chisel the damn thing off at the end of the day."

"Being a cop's really not that much different," Melanie said. "During the course of the day I'll say 'yes sir' and 'no sir' to any number of people I'd just as soon punch."

"What I get tired of—really tired of—is the creeps who suggest that we can put together one hell of a deal if only I'd have sex with them."

"Met a few of those myself," Melanie said. "Guys think they

can get out of a traffic ticket by laying on the charm. Just know they're irresistible."

Before Tyleen could respond, her phone rang and she was instantly engaged in conversation. Glancing at Melanie, she used a finger to push her lips into a silly fixed grin. Her smile firmly in place, Tyleen said, "Lunch Tuesday? Sure, Roj, I'd be delighted. Where'd you like to go?"

Suddenly Melanie's attention was drawn to the man in a dark raincoat who had just stepped off the elevator. Carrying an umbrella and wearing a bowler hat, he looked like John Steed. But whereas Steed was the consummate English gentleman, this guy was suspicious. Melanie watched him, uncertain what about the man made her uneasy.

He was standing with his back to her, studying the list of offices on the seventh floor. Melanie waited for him to turn, so she could get a better look at his face. Slowly, almost reluctantly it seemed, he moved away from the glass-encased list, exposing his profile.

It was not Robert Heckly's face.

This man was more square-faced and darker-haired; he was older, and there was no dimple on his chin. She mentally added makeup to the photographs of Heckly, filled in the dimple, concluding that the transformation, though difficult, was possible.

The man paused, seemed to be studying the name of the advertising agency, and then his eyes made an inconspicuous but careful study of the office.

He was holding the umbrella in his right hand.

His left had not moved.

Tyleen was still on the phone, talking about thirty-second spots. Her words faded into the background, becoming a dull buzz.

The man turned, walked to the entrance to the stairs, glanced around to see who might be watching, then opened the door and stepped into the stairwell.

Melanie reached for the phone, then hesitated. How long would it take the San Francisco police to get here? And what was she going to tell them, that there was a guy who looked like John Steed who was using the stairs instead of the elevator?

Melanie made her decision. Instantly she was on her feet and out the door, stepping into the stairwell, her fingers slipping under her jacket and resting on the butt of her nine-millimeter automatic.

Pausing, she heard footfalls above her. She started upward, moving as silently as possible.

As she rounded the turn between the seventh and eighth floors, she looked upward, seeing nothing. She increased her speed, moving past the door to the eighth floor. She kept climbing, and after a few moments, she was breathing heavily. By the time she was midway between the ninth and tenth floors, she had to stop and rest. And she realized that she would have to have caught up with the man by now if he was still in the stairwell. Which meant he was either on the eighth or ninth floor.

Below her a door opened. The man with the bowler stepped into the stairwell, looked up at her, and started toward her.

"Excuse me, miss," he said, "but I seem to be lost. Do you think you could help me?" Using his right hand, he unbuttoned the top button of his raincoat.

Melanie watched him, transfixed, her fear-numbed brain refusing to function.

The Best Motel on the Interstate was not on the interstate. It was half a mile from the highway, at the edge of a nondescript San Francisco bedroom community. The place wasn't much to look at, an L-shaped one-story structure with peeling paint. The sign out front proclaimed "low rates."

Tuffle met Cotter out front. "Koz is on the way," he said. "Vickers is watching the back, and I've asked for backup from the locals and the highway patrol. They've been told it's a silent approach situation and that they should keep marked units out of sight."

Cotter nodded his approval. "Tell me about Heckly."

"It was the name that tipped Vickers off," Tuffle said. "H. Lee

Roberts. He showed the manager Heckly's photo, and she made a positive ID. He's in room three."

"Is he there now?" He wasn't. Cotter could feel it. Heckly was long gone.

"Manager didn't know for sure," Tuffle replied. "Phoning his room's not an option. This is cut-rate accommodations. No phones."

"How many of the other rooms are occupied?"

"None, according to the manager. She says she doesn't have any kitchenettes or anything like that, so most of her customers are just for one night, and they've all gone. She says Heckly is the first weekly-paying guest she'd had in nearly a year."

Cotter tried to establish the mental link with Heckly. Nothing happened. For just an instant, he thought he felt Heckly's presence, but then there was nothing, no indication of whether the madman was near or far — or even that he existed at all.

It was just like last time. Kozlovski arrived, followed by Captain Zinn. They met with state troopers and sheriff's officers and decided how to go about it. They concluded the sheriff's SWAT guys should go in with everyone else standing by to provide cover.

A sheriff's captain used the bullhorn to inform Heckly that he was surrounded and that he had no choice but to surrender. When that got no response from room three, tear gas was fired through the window. Heavily armed cops watched intently, ready to do whatever they had to do.

They were wasting their time. Cotter knew it with all the certainty he knew the sun would set. Heckly might be sitting in a bar half a block away, laughing his ass off, but he wasn't in that room.

Donning their gas masks, four cops dressed in traditional SWAT team black moved in a crouch to the door. One of them used the keys the manager had provided, the door swung open, and ninjas swarmed inside.

A moment later the SWAT team leader emerged. Removing his gas mask, he said, "Suspect's gone."

Cotter gave a barely perceptible nod, directed at himself.

"But there's a body inside," the SWAT guy added.

***

When the tear gas had been cleared out of the room, Cotter and some of the other cops entered it. The corpse was on the bed, a dark-haired woman wearing jeans and a Western shirt. She was on her back, arms angled away from her torso as if she'd been making an angel in the snow. There was no blood, no indication of mutilation. Her head was turned to the side, making her face visible.

The dead woman was the only thing in the room that didn't belong there.

One of the sheriff's men said, "I know her. Her name's Georgette or Paulette or something like that. She hangs out over at the Shootin' Iron on Syler Road. It's a stomper joint—you know, a cowboy bar."

"Where all the ranch hands hang out," Kozlovski said.

The deputy, a young blond guy, looked at him funny but didn't say anything.

The case belonged to the sheriff's officers, so people from other jurisdictions, including Cotter, had to stay in the background and let them handle it. A plain-clothes sergeant named Muller took charge.

The medical examiner arrived, a tired-looking woman introduced as Dr. Abigail Stapleton. She rolled the corpse over and said, "Strangulation. Look at the neck."

"He usually uses a knife," Cotter said.

"No sign of it yet," replied the ME. "Let's see what's under her clothes."

One of the deputies raised the body into a sitting position, and the doctor removed the Western shirt. Georgette or Paulette was small-breasted and hadn't worn a bra.

"Help me with her pants," Dr. Stapleton said.

Again the deputy obliged, and the dead woman's tight-fitting jeans were pulled off. Still no signs of knife work. The ME pulled down the victim's panties.

The dead woman's pubic hair had been shaved, presumably with an electric clipper. The hair was a uniform quarter inch in length except for a small portion that had been shaved away completely, forming a shape.

The letter *C*.

"What the hell," one of the deputies said.

The last time Heckly had used the letter it had stood for "cheat." But Cotter felt this *C* meant something else, although he didn't know what.

"Cunt?" one of the cops said.

"It's in the right place," said another, who immediately flinched, glanced at Dr. Stapleton, and blushed. As if a woman who cut up corpses for a living had never heard the slang terms for vagina.

"Sorry, ma'am," the deputy said. "My mother didn't raise me to talk that way in front of a woman."

Dr. Stapleton looked at him as if he were something puzzling she'd just discovered during an autopsy.

After the body was removed, the lab crew from the sheriff's office went back into the room to remove the sheets from the bed. The bedding would be taken to the lab for analysis, then held as evidence. Cotter, Vickers, Kozlovski, Tuffle, and Captain Zinn gathered outside room three to compare notes.

"I've talked to the undersheriff," Zinn said. "We've agreed to let each other know right away if anything significant breaks." He pulled out a small notebook. "They've learned that the victim's name is Jeanette Leyland. She's divorced and has a three-year-old daughter, who was staying with a woman who sometimes takes care of her. Preliminary estimate puts the time of death at about twelve hours ago. Uh, let's see . . . Leyland was a shipping clerk at a electrical parts warehouse in San Francisco. Apparently she often went to a local bar called the Shootin' Iron, where she picked up men."

"She picked up the wrong one this time," Vickers said. He was a pale young man with black hair, a sharply pointed nose, and the calculating look Cotter associated with car salesmen and crooked accountants. Temporarily in plain clothes, he was wearing a trenchcoat and a fedora. He looked like a character from a George Raft movie.

Tuffle was shaking his head. "This guy is having fun with us. He kills people just to leave us messages. Then we find the bodies just when he wants us to."

"And he uses a thinly disguised alias, just to make sure we get the message," Kozlovski said.

"He's making us look like dorks," Tuffle said.

"We'll get the bastard," Kozlovski said, but his eyes were full of doubt. The troops were becoming demoralized.

Cotter said, "All this is high-risk for Heckly. He's taking a lot of chances. When someone does that, it's only a matter of time before he screws up." Words to give hope, build morale. Cotter wondered whether he believed any of them.

Vickers said, "We'll get the scumbag."

Scumbag? Cotter thought. Somehow it didn't seem to fit. The term made sense applied to some career armed robber/drug addict who'd murder someone for pocket change. But Heckly was in another class entirely. You had your once-in-a-hundred-years flood. Heckly was the once-in-a-hundred-years criminal.

"We're starting to believe Heckly's own hype," Cotter said. "He's a smart scumbag, one with a crazy plan. But he's still a scumbag."

"Amen," Vickers said.

"Let's get back to checking motels," Cotter said. "I want every place he could possibly stay to have his picture, and I want the people working at those places to know we are extremely anxious to hear from them if he shows up."

Before they had a chance to move, one of the local officers emerged from room three and said, "There's something here you'd better see."

The Tres Cerros officers crowded into the room. The mattress had been removed from the bed, exposing the box springs—on which had been left a message in spray paint, like street gang graffiti on a wall. The large red letters said:

C IS FOR CINDY

Thirty-one

Still unnerved by what had happened, Melanie Gunderson sat in Cindy's office, shaking her head. "A flasher," she said. "A goddamned flasher."

"Anyone would have been scared if they thought they were face-to-face with Heckly in a stairwell," Cindy said.

"I damn near shot him," Gunderson said. "He was nothing but a weenie waver, and I very nearly blew him away."

She recalled how the man had begun unbuttoning his raincoat, how the gun was suddenly in her shaking hand, her finger applying pressure to the trigger.

"He had the top button buttoned and the belt loosely tied at the waist," she said. "He undid those two things and flashed me. All he had on underneath was the bottom part of his pants legs, held there by some kind of suspenders or garters or whatever. Beyond that he was naked as a jaybird."

"Unbelievable," Cindy said. She was sitting at her desk. Melanie was in a plush visitor's chair.

Gunderson said, "The cop who came to collect him said the guy does this all the time, going around wearing nothing but an overcoat, a bowler hat, and the bottom two feet of his pants legs. One time at Fisherman's Wharf he flashed a whole troop of Girl Scouts from Sacramento."

"Sick," Cindy said.

"But not as sick as Heckly. I've handled lots of flashers. Basically, it's no big deal. But when I thought this guy was Heckly, when I remembered what he did to Cotter's family . . . well, I might as well say it, I freaked, I panicked."

"I don't blame you."

"But I'm supposed to be a professional. I'm supposed to know better."

"You handled it just fine."

"Then how come I'm sitting here shaking?"

"Because you had a harrowing experience."

"For a second I froze, stood there as rigid as a marble statue. Then I snapped out of it and damn near killed a guy for waving his weenie at me."

"This whole business has us on edge. I'm jumping at shadows, too."

Melanie Gunderson sighed. "If you'd like to have someone else on this job, someone more reliable, I'll understand."

"I like having you."

"But—"

"No buts, I'll keep you."

"Thanks," Gunderson said. "Now all I have to do is face Cotter."

"Mike has complete confidence in you."

"After today, he—"

". . . Will *still* have complete confidence in you—trust me."

There was a light rap on the closed office door; then, before Cindy could respond, it opened and Cotter hurried in.

"I need to talk to you right away," he said to Cindy.

"Excuse me," Gunderson said, rising, "I'll get back to my desk."

"No, no," Cotter said. "Stay. This concerns you, too."

"Mike," Cindy said, "something's happened, hasn't it?"

For a moment he just stood there, studying her, his eyes full of concern. Finally he said, "Thank goodness you're all right. This whole thing's bad enough, but if I lost you . . ."

"What happened?" Cindy asked, suddenly very rigid in her chair.

He told her about the latest message from Heckly.

Although the office was comfortable, Cindy shuddered, then wrapped her arms around herself as if trying to keep warm.

"You've got to let us take you somewhere safe," Cotter said.

"But . . . I don't know what to do, Mike. I really don't. If I go into hiding, I'm walking away from my life—from you, from my business, from everything—but I'll have admit, I'm scared to death. I mean, this lunatic has used my name. He plans to hurt me. He's put it in writing."

"There might be a way you could still run the business," Cotter said.

"Could I be face-to-face with people?"

"No, of course not. But you could talk to them over a secure phone. And a lot of the paperwork could be faxed."

"Mike, it's not the same. Sometimes you have to meet the people you deal with."

"We're talking about your life," Melanie Gunderson said softly.

"Yes, but . . ." She shook her head. "The business isn't worth dying for, is it?" She glanced at Gunderson, then shifted her gaze to Cotter. "I'll be alone."

"Not alone," Cotter said. "You'll have police officers with you twenty-four hours a day."

"No leaning on each other."

"I'll call you every evening."

"We can tell the clients you're sick," Gunderson said. "The flu or something."

Cindy nodded. "Give me a day or two to get things organized."

Cotter would have preferred to take Cindy away that instant, but he didn't want to push her too hard. Not many people were in a position to simply drop everything and walk away from their lives. Arrangements had to be made, affairs put in order. She had agreed to go into hiding; that was the main thing.

"I could be holed up somewhere forever," Cindy said miserably. "There's no guarantee Heckly will be caught anytime soon. It could be weeks, months, even years." She looked at her watch. "Oh, my God. I've got to go. I'm late for a meeting with a client."

"I'll go with you," Cotter said.

"Mike, I'll be tied up all afternoon. Can you stay away that long?"

Cotter hesitated, clearly reluctant to let her out of his sight. "No," he admitted. "I can't. I have to get back."

"Can you use a personal secretary at this meeting?" Gunderson asked.

"Yes," Cindy said, plainly relieved. "I think taking along my new secretary would be an excellent idea."

When she and Cindy Brekke left a few moments later, Melanie Gunderson found she was seeing Heckly everywhere she looked. A guy was working on the soft drink machine at the end of the hall. She watched him as they waited for the elevator. He was

242

about twenty, with curly red hair, and much heavier than Heckly, but she watched him anyway, waiting for him to use his left hand. He was on his knees, reaching into the machine's works with his right hand, not using the left. When the elevator arrived he still hadn't used it, but then she had discovered that people often didn't use their left hands while she was watching them.

The elevator arrived and the two women stepped aboard. The man fixing the soft drink machine glanced over his shoulder at them, made momentary eye contact, then looked away.

Inside the elevator were a man and a woman, both dressed expensively. The man was about sixty, gray-haired, blue-eyed, and square-jawed. Cindy recognized him, and they exchanged greetings. He got off on the third floor, and two other men got on. They were in their thirties and didn't look anything like Heckly either. Even so, Melanie watched them warily, paying special attention to each one's left arm.

She and Cindy took the elevator to the underground parking area. A man was sweeping the concrete floor with a large push broom. He was an elderly Hispanic with curly salt-and-pepper hair. Even Heckly couldn't disguise himself that well, Gunderson decided. And he was sweeping with both hands. The man paid no attention to the two women as they headed for the silver Mercedes two rows over.

Melanie shifted her attention from the janitor to the two men approaching from the left. They looked harmless enough, middle-aged guys in business suits, one carrying a briefcase, the other a large manila envelope. The one with the briefcase glanced at Cindy as they passed, but the look he gave her was lascivious, not murderous, his eyes sliding down her body and lingering on her legs. Melanie Gunderson got looks like that herself from time to time—usually from male cops unaware of her sexual preferences—but she was hardly in Cindy Brekke's league. Melanie supposed she could look in the mirror and find cute; Cindy, on the other hand, was centerfold material.

She allowed herself a surreptitious glance at Cindy's sleek, slender form, let her eyes travel down to the well-turned ankles, then stopped herself. She thought, *I'm just looking, Leandra, okay? Nothing to get jealous about.*

When they were in the Mercedes with the doors locked, both

243

women let out a sigh of relief.

Robert Heckly watched as the silver Mercedes backed out of its assigned parking space, glided along the row of parked cars, rolled up the exit ramp, and disappeared into the city. He pushed the dirt he'd been sweeping up into a corner, his right arm doing the actual work while his left hand rested uselessly on the broom handle. It created the illusion of an able-bodied man sweeping the floor. He had learned how to manipulate people's perceptions back in New Jersey, at the Issington Community Theater. He had at one time been on its board of directors, and he had also been a volunteer actor, makeup artist, and set designer. Leaning the broom against the wall, he headed for the elevator.

He got off on the seventh floor. A man was repairing the soft-drink machine. He seemed totally preoccupied, unaware of passersby. Heckly paused in front of the office of Brekke and Associates, looking in through the glass entrance. He saw the receptionist, a small woman with jet-black hair. Someone was talking to her, a tall, attractive black woman wearing an eye-catching green dress. The two were smiling and laughing, unaware that they were being watched.

"Help you with something?"

Heckly turned to find a policeman eyeing him suspiciously. "I'm looking for a lawyer," he said with a heavy Hispanic accent.

"This is an advertising agency."

"I don' need no advertising. I need a lawyer."

"There's no attorneys on this floor."

"Which floor are the lawyers on?"

"Which lawyers you looking for?" The cop was in his mid-twenties, a linebacker-type with hard eyes, who constantly fingered his baton as if he could hardly wait to crack a few skulls.

"Don' know. I represent the tenants. We're going to fight the landlord. He don' ever fix nothing."

"The lawyers here don't do that kind of stuff," the cop said.

"No? Why not?"

"These are big-time lawyers. They'll charge you hundreds of dollars an hour."

"We don' got that much."

"Try Legal Aid."

"Where's that?"

"I don't know. You'll have to look it up."

Heckly let the cop steer him onto the elevator. As the car descended, he considered what he had discovered. The cop he'd just encountered hadn't been around the last time he'd inspected the seventh floor, which meant the cop probably just checked in from time to time.

The woman who'd left with Cindy Brekke a few moments ago was also a cop. He could tell by the way she stuck close, protectively, her eyes taking in everything in the vicinity. He'd noticed the way men eyed Brekke, and he'd seen the woman cop look at her the same way. But then, this was San Francisco. What did one expect?

He took the elevator to the parking area. As he stepped out of the car, he was whistling softly to himself.

"I'm sorry," Cotter said. "If it wasn't for me, you wouldn't be in this situation."

"You didn't create Heckly," Cindy replied. "Somehow, in some way we'll probably never understand, his brain got put together wrong. No one can blame you for that. You're the victim in all this, and I'm getting tired of people trying to blame the victims all the time."

They were eating at Cindy's kitchen table. Cotter had made a low-calorie version of chicken paprika. It was a good recipe, but they were consuming it with all the enthusiasm of children being forced to eat their brussels sprouts.

"I felt sorry for Melanie today."

"She shouldn't have followed him into the stairwell. Thank goodness she didn't shoot the flasher."

"Don't be too hard on her," Cindy said.

"If it had been Heckly, she'd probably be dead right now, with a letter on her corpse — '*D* is for dead cop.'"

"What would you have done differently?"

"Given the circumstances, the need to make an instant decision, I don't know."

"So you might have done exactly what she did?"

"I might."

"So cut her some slack."

"Cindy, I'm not mad at her. I'm worried about her. I put her in that situation because I thought she was the best person for the job—and I still do. She took the assignment because I wanted her to, and because she's a friend. That sort of makes me responsible for what happens to her."

"It gives you someone else to worry about—besides me."

"Yes."

"You can't be responsible for the whole world."

"But this is Heckly, and if—"

"You're not responsible for Heckly."

"—I hadn't broken his arm—"

"You were fighting for your life."

"—none of the other things that have happened would have occurred."

"Bullshit."

Cotter worked up a smile, hoped it was at least partially genuine. "I love it when you say bullshit."

"Bullshit."

"Thank you."

Cindy laughed, shaking her head. "How can you clown around when there's a diabolical lunatic out there who wants to kill us?"

"Can you think of a better time?"

"No, I guess not."

They picked at their food in silence.

Noodles and green peas accompanied the chicken paprika. Studying her plate, Cindy said, "What's the origin of this dish?"

"The chicken paprika? It's Hungarian."

She looked up. "Just think, Eva Gabor may have eaten this same meal in her native country."

"I suppose that's possible," Cotter said.

"Actual Hungarians could be dining on this very same dish."

"As we speak?" Cotter said.

"As we speak."

"Well, there's the time difference. It's the wee hours of the morning there."

"Maybe some Hungarians are late eaters."

"I've checked with the phone company," Cotter said, steering the conversation back to the matter at hand. "They can have the phone and fax lines installed and ready to go tomorrow morning."

"Mike . . ."

"What?"

"Tell me this is going to work and that everything will be all right." Her eyes were filling with fear and uncertainty.

"You'll be fine. I think we can even arrange to have you get together with your clients, if it's absolutely necessary."

"How?"

"You'll meet them somewhere. Not the office. A restaurant, maybe. We'll check the place out to make sure it's safe, then drive you there, making sure you're not being followed. Same thing on the way back. We'll be careful, make sure you're not tailed."

"That might work," Cindy said.

"At the hideaway, you'll have phone and fax, and twenty-four-hour protection."

"I guess I really wouldn't be out of touch."

"No."

She shivered. "I'm starting to look at every strange man I encounter as if he were a murderous madman. I jump at small noises. I'm not that much use at the agency when I'm like this anyway."

"You'll be well hidden and guarded."

"And if Heckly is still out there a month from now? Or several months from now? What then? How long do I hide? How long will the city of Tres Cerros provide me with police protection?"

"I don't know," Cotter said. "All I can tell you is that this is what I think we should do right now."

"Then we wait and see?"

"Then we wait and see."

Cindy sighed. "I'm going to miss you, big guy."

"I won't be far away."

Thirty-two

In the morning, Cindy said that she needed to spend at least half a day at the office to clear up a few details and to explain in person to her staff why she was going into hiding. After that, she'd be ready. Cotter sent Kozlovski, Tuffle, and Gunderson with her and told them to stay with her until it was time to move her to the safehouse.

Captain Zinn arranged for him to keep Gunderson and the three officers on loan from the patrol division. With Kozlovski and Tuffle, that gave him six people to do what had to be done—seven, if he included himself. They were going to be working some very long hours, and the officers would be spending a lot of time away from home, especially Gunderson.

"I hope you know what I went through to get these," Captain Zinn said, stepping into Cotter's cubicle. He lay what looked like three hand-held transmitter-receivers on the desk.

"No gaps in the frequency coverage?" Cotter asked, studying one of them. It had one of those weird, stubby rubber antennas protruding from the top.

"No. It'll register a signal on any radio frequency in the spectrum, and give you a readout on it."

The devices would enable them to check their cars for the presence of transmitters that sent out a homing signal. Heckly was smart enough to think of it, and Cotter intended to be prepared. The idea was to think of anything Heckly might come up with and counter it before hand. For Cotter, it was going to be a nerve-wracking contest, because Cindy's life depended on how well he performed.

"I heard from the sheriff's office," Cotter said. "They found several witnesses who saw Jeannette Leyland leave with Heckly.

Half a dozen positive IDs of Heckly's photo. Also, Heckly's prints were all over the motel room."

"We already knew it was him," Zinn said. "I don't suppose they got anything new."

"Only what Heckly intended them to get."

Zinn sighed. "As usual."

It was two in the afternoon before Cindy was ready for the journey to her hideaway. Cotter joined Kozlovski, Tuffle, and Gunderson in Cindy's private office. The three police officers were looking bored and somewhat restless.

"Mike," Cindy said. "I'm sorry to keep everybody waiting, but there's so much to do, so much that only I can handle."

"Who are you putting in charge?" Cotter asked.

"Tyleen. And that's a little bit of a problem, because she's technically junior to some of the others. The thing is, she's got the best head on her shoulders. She's the most organized, the one who would make the best leader. It's just that there are so many sensitive egos in this business."

"If she's a good leader, she won't antagonize anybody."

"But these are advertising people. They're—"

"They're going to get along without you for a while."

Cindy drew in a deep breath and nodded.

"Are you ready to go?"

"Let me tell Tyleen one final thing." Giving him an apologetic look, she dashed from the room. Gunderson, who wasn't letting Cindy out of her sight, followed her.

Cindy returned a few moments later, proclaiming she was ready. "I'll have to go by my apartment for some things," she said.

"Give us a list," Cotter said. "I don't want you going back there."

Cindy looked as though she was about to protest, but she apparently thought better of it and nodded. "Let's go," she said.

Cindy took her own car, and the police officers followed in three others. Before leaving, Cotter checked all the vehicles for homing devices; all were clean.

They followed a prearranged route that involved abruptly doubling back a number of times. The three police cars took turns dropping back to make absolutely sure no one was following them.

What would normally have been a forty-five-minute trip took over two hours. But when they arrived at their destination, they were satisfied that no one had followed them.

Cindy's new home was a four-story apartment building in Tres Cerros. Built in the fifties, it was white with a Spanish tile roof—a real one, with thick red ceramic tiles that probably weighed a ton. A number of identical buildings were scattered around the city, all built by the same contractor at about the same time. A couple had been converted into condos, but most were still renting to people in the middle income bracket.

The one problem Cotter saw with it was that there were others around, people who could be endangered if Heckly somehow discovered where Cindy was hiding. But then, this was what they'd been able to get. And the idea was to make sure Cindy wasn't found.

Parking for tenants was provided in the back of the building, beneath a roof which extended from the rear wall of the structure for its entire length, creating a carport wide enough to hold several vehicles parked abreast. They left Cindy's Mercedes there, and went upstairs to her temporary home.

"This is nice," she said after a quick perusal of the apartment.

The place had hardwood floors and throw rugs, walls of genuine plaster, and a view of the neighborhood that was limited at that particular moment by fog.

"They don't make buildings like this anymore," Cindy said. "I pay a fortune for a place that's mainly wallboard and plastic. In a lot of ways this is nicer."

"Yours is the bedroom on the left," Mike said. "The other one has a good view of the street, and we need to have access to it."

"Okay by me. You ready for my list of the things I'll need?"

"I'm ready."

Sitting down on the couch, she took a notebook from her purse and began writing. When she was finished, she tore off the page and handed it to Cotter.

"What if I need things that can't be faxed?" she asked, looking up at Cotter.

"We'll arrange a messenger service. It's going to be complicated, so it would be good if you didn't do it too often."

"What do I do if I need to use it?"

"Just tell us, and we'll arrange it."

She rose, slipping her arms around him. "Thank you," she said, "for doing all this for me."

"There's nothing I wouldn't do for you."

"I know that."

"Good."

"This is scary," she said.

"You'll be safe here."

Realizing that three cops were in the room with them, they separated.

"I'll get these things," Cotter said.

He had to force himself to walk out the door and leave Cindy in the hands of others—even though he was confident they were good hands.

It was about two A.M. as Robert Heckly sat in a rust-pocked vintage Chevy, studying the twelfth-floor window of Cindy Brekke's apartment. Her car was not in its parking space. The window he was observing was dark. Cotter was hiding her somewhere.

Heckly started the car, drove until he came to a through street, and headed north. He had expected Cotter to hide Cindy. It was part of the game they were playing, a treasure hunt with Cindy as the prize.

Heckly expected to win.

As he drove, his thoughts wandered. He recalled those fifteen years as a guest of the State of Texas. Endless days of television and ping-pong and softball games no one really wanted to play. Canned peas nearly every day for lunch, usually accompanied by chewy meatloaf and sticky macaroni in a yellow goo. Half the inmates walking around like zombies, zonked on drugs.

The idea was to keep the "patients" occupied and tranquil—especially tranquil.

The guards and orderlies seemed nearly as unhappy at having to be there as the inmates were. But unlike the prisoners, they had someone to take their frustrations out on. There was a room with padded walls that the guards called the lesson room.

Heckly had never been in that room.

What you had done to get into prison didn't seem to matter much to the guards. It was what happened within the three fences that determined how you got along with them. They were stupid and brutish, often high on their own special variety of chemicals, and he found them easy to manipulate.

Like Leo Duver.

On the day of Heckly's escape, Duver was waiting for him in his Trans Am at the spot where the road dipped into the bed of a dry wash, about two miles from the institution. Heckly had Stiller's wife as a hostage, and he was driving the Stillers' car. As he came to the wash, he flashed the headlights; Duver pulled in behind him. The big redneck had no intention of letting Heckly out of his sight until he got his money.

Couldn't pull a fast one on a smart man like Leo Duver.

Heckly had glanced at Mrs. Stiller, who'd stared straight ahead, as rigid as a statue. She was a middle-aged woman, neither pretty nor plain, wearing a blue dress. It was the first really good look he'd had at her. The inmates rarely saw her. She probably had to spend her days sitting in the house, watching television or playing bridge with the other wives. An existence remarkably similar to that of the inmates.

"What are you going to do to me?" she asked, her voice a frightened whisper.

He didn't respond. There didn't seem to be any point.

"Please," she said. "I've never done anything to harm you."

Appealing to his conscience, his basic good nature. Foolish woman. Her psychiatrist husband would have known better.

"I haven't decided yet what to do with you," he said. "A lot of it depends on you."

"W-what do you want me to do?" she asked.

"Just do whatever I tell you to do, try hard to be cooperative, and that will weigh heavily in your favor when I make up my mind."

"If I'm good, will you let me go?"

"Anything's possible."

"I'll do whatever you say."

"Don't even think about trying to jump out of the car. I might not be able to stop you, but you'd probably injure yourself. Also, do you see those headlights behind us?"

She glanced out the back window. "Yes."

"That's my accomplice. You wouldn't get anywhere even if you did survive the jump. And let's face it, there's nowhere out here for you to go, nobody to help you."

"I won't do anything like that."

"Good. Because it would weigh heavily against you when I make up my mind."

She nodded.

"Turn on the radio."

She obeyed.

"Now find a talk show."

She turned the dial until Larry King's voice was coming from the speaker. "That okay?" she asked.

"That's just fine."

"Anything else?"

"I can't hear the radio if you keep talking."

"I'm sorry," she said.

He drove into the mountains with Duver following. Finally the redneck started flashing his lights, and Heckly pulled over. He got out and walked back to Duver's car.

"Where the hell are you going?" Duver asked. "There are sure as hell no banks out here."

"We're taking a detour."

"A detour to where?"

"Where it's isolated."

"Why?" Duver asked, frowning.

"So I can dispose of my companion."

Duver's frown deepened. "What do you mean by dispose of?"

"What do you think I mean?"

"Hold it. I didn't agree to being involved in a murder."

"You object?"

Duver hesitated. "She doesn't know who I am, does she?"

"No."

"Well, I object to killing her. Why can't you just tie her up and leave her somewhere? You're out. You've got a good head start. All you have to do is give me my share of the money, and you can disappear."

"That's what we'll do, then."

The guard nodded, satisfied. "Hey, you just left her up there. Aren't you afraid she'll try to get away?"

"No," Heckly said, and returned to the other car.

After driving another few miles, Heckly pulled off on a narrow dirt road.

"What . . . what are we going to do here?" Willa Stiller asked. She was shivering.

"You've been very cooperative, Willa. And I promised my associate in the other car that I'd just tie you up and leave you here."

Though still trembling, she was visibly relieved.

"Get out of the car."

She instantly obeyed.

Heckly reached under the seat, getting the long, sharp knife he'd taken from the Stillers' kitchen. Duver was getting out of the car. Heckly and the woman reached the rear of the car at the same time. He stepped toward her, the knife arcing upward, penetrating the skin beneath her ribs, the blade continuing its journey until it penetrated her heart.

She emitted a single gasp, her eyes opening wide in shock, and then Willa Stiller collapsed at his feet.

"Hey!" Duver said. "Shit! You promised that—"

Heckly silenced him with a karate kick. Two more followed it, and Duver lay on the rocky ground unconscious. He had kept his word to Willa Stiller. She had cooperated, and her death had been quick and painless.

But he had lied to the big redneck.

Leo Duver's death would be slow and enjoyable.

When it was over, with Leo's screams still lingering in his ears, Heckly put both bodies into Duver's car and drove farther into the desolate country. He left the bodies a few miles apart in places humans rarely frequented. Hikers got lost out here, and their remains would go undiscovered for months—sometimes for years, by which time they'd been reduced to scattered bones.

He'd left the keys in Duver's car. The Pontiac Trans Am wasn't new, but it was in reasonably good shape. And from what he'd gathered from talking to one of his fellow inmates at the Southwestern State Hospital—a young man named Gonzales who'd been a member of a Houston street gang—the model was a favorite of Hispanic teenagers. Someone would discover it, find it too inviting to pass up, and in a day or two it would most likely be in Mexico. If it was found by an honest citizen who notified the police, so be it. A guard quit his job, and then his car was found abandoned in the mountains. Such things happened. And a search of the area around the Trans Am would turn up nothing, for the bodies were many miles from the car. The authorities would tow the car away and promptly lose interest.

He drove the Stillers' old Datsun to El Paso, where he disabled the engine, then called a wrecking yard and said he had an old car that had blown its engine, and he wanted it picked up and crushed. The man on the other end of the line said he'd come for it, but he'd have to charge him for hauling it off. He'd deduct the value of the car, but it would still cost him.

Heckly said okay. "Is your crusher the kind that makes them into a cube?"

"Yeah."

"Can I watch?"

"You that mad at that car?"

"Uh-huh."

"Cost you another twenty-five bucks."

"Okay."

Heckly's thoughts returned to the present as he stopped at a red light on the outskirts of Tres Cerros. He was heading for Petal Parker's apartment. The light turned green, and he stepped on the gas, the engine muttering loudly through the leaky exhaust system. Petal said there was a hole in the muffler. The car was hers. He and Petal were living together.

Her place was in Colmer, in an old house that had been converted into apartments. The neighborhood was mixed: white, black, Hispanic, and Asian. The only requirement for living here was poverty—or a willingness to expose oneself to street gangs and other violent types. Heckly parked the car at the curb. Its big V-8 engine dieseled, thunking and sputtering and spewing out a cloud of smoke like some fire-breathing beast in its death throes. Finally it emitted a last grumble and died.

Petal lived on the ground floor. As he walked toward the door, something clanked on the ground to his left. It was a beer can. Members of a motorcycle gang occupied the apartment above Petal's, and they tossed the empties out the window. The pile was impressive.

"Where were you?" Petal demanded as he stepped inside. "You said were just going for a short while."

She was braless beneath her checked shirt. On younger women this usually resulted in an enticing jiggle. Petal just sagged.

"I had some errands to run," he said.

Petal, as her name suggested, was a product of the sixties, an aging flower child whose moment in the sun had come and gone. Her parents had named her Barbara Jean, a name she so disliked that she'd legally changed it—this after a heated argument with her parents, who had strongly disapproved of her hippie life-style.

To her, the squalid neighborhood typified the oppression of the underclass in the capitalist society. Strangely, Petal liked it here; she saw the neighborhood as a place that was teeming with real people, individuals who were true to themselves, whose souls were unsullied by the corruption of the giant corporations and their greedy minions—despite the circumstances in which they were forced to live. She ate only organic foods, reread *The Hobbit* every few months, and had spent two years in a mental institution. She always wore jeans and did her hair in a long gray-brown braid.

As she stood there, her eyes demanding a better explanation, Heckly considered killing her and leaving her body for Cotter to find. With a letter on it. Perhaps a *P.* For "pain in the ass."

But then, it didn't fit the plan.

"It's all right," he said. "Nothing to get mad about."

"What were you doing?"

"Errands. Personal errands."

"You have secrets from me."

"I do things that don't concern you."

"Who were you with?"

Although he'd only been living with her a few days, Petal was extremely possessive. She had a fear of abandonment and rejection. Her clinging was so extreme it had probably caused the very rejection she feared.

"No one," he answered.

"Uh-huh. Sure. Who was she?"

"There was no she," Heckly said. "But if you're not going to trust me, I shouldn't stay here." He turned toward the door.

"No," Petal said quickly. "Don't go. I'm sorry. I do trust you."

"You sure?"

"Yes. I told you, I'm sorry."

"All right. I forgive you."

He stepped forward, taking her in his arms. She seemed stiff, reluctant.

"You'll stay with me, won't you?" she said. "You won't leave."

"Of course I wouldn't leave, Petal. Unless you didn't trust me."

"I . . . I trust you."

"You sure?"

"Yes, I'm sure."

"No more questioning me when I have errands to run?"

"No more. I promise."

"Good."

She finally relaxed and returned his hug. Heckly found it as exciting as holding a sack of animal feed.

"I'll have errands to do the next few days," he said. "Sometimes I'll be out at night as well. I'll need the car."

"It's okay," she said. "I trust you."

He pulled off his wig. It was darker, longer, and fuller than his natural hair, and altered his appearance significantly.

"You audition for the part yet?" Petal asked.

He had told her that he was an actor, and that before auditioning for a part, he lived it, completely submersed himself in it, even trying to look like the character he would portray. To Petal, this was completely plausible. He removed the fake moustache, and she kissed him.

"The audition's a few weeks off yet," he said.

"You won't leave me, will you?"

"Of course not, Petal," he said. "We're kindred spirits, you and I. People who see life as it really is."

"We haven't sold out to the system," Petal said.

"No, not us. Never."

"Fuck the system," Petal said.

"Power to the people."

"Right on," Petal said, making a power fist. The woman was an anachronism. Today's young people would probably find her strange and avoid her. They had no concept of what had transpired in the world in which Petal Parker still lived; it was ancient history, no longer relevant.

"Will you be an eighty-year-old flower child, Petal?" he asked.

"The world would be better off with more flower children. Love instead of exploitation, cruelty, destruction of the environment. Love instead of violence."

"Love instead of violence," he echoed. "It *would* be better, wouldn't it?"

The irony did not escape him. Robert Heckly had never loved anyone, with the possible exception of himself. And he thrived on the violence he inflicted on others. He knew these things about himself and was entirely comfortable with them.

"Are you ready to go to sleep?" he asked.

"Yes," she said. "I'm tired."

They had sex in Petal's old iron-framed bed. Heckly didn't enjoy it. But to Petal it was an act of love. Afterward she clung to him while he studied the cracks in the ceiling and refined his plans.

The morning demonstrated the wisdom of moving in with

Petal. Using her car, he drove to a coffee shop and ordered a cup of dark-roasted Columbian and some doughnuts. Petal wouldn't allow coffee in her apartment—it was bad for you and the Latin American coffee pickers were exploited. Her typical breakfast consisted of slices of organically grown melon and unbuttered whole wheat toast.

The first thing he did was buy a newspaper. Petal never read the paper and, since she didn't own a TV set, never watched the news. Therefore he wouldn't have to worry about her seeing what was on the front page of the Tres Cerros *Times-Courier*. The headline asked:

HAVE YOU SEEN THIS MAN?

Beneath that was his photo, with the caption "Authorities are seeking escaped Texas mental patient Robert Heckly in connection with a series of killings in the Tres Cerros area." The story described the local murders, then detailed Heckly's past exploits, starting with the events that had occurred in New Jersey.

The paragraph about the murder of a Texas state policeman's family did not mention that the cop was now living in Tres Cerros under an assumed name.

There was no mention of Cindy Brekke.

Heckly was pleased with the way his foresight had paid off. He had known that sooner or later Cotter would give his photo to the press. But Petal lived in a neighborhood where people respected each other's privacy, minded their own business, and had an abiding distrust of the police. In such a place no one would see through his disguise because no one would want to. Only Petal knew what he really looked like. And Petal didn't own a TV set, didn't read the papers. She still talked about her preference for the Soviet order over the capitalist system. She didn't seem to know that the Soviet Union no longer existed—or she was unwilling to accept it.

Heckly hadn't been sure what he'd been looking for when he'd stepped into that left-wing bookstore full of anti-American propaganda and gay/lesbian magazines. What he had found was Petal, who had exceeded his wildest expectations.

His attitude toward her was changing. At first it was mocking, telling Petal how much alike they were while telling himself how stupid she was. But as he sat in the coffee shop, thinking about her, he realized that he was beginning to find her repulsive. She didn't shave her legs, and big tufts of hair protruded from under her arms. She usually had a vaguely stale odor, as if bathing was reserved for the capitalist pigs.

Although killing her had not originally been part of the plan, the plan was fluid. It could be changed.

He washed a bite of fresh powdered doughnut down with Columbian coffee, not caring one whit that it had been picked by exploited Latin American peasants. And he began to fantasize about killing Petal Parker.

Doing it slowly.

While he stared into her muddy brown eyes.

And ignored her pleas for mercy.

Thirty-three

For Heckly it was a busy day. At a company that specialized in security equipment he purchased a tiny magnetically attached transmitter and a directional receiver that operated on the same frequency. The man who sold it to him was very discreet, answering his questions but not inquiring about his reasons for wanting what he was buying.

Next he went to the Radio Shack in the Three Hills Mall and bought a scanner, which he programmed to monitor the frequencies used by the Tres Cerros police.

Then he parked near the police station. He had time to learn where Cindy Brekke was. He was sure that with patience he would find her.

He spent the entire day watching the comings and goings of cops and listening to them talk on the radio.

At nightfall he moved to a spot across the street from a small duplex. Cotter's unmarked car pulled into the graveled parking lot about nine. The policeman was using his old apartment, now that Cindy Brekke was in hiding. She wasn't here. Heckly had watched the place long enough to be sure of that.

He waited until he was certain no trap had been set for him here; then he slipped through the shadows and attached the transmitter to the rear bumper of Cotter's car.

When Cotter awoke, he rolled over and reached for Cindy, finding only the cool smoothness of the sheets. Then he realized that Cindy was in an apartment across town, where she was being guarded around the clock.

He sat up, putting his feet on the floor, noting the cheap dresser, the worn carpeting, the dark smudges around the light switch, the unadorned walls on which rectangles of discoloration marked the places where previous tenants had hung pictures. The apartment had that musty, unused odor of a place that's been closed up and vacant for a long time.

It reminded him of how lonely he'd been living here.

And of how lonely he'd be again if anything happened to Cindy.

It can't happen again, he thought. *Not twice in the same lifetime.*

He shook some of the sleep from his head, and he realized that it was up to him to make sure it didn't happen again. A chill slithered through him, and for an instant he felt overmatched, incapable of competing with Robert Heckly. Then he reminded himself that Heckly was just a man. A clever, insane man, but a man nonetheless, as vulnerable as any other.

Slipping on a robe, Cotter went into the kitchen and put water and Hills Brothers into the coffeemaker. The apartment came with an ancient refrigerator that had to be defrosted and a gas stove whose right rear burner emitted flames that were orange instead of blue. Though basically a dump, the place rented for $850 a month. A similar place in Colmer would have gone for less than half that, but the department required its officers to live in the city so they'd be available in case of an emergency.

He considered staying at Cindy's place, deciding against it because he'd been afraid it would seem too lonely without Cindy there. He sighed. It couldn't possibly be any more lonely than this.

After a shower, he cooked bacon and eggs for breakfast, just because it had been so long since he'd had anything like that—Cindy didn't eat foods so high in fat and cholesterol. But instead of being a rare treat, the breakfast seemed greasy and unappetizing. He consumed half of it and decided he'd had enough.

He was on his way out the door when the phone rang. It was an old rotary-dial model—made in the USA by Western Electric and built to last forever—which could go anywhere in the apartment by virtue of its twenty-five-foot cord. At the moment it was sitting on the arm of the sofa. Cotter lifted the receiver.

"Hi," Cindy said, "it's me."

"I was going to wait and call you from the office," he said. "Just in case you were sleeping in."

"That's a little hard to do when you're in a strange place and you have police officers just outside your bedroom door—not to mention the serial killer who's just put your name on the top of his list of people he'd love to meet."

"We're going to make sure that doesn't happen," Cotter said.

"I've been scared right along, Mike. But last night, here in these circumstances . . . it really brought it home. The danger. That Heckly could—"

"He won't. We won't let him."

Cindy made a peculiar noise. Cotter thought she'd shuddered. She said, "Did you sleep okay—without me?"

"It would have been much better with you," Cotter replied.

"I've discovered I don't like sleeping alone," Cindy said. "I'm not used to it. I don't want to get used to it. Without you, the bed is just so . . . so empty. That's a complicated way of saying I miss you."

"I miss you, too," Cotter said softly.

She took a slow breath. "You know what's crazy? All my communication with the office is by fax. I mean, we could just as easily talk over the phone, but we don't. We fax memos back and forth."

"How's Tyleen doing?"

"She seems to have really taken hold of things. The resentment I was worried about hasn't materialized. Apparently Tyleen has done a remarkable job of handling any dented egos—at least, as far as I can tell from here."

"I give all the credit to you—for picking the right person."

"You'd support me if I put King Kong in charge."

"Well, I *am* just a tiny bit biased when it comes to you."

"Just a tiny bit?"

"Okay, I'm extremely biased when it comes to you."

"That's better," Cindy said. "Will I see you today?"

"I shouldn't go there any more than is absolutely necessary; you know that. Heckly could be watching me, hoping I'll lead him to you."

"Can't you do something to make sure you're not followed?"

"Unfortunately, the only way to be one-hundred-percent sure I don't lead Heckly to you is not to go."

"Mike . . ."

"You'll see me. I just shouldn't do it too often."

"But you will be here—at least every so often."

"You kidding? If I don't see you soon I'm going to burst."

"Don't burst," Cindy said. "But don't take too long, either."

"I'll let you know," he said.

They hung up reluctantly.

For a moment, Cotter stood there staring at the phone, emptiness and loneliness filling the apartment, engulfing him. Then old questions began to circle in his brain. *Why me? What did I do to deserve Heckly?*

But these questions were unanswerable, products of self-pity. If he gave in to this mood, Cotter realized, he would sink into a morass of dejection, which would only make it harder for him to deal with the situation. He shook his head, as if trying to fling off the despondence that had started settling over him.

He quickly washed the breakfast dishes, then pulled on his coat and stepped out into a beautifully bright and sunny morning. Reaching beneath the front seat of the unmarked Dodge, he got the signal detector, switched it on, and started to walk around the car with it. The device instantly came to life, emitting a beep as it displayed the frequency it was receiving. Cotter stopped in mid-stride, transfixed. He'd gotten the signal detectors as a precaution, because he wanted to think of every move Heckly might make and be prepared for it. Now that his foresight had paid off, he stared at the rectangular object in his hand, not really believing it.

Finally he climbed into the car, started the engine, and picked up the microphone. "Three-thirty-eight to Control."

Parked out of sight around the corner, Heckly listened over his scanner as the dispatcher responded, "Go ahead, three-thirty-eight.

"Ten-eight, ten-nineteen." Which meant Cotter was in his unit and on his way to the station.

"Ten-four, three-thirty-eight."

Heckly had started to recognize the voices of the various women who worked as dispatchers. He found himself wondering what they looked like. This one was less efficient-sounding than most of the others, a young woman with a melodic quality to her speech. He pictured her as slightly overweight with blond curls and baby blue eyes.

He listened as the intensity of the beeping tone emitted by the receiver decreased, showing a reduction in signal strength. The device was about the size of a pocket tape recorder. It hung from a knob on the dash. Connected to the receiver by a wire and held to the top of the dash with a suction cup was a small dish antenna. It was highly directional, and by rotating it and listening to the beeping tone, he could tell from which direction the signal was coming, which meant he could tell which direction to travel to find Cotter. Simple by modern standards, but quite efficient.

He stayed well back, out of Cotter's sight. He knew where the detective was going, and this was an opportunity to familiarize himself with the tracking device.

The neighborhood was old by Tres Cerros standards, though by no means seedy. Two-story clapboard houses like those in any Eastern or Midwestern city lined the street, white houses with shutters and trim painted green or blue or yellow. Huge trees stood in the yards, their thick roots making roller coasters out of the sidewalks. This was the closest you could come to reasonably priced housing in the community—if housing anywhere in California could be said to be reasonable.

"Three-thirty-eight to Control."

"Three-thirty-eight," the dispatcher said in acknowledgment.

"Signal eighty-four."

"Ten-four."

Heckly frowned. Signal eighty-four? He'd never heard that before.

A few seconds later, the beeping tone abruptly grew softer, indicating that Cotter had changed direction. Could signal eighty-four mean he'd changed his mind, that he was on his way to visit Cindy?

Ahead was Peninsula Avenue. The police station was to the left. Turning the dish antenna, Heckly discovered that Cotter had gone right. He followed.

As he drove along Peninsula Avenue, Cotter tried to establish the link with Heckly. The signal was not there. It hadn't been there for days. Perhaps the phenomenon was a transitory thing, and now it was gone, never to be regained.

Or Heckly wasn't following him.

But Cotter desperately wanted Heckly to follow him, for he was leading the madman into a trap. Signal eighty-four had been the cue to set it in motion. Cotter was heading for a dead-end street off Golden Avenue. Other unmarked units would be moving into the area. A special highway patrol plane would provide aerial surveillance. The small, light aircraft could fly at extremely slow speeds; it was much quieter than a helicopter, much less likely to call attention to itself.

As soon as the plane was overhead and everyone on the ground was in position, the dispatcher would give him a signal eighty-five. The whole operation was being run with a special set of radio codes Cotter had made up in case Heckly was monitoring their transmissions.

Cat and mouse. Except that neither Cotter nor Heckly wanted to be the mouse.

Hurry up, Cotter thought. Before Heckly gets suspicious.

Heckly was driving a Mercury Sable he'd borrowed from the parking lot of a strip mall, where he'd found it with the keys in the ignition and the door unlocked. The careless owner would have reported it stolen almost immediately, so Heckly had switched license plates with a Subaru. People usually didn't notice their license plates, so there was a good chance the Subaru's owner would be unaware of the switch, at least for a while.

He was using a stolen car for two reasons. The first was that Petal's old clunker wasn't up to a quick getaway if the need for one arose. The second was that there was always the chance that someone would get the license number of the car he was driving, and he didn't want to lead them to Petal, who was providing him with the perfect hiding place, while the cops were probably still looking for him in motels.

A shadow crossed the street in front of him. Looking up, he saw a light plane.

Cotter had been driving at a leisurely pace for fifteen minutes now. He was still on Peninsula Avenue, nearing the outskirts of Tres Cerros. Towering signs rose from at least half a dozen motels like neon stilt walkers hoping to catch the attention of people on the freeway. The Peninsula Avenue interchange was just ahead.

"All purple units, signal eighty-five," the dispatcher said.

Purple units? Heckly wondered. It was another unfamiliar code. He felt his brow crawl into a frown. He didn't like things that were unfamiliar.

Then the dispatcher said, "All green units clear for code seven starting at eleven."

That he understood. Code seven meant a meal break. Apparently the Tres Cerros police had started assigning cars to groups designated by colors. If the green group was having lunch, the other groups would still be on patrol. The unfamiliar signals were probably part of the same new procedure.

As he crossed the freeway, the beeping of the receiver abruptly diminished. Then, to his left, he saw Cotter's brown Dodge, on the other part of the overpass, going back the way they had just come. It was the perfect maneuver for trying to determine whether he was being followed. But it would work only if the follower was staying close, keeping you in sight.

Heckly smiled.

Cotter was doing all the things he should do if he was trying to make absolutely sure he wasn't being tailed. That's what Heckly would expect him to do if he was on his way to Cindy's hiding place. And Heckly would continue following him as long as he believed Cotter would lead him to Cindy.

So Cotter made an abrupt U-turn and sped onto the freeway, merged with traffic, got into the fast lane, kicked it up to eighty, then got off at the next exit and headed toward the center of town on Wilson Boulevard. After three blocks, he turned right, then right again, then again, which took him back to Wilson. He turned left on Wilson and sped back toward the freeway. He saw no sign of Heckly.

"Purple four-nine-four to control."

"Go ahead, purple."

"I have more data on that vehicle the captain was interested in."

More important information disguised as ordinary cop radio chatter. Four-nine-four was the highway patrol's eye in the sky.

"It's number twelve on the list," the officer in the plane said. "Charles, seven."

Cotter had made up a list of automobile makes and colors, assigning number and letter codes to each. Twelfth on the list was Mercury. C meant a Sable; seven was from the list of colors and meant green. The cops in the air had spotted a tail, a green Mercury Sable.

"Code eighty-nine," the cop in the sky said. Heckly was still following, heading into the trap.

The beeping dropped in intensity, and Heckly rotated the antenna until the sound increased. Cotter had changed direction. At the next intersection, Heckly turned right.

Again he caught a glimpse of the small plane. It was blue, very small, probably one of those aircraft capable of flying so slow that it could practically land in a tennis court. No doubt some people with a new toy, taking an aerial tour of the city.

Again Cotter changed direction, heading to the left. Heckly followed. Ahead was an underpass, and beyond it was the warehouse for a moving company. He passed under the freeway, turned left, then right. This part of town was a warren of warehouses and streets that had been interrupted by the freeway. A sign informed him that he was heading for a dead end.

Heckly jammed on the brakes, his mind working furiously.

The cops were talking in unusual codes.

A plane was overhead.

He was heading into an area from which escape could be extremely difficult.

A trap.

"Signal ninety-one," a male voice said over the police radio. It came from the airplane, Heckly realized. He scanned the area, looking for police cars, seeing nothing suspicious. They were staying back, letting the plane keep track of him, waiting to close the trap up ahead somewhere.

"We've still got a signal ninety-one here," the cop said over the radio.

Cotter had invented a whole new code, just in case he was being overheard. He had found the transmitter on his car and turned it into a trap. Heckly made a U-turn, then headed back the way he had come.

"He's made us!" the cop in the air shouted. "He's heading on Mulberry," toward the freeway.

Cotter's excited voice came on the radio. "Give it out, Control. Mulberry and the freeway."

"All units," the dispatcher said, "be advised detective units are in pursuit of a green Mercury Sable in the vicinity of Mulberry and the freeway."

No more fake codes, Heckly thought. Now it was just an ordinary case of him fleeing and the cops chasing.

Heckly skidded around two corners; then the freeway overpass loomed ahead. Beyond it were the lights of an approaching police car.

More flashing lights appeared in the rearview mirror. There were no cross streets. No entrance ramp leading to the freeway.

Putting the accelerator on the floor, Heckly built up as much speed as he could, then jumped the curb, the Sable bouncing up the freeway embankment, its wheels spinning, its motor screaming. On the scanner, cops were all yelling at once. The Mercury was barely moving by the time it reached the top of the embankment, but he made it. Tires still spinning, he roared onto the pavement. Horns honked and tires squealed.

And then he was speeding away.

"Northbound on the freeway!" the cop in the air hollered, and then they were all giving their locations, the cop frequency filled with loud, confused voices.

Heckly swerved around cars as fast as the Sable's V-6 would go. Ahead was an exit, and he took it, cutting in front of a station wagon, and then speeding down the exit ramp. When he reached the surface street, he turned left, under the freeway.

"Westbound on Miller," the cop in the plane said over the radio.

His name was Randy Donaldson. He and the pilot, Sergeant Toomis, were squeezed into a cockpit so small they were literally rubbing elbows with each other.

Donaldson watched as the green Sable sped under the freeway and disappeared. A white van entered the underpass from the other direction, and for a few moments neither vehicle was visible. Then the van emerged from the other side of the underpass. Where was the green car?

"He drove under the freeway, and he's still there," Donaldson said over the radio.

He watched as police cars sealed off both ends of the underpass. They had him now.

"I can see his car," a cop reported excitedly. "It's turned sideways in the road."

"Three-thirty-eight to the units at the freeway. Wait for backup. This subject is ten-thirty-five." Dangerous.

Cotter made his way along streets that twisted and dead-ended where the freeway had sliced through the area like a knife. The neighborhood was full of small wholesalers. He passed places that specialized in plumbing fixtures and power tools and even fasteners. It was like a maze in which he had to constantly watch out for slow-moving trucks, which pulled out of loading areas and claimed the streets as if daring anyone in anything as small as a car to challenge them. Cotter's siren and lights seemed to make little impression on the drivers.

When he finally got to the underpass where Heckly was trapped, he found half a dozen squad cars blocking the road, officers crouching behind them with their weapons drawn.

He's not here!

The realization hit Cotter like a hammer blow. Stunned, he got out of his car and walked toward the officers, trying to find the link with Heckly. He got a slight hint of the man, and then it slipped away. A vague feeling of elation, of freedom.

"Mike," Kozlovski said, joining him. "We can't see him, but he went in and never came out, so he's got to be there."

He did come out. Somehow.

"Okay," Cotter said. "Let's get him."

"You want the SWAT guys, or should we do it?"

"There's no hostages or anything," Cotter said. "Let's take the son-of-a-bitch."

Kozlovski nodded approvingly.

Cotter had taken his hand-held radio with him. He raised it to his mouth and pressed the transmit button. "This is three-thirty-eight. How many of you on the west side?"

"Seven," came the reply.

"Holler when you're ready."

When everyone had prepared to move into the underpass, Cotter shouted a warning to Heckly. He had to do it this way because it was always possible he was wrong, that Heckly was hiding in the car, waiting for them to come for him. Also, he had to go through the motions because there was no way he could say, "Forget it, guys. I've used my psychic powers, and I know he's not in there."

They moved in.

And found an empty green car. No one in the trunk. No one scrunched down on the floor.

No manholes or other exits in the underpass.

Kozlovski was the first to contact the plane and report what they'd found. "You guys asleep up there or what?"

"No one came out," came the reply from the sky. "We'd have seen them."

"Come on, Donaldson," Kozlovski snapped. "He ain't here,

and he goddamned well didn't tell fuckin' Scotty to beam him up."

"No other vehicles came out of there?" Cotter asked.

"No, just a van that entered from the other direction at about the same time the Sable did."

"What van?" Cotter demanded.

"A white one. But . . . Jesus, he couldn't have. There wasn't time."

But they all knew that somehow Heckly had managed to do it.

Thirty-four

"He . . . he . . . he just popped the release on my seatbelt and shoved me over and . . . and . . . and took over."

The woman was about thirty. She had blond hair that had been permed into a mass of tight curls. Her big hazel eyes were filled with terror that was only slowly subsiding. Her name was Veronica Gibbings.

She was using the side of her white van for support. Cotter, Kozlovski, and two uniformed officers were listening to her story. Other cops were scouring the neighborhood for any sign of Heckly. The drone of the Highway Patrol airplane wafted down from above.

"I . . . I didn't know what would happen. I . . . I was afraid what would happen to the children."

A boy and a girl stood beside her. He was about nine, and she was about two years younger. The girl looked confused, as if puzzled by her mother's reaction. Obviously brother and sister, they both had their mother's blond hair and hazel eyes, as well as freckles, which she didn't have.

"Wow," the boy said. "We were hijacked by a real crook." He seemed awed to have been part of such a thing.

The mother looked at him, looked at Cotter, and shivered. She appeared as though she might faint.

The boy said, "The man turned his car sideways in the road, and then he ran up yelling for help. But he didn't really need help. He was just trying to trick my mom." He looked at her as if to say, *Worked, too, didn't it?* "When she rolled down the window, he grabbed the door and climbed in and started driving."

"Did he say anything?" Cotter asked. So far, the boy was proving a better witness than his mother, and he was anxious to tell them all about it, so Cotter decided to let him.

"Just that we should keep quiet if we didn't want to get hurt." He grinned. "Just like the bad guys on TV."

"Then what happened?"

"He drove us here, and then he told us to stay in the van, and then he got out."

They were in a Little League field, behind second base. Heckly had jumped the curb between home plate and third base and driven to the edge of the outfield.

"Which way'd he go?" Cotter asked.

"That way," the boy replied, pointing toward the right-field corner.

"Did he have a car?"

The boy shook his head. "Nope. He just walked until he disappeared."

"What was he wearing?"

"Just regular clothes."

"What color?"

"Ummmm," the boy said, scrunching up his face in thought. "His shirt was green and his jacket was gray and his pants were . . . what do you call it? You know, sort of like army guys wear sometimes."

"Khaki?"

"Yeah, that's it."

Cotter gave out this information over his portable radio.

"After he left, we just sat here," the boy said. "We didn't knock on a door or ask to use the phone or anything. My mom was afraid to move." He looked at her as if he were ashamed of her.

A tear trickled down Veronica Gibbings' cheek, and then she began to sob.

Tyleen Windley thought everyone else had already left the office, but when she stepped into the reception area, she found Dominique putting the cover on her word processor.

"Thought I was the only one working late," Tyleen said.

"At five minutes till five, Cindy called with two letters she wanted to get out right away."

"Who to?"

Dominique named two Madison Avenue agencies Cindy's firm sometimes worked with when an Eastern connection was needed.

"I thought I was in charge."

"She's not going around you, Ty. She's frightened and confused, and she just wants to keep her finger in. Besides, she said I should be sure to give you copies of both letters."

"You ready?" Tyleen asked. "I've got to lock up."

As the two women got their coats from the small closet near the main entrance, Dominique said, "You don't have to do everything yourself, Ty. I can lock up. Operating the key doesn't require an executive decision, you know."

"Have I been that bad?"

"Let's just say you're taking your responsibility very seriously."

"I want to help Cindy. I'm worried about her."

Tyleen locked the office, and they walked to the elevator. Dominique pushed the down button.

"Am I being heavy handed?" Tyleen asked.

"No, no. Everyone thinks you're doing great—even the big egos like Beryl are happy. You've just got to learn to relax, that's all. You'll give yourself ulcers."

The elevator arrived. They stepped into the car, and Tyleen pressed the button for the underground parking area.

"Hit One for me," Dominique said.

"You need a ride?"

"Thanks, but there's no need for you to bother. It's only a twenty-minute bus ride."

"You sure?"

Dominique said she was. Then she added, "This is something, isn't it, this whole thing with Cindy?"

"There's a hell of a lot of crazy people out there," Tyleen said.

"But why threaten Cindy? What did she ever do?"

"What did any victim ever do?"

"At least she's got that policeman boyfriend of hers to look out for her," Dominique said.

"I think he's involved in it somehow."

"The big cop? You mean, this crazy person is really after him?"

"I don't know," Tyleen replied. "I just think he's involved in some way—beyond simply protecting Cindy."

"Do you know where they've taken her?"

"No idea, except that it's a Tres Cerros phone number. Someone's threatened her, and she's taking it real seriously. That's all I know."

The elevator stopped on the first floor, and Dominique got off. "See you tomorrow," she said, and disappeared into the lobby.

Tyleen got off in the underground parking area. There were only a few cars there now, and the place seemed musty and deserted. Her heels clicked loudly on the concrete, echoed back at her from the shadows.

She saw movement from the corner of her eye, but when she looked in that direction, there was nothing there. Her red Ford was fifty feet in front of her, a gleaming metal sanctuary. Tyleen picked up her pace, her heels clicking like a metronome set on fast.

Reaching the car, she inserted the key in the lock, pulled open the door, then hesitated, making sure no one was hiding in the backseat, ready to grab her as soon as she was behind the wheel. No one was there.

Tyleen tossed her purse into the car, then started to climb in after it.

And something grabbed her, pulled her back out again.

A hand clamped her mouth closed.

"T is not for Tyleen," a voice said.

Dominique Long stood at the curb, peering down the street, waiting for the familiar boxy shape of her bus to appear at the end of the block. An unshaven man in a worn peacoat was the only other person at the bus stop. Ordinarily, he would have been sufficiently unsavory to make her nervous, but after her conversation with Tyleen about some lunatic threatening Cindy, Dominique was glad not to be there alone.

It was about six o'clock, twilight, and a cool breeze blew through the canyons of the city. Dominique squeezed her coat together at the collar.

To her left was the ramp that led from the underground parking area. Tyleen's red car should have appeared by now. Perhaps she was talking to someone, or maybe she'd gone back to the office for some forgotten papers. Dominique's bus rounded the corner at the end of the block and rolled toward her, spewing black diesel fumes. As she watched it approach, she thought she heard a scream from the direction of the parking area.

Then, a block or two away, a siren let out a short *whoop*, probably a police officer pulling someone over. And Dominique realized that what she had heard just a moment before was a siren.

The bus arrived with a hiss of air brakes, and its doors flapped open. Dominique climbed on board, depositing her money as she stepped into the waiting warmth.

She took a seat near the front. The man in the peacoat remained on the sidewalk, apparently waiting for a different bus. She glanced back toward the ramp leading to the parking area, still somewhat apprehensive.

Come on, she scolded, it was just a siren.

And she put the matter out of her mind.

Cindy Brekke sat on the nubby living room couch, thinking that her formerly well-ordered life had suddenly become a swirling mass of uncertainties, carrying her along like a fast current that at any moment might dash her against some unseen rocks or sweep her over the edge of a high waterfall.

Detective Kozlovski sat in a recliner, reading a two-day-old issue of the *San Francisco Chronicle*. In the bedroom that overlooked the street, a cop named Anislov was sitting on a wooden chair that he'd turned backward, staring out the window. Every so often he'd raise a pair of binoculars to his eyes, then quickly jot down a license number or some other scrap of data. They were trying to get a feel for the neighborhood, learn its patterns, discover who regularly frequented the area. The only way to know when something's out of place, Kozlovski had explained, is to become familiar with how things are supposed to be.

Cindy found it awkward living with strangers twenty-four hours a day. She had little in common with her guards, and she usually had no idea what to say to them. Sometimes they engaged in shop talk and gossip—so-and-so flunking the sergeant's exam, officer X sleeping with officer Y, officer Z getting a divorce. Cindy, an outsider, had absolutely no idea who they were talking about. And when they weren't talking about things like that, they were talking about football, a sport Cindy had never had the slightest bit of interest in. Besides, it was spring, time for baseball. Didn't people know that the Super Bowl, the official culmination of the pro football season, had been played back in January?

Once, she'd considered describing for them in detail Margot Fonteyn's performance in *Swan Lake*, just to show them what it was like to be a bored listener, but she hadn't actually done it. These people were working extremely long hours to protect her, and they were prepared to risk their lives in the performance of that duty, if necessary. She owed them not only her gratitude, but common courtesy as well. So she let Dame Margot dance in her imagination and kept her out of the conversation. And when her protectors talked enthusiastically about someone she'd never heard of throwing the "bomb," Cindy smiled and tried to look appreciative of the bomb thrower's feat.

Although the days were boring, the nights were scary. She knew that every thunk and groan of the old building didn't mean Heckly was standing over her bed in the dark room, ready to turn her into steaks and chops. The rational portion of her brain knew that. But there was another, more primitive part that wasn't swayed by mere logic, a part that made her cringe at every sound, brace herself for the slash of the blade.

The phone rang. It was on the floor by the coffee table. Kozlovski leaned forward and answered it.

"Uh-huh," he said. "Who's calling?" Standing, he handed the phone to Cindy. "Your office."

"This is Cindy," she said.

"Hello, Cindy."

She hadn't expected a man. The only one in the office was an artist named Jamie Tolliver, a good-looking young man with soft eyes who always wore at least two rings on his left ear and frequently marched in gay-rights parades.

"Jam?" she said.

"No, Cindy, not Jam. I'm not really from your office."

An icy hand squeezed her soul. "Who . . . who . . ."

"You know who this is, Cindy."

Kozlovski looked up. She motioned frantically for him to listen in on the kitchen extension. Instantly getting the message, he was out of his chair and through the doorway. There was a barely audible click as he lifted the receiver.

"I see the police have joined us," the man said.

"How . . . how did you get this number?" Cindy asked.

"Aren't the police going to say anything?" He paused. "All right, you can pretend you're not there, if it makes you feel better."

"How—"

"How did I get the number? It was given to me."

"Who—"

"Who gave it to me? Tyleen."

"Tyleen?"

"You know, tall, attractive, African-American."

"What have you done to her?" Cindy demanded.

"You'll see."

"Have you hurt Tyleen?"

"Be patient, Cindy. All will be discovered in time."

"All . . . all *what* will be discovered in time?"

"You're not trying to trace this, are you?"

"All *what* will be discovered in time?" Cindy demanded. "What have you done?"

"No, you wouldn't have thought to set up a trace on this line, because you would never have figured that I'd get the number."

"What have you done to Tyleen?" Cindy said, her voice becoming shrill.

"You'll find out shortly. But in the meantime I'll give you a clue. *T* is not for Tyleen."

The line clicked and went dead.

279

Thirty-five

"She's alive," Cotter said, holding Cindy. She was shaking.

"How . . . how badly was she hurt?" Her voice was small and tremulous, like a frightened child's.

"She's listed in serious but stable condition."

"What did he do to her?"

"Stabbed her several times."

Cindy shuddered. "Oh, God. Poor Tyleen. She's not even involved in any of this. She's an innocent bystander."

"The victims of people like Heckly usually are," Cotter said softly.

Kozlovski and Anislov were in the bedroom, keeping an eye on the street and giving Cotter and Cindy some privacy.

Cindy said, "What did he mean, '*T* is not for Tyleen'?"

Cotter hesitated, then said, "He left a message. Written on the windshield in blood. It said, '*T* is for the trap you set for me.' "

"It made him mad, and he took it out on Tyleen?"

"That's the way he works. He hurts the people you care about."

"Mike . . . he's got the phone number here."

"It won't help him. It's an unlisted number. He can tell it's in Tres Cerros, but that's all."

"I'm afraid."

"He can't find you here."

"You sure? Can't the phone company tell him?"

"The information operators don't have a listing for this number. They can't even give it out by mistake."

Cindy just held him, shivering. He'd never seen her like this, so vulnerable and helpless. But then, that was the effect Heckly wanted to have. And, as Cotter knew only too well, Heckly was a master at inflicting it.

"Change the number," Cindy said. "Please. I don't think I could bear to hear his voice again."

"We need to keep this number. We can put a trace on it, and if he phones here again, we'll get an instant readout on the location he's calling from—just as with 911 calls."

Cindy drew in a slow breath. "What do you want me to do," she said, "if he calls again?"

"Just keep him talking as long as you can."

Heckly had no intention of calling again. One of his reasons for phoning Cindy Brekke had been to note any background sounds. A ship's horn, a train, trucks gearing down for an upgrade. Something, anything. But there had been nothing audible in the background.

If he called the number again, his location would be traced. *Sorry, Cindy,* he thought, *but we won't be able to talk anymore.*

Heckly was parked across the street from the police station, watching the cops. He knew Cotter would never lead him to Cindy. Cotter was much too cautious for that. But Cotter wasn't the only cop involved in protecting Cindy Brekke, which was why Heckly was watching the police station, why he listened to the police frequencies whenever he wasn't asleep.

Petal didn't like hearing the police calls; she said listening to the cops made her nervous. But then, Heckly didn't care what Petal liked.

He was in a white Honda today. He tried to change cars daily, so the cops didn't become suspicious seeing the same vehicle all the time. Although most people weren't so careless, there were always an obliging few who, through foolishness or forgetfulness, left the keys in their unlocked cars.

Heckly had even found a Maserati in the parking lot of a supermarket, with the keys dangling from the ignition. It had been fun to drive such a car—not to mention easy getting away from Cotter when the policeman had spotted him near Cindy Brekke's apartment.

"David-six, Control," came over the scanner, and Heckly turned the volume up a notch.

"Go ahead, David-six."

"Ten-eight, en route assignment."

"Ten-four."

David-six was one of the patrol units that didn't go on routine patrol, but did something else. There were two others, Edward-four and Adam-nine. Heckly watched as the black-and-white patrol car pulled out of the police parking area and headed south. Easing away from the curb, Heckly followed.

A lone cop was in the cruiser. It was hard to tell from the back of his head, but he looked young, and he wore his hair in a flattop. Making a statement: *I'm a macho cop.*

The police car took its time, continuing south for about five minutes, then turning left on a one-way street. Heckly stayed behind him. The officer continued eastward until he was in a sparsely populated area crisscrossed with ravines. He turned left onto a narrow paved road.

Then Heckly saw the sign. In blue letters on a cream background it proclaimed:

TRES CERROS POLICE DEPARTMENT
POLICE FIRING RANGE

It had at least half a dozen bullet holes in it.

Heckly turned around. He could see the range, which consisted of an embankment with targets set up, a long table where shooters stood, and some lights on poles so the place could be used at night. It had a chemical toilet, one of those portable things you always saw at construction sites. There was nowhere here to hide Cindy Brekke. And there had certainly been no shooting in the background when he'd talked to her on the phone.

"Did you get the part?" Petal asked when he got back to her apartment.

"They'll let me know."

"Will you need the car tomorrow?"

"Yes."

"More auditions?"

"Of course. If I get one of the parts, maybe we can move there, to San Francisco."

Petal frowned. "It's not like it used to be."

"No more flower children."

"No," she said. "But there are no more flower children anywhere."

"So then, what's wrong with San Francisco?"

"It's just too sad to go there and be reminded of the way it was."

"Well, we don't have to live there."

She nodded, but she was looking inward, communicating with herself. "I need the car tomorrow," she said.

"Why?"

"To buy groceries."

Petal lived on disability payments—the impairment presumably mental, since there didn't seem to be anything wrong with her physically that would keep her from working. As far as he could tell, she spent it all on rent and food, with nothing left over.

"What do you need? I'll pick it up."

She shook her head. "You wouldn't get the right things."

"Why not?"

"I only shop at the co-op. They carry nothing but organic produce. None of their things have been contaminated by the big fascist corporations."

"I have more auditions tomorrow," he said. "In San Jose."

Petal pouted. "I don't like San Jose."

Deciding the conversation was going nowhere, Heckly sat down on the threadbare couch and turned on the portable scanner.

"Eleven-ninety-four Sequoia Circle," the dispatcher said. "Three-fourteen just occurred. Subject is described as a white male, about twenty, wearing blue jeans and a black cap."

Three-fourteen meant indecent exposure. It had taken almost no time at all to learn the codes, a few hours of listening and a little common sense.

"I hate that," Petal said, covering her ears.

"I told you how much competition there is for the part of the policeman in this play. I need to listen so I can learn how police officers talk and think. It's the only way I'll get the part."

"All those pig voices."

"All cops are pigs?"

"Yes," she snapped, her face reddening with anger. "How can you listen to them? They're agents of the fucking fascist establishment!"

"You shouldn't let it bother you," he said.

"I hate the fucking pigs!" She spat out the words, her hands balling into fists. She glared at him for a moment, then whirled and stormed out of the room.

Clearly Petal wasn't always the insecure clinging vine he'd met at the iconoclastic bookstore. She had abrupt and unpredictable mood swings. Petal would require closer watching and more careful manipulation than he'd anticipated.

Petal was agitated the rest of the day. He made love to her that night, hoping to mollify her, as sex usually left her contented and snuggly. He awoke the next morning to find the bed empty.

When he went into the kitchen, she was sitting at the table, frowning at her cup of herbal tea. "Good morning, Petal," he said cheerfully.

She looked at him, her eyes filled with things he was unable to read.

"What's on your mind, Petal? Want to tell me what's bothering you?"

"Took the garbage out," she said.

"That's nice. Wouldn't want it hanging around, would we?"

"I know," she said flatly.

"What do you know, Petal?"

She got up, fished a crumpled newspaper out of the garbage, and flung it at him. *"This* was in the dumpster. I don't usually pay any attention to the newspaper, but I couldn't hardly miss your picture, could I?"

He unfolded the paper and there he was, looking back at himself from the front page.

"You cut up that pig's family, like it says?"

"Do you really think I'd do a thing like that, Petal?"

"The article said the guy they're looking for had a bad left arm. Just like you."

"Do you think the fascist establishment newspapers tell the truth, Petal?"

"I think you'd better leave. I got no use for the pigs, but that cop's family wasn't involved. I don't think I could live with someone who'd do something like that."

"So, you haven't called the police."

"Me, call the pigs? Not if I was being raped and murdered right outside the pig station. Besides, if you don't go, I'll get the bikers upstairs to help me. I'm a friend of theirs. They take me riding sometimes."

"So no one knows but you, Petal."

"Don't get any smart ideas," she said, pulling a gun from under her shirt. A .22 automatic. Not the sort of weapon that tore a person apart, but deadly nonetheless.

"And I thought you were a pacifist."

"I am, but I also have enough sense to protect myself."

"War's bad, but blowing away the person you slept with last night is okay."

"The only thing that's okay is your leaving." She motioned with the gun. He was supposed to go now.

"Can I at least get my things?" he said, rising.

"I'll put them on the porch. You can pick them up later."

"Don't you want these?" he asked, holding up her car keys.

"Yes," she said, reaching for them.

Heckly kicked the gun out of her hand. Surprise registered on her face, and her mouth opened, but before she could make a sound, a second kick sent her flying backward and crashing against the refrigerator.

Thirty-six

The official police parking lot was behind the station. It had only one exit, and Heckly was parked across the street from it, monitoring the police channels and watching.

He had left Petal in the bathtub. Despite the fact that the building was full of unsavory occupants, no one seemed to bother her, and it was unlikely that anyone would discover her body for a while. Not that it mattered, since he had no intention of going back there. He'd left her car in the parking lot of the Three Hills Mall, where he'd found the Cherokee he was driving today—keys dangling from the ignition.

The license tag had been borrowed from a Volkswagen.

"Edward-four's ten-eight, en route special assignment," the female voice of a police officer said over the radio.

Heckly followed the black-and-white. It led him to Martin Luther King High School, a shiny new complex with carefully tended grass and shrubs. In this prosperous lily-white city, there were probably very few of King's African-American brothers and sisters among the student body here.

An hour and a half later, the woman emerged and drove to Daniels Middle School. Again she remained inside for over an hour. Apparently her special assignment was telling kids to just say no to drugs or something like that.

He didn't follow her to her next stop.

"That's not him," Jake Byrd said, looking at Heckly's picture. "The guy staying with Petal had more hair, and it was darker, and he had a moustache. And he didn't have that thing on his chin, that dimple." He returned the photo to Cotter.

286

They were standing in the dingy, musty hallway outside Petal's apartment. The walls, once white, were uniformly the brown of a smoker's tobacco-stained fingers. The finish had long ago worn off the wood floor, which squeaked and sagged when Cotter walked on it.

Byrd was wearing bib overalls with no shirt underneath, exposing a thick tangle of dark chest hair and massive tattooed arms. Most of his weight was from fat, which made both his face and his overall form round. Lined up outside were about half a dozen chopped Harleys. One was his.

"Normally I wouldn't go into her place," the biker said. "But Petal came up early this morning and said she'd learned something about this guy that was living with her, and she was worried."

"She say what she'd learned?" Cotter asked.

"No, just that she was scared and that she wanted some of us to come down later and check on her, just in case she needed help getting the guy to leave. Petal was kinda weird—always talking about health food and socialism and shit like that—but she was a pretty good neighbor, so I said we'd help her out."

Byrd rubbed his right arm in the vicinity of a large tattoo, a dagger dripping blood. "Anyway," he continued, "when I came down to check on her, I knocked and nobody answered. I tried the door, and it was locked. I got to thinking about how she looked really worried when she talked to me, so I decided to go in. The locks in this building are a friggin' joke. So I just slipped the lock and went inside. At first I thought she wasn't there, but then I looked in the bathroom, and there she was with this note resting on her chest. She was obviously dead—I mean, with her eyes all dull and staring the way they were. So I got the hell out of there and called you guys."

He rubbed the other arm, massaging a tattoo composed of an eye, a heart, and a cat. I love pussy. Cute.

Cotter thanked Byrd for his help and went back inside. It was a small three-room apartment with threadbare furniture. Cobwebs hung in ropy strands from the corners of the ceiling; a thin layer of dust covered almost everything in the place. Petal Parker hadn't been into housekeeping.

Although the homicide was in Colmer's jurisdiction, it had been agreed that the investigation should be a joint effort and that Tres Cerros, which had much better facilities, would handle the labwork. With two stony-faced Colmer detectives looking on, Cheech and Chong were collecting samples and taking crime-scene photos.

Kozlovski appeared in the bedroom doorway. "Look what we found in here," he said.

When Cotter joined him, he moved to the tiny closet. A few K-mart-quality sweaters and blouses hung from the piece of steel water pipe that served as a hanger rod. Below them, on the floor, was a typewriter. An Adler manual.

"Looks like he's through sending us smartass letters," Kozlovski said.

"He's telling us the game is coming to an end," Cotter replied.

Inwardly Cotter shuddered. If the game was nearly over, it meant Heckly had concluded that it was time for the *coup de grâce*. That meant he would make his move against Cindy. Cotter had done his best. He'd hidden Cindy as well as he could, tried to think of Heckly's every possible move and allow for it, plan to counter it. But no one could foresee every possibility. There were too many unknowns, and each one represented a chance for Heckly to outwit him.

The trap he'd set when he'd discovered the homing transmitter on his car was a case in point. He should have captured Heckly. The woman in the station wagon going through the underpass at that exact moment was unpredictable. But it had happened. And Heckly was still free to go for his *coup de grâce*.

In its original meaning, the term meant "death stroke." Cotter winced.

"Arrogant son-of-a-bitch," Kozlovski muttered, still looking at the typewriter.

"You should be home, getting some rest," Cotter said. "I can handle this."

Kozlovski grinned. "Someone has to make sure you don't mess it all up."

"You're guarding Cindy from noon to midnight."

"I'm afraid I'll get lazy with all that free time."

"Yeah."

"Hey, I've been with you on this thing since the beginning. We're in it together." Which was pretty much what Cindy had said.

"I appreciate that," Cotter said.

Kozlovski shrugged.

Cotter hoped he deserved the loyalty of people like Kozlovski and Cindy. As he stood there staring at the Adler typewriter, now-familiar self-doubts churned in his core like an icy whirlpool. It wouldn't take much to mess this thing up, he knew. If he did, if he let Heckly outwit him, the monster would keep on killing. And Cindy would be one of his victims.

And it would all be his fault.

Conrad Isley from the medical examiner's office arrived. Thin to the point of gauntness, he had a prominent Adam's apple, a large, hooked nose, and incisors that were unusually long and sharp. He had several nicknames, including the Count (as in Dracula) and Ichabod Crane.

"Apparently strangled," he said when he was done. "There are a few bruises, but they probably wouldn't have caused serious injury. She's been dead a couple of hours."

After Isley was gone, Cotter stepped into the bathroom. He'd seen the victim when he'd first arrived, but now he wanted to get a second impression of the scene, absorb any details he might have missed the first time.

Fully clothed, Petal Parker lay in the bathtub, staring at the ceiling with lifeless eyes. She might have been cute at nineteen, but she had clearly become drab and plain as she'd aged. In a society that judged women by their appearance, she had done nothing to alter hers. She wore no makeup, and she had on jeans and a man's shirt. She wore her graying hair in a braid, which had been pulled around to the front so that its end, secured with a green rubber band, rested on the top button of her shirt like the tail of a comma.

Heckly had eviscerated Sheri Vanvleet in the shower, then laid her out on a bed in a macabre display. He'd done the opposite with Petal Parker, strangling her, then putting her in the bathtub. More acts intended simply to confound?

Cotter sensed that Petal had been laid out this way hurriedly. Compared to the other grim scenes left for him to find, this one seemed to lack style. Perhaps her death had been unplanned. Or maybe circumstances had caused the madman to strike before he'd intended to.

Petal had gone to the motorcycle gang upstairs to say she might need help. Had she somehow forced Heckly's hand?

Rushed or not, Heckly had made sure that Petal Parker had become another limb on the bramble-bush, another thorn to prick Cotter.

Encased in a transparent evidence bag now in possession of the lab crew was the note that had been jammed into Petal Parker's breast pocket. Scrawled in pencil were the words:

P is for pain in the ass.

"Adam-nine's ten-eight, en route special assignment."

Heckly watched as the unmarked car pulled out of the police parking lot, turned left, and headed into the night. He had learned that marked units driven by uniformed officers had code names like Edward-five or David-two or Charles-six. Detectives, who drove unmarked cars, had numbers only—Cotter's three-thirty-eight, for example.

But Adam-nine had just left in a gray Ford, an unmarked car. For a special assignment. Heckly followed in the Cherokee.

The Ford traveled slowly, the cop driving not taking any actions to thwart potential followers. But then, although it made sense for Cotter and the officers associated with him to be cautious, an ordinary cop, a stranger to the investigation, would see no reason to be so careful. Or so Heckly hoped.

After he'd quit following the cop who was visiting schools, he'd had a burger for lunch, and he'd been watching the police station continuously ever since. It was about quarter to eight now, and the darkness would make his job easier, for he would be just another set of anonymous headlights in the cop's rearview mirror.

Heckly shifted his position. He'd been in the car all day. He was stiff and sore. Not that it mattered. A few stiff joints were a small price to pay for the satisfaction he would get from killing Cindy Brekke. It was payment due for the mangled, useless arm.

Fifteen years to think about it.

Fantasize the various ways it could happen.

Savor each and every one.

He didn't know yet how it would happen, because he hadn't found her yet. But he would find her. Maybe tonight. And he did know what tools he would use. He also knew where he would buy them. The place was in the Tres Cerros Yellow Pages, under the heading "Surgical Equipment and Supplies."

He allowed a blue compact to get between him and the Ford. The cop was southbound on a divided street with a landscaped island. A few wisps of fog swirled in front of the Cherokee, but the mist didn't look as though it would be heavy tonight. Ahead the traffic signal turned amber. The gray Ford sped up, the cop running the orange light.

The compact in front of Heckly braked.

He started to change lanes, then realized there was no way he could make the light, so he jammed on the brakes, the tires squealing as the car came to a shuddering stop.

Ahead the Ford's taillights grew smaller.

Then they turned left and disappeared.

When the light changed, he passed the compact and accelerated. Reaching the intersection where the Ford had disappeared, he made the same left turn. The gray car was nowhere in sight.

He slammed the steering wheel with his palm, anger, hot and electric, shooting through him. This could have been it! A uniformed cop in an unmarked unit on a special assignment. And he was gone. Heckly pulled to the curb in front of an H & R Block office, then simply sat there, overwhelmed with rage.

As quickly as it had come, it faded, the heat dissipating as though some internal valve had opened, flooding him with coolness.

No matter, he told himself calmly. He could follow Adam-nine again tomorrow. No reason to get impatient. He would prevail. Those with superior minds always did.

Besides, the longer it took, the more time to anticipate the ending, imagine every detail.

Heckly pulled away from the curb. He was on a wide undivided thoroughfare, lined with the usual array of small businesses. Neon winked and blinked colorfully in an attempt to get his attention. He drove for four or five blocks, seeing no sign of the gray Ford, then gave up and turned around. Tomorrow he would stay closer, not let another car get between him and Adam-nine.

Then he spotted it. In the parking lot of a small Italian restaurant. A gray Ford with two short antennas by the trunk lid. Heckly drove past the place, turned around, and parked in the lot belonging to the auto-parts store across the street. He'd been waiting only about five minutes when a young man in civilian clothes came out carrying two pizza boxes. He unlocked the Ford, put the pizzas in the passenger seat, and slipped behind the wheel.

When the gray Ford pulled onto the street and continued in the same direction it had been traveling earlier, Heckly followed.

The Ford stayed on through streets until it was in West Tres Cerros, where it entered a neighborhood of older apartment buildings. It pulled into a drive belonging to a white four-story apartment house with a roof of red Spanish tiles. Heckly drove around the block, discovering that the rear of the building was also accessible from an alley. He drove around the block again, getting to know it, looking for signs of a trap. Satisfied that no surprises awaited him, he pulled into the alley.

As he passed the white apartment building, he spotted the unmarked Ford. And then he saw the silver Mercedes.

"Hello," he said softly.

And a warm, tingly glow settled over him.

Thirty-seven

Heckly spent the night in a place he was sure no one would ever look for him: the South Colmer Rescue Mission. The bums smelled bad, and they snored loudly, spewing out foul alcohol-scented breath, but no one gave him a second glance. He had dressed in filthy, tattered clothes, smeared dirt in a few strategic places, donned a gray-streaked beard. He fit right in.

He had also discovered that between them, Tres Cerros and Colmer had an inordinate number of public buildings where he could lock himself in a men's room stall, hang a small mirror on the back of the door, and put his makeup artistry to good use. In a pinch he could even use the toilet bowl for dying his hair.

Shortly after dawn, he was parked down the block from the white apartment house with the roof of genuine red clay tiles. He'd seen identical buildings in other parts of town, which led him to believe the Spanish look had been the rage here at one time—before concrete, steel, and glass had become the universal building materials.

Today he was in a yellow pickup, which he'd borrowed from a Colmer driveway. The floor had been covered with beer bottles, which had rolled around, clanking against each other annoyingly until he'd stopped to toss them into a dumpster. Until he'd aired it out by driving with the window open, the truck's cab had smelled a lot like the rescue mission. Heckly assumed the driver had come home too drunk to think straight. The keys had been lying on the seat in plain sight.

He spent the day watching the place. Cops came and went, always in unmarked cars with antennas that gave them away. Knowing he couldn't stay in one spot too long, he toured the neighborhood, looking for a good place to station himself. A block over from the white apartment house, he found a home for sale. Two stories, light blue with dark blue trim, the paint peeling. And it was vacant.

After a quick visit to a nearby hardware store, he returned with a long ladder, brushes, and other painter's supplies, and several cans of blue paint. From the ground he could see the red tile roof of the building where the cops were hiding Cindy Brekke. From the ladder he could see almost the entire building.

Shortly after five o'clock, Cotter showed up.

To avoid arousing suspicion, Heckly had to leave the job by dusk, since no painter would work in the dark. He maintained his vigil from the pickup. The cops weren't patrolling the neighborhood, he had discovered, so sure were they that their hideaway could not be found. They had allowed themselves to become overconfident. Always a mistake.

About eight o'clock, Adam-nine showed up with pizza boxes. Earlier pizza had been delivered to the building, apparently to someone other than the cops. He wondered why the police officers didn't have theirs delivered, concluding that they had some kind of a deal going with the Italian restaurant where Adam-nine made his nightly stops.

He already knew which apartment Cindy Brekke was in. He'd seen one of the cops look out the window.

Although he spent the night at the rescue mission among society's castoffs, Robert Heckly was wearing a sports jacket and tie the next morning when he stood in front of the white building with the red tile roof. It was identical to the apartment house in which the police were attempting to hide Cindy Brekke. Out front was a sign stating that an apartment was available and giving the number of a rental agent.

As he approached the door, a man wearing a blue blazer with a red tie and gray slacks emerged from the building.

"Mr. Jacobs?" the man asked.

"Yes. I take it you're Hiram Sebastian."

"That's me. Come on in, and I'll show you the place. It's on the top floor, so we'd better take the elevator."

The building was old, but well maintained. Hardwood wainscoting covered the bottom three feet of the wall in the small lobby. The switch plates were solid brass. So was the plate for the elevator call button. Incandescent lights were suspended from the high ceiling like upside-down mushrooms on long, thin stems. The elevator had one of those collapsible grates for its inside door. It formed a pattern of repeating diamond shapes when the rental agent pulled it closed.

"Buildings like this have something the new places just don't have," he said, pushing the button for the fourth floor.

The vintage elevator lurched, then began rising, its works making squeaks and rattles.

"Everything in this building was made to last," the agent said. "New buildings, they're falling apart in a couple of years. Twenty years from now, this building will still be here, still look just about like it does now."

"I've seen other buildings just like this one," Heckly said. "Is it just the outward appearance, or are they absolutely identical?"

"They're the same right down to the last nail," the agent said as the elevator arrived at the fourth floor. He slid the metal grate out of the way. "Built by John Morton. You from around here?"

"Ohio."

"Oh. Well, you probably wouldn't have heard of him, then. Morton family's old money—old by California standards, anyway. They were into logging, shipping, banking, and real estate. At one time they—ah, here we are." He slid a key into the lock of apartment 4-C.

"You were telling me about the other buildings," Heckly said. "You said they were identical to this one."

"Floor plan, fixtures, trim, you name it."

"Even things like the doorknobs and locks?"

"Exactly the same. Morton bought nothing but quality building supplies, but he tried to save money by buying in bulk. I'm afraid you won't be able to appreciate the view, as foggy as it is this morning, but on a clear day you can see the boats on the bay."

Heckly moved to the window, looked out on the mist-shrouded neighborhood. "I'm sure it would be lovely on a clear day."

"Notice that the only cracks in the walls are hairline, barely noticeable. That shows you how tough this building is. It's been here through a lot of tremors. A lot of buildings this age have cracks you could drive a truck through. Let me show you the kitchen. It's been completely renovated."

Heckly looked at the gleaming ceramic tile counters and the built-in dishwasher, then moved on, nodding appreciatively as the agent pointed out the lavish use of thick wood trim, the hardwood floors, and the two spacious bedrooms.

"They're asking two, but on an extended lease, I'm pretty sure we can get it done for seventeen-hundred. Of course, there would be the usual deposits." He looked at Heckly expectantly.

Heckly took the agent's card and said he'd let him know.

He drove away in a stolen Chrysler Le Baron, having learned the exact layout of the building in which Cindy Brekke was hiding and knowing what kind of locks it had.

It was early afternoon when he showed up at the house for sale a block over from Cindy Brekke's hiding place. He was using the same stolen pickup because a real painter would use a single vehicle. Overnight he'd left it in a neighborhood of apartment buildings where people often parked on the street.

He'd left his paint, brushes, and ladder in the backyard. Gathering together what he needed, he went to work, painting the underside of the eaves. Every time he reached one of the second-story windows, he tried it, thinking that people would be less careful with windows on the upper floor. He was right. The third one he tried resisted for a moment, then slid upward. Heckly climbed into a bedroom with ponies happily frolicking on the walls. Down at a child's level, the ponies were entangled in purple crayon squiggles.

It reminded him of his own boyhood wallpaper, the room in which he and Winnie London had played until Winnie had hit him with the toy. He recalled Winnie's fingers in the crack of the door, swelling, turning that pretty shade of purple.

The house was empty, the furniture and pictures and appliances presumably having gone with the owners. In the kitchen he found a remote control for the door of the detached garage. Unlocking the kitchen door, he stepped into the backyard.

He now had a place from which he could watch Cindy Brekke's hiding place twenty-four hours a day. There was no reason the same painter doing the exterior of a house couldn't do the interior.

He bought some paint the same colors as the interior trim and walls. He also bought a lock similar to the ones John Morton had put into his apartment buildings. The exact model was no longer manufactured, but the one he found was close enough. He set to work with the lock picks he'd acquired from one of the residents of the rescue mission.

He'd learned how to pick a lock when he was a teenager. Not because he was aspiring to become a criminal, but for the same reason a bright fourteen-year-old with a home computer would try to hack his way into the mainframe at the Pentagon. It was the challenge of the thing. You wanted to see whether you could actually do it. As a boy he'd been a whiz at picking locks.

Sitting in a chair by an upstairs window that afforded a good view of the white apartment house, he practiced picking the lock while he monitored the police frequencies. It took him nearly fifteen minutes because he had to handle both picks with one hand. But he got it done.

As the day wore on, he got better at it.

It was like riding a bicycle. Once you learned how, you never forgot.

As he sat by the window, practicing with the lock picks, he had plenty of time to think. His mind wandered through his life, picking out the high points, presenting them to him in a series of grisly snapshots, like an advertisement for a particularly gruesome horror movie.

Gruesome to others. Not to him.

He saw his mother falling down the stairs. Heard the *smack* of the two-by-four as it made contact with his father's flesh. Saw the expression on Leo Duver's face when he placed the blade of a sharp knife against the redneck's throat, the guard knowing he was going to die, but a part of him refusing to accept it, searching frantically for some tiny ray of hope. It was only after that desperation had all drained away, leaving nothing but resignation and hopelessness, that Heckly had ended it.

Duver's screams had echoed in the mountains, but there had been no one to hear them—no one except Heckly.

There were others, too. Many that no one knew about. The woman in Austin, for instance. A man in North Carolina. The bum in San Diego. Thornton Hollingsworth and his wife.

And he saw the fear and terror and confusion in the eyes of the little girl as she watched him cut up her mother and brother.

Which brought his thoughts to that day fifteen years ago when it had all begun.

His left arm useless and throbbing with intense pain, he sped through the flat Texas landscape, uncertain where he was going. He had to get off the highway. He had to avoid main roads altogether. The cop would radio in a description of both him and the car.

Ahead was a county road. He took it, speeding past oil wells and small farms. A jolt of pain shot up through his arm, making him gasp. The car swerved, but he regained control of it.

The county highway intersected with a farm route, and he took the smaller road. His arm rested on the seat, the slightest movement sending waves of incredible pain shooting through the injured limb. His elbow was red and swollen, and from that point downward everything seemed out of whack, as if all the parts were out of alignment. He didn't know whether any bones were broken, but he was sure the muscles were torn, the joints badly damaged.

A doctor would probably tell him that a series of operations necessary, and that even after surgery, the arm would probably never fully recover. But then, he could not seek medical attention, for walking into a doctor's office would be tantamount to walking into a police station.

The goddamn cop had ruined his arm.

Anger bubbled through him, then instantly subsided. He had no time now for rancor. He had to hole up somewhere, think things through, make plans.

He slowed for a tractor pulling a rusty, rattling piece of farm equipment. The road was narrow, with room neither for him to pass nor for the farmer to pull over. Heckly followed the clanking contraption at twenty miles an hour until the farmer reached his turnoff and left the road.

As Heckly sped up, he hit a pothole, jarring the car and sending a searing jolt of pain through his arm.

How had it happened? How had he let the stupid cop do this to him? Never before had he had any difficulty in a fight. He was highly skilled in fighting, a holder of a black belt in karate, and he was a disciple of other martial arts as well. How had the cop done this to him?

Luck, he decided. Sheer luck.

He pictured the cop holding on with bulldog tenacity. He could have pounded the ignorant slob into a pulp, and he still wouldn't have let go. If the pain hadn't clouded his judgment, he could have killed the son-of-a-bitch.

But then, it wasn't too late to make sure the cop learned to regret what he'd done. Truly regret it.

Heckly followed farm roads for forty-five minutes. Eventually the sky ahead of him began to take on a grimy look, and he realized he was heading toward Houston. He didn't want to go into Houston in a car every cop in the area would be looking for, so when he saw a narrow dirt road ahead, he took it.

The maintained portion of the road ended in a clump of trees, with three little-used tracks heading off in different directions. He took the one on the right. It led him to a pair of buildings, a shack and a dilapidated barn. There was a pickup outside, a twenty-year-old Chevy with a cracked windshield and baseball-sized rust holes in its side.

A scruffy old man emerged. Wearing suspenders and a floppy hat, he looked like a character out of Snuffy Smith.

"What you want?" the old man asked.

"I'm lost," Heckly said, getting out of the car.

"Just go back the way you came."

"I need to use your phone."

"Ain't got no phone. What happened to your arm?"

"Skiing accident."

"Skiing?" The old man looked perplexed, as if uncertain whether the stranger was serious or poking fun at him. His face was covered with white stubble. His skin was wrinkled and sticky looking.

"How come you don't have a phone?"

"What would I want with one? Ain't nobody here but me, and I got nobody to talk to."

"That right?" Heckly said, thinking the barn would be a good place to hide the car. "You must be one of those hermits."

"What of it?" the man asked belligerently.

"Did you know this is the day you're going to die?" Heckly asked. It was a rhetorical question.

That evening, as Heckly watched the white apartment house, Adam-nine showed up, bringing the customary two pizzas with him. Around nine a car with an illuminated Guido's Pizza sign pulled up in front of the building. A kid carrying a black pizza-delivery container hurried inside. Clearly the place had been home to pizza lovers even before the cops moved in.

Heckly had broken off his vigil long enough to buy a sleeping bag. He spent the night on the floor, near the window through which he'd been watching the white apartment building.

He was studying the apartment house through binoculars the next day when, from downstairs, a woman's voice called, "Is anyone here?"

Switching off his scanner, he concealed both it and the binoculars under the dropcloth he'd laid out, then hurried downstairs. In the living room he discovered a pretty blond woman wearing a green blazer that had the logo of a real estate firm on the breast pocket. She was accompanied by a conservatively dressed middle-aged couple.

"Hi," Heckly said. "Go ahead and look around. I'll try to stay out of your way. Be careful upstairs. Wet paint."

The real estate woman frowned. "You're painting the house?"

"Yes, ma'am. Inside and out. I've even started working nights on it."

"Who hired you?"

"The owner."

"The Koenigs?"

"Yes, ma'am, the Koenigs."

"Where'd you get the key?"

"He'd left one with the neighbors. All I had to do was pick it up."

"I wonder why they didn't tell us."

"Got no idea about that."

"Well," she said as her frown faded. "The place certainly needs it. We advised the Koenigs to paint it, but they didn't want to spend the money."

"Guess they changed their mind, huh?"

"Guess so," she said. Then, as if suddenly remembering they were there, she turned to the couple and said, "Well, I told you this was a nice house that needed a little painting, but I guess the painting part's been taken care of. Come on, we'll take a look around."

"Frank-three to Control, we're ten-ninety-seven on Arrow Street."

"Ten-four, Frank-three."

The black-and-white Tres Cerros police cruiser was driven by patrol officer Sandy Cassidy, who was accompanied by officer Edmundo Lucero. They got out of the patrol car and walked toward the two-story blue house. It was nearly dusk, one of those days when the temperature had abruptly plunged about twenty-five degrees for no apparent reason.

"I don't understand why this town's growing as fast as it is," Lucero said. "With weather like this, who'd want to come here?"

"You did."

"Can I help it if this is where my car broke down? I was heading for San Francisco. Wanted to put some flowers in my hair."

"You'd look silly with flowers in your hair. Besides, the weather's exactly the same in San Francisco."

"Yeah, but there's a lot more to do, so you don't notice it as much."

They'd been dispatched to the house on Arrow Street because the real estate agent had found a man painting the place, claiming he'd been hired by the owner, who had moved to Seattle. But when the real estate agent had checked with the owner, he denied having hired a painter.

There was no sign of anyone at the house, although someone had been painting it. A lot of the trim and a portion of the eaves had received a fresh coat of blue. "Doesn't make any sense," Lucero said. "Who the hell breaks into an empty house so he can paint it?"

"The quality of criminals just isn't what it used to be," Cassidy said.

Lucero gave her a funny look "You think they've forgotten how to steal? Hey, I've got more faith in our crooks than that."

They checked the doors and windows, finding everything locked. Shining their flashlights in through the window of the locked garage, they spotted a ladder and some cans of paint.

Lucero shrugged. "My kitchen needs painting. Think I can get him to break into my house next?"

"Maybe you could run an ad in the personals."

They reported what they'd found and resumed patrolling their assigned district, unaware of the activity in the white apartment building whose red tile roof was visible above the tops of the neighboring homes.

Sixteen-year-old Joshua Reiner drove his vintage Pontiac sedan into the alley behind Guido's Pizza and parked outside the rear entrance. He switched off the lighted sign that was held to the Pontiac's roof by a suction mount and drew its power from the cigarette lighter.

Joshua sighed. He's saved the money he'd earned mowing lawns and the money his Aunt Emily had given him, and his dad had said he could buy the car if he could get the insurance, which for a sixteen-year-old in the State of California was approximately a million dollars a year. His dad had advanced him the money for the policy, but he had to pay it back, which meant he had to have a job, which, as it turned out, meant that the only time he got to drive the car was when he was delivering pizzas.

He told all his friends about the chicks that offered him their bodies when he'd showed up with pizza, but it was total bullshit. Guys usually paid for the pizza. Sometimes they demanded to know why it had taken so long. Half the time they didn't offer a tip.

Guido was an asshole. He yelled at the delivery boys all the time, and he paid them less than the minimum wage, saying he didn't have to pay any more than that because they got tips.

Yeah, sure.

As Joshua stepped into the kitchen, he was engulfed by the steamy aroma of tomato sauce and mozzarella. Using a wooden paddle, Guido removed a pizza from the long stainless steel oven, slipped it onto the cutting surface, and attacked it with the slicing wheel. Looking up, he spotted Joshua, who was heading to the men's room to take a much-needed leak.

"So what the hell took you so long?" Guido asked. He was maybe five-three, pudgy, and had curly hair that always looked greasy and a face that was always red, as if overheated.

"Making a delivery."

"Jesus! You walk?"

"I went right there and came right back."

Guido looked at him as if to say, *Do you really expect me to believe that shit?*

"Well, I did," Joshua said.

"Here," Guido said, shoving a pizza box into Joshua's hands. "Do you think you can get it there before it gets cold?"

"Where does it go?"

"Jesus, read the fucking slip, why don't ya? What's with you guys, you don't know how to read a goddamned delivery slip?"

Joshua headed for the back door.

"Move it!" Guido shouted. "The customer ain't paying for cold pizza. No wonder you guys complain about not getting tips.

Who's going to tip for a pizza that's cold and two hours late?"

As he stepped into the night air, the sensation that something was wrong settled over him. He hesitated, his eyes scanning the shadows, but nothing seemed amiss. Dismissing it as nothing, he shoved the insulated pizza box into the Pontiac's passenger seat and slid behind the wheel, switching on the Guido's Pizza sign. He checked the delivery slip. Arlington Drive, six blocks away. Then he realized he'd never make it to Arlington Drive without taking a leak.

He hesitated, knowing Guido was going to be furious, but then he dashed back inside, because the need was urgent.

Guido looked up. "What the—"

"Sorry, it's an emergency." And then he was through kitchen and into the short hallway leading to the john. When he'd relieved himself, he hurried out, not looking at Guido, who muttered something incomprehensible back.

He was back in his car, buckling the seatbelt, before he realized that something was wrong.

The pizza sign's power cord no longer came in through the window and plugged into the cigarette lighter socket. Quickly climbing out of the car, he looked at the roof. The illuminated Guido's Pizza sign was gone.

"Sixty-five bucks," Guido had said. "You lose that sign or you break it, and you pay for it. Got it?"

Yeah, Joshua thought, *I got it.*

Then his eyes settled on the passenger seat. The pizza was gone, delivery case and all. He had no idea what the case might be worth, but he knew who would be expected to pay for it. Reluctantly, he went back inside.

"I think you better call the police," he said, wishing he was still ten, playing in Little League and riding his bicycle instead of worrying about car insurance. Life could be a real bitch when you got older and had responsibilities.

Cotter lay in bed, watching the shadows on the ceiling. They made cats and dogs and buildings and monsters, changing as cars passed by or pulled into driveways. Whereas the ceiling in

Cindy's twelfth-floor bedroom was static, here at ground level the shadows were shape changers, constantly in a state of flux. And instead of elevator noises, there were street sounds: engines revving, doors slamming, dogs barking, words being exchanged. It was the difference between life in the ivory tower of a luxury high-rise and life among the teeming masses.

He rolled over, nagged by doubts. Was he handling things correctly? With everyone tied up guarding Cindy, the only investigating being done was what he was able to do himself. Would more people working on it turn up Heckly? The madman had to be staying somewhere.

On the other hand, he worried whether Cindy was well enough protected. If anything happened to her . . .

He shuddered at the prospect.

He saw Cindy much less than he wanted to. But every time he visited the white apartment building, he was taking a risk. He was careful, always checking for a transmitter on his car, doubling back repeatedly, constantly watching the rearview mirror. But no precautions were foolproof.

Again he rolled over. The shadows on the ceiling seemed to form a claw now, slowly reaching across the surface to perform some unspeakable evil.

And then it hit him, washing over him like a giant ocean wave, overwhelming his every sense. The link that had been inoperative for many days suddenly reestablished itself. With a vengeance.

He was falling into the bottomless blackness.

And he had gone too far. He was in the place where the madness lived. He tried to close his mind to the bizarre feelings swirling around him, all of them so horribly, horribly wrong, but it was impossible to tune them out.

It was like being in a vast computer programmed by the likes of Hitler and Charles Manson, and the people who put bombs on airplanes or used children for target practice. A committee of them, all putting their inner selves into the machine. The computer would spew out as truth answers filtered through the frames of reference of the committee members.

It was a machine filled with surreal monsters, a Frankenstein of a machine.

Abruptly the link was severed, but not before he learned something very important.

For a moment, too drained to move, he simply lay there, breathing rapidly, his fists squeezed into balls. Then he quickly got up, grabbed a small suitcase, put it on the bed, and started throwing clothes into it.

"I hope I know what I'm doing," he said, and was surprised by the shakiness of his voice.

Thirty-eight

It was Friday night when a seven-year-old Mitsubishi two-door pulled up in front of the white apartment building with the red Spanish tile roof. Robert Heckly switched off the engine and the Guido's Pizza sign. Picking up the pizza-delivery case, he walked toward the apartment house, knowing the cops would be watching him from a dimly lighted third floor window. He was not worried about being recognized, for he wore a blond wig tied in a ponytail and a wispy moustache of the same color. And he'd enlarged his nose, altered the contours of his face, hidden the dimple in his chin, added a smattering of freckles.

Besides, they were not expecting him. They thought Cindy was quite safe here.

Like the delivery people he'd watched, Heckly carried the pizza case horizontally, supported by a single arm. Although he'd eaten the pizza immediately after stealing it, the case was not empty. It contained surgical equipment.

Heckly glanced up, checking the living room window of 3-C, making sure it was still dark. The lights in the living room had gone off half an hour ago. Which meant Cindy had gone to bed, and the cops were in the other bedroom.

There was nothing between him and Cindy except a lock he knew how to pick and an empty living room.

There were no buzzers or other security measures for him to bother with. The building had been constructed in less dangerous times, and no one had changed it. Being careful not to seem awkward, he used his one good arm to both hold the pizza case and pull open the door.

He had the elevator to himself as he ascended to the third floor. The layout was identical to that of the building he'd visited. The walls of the hallway were even the same shade of creamy white. Each floor had four apartments.

No light showed beneath the door of apartment 3-C.

Putting down the pizza case, Heckly checked the lock, finding it was exactly like those in the other building. He ran back to the elevator and pushed the basement button. The machine began its rattling, clanking descent. It was old and slow as well as noisy. It would cover the sounds of his picking the lock as long as he worked quickly enough. Slipping the picks out of his pocket, he hurried to the door of 3-C and went to work.

The elevator whined and clattered its way downward.

The lock was primitive, barely more sophisticated than the nineteenth-century invention of Linus Yale, and he quickly worked the tumblers into the right position and turned the cylinder.

The living room was dark, vacant. Picking up the pizza case, Heckly moved into the apartment, silently closing the door behind him. The door to the bedroom occupied by the guards was closed, a dim strip of light at its bottom.

"Fifteen-two, fifteen-four, and a pair's six," said a male voice from the other side of the door.

"You going to skunk me again?" another man said.

"Not with six point hands, I'm not."

"First one you've had all night that didn't have at least twelve points."

"Quit complaining and count your cards."

He had five in his hand and three in the crib. Heckly heard the sound of cards being shuffled.

"The pizza guy hasn't come out yet."

"Give him time. He's got to make change, and he needs a few moments to act real nice so he can earn a tip for his trouble."

Heckly moved to the other closed door. No light showed beneath it. He put his ear against it, hearing nothing. He felt the weight of the .22 automatic he'd taken from Petal in his jacket pocket. He didn't like guns much, but he'd brought it along this time just in case he needed it.

Noiselessly, he opened the door and stepped into the darkened room.

There she was, asleep in the bed. A lump under the covers, blond hair showing at top. *Hello, Cindy*, he thought.

He put the pizza case down beside the bed, opening it silently. Even in the darkened room, there was enough light to show the glitter of stainless steel surgeon's tools. He took out one that was long and tapered to a sharp point. One quick thrust to kill her, and then he could take his time with the rest. When he'd imagined how this would go, he'd pictured himself doing it in some secluded place, where he could take his time and no one would hear Cindy's screams. He'd even considered making an audio tape of the event, one copy for him and one for Cotter. Alas, these circumstances did not permit that.

He studied the darkened room, feeling the silent relationship between him and his victim, savoring the moment. Victory was at hand.

No one knew he was here, and it was unlikely the cops would look into Cindy's private bedroom. They would be shocked at what they found in the morning. And they would know how thoroughly he had outsmarted them. He moved a little closer to the bed, reached for the covers, planning to pull them down and kill Cindy in one quick, silent movement.

The lights came on.

Two cops stood in the doorway, aiming guns at him.

Cindy Brekke was sitting up in bed, and she, too, was pointing a gun at him. Except it wasn't really Cindy, he realized suddenly. With one hand she pulled off her blond wig, revealing red hair. It was the cop who'd been guarding her in San Francisco.

And then Cotter was there too, staring at him, his eyes simmering with loathing.

"Drop it," one of the cops said. "I would truly love to blow your ass away. It might very well be the high point of my life. You've got about two seconds to decide which way you're going to go."

Heckly dropped the surgical instrument.

Then Cotter was standing over him, staring down at him, his mouth drawn into a crooked line, as if he were repulsed by what he saw.

All the other cops were standing back, giving Cotter the chance to do whatever he was going to do. It was as if he and Cotter were the only ones here, just the two of them in their own private world. If Cotter killed him, all the other cops would testify it was self-defense.

Heckly waited to see what would happen. *Stay calm,* a part of him urged. *These dimwits only think they've beaten you.*

Still it was just him and Cotter, tension hanging in the air, the big cop standing over him, looking at him as if he were something unclean and disgusting.

Then Cotter reached inside his jacket, but what emerged was only his fingers in the shape of a gun. He aimed the finger gun at Heckly and pulled the imaginary trigger, his lips forming the word bang.

For an instant, Heckly thought he felt the bullet.

"I just wanted to see what it would feel like," Cotter said.

He motioned to the other cops, who stepped forward and grabbed Heckly, pulling him to his feet.

And something inside Robert Heckly screamed, *No, you are not going to let these pathetic assholes win!* He saw a human shape to his left, and gave it a karate kick, spinning away from the hands that held him. He leapt over the downed form of the cop he'd kicked and flung himself at the door, knocking someone out of his way, delivering a karate blow to someone else—Cotter, he thought.

And then he was in the living room, rushing toward the door. Raised, confused voices came from behind him.

He reached the door, turned the knob.

Cotter was on the floor, his thoughts whirling. As he got to his feet, he realized that he'd known what Heckly was going to do before he did it. He'd *known* the madman would break free, use his martial arts skills, try to escape.

At least he'd have known it if he'd properly interpreted the sensations that had flooded his mind an instant before Heckly had made his move.

Heckly was through the door. Cops were scrambling after him. Cotter dashed after them.

* * *

More shouts, the sounds of the cops coming after him. Heckly thought about using the automatic he was carrying, but he knew that if he drew it, the cops would gun him down. And even in the panic of the present circumstances, Robert Heckly was a planner. He wanted to live to fight another day. Forgetting about the gun, he yanked open the door, plunged through it, and headed for the stairs.

A loud bang.

Pieces of plaster exploded from the wall near his head. And then he was on the stairs, taking them four and five steps at a time. He missed a step, his feet slipping out from under him, his butt hitting the stairs, then bouncing and sliding downward. He scrambled to his feet, plunging down the next flight of stairs. Although he didn't dare turn around and look, he knew they were behind him, because they'd never give up. He was the ultimate bad guy, the one who'd turned a cop's wife and kid into chops and roasts and briskets.

He reached the ground floor, expecting to find a squad of cops waiting for him, but no one was there, and he hurried to the door, flinging it open and rushing into the night. He heard them now, coming after him. Footfalls, heavy breathing.

Across the street was the Mitsubishi with the Guido's Pizza sign on the roof. Realizing he didn't have time to get into the car and get it started before his pursuers reached him, he stayed on the sidewalk and ran, channeling all his energy into his legs. He heard a shout, but it wasn't close. All that jogging was paying off.

From behind him came the sound of an engine revving, tires squealing.

Rounding the corner at the end of the block, he spotted an alley and rushed into it. The alley was dark, and its shadows engulfed him protectively. He passed garbage cans and rear gates. Somewhere a dog barked. Heckly slipped over a wall into a dark backyard. He hesitated, listening. Cars roared by on the street. And one was moving down the alley. He could hear the police radio, voices talking in numbers.

Moving as quietly as he could, he made his way through the yard. He stepped on something, a child's toy, he thought, and it cracked loudly underfoot. No lights came on. No dobermans appeared out of the gloom with bared teeth. He thought he heard a sound come from near the spot where he'd climbed over the wall, but staring into the gloom, he could see nothing but shadows.

He left the yard through the front gate, made sure no one was coming, then darted across the street. Slipping between two houses, he entered another backyard. This one wasn't fenced. A dog in the next yard started barking furiously. He quickly made his way into the alley. More dogs began to bark.

The alley was lined with walls. Heckly thought about climbing over one of them, but he didn't know which yards contained dogs and which didn't. They were making a clamor that could be heard for blocks. He picked up speed. He was vulnerable here.

Light at the end of the alley.

Someone with a flashlight.

A cop.

Heckly spotted a gate. Hoping there was no dog behind it, he slipped into the yard. Nothing happened. He crouched, pulling out the .22-caliber revolver. He could hear the quiet *scrinch-scrunch* of shoe soles on the sandy pavement of the alley. And in the distance, the sound of an engine idling. The glow from the flashlight was making the shadows in the yard lengthen and shorten and shift position.

The cop was directly opposite him, on the other side of the wall. It was about six feet high. The cop could not see over it. Heckly put away the gun. If he used it, other officers would hear the shot and come running.

The cop reached the gate, shined his light into the yard, kept moving. Heckly quietly opened the gate, moved up behind the cop, and put him in a hold that choked off the flow of blood through the carotid artery. The cop struggled, but in only a couple of moments his efforts became weak, and then he was unconscious. Heckly headed for the car he'd heard idling at the end of the alley.

Then he saw it ahead of him, a nondescript sedan. Moving closer, he saw the two antennas of its rear end. Suddenly, powerful arms grabbed him from behind, spun him around. His hand found the pistol in his coat pocket, pulled it out.

It was knocked from his hand.

"Surprise," Cotter said.

Instantly Heckly sized up the situation. They were alone, he and Cotter. After fifteen years, it was just the two of them. Though he had the use of only one arm, Heckly was an expert. And this time, he would prevail.

"No, you won't," Cotter said.

Stunned, Heckly stared at the shadowy shape in front of him. Could Cotter read his mind?

"You're wondering whether I can read your mind," Cotter said. "Not quite. But I can sense things."

Heckly slipped to the side, unleashing a karate kick. Strong fingers gripped his shoe and held it, forcing him to hop backward. A sharp twist to his foot, and he was on the ground.

Heckly scrambled to his feet, instantly assuming the fighting stance, his good hand ready to deliver a deadly karate blow. Cotter moved in close, and Heckly attacked with a series of kicks and chops that all connected with nothing but the night air.

He whirled, tried again. Missed again.

The presence in his head had been coming and going. He'd learned to ignore it. But now it had hummed into life as if someone had switched on a vibrator inside his skull.

"Stop it!" he shouted.

"Is that what Julie and Sean yelled?" Cotter asked. "Did they plead with you to stop?"

The sensation became worse, as if someone were inside his head with an electric drill, using it on his nerve endings.

"Stop it!" Heckly yelled.

"Fuck you," Cotter said.

Lights danced in front of Heckly's eyes.

Bolts of agony exploded in his head. And then he was running down the alley, holding his head, weaving, stumbling.

"This is for Julie," Cotter said, and Heckly thought his brain had exploded. He turned, flailed the air, and collided with a garbage can.

"This is for Sean." Cotter's voice seemed to be everywhere, above him, below him, inside him. Fire burned through Heckly's head. He screamed.

"This is for Jennifer."

Thunderclaps, each one followed by agony.

"Stop," Heckly whimpered. "Stop."

Then Cotter was there, holding him, breathing into his face. "This is for what you wanted to do to Cindy."

Heckly felt himself spun by powerful hands, slammed face-first into the wall.

The officer Heckly had used the choke hold on was Vickers. Cotter made sure he was okay, then used the radio in the unmarked car to inform the other officers of what had happened. The first one to arrive was Melanie Gunderson.

Heckly was on the ground, handcuffed, staring into the night as if he were peering into another dimension. Gunderson stood over him, shining her flashlight into his face.

"He collided with a wall," Cotter said.

"Armed and dangerous, resisting arrest." She shrugged. "Besides, he doesn't look too badly hurt."

"Except for knocking the gun out of his hand, that's the only physical thing I did to him."

Gunderson nodded. But when she looked at Cotter again, there was something unreadable in her eyes.

She said, "You didn't have your gun tonight, did you?"

"No. I was afraid I'd do something with it I might regret later."

"You didn't need it," she said.

"As it turned out," Cotter replied.

"Is it truly over?" Cindy asked.

She and Cotter were holding each other. They stood in the living room of an apartment identical to the one in which

Heckly had been caught. That the apartment buildings should be twins had been Cotter's idea. Unable to be absolutely certain the link between him and Heckly was a one-way thing, he'd decided not to take any chances. If Heckly had managed to get an image of Cindy's hiding place from Cotter, he would have seen a white apartment house with a red Spanish-tile roof. Just like the one in which the trap had been set.

"It's truly over," Cotter said.

"I wish I could believe that."

"He's in the hospital, being treated for minor cuts and scrapes. From there he goes to a maximum-security lockup."

"He escaped from a maximum security place once before."

"He'll be carefully guarded. He's not going anywhere."

Cindy buried her face in his shirtfront. She started shaking; Cotter realized his shirt was getting wet. Cindy was letting it all out, shedding the emotional strain of the past few weeks. He just held her, silently offering her his strength while her tears of relief soaked through his shirt.

Epilogue

"I visited Tyleen at the hospital today," Cindy told Cotter as he stepped through the door of her apartment. "She's sitting up in bed now, and most of the tubes have been removed. She looks much better."

"Any word on when she will be released?" Cotter asked.

"Probably in a few days."

They hugged each other. It seemed to Cotter they'd been doing that a lot in the two weeks since Heckly's capture—gently touching each other every chance they got, as if reaffirming that they were whole, safe.

"How did it go today?" Cindy asked.

Cotter had spent the afternoon with Dr. Ventana. "We did the Zener cards again. Same results as last time. I got almost all the circles."

Cindy frowned. "Does she have any idea what it means?"

"No. She says she's never seen anything like it."

Cindy led him to the couch. "I've been thinking about that. Couldn't this business with the circles mean your ESP is limited, that you have a powerful ability but only in a narrowly defined area?"

"I do. The reception of telepathically transmitted circles."

"In a way, the circles are like your link with Heckly. It only works with one shape, circles. And—"

"And with one person. But that part's understandable. The relationship between Heckly and me involved some powerful emotions. That doesn't explain the circles."

"No," Cindy said thoughtfully. "But I think this . . . this ability of yours is still there, within you. And I think it may surface again, if all the conditions are right."

"Maybe Dr. Ventana will be able to shed some light on all this," Cotter said. "She says she's planning some very sophisticated experiments."

"When will she do them?"

"Starting the day after tomorrow. Apparently it'll take a few weeks to do everything."

Kissing him gently, Cindy said, "I'm glad you're home, big guy. Ever since all this happened, I don't like being away from you, even for a few seconds."

"Does this mean we're becoming inseparable?"

"I hope so."

"Me, too." He kissed her forehead. "That's my favorite part."

"Uh, most men would probably choose something a little lower."

"But that's the part that loves me."

She grinned at him. "Cotter, you're such a hopeless romantic."

Cotter managed a smile of his own, but he felt it fading almost immediately. Although he had tried not to admit it to himself, he was still troubled by what had transpired between him and Heckly.

"Something on your mind?" Cindy asked.

"Well . . ."

"Out with it."

"There are some things about that night that worry me."

"What things?"

"I did something that night," he said.

She searched his face. "What, Mike? What did you do?"

He took a deep breath. "Being in the same room with Heckly . . . well, it made the link come alive. I was in his head, knowing what he was going to do before he did it. That's how I was able to find him. I could sense his relative bearing, his distance."

"You told me about that," she said.

"But I haven't told you the rest. When I caught up with him, I found out I could use the link to hurt him. And I did. I sent pain into his head. You could see how agonizing it was by the way he was acting. He was stumbling, bumping into things. He pleaded for me to stop."

Cindy hugged him tightly, telling him it was okay, she understood.

"I didn't stop. I gave him more pain. It was just so easy . . . and so damned satisfying."

"Mike, under the circumstances . . ."

"It's not that Heckly didn't deserve it. He did. What worries me is how easy it was to be cruel and totally without compassion—just like him."

"You're not just like him, Mike. Not the least little bit."

"I gave him intense pain, and it was unnecessary. I could have cuffed him at any time. But I kept on doing it, and—at least for a while—I couldn't stop myself. Suddenly I had this power, and I felt compelled to use it. I liked hurting him. And that's what worries me. Heckly's supposed to be the one with no conscience, the one who enjoys inflicting pain."

"Mike, who wouldn't want revenge after what he did to you? Anyone would have done what you did."

"But only I had the power to do it. The last time I saw him, he was staring off into space, as if . . . as if his brain was burnt out. I guess I'm just a little afraid of what I became that night. It's an awesome power. And it's very easy to abuse."

"Mike . . . I can see how this would frighten you. It would frighten me, too. It would frighten anyone with any sense. But the fact that you feel this way, that you're so worried about it, proves your conscience is in good working order."

Cotter was silent for a moment; then he said, "Does it bother you that . . . that I'm different?"

"Bother me? Of course not. You're still the same kind, gentle man I fell in love with."

"I may also be a . . . well, a weirdo of sorts. I—"

"If you're a weirdo, I wish we all were. The world would be a better place." She looked at him lovingly. "Hey, if you can read my thoughts, then you know what I think about you."

"I can't read your thoughts. And I wouldn't if I could."

"Well, then I'll have to tell you what I'm thinking. Let's just say I'm not about to step down as the president of your fan club, big guy."

Cotter was no longer linked to the madman and hadn't been

since that night. He had severed the connection. Permanently.

Heckly was being kept in an isolation cell, under twenty-four-hour guard. Having recovered from the encounter with Cotter in the alley, he spent most of his time reading and plotting strategy with his lawyer. He had been charged with numerous counts of murder in California, and in Texas with the death of Willa Stiller. In California, Heckly might be declared incompetent to stand trial. In Texas, however, times had changed in the past fifteen years. Juries there were all hanging juries these days. Heckly could well get a lethal injection.

Cotter hoped so.

If Heckly had escaped once, he could do it again.

And that was a chance the world should not have to take.

He said, "Fan club, huh? I like that. Do I get to have groupies?"

"Certainly, but they all have to be about fifteen, and you have to share them fifty-fifty with a rock group called the Baby-Crushing Planet Destroyers."

"Is there such a group?"

"Probably."

"Mumpf," Cotter said.

"Last time I got double mumpf," Cindy replied.

"You can have all the mumpf you can handle," Cotter said.

"Promise?"

"Yeah, I promise."

Cotter had absolutely no idea what they were talking about, but it was nice to be able to say dumb things again, to be able to know that just *maybe* life could be normal again—as normal as it could be for him.

*"MIND-BOGGLING... THE SUSPENSE IS UNBEARABLE...
DORIS MILES DISNEY WILL KEEP YOU
ON THE EDGE OF YOUR SEAT..."*

THE MYSTERIES OF DORIS MILES DISNEY

THE DAY MISS BESSIE LEWIS DISAPPEARED	(2080-5, $2.95/$4.50)
THE HOSPITALITY OF THE HOUSE	(2738-9, $3.50/$4.50)
THE LAST STRAW	(2286-7, $2.95/$3.95)
THE MAGIC GRANDFATHER	(2584-X, $2.95/$3.95)
MRS. MEEKER'S MONEY	(2212-3, $2.95/$3.95)
NO NEXT OF KIN	(2969-1, $3.50/$4.50)
ONLY COUPLES NEED APPLY	(2438-X, $2.95/$3.95)
SHADOW OF A MAN	(3077-0, $3.50/$4.50)
THAT WHICH IS CROOKED	(2848-2, $3.50/$4.50)
THREE'S A CROWD	(2079-1, $2.95/$3.95)
WHO RIDES A TIGER	(2799-0, $3.50/$4.50)

Available wherever paperbacks are sold, or order direct from the Publisher. Send cover price plus 50¢ per copy for mailing and handling to Zebra Books, Dept. 3939, 475 Park Avenue South, New York, N.Y. 10016. Residents of New York and Tennessee must include sales tax. DO NOT SEND CASH. For a free Zebra/Pinnacle catalog please write to the above address.